TEA WITH GRACE

A Story of Synchronicity
And Platonic Love

OREST STOCCO

TEA WITH GRACE

ISBN 978-0-9920112-2-2

Edited by Penny Lynn Cates

Cover Design by Penny Lynn Cates

*"Love is born into every human being;
it calls back the halves of our original nature together; it tries to
make one out of two and heal the wound of human nature."*

—Plato, *Symposium*

CHAPTERS

1. GRACE KENDAL

Grace Kendal, whose eyes are her most distinctive physical feature, one pale blue and the other dark brown, is a devout Roman Catholic, a former Sister of Mercy, a loving wife and mother of a boy and girl, both adopted in infancy and now in their early twenties, a semi-retired high school English teacher, and a caring, compassionate woman.

I'm a painting contractor in my early fifties, a former Roman Catholic who left the Church in my early twenties because I outgrew my Christian faith, unmarried but coupled with Cathy Collingwood, the love of my life, a spiritual eclectic and writer by avocation, and I got to know Grace Kendal intimately while painting her house.

Grace and her husband Brandon and their son Michael had just moved to Ontario from St. John's Newfoundland. Their daughter Kathleen, who was still taking courses in her social work field, remained in St. John's.

Still too energetic for retirement and with too much left to give to the profession he loved, Grace's husband procured a new position as principal of the St. Jude's Roman Catholic School in my hometown after his position on the Catholic School Board in Newfoundland was terminated when the provincial government did away with the Separate School Board, and he contracted me to paint the new house that he and his wife had just purchased on McCrady Avenue which overlooked St. Jude and Lake Superior.

A former monk who had also outgrown his religious commitment, both he and Grace had lived the disciplined Christian life with vows of poverty, chastity, and obedience for over twenty years, meeting providentially in the same school where they taught after leaving their order, and falling in love; and it was obvious from my first impressions that they were good people whom I would be privileged to work for.

But something apart from their obvious goodness fascinated me, and it was not until I began conversing with Grace as I worked in her home and over tea during my breaks in the dining room that she had difficulty deciding what color to paint that it finally dawned upon me that they both lived the spiritual life of Christianity consciously.

I too lived the spiritual life consciously, but not within the context of Christianity. Nevertheless, the spiritual life is the spiritual life regardless which context it is lived in, and this was the common bond that I came to recognize in my daily conversations with the engaging former Sister of Mercy.

A number of times our conversations evolved into dialogues that almost became full-blown dialectical discourses, but not quite; and it wasn't until the last conversation that we had over tea in her freshly painted Tempting Teal dining room as I was about to leave for another job that we both felt a sudden pang of loss.

"Oriano, I'm going to miss our conversations," she said, with a long sigh; and I, sadly, was forced to agree with her.

I did have to return to paint the washroom on the main floor and her son's bedroom, which I had to put off for a few days because I was committed to do a drywall taping job in the city, so I knew that we would be talking again at least one more time; but on my long drive to my little job in the city I became possessed by my idea to initiate the literary project with the former Sister of Mercy which would allow us to continue our fascinating conversations, and I seriously pondered the possibility for the next few days.

Being very familiar with Plato's dialogues, which I had discovered at the tender age of fifteen when I purchased an encyclopedic set of books called *The Great Books of the Western World* that one of my older brothers had to sign for, as well as from personal discourses that I had with an agnostic friend and an atheist friend which I rendered into my novel *The Other Side,* I knew that dialogues that evolved into dialectical discourses could take one to such Socratic heights that one might have difficulty breathing the rarified air, so I had to weigh my idea of discoursing with a devout Roman Catholic very carefully; I was, after all, a non-believer of many Christian premises.

Because I had to reason my way through so many heartbreaking impasses in my search for the path best suited to my irrepressible, if not pathological need for authenticity, I was not afraid

2

to go wherever the unpredictable spirit of dialectical discourse would take us; but could Grace? Would the former Bride of Christ have the courage to suspend her Christian faith and let divine reason be her guide? I honestly didn't know.

It was presumptuous of me, presupposing that her faith would have to be suspended to fly on the wings of untrammeled reason; but having been down that road more times than I cared to remember I knew what she would be up against, and I wasn't at all sure I could enjoin her in such a perilous endeavor.

And it would be perilous. As my literary mentor "Papa" Hemingway once confessed, one never knows what lies inside himself until he goes there. But Grace inspired confidence in me. She was, after all, a Sister of Mercy for twenty years. That spoke volumes about her contemplative life. But what impressed me most was the ease with which our conversations flowed. From our very first talk we disclosed details about our lives that one would not normally reveal until a friendship has been well established; and that, upon reflection, I attributed to instant mutual trust.

That's why I wanted to continue our conversations. On the phone one morning while talking about painting her basement washroom she told me that if we were neighbors she could see us socializing and becoming very good friends.

I agreed. But there was no reason not to still be friends, was there? If not socially, why not Platonically? Grace did, after all, fascinate me intellectually because I had never met a genuine Christian before. And she had told me on more than one occasion that she found me deep and full of so much Light that—she didn't know what.

"I did tell you that I was a Light-bringer," I said to her when she made that comment the first time, and then I laughed to make light of the implication.

It was private humor. I had changed three bulbs in her house, and as I screwed in the new bulb in her basement stairwell and it shone brightly in the landing I made the comment that I was a Light-bringer in synchronistic response to her comment.

I had said something in reference to her daughter that led Grace to say that I was full of so much Light—her metaphor for

3

wisdom; and I simply played upon this, as I often do with many things that people say to me.

I do have a rich and spontaneous sense of humor; one that crosses all boundaries in life. This is probably the most charming aspect of my personality, and I exploit it for whatever purpose I deem necessary; especially for literary gain. In short, I use my quick wit to draw people out; and I drew Grace Kendal out with little effort because she was so appreciative of my spontaneous and unpredictable sense of humor.

"You're always upbeat, Oriano," she told me after my first week of working at her house. "You lift my spirits."

"I have a way of doing that," I replied, with a generous smile. " I just happen to be a person who sees life in a positive light."

But so did Grace. She was merely exhausted from her move from Newfoundland; that was all. While her husband settled into his new position as principal of St. Jude's Roman Catholic School Grace had to stay behind to find her daughter a suitable apartment in St. John's and get her moved in, and she was responsible for all the packing and moving and then unpacking and bringing her new house in St. Jude up to the high standards that she was accustomed to and which endeared her to me from the moment we first met.

I love people who aspire to excellence, and Grace's whole life impressed me as one indefatigable effort to personal excellence. It was well defined by her Christian faith, mind you; but excellence is excellence by whatever name, and it enriches one's life aesthetically—and spiritually, as I painfully learned from the sayings of Jesus.

And that was another reason why Grace and I empathized intellectually; we both appreciated the cryptic, paradoxical, and life-transforming sayings of Jesus—an appreciation that we both knew could only be born of hard-won experience.

Indeed, we both quoted the same saying on separate occasions and smiled at our intimate familiarity with one of the most mind-boggling sayings in the Gospels that reflects the complete message of Christ's teaching of salvation which St. Paul rendered into his soul-searing admonition to "die daily" — ***"For whosoever will save his***

4

life shall lose it; and whosoever will lose his life for my sake shall find it" (Math. 16:24).

And this puzzled Grace. She assumed that I was Roman Catholic. But given our conversations I sensed her suspicion that she might be wrong about me; that's why she came right out and said to me one day over tea during my afternoon break: "You're a Christian, aren't you? If you had to sign what religion you belong to on an official document, you'd write in Christian; wouldn't you?"

How desperately she wanted for me to be a Christian, and how painful it was for me to tell her that I was not. "I'm sorry to disappoint you, Grace; but I couldn't write Christian in the little box. I've outgrown my Christian faith."

I expected her to pursue this. I certainly would have had someone asked me that question, but Grace didn't; and this puzzled me. Which was another reason why I wanted to pursue further dialogues with her—because I wanted her to see the real me.

I saw the real her. Grace was a genuine Christian, and I even told her so. On the morning that I dropped by to pick up my tools for my small job in the city we had a cup of tea and she, dying of curiosity to know what impression I had formed of her while painting her house (and acutely conscious of the fact that she might see herself in one of my stories one day), came right out and asked me, "So, tell me Oriano; what do you think of me?"

"I don't have to think, Grace. The distilled essence of my impressions of you is that you have given me a healthy new respect for Christianity," I calmly replied.

This could not have pleased the former Sister of Mercy more. "Oh good! I'm so thankful for that! I try to live the life of Christ. I try so hard…"

I have no doubt that there are many genuine Christians in the world, but I never met one until I met Grace Kendal. As I very boldly and thoughtlessly said to her one day, "I would not wish Christianity upon any person."

Once again, she did not pursue this astonishing statement (yet another reason why I wanted to initiate a Platonic relationship with her); but feeling like I had left a ball suspended in mid air, I amplified

5

my comment: "The sayings of Jesus are so difficult, if not impossible to live by that I would not wish them upon anybody."

She smiled her beatific smile that radiated so much sympathetic understanding that it endeared her all the more to me, but she said nothing. I did however feel her lock up that piece of information in the back of her mind to call up should the occasion ever arise to probe deeper into my life which, upon reflection, leaves me to wonder if she had not set me up to continue our talks after I completed painting her house.

But I knew that Grace did not have a devious bone in her body, so something else was at play. In fact, on several occasions I said to her that I felt there was some mysterious symbolic reason for our meeting, something synchronistic that went well beyond the meeting of two engaging minds; but I didn't know what.

It felt like Soul meeting Soul; a kind of instant spiritual recognition. Only she had come to me from her own devoutly and clearly defined Roman Catholic faith, and I had come to her from my own spiritual path; and this excited both of us enough to initiate spontaneous, easy-flowing conversation every day that I worked at her house.

I enjoy and am becoming more versed each day in the language of life (what the Catholic monks used to call "reading the book of the world"), and in my daily talks with Grace I sensed a play unfolding before my very eyes—a symbolic drama directed by Someone on High that I later came to call the "omniscient guiding force of life."

I didn't dwell on the image, though; because I did not want to set myself up for disappointment. But I could not shake the idea. And that was possibly the most compelling reason to ask her if she would like to engage in a Platonic dialogue with me after my job was done; a friendship of mutual intellectual curiosity.

I honestly wanted to engage her Christian mind with my eclectic mind in a dialectical discourse. The very idea excited me. Not that I wanted to test my personal philosophy with her resolute Christian faith; that did not interest me in the least.

I had died daily. I had been reborn. I was no longer a seeker; I was a doer. I lived my own life come what may, and I let others live theirs; but it excited me to know what kind of insights we could give birth to when our two minds engaged in Platonic inquiry.

It had been years since anyone had engaged my mind like Grace had (and possibly I hers); and she had barely scraped the surface of my life. I had tried many times to initiate talks of a dialectical nature, especially with my agnostic and atheist friends; but how quickly they fell from those heady heights where ethereal ideas become reality.

But with Grace it was a whole different ball game, because she was aware of those rarified heights. Her Christian faith had lifted her beautiful soul high enough to catch a glimpse of that place we all know deep within to be our spiritual home, and she wanted desperately to reside there permanently; but her path was still a daily struggle.

And it puzzled her to no end that I could be so calm, so casual and indifferent to these rarified heights of spiritual awareness; as though it was the most natural thing in the world to be free of life's travails. But I wasn't free, of course. I, too, had to deal with life's daily struggles. But I knew something that she did not know; or, rather, I knew something about the spiritual life that lay outside the narrow confines of her Christian paradigm.

And that was another reason why I wanted to engage her in a Platonic dialogue. Not that I wanted to convert her to my way of thinking. God forbid such presumption; I merely wanted Grace to see that life—meaning spiritual salvation—also existed outside her Christian box. That, then, was the working premise for the series of Platonic dialogues that I wanted to initiate with the former Sister of Mercy...

When the idea first came to me I shuddered, because I am very familiar with the confrontational nature of dialectical inquiry. When dialectical inquiry is given free reign it can ascend to such heights that it can make one dizzy (if not giddy) with rational clarity—but only at the expense of everything that hinders soul from ascending. In other words, as the Sufis say, "one must unlearn to learn." But how many people have the courage to let go of their false beliefs to dwell in the lofty heights of truth?

That's why they condemned Socrates (and crucified Jesus); and that's why I have been so presumptuous in my conviction that to be a genuine Christian one must have transcended their false nature, which within the paradigm of Christian faith can only be done by dying daily. And with "fear and trembling," as St. Paul said.

Gurdjieff said that to speak the truth is the most difficult thing in the world to do, because to speak the truth one must be able to see the truth from the lie in oneself; and herein lies the crux of the matter, for *"godly sorrow worketh repentance unto salvation not to be repented of, but the salvation of the world worketh death. For behold, this selfsame thing, that ye sorrowed after a godly sort, what carefulness it wrought in you, yea, what clearing of yourselves, yea, what indignation, yea, what fear, yea, what vehement desire, yea, what zeal, yea, what revenge!"* (II Cor. 10-11)

This "selfsame thing" that St. Paul talks about is not as cryptic as it sounds. It is St. Paul's creative way of revealing the dual nature of man—the lower material self and the higher spiritual self; and unless one transcends the material self by dying daily one will never realize his spiritual self. And that's what I saw in the former Sister of Mercy.

Grace was a woman who had also died daily, and in her I saw the gentle soul that she had become. Gentle, but as I said to her one day in her kitchen as I rolled the cool but warm Tempting Teal onto her adjoining dining room walls, "Behind that gentle exterior lies an indomitable spirit." She smiled her beatific smile, delighted to be seen truly; but having been humbled by the Way of the Cross, she said nothing.

We understood each other. We both saw genuine people in each other. That was the instant recognition of Soul meeting Soul. And that was why we had instant Platonic rapport. And I wanted to continue that. I wanted to know how it was that she had come to that authentic state in herself that had cost me so dearly to realize—that purity of consciousness where the spiritual self is unhampered by the egoic nature of the lower self.

Because that's what it was all about in the end. That's what all of the hullabaloo about salvation was about—the transformation of our false consciousness. And Grace, by whatever other Christian means she had realized it, was authentic.

And how refreshing it was to meet an authentic person. How far and few they were, for "the pursuit of the unhypocritical life," as Jungian psychotherapist Jeremiah Abrams calls "shadow work," can try the most hardy soul. But should one reach the heights, which in one of my books I referred to as analogical mountain climbing, one takes on an aura of child-like innocence and becomes, in spite of themselves, a bringer of Light.

There is nothing mystical about this. All genuine people are channels for the Light of God. But becoming genuine—*'aye, there's the rub that makes calamity of so great a fortune!'* Not that a person who has realized his authentic self is not subject to moments of falseness; we certainly are. But the burden that this places upon our conscience is so heavy that we will do anything—and I mean anything!—to rid ourselves of our guilt.

This was one of the conversations that I had with Grace one day; the question of personal guilt. She wasn't sure she had done enough for her daughter, whom she suspected was born "fetal alcohol affected." She did find some consolation in Kathleen's therapist who told her that were she and Brandon not the nurturing and loving parents they were her daughter would almost certainly have ended up on the streets, or in jail; but Grace being Grace, this wasn't good enough.

She wanted better for her daughter. Always better. And this, she realized, was her cross. But it did take its toll on her. In her basement one morning as I was about to apply the second coat of soft Dusty Rose to her cupboard doors, she opened up to me about the pain and suffering that Kathleen had put her through, and fighting back tears she said to me, "Oh Oriano, I don't know what I possibly could have done to deserve this..."

Keeping whatever I had to say to Grace always within the context of the Christian paradigm, I smiled sympathetically and said, "Just look at it as penance, Grace."

She smiled back. "You're right. It is penance." And in an instant she shouldered her cross once again and supported it with the dignity that made her Grace.

How delightful it was for me to see a person take on such an oppressive burden with so much dignity. Had only I been as dignified when I struggled with my father's demons. I confess; I was not dignified. I tore into my father with the courage of blind conviction and wrestled with his alcoholic demons until only one of us was left standing. I put my father in the hospital with a brain aneurism and narrowly escaped the furies of patricide.

But that was my way. As my father once described me to one of my cousins who had just emigrated from Italy, *"Se Oriano deve andare al diavolo per ottenere qualcosa che ha bisogno, allora è lì che andrà."* In English it meant that if I had to go to hell to get what I needed, then that's where I would go.

I wasn't afraid of anything, and I did go through hell many times to find my authentic self. That's what gave birth to the hardest saying of my life: *the shortest way to God is through hell.* So I know what price one must pay for liberation from the spiritually suffocating constraints of one's false consciousness, and I admired Grace for the cross that she had so freely chosen to bear.

This does not mean that she was always calm and poised with her cross on her shoulders. Kathleen did come home for a ten day visit while I was painting, and one morning I was downstairs working when I heard Grace and her daughter going at it. Grace exclaimed, *"This is my house and I don't want you taking it over!"*

"It's dad's house too, and he said I can do it!" Kathleen screamed back.

I shut the basement door to respect their privacy; but Grace, suspecting that I had heard their argument, tried to put a kinder, gentler face on it.

I understood her need to paper over it, but she wasn't really papering over it; she was merely putting it all into context for me to understand the nature of her cross. But I did understand, and I simply said, "Grace, what can you do? I know how much you love your daughter; but you can't let her walk all over you."

Once again, Grace smiled. This time her smile compelled her to say yet again, "Oriano, you're full of so much Light—"

It was her personal cross. She knew it, I knew it, and I had no desire whatsoever to interfere in her karmic life; so I simply referred to it as her penance because Christianity, whose fundamental tenet is forgiveness of sins, does not acknowledge the Spiritual Law of Karma. And that, I'm sure, would be one of the subjects that we would inevitably touch upon should we enjoin in a Platonic relationship after I painted her house.

But the more I thought about it, the more apprehensive I became. Grace did tell me one day over tea during my morning break that one of her favorite sayings which she had learned while still a young Sister of Mercy was, "When in doubt, don't act." Ironically however, I wasn't doubtful for myself; I was doubtful for the people around us.

What would Grace's husband think of my literary project—whatever that entailed? And my Cathy, who in spite of our complete trust in each other's love always shrunk in fearful apprehension whenever I showed a passing interest in another woman, however innocent; how would she respond? Not that my literary project with Grace would ever threaten my love for Cathy; it was just her insecure feminine nature.

Married for seventeen and a half years to a man she had long ceased to love, one of the first things that Cathy asked me when we first met was if I believed in love. "Yes, of course I do," I replied, with that blind conceit that years later prompted her to say to me, "You were so full of yourself you didn't have any room in your life for anyone else."

Cathy finally divorced her husband. She was motivated to leave him because her brother, whom she was very close to, died of cancer. He was only thirty-five years old. "There has to be more to life than this," she concluded, as they lay her brother into his grave; so she left her husband to find the meaning of her life.

Coincidentally, Grace also had a brother who died of cancer at an early age; and this helped make up her mind to leave the Sisters of Mercy which had ceased to nourish her soul. Like Cathy, Grace wanted more meaning out of life; and she agonized no less to leave the security of her Order than Cathy did to leave the security of her loveless marriage.

But such is the mystery of the spiritual life. We all agonize over decisions that are going to affect our spiritual destiny.

Unfortunately, we can't all make these decisions. This is why the sage of Walden Pond Henry David Thoreau came to the sad conclusion that most people live a life of quiet desperation.

It takes an incredible amount of courage to live our own life. People know this, but they repress this knowledge. They do not want to think about it because it forces them to see their own cowardice. And rather than stare into the face of their own fear, they project it onto life by resentfully denying those who dare to live their own life.

But not everyone is karmically ready for the spiritual journey to wholeness, and Cathy, having embarked upon this incredible journey with me, was forgiven her insecurity; but I confess my stupidity for even discussing my idea with her in the first place.

"I don't want to talk about it," she said to me on our drive to the city for groceries Saturday morning a day or two after the idea began to possess me.

"Why not?" I foolishly asked.

"Because I don't like the idea. I think it's invasive."

"But I'm going to be up front about the whole thing. It would be a mutual decision, Cathy. There's no other agenda."

"I still don't think it's right," she insisted.

"Why?"

"I don't want to talk about it."

"Fair enough," I said, and dropped the subject.

There was no point discussing it. Cathy had no idea what a Platonic relationship entailed. She was not an intellectual and had never experienced the exciting dialectical play of ideas. Cathy was, as I described her to Grace one day when she asked me about her, "at heart a country girl unhampered by sophistication."

And yet, despite the fact that she was not a thinker in the philosophical sense she resented being told that she was not; and although this frustrated the hell out of me in the early stages of our relationship, I find it amusing today because it is so indicative of that irritating quality that women who have yet to realize their own identity posses; and men also, to be perfectly fair, and so I promised myself not to bring up the subject again.

It was my literary project, inspired by my Muse; and if there was one thing that I had learned in all my years of writing it was to never turn my back on my Muse.

Grace understood this. This is why she admired me for getting up every morning at four o'clock to write before going to work my trade at nine. She taught English literature in high school. We talked about writers and the creative process. We spoke the same language. But my idea went well beyond our mutual interest in literature; it had to do with a divinely ordained meeting of two very different minds.

Grace was a devout Christian. I was a spiritual eclectic. And the meeting of our minds inspired such spontaneous insights that they made me laugh. Like the concept of "ghost busting" that I came up with to describe the workmanship on Grace's new house by the original owner who obviously had little idea of what the virtue of work was all about. With every imperfection that I cleaned up (like removing tacky wallpaper that covered up drywall deficiencies that I had to correct before painting the walls) I would say to Grace, "We've just busted another Tommy Ping ghost!"

Tommy Ping was the original owner; and I must have busted a dozen Tommy Ping ghosts before I came upon the slanted tie rack in the master bedroom closet that instantly broke me up and which gave Grace such guilty pleasure that she had to call her husband at the school to share my comment with him; and he bowled over with laughter.

"Tommy Ping did it again," I said out loud when I started painting the closet. I spotted the slanted tie rack and broke into a fit of laughter. Grace was downstairs. She heard me laughing and wondered what I was laughing at. I had to share my humor with her. "Hey Grace," I yelled down the stairs. "Did you see this tie rack in here?"

"Yes, we did. Can you believe it?"

"Only a slanty-eyed Chinaman could have put that up!" I yelled back down, and broke into another fit of irrepressible laughter.

I heard Grace laughing. She couldn't repress it. She had to come up the stairs and share her laughter with me.

"I don't mean to sound racist, Grace; but this is so apropos," I said, and we both broke into a fit of fresh laughter.

13

"Oriano, what would people think if they heard us talking like this?"

"Who cares? I know I'm not a racist, and I don't see you being racist; so what does it matter? It was just too good to pass up, Grace. I couldn't let that one by."

"Another Tommy Ping ghost," she repeated, with a delicious smile.

That was why I didn't feel uncomfortable proposing my idea to her, there was no tension between us; and I simply wanted to see if I could elevate our exciting talks to a Platonic level just to see where they would take us. It was literary curiosity, pure and simple; but I still had to ask myself: am I being presumptuous?

Of course I was being presumptuous. But what is a writer without presumption? Is he not just another compiler of other people's lives, thoughts, and ideas? An Updike without the genius of his art? A Hemingway without imagination? A Chekov without irony?

Everyone is fond of quoting the Preacher's iconic words that there is nothing new under the sun, but they have not experienced the spirit of Platonic inquiry. They do not know that the intermingling of thoughts can give birth to new insights and ideas that do not exist under the sun; and I saw in Grace Kendal the Christian I had been waiting years to dialogue with, and I could not let that opportunity pass me by.

Besides, Grace had miraculously restored my respect for Christianity. Not my respect for Jesus Christ, whom I loved and admired; but my respect for the religion whose ossified thinking stubbornly continued to retard the spiritual consciousness of the world.

"But you do believe in Jesus Christ?" Grace asked me the day after I told her that I could not fill in the little box in the official document with the word Christian.

"Like the Gnostic Gospels tell us," I replied, without hesitation (we had come too far in our talks for that), "I believe Jesus Christ was a teacher of the Way. He wasn't the only teacher of the Way; but he was a great teacher of the Way. Perhaps the best."

14

Grace looked at me with the same mixture of curiosity and perplexity in her eyes that I continued to inspire in her. She knew that I had not come by my beliefs lightly, and she wasn't quite sure she should pursue it any further.

Sensing her hesitation, I thanked her for the tea and went back to work hoping to pick up the subject another time—yet another reason to continue our talks.

We had left too many things unsaid, too many subjects cut short by one thing or another; and I simply had to give her the opportunity to satisfy her curiosity about me. But how would she react to the idea of recording our talks?

Would she be self-conscious? Could she trust in her own beliefs enough to hear herself speaking them out as I taped her gentle voice on my recorder? I knew that I intrigued her, and I knew she would welcome the opportunity to further delve into my private life; but would she be willing to allow a recorded transcript of our talks?

I wouldn't know until I asked her, so my literary project was up in the air. I hoped that she would; but if she didn't, I would have to resort to Plan B…

Grace wanted to have Cathy and me over for dinner when she got her house in order (she wanted to cook us a "down-home Newfie dish"), and I accepted her invitation; so that opened the door for further dialogue. I would simply initiate the dialogue to flow in the direction that would resolve many of the questions that we had left unanswered.

But I preferred to be open about it. I preferred Grace to know that I wanted to keep a record of our talks. I had already told her that she had inspired a character in a short story that I had just written (but was going to rework having learned so much more about her), so I had no hidden agenda—

"There's no point denying it," I said to her. "You know very well that a writer draws upon everything that touches his life; and you interest me very much. But I will tell you one thing about the way I write, though. I use real people to inspire my characters; but they take on a life of their own in my stories. And that is one of the most

15

exciting things about creative writing—watching my characters come to life on their own volition."

But knowing this was that why Grace didn't pursue some of the subjects that were left unresolved? Was she being coy with me?

I didn't think so, because Grace had opened up to me so much at times that I was forced to smile at her unabashed candor. In short, I sensed in Grace Kendal a woman who was comfortable with the woman she had become, and she wasn't afraid to speak about her life; that's why I wanted to pursue our talks.

I, too, was comfortable with who I had become. I had nothing to hide (although, like Hemingway, there were things about my life that I reserved for my fiction); and this level of personal comfort—unlike most people that are afraid of being seen for who they really are—was another reason why Grace and I could be so open with each other.

I did however deliberately excite her curiosity by keeping our conversations always within the context of the Christian paradigm, which I confess was difficult to do at times; but I had no desire to reveal the parameters of my own spiritual path. The footings of our Platonic relationship weren't strong enough yet to support that; but they could be. I saw in my literary project the possibility of an original structure of Christian and eclectic thought, and I was dying to see what this dialectic would look like.

So there was a mystique about me. I didn't create this mystique intentionally; I did it simply to establish a sense of conversational ease. And it delighted me watching Grace find her way deeper into my private life with every disclosure that I made about myself.

Or had I read her wrong? Had I merely seen what I wanted to see in Grace—a former bride of Jesus Christ unafraid to risk her faith in philosophical inquiry?

I had done that before, reading a woman completely wrong; and what a shock it was when it dawned upon me that the image I had in my mind did not coincide with the woman I had been in love with for a whole year. *Had I fallen in Platonic love with Grace?*

I had never experienced that before; not in real life, anyway. I had fallen in love with many great minds in my search for

16

authenticity—Socrates, Sartre, Camus, Nietzsche, Gurdjieff (mostly through the writings of his students, like P. D. Ouspensky, Dr. Maurice Nicoll, and C. S. Nott to name just a few), and Carl Gustav Jung whose *Memories, Dreams, Reflections* introduced me to his depth psychology that shed beams of light upon my lonely path, and Wordsworth, Rumi, and Paul Twitchell—many, many minds; but the only reason I fell in love with these great minds was because they all pointed me to the Way, and it was the Way itself that I was actually in love with!

But with Grace Kendal it was different. She lived the way of Jesus Christ according to her strict Roman Catholic faith, not the Way in itself, something that Grace had not yet come to fathom; so I honestly don't think I fell in love with her Platonically. I was merely excited by the possibility of a Platonic relationship with her, that's all.

"I know what Jesus said, Grace," I said to her in her dining room one day. I had the extension pole in my hands and was rolling the Tempting Teal onto the other two walls that I had suggested she also paint in the same color to create the illusion of a separate room from the attached kitchen that I was going to paint off-white; but I stopped rolling and turned to her. "Jesus said, *'I am the way, the truth, and the life,'* and I believe him. But he was not the only Way-shower, Grace. The Way does not belong to any one person. The Way just IS. It is neither above you, nor below you. It is not to your right, or to your left. It is not within you, nor without; the Way just IS. And it is wrong for Christianity to claim the Way as its own. It's simply wrong."

"But Jesus died on the cross for the sins of the world, Oriano," Grace responded, with that look of inexplicable curiosity in her anomalous eyes. "You can't deny that—"

"Maybe he died on the cross, maybe he didn't; history is mixed on that subject. But what does the death of one man two thousand years ago have to do with my salvation? I love and admire Jesus for his commitment to the Way, Grace; but he's not my savior."

"If you don't mind me asking, Oriano; who is your savior? Or do you have one?"

"I do and I don't. I've found myself, Grace. I know who I am. Let me see if I can put this into some kind of philosophical context for you. Are you familiar with Sartre?"

"Just in passing. I've never read him."

"Sartre was a philosopher and an atheist. I didn't share his atheism because I've always believed in God; but despite his atheism, Sartre pointed me to the Way with his incredible commitment to intellectual integrity. Tragically his commitment—*engagement,* to use his word, which means more than commitment—was to his enormous ego; but what the hey, it was integrity. And I loved him for that. So I latched onto his philosophical concept of *good faith* and made it a part of my own ethic. But Sartre couldn't take me any further in my search for myself than his irreconcilable dilemma of *being* and *non-being.* 'I am what I am not, and I am not what I am,' he concluded his philosophy. But I couldn't live a philosophy that left me so unresolved; so I was forced to drop existentialism and move on. But it did open me up to more of the Way. That's how I found another teaching which prepared me for another teaching of the Way, and so on and so on until I found the perennial philosophy of the Way; so I don't have a personal savior, as such. I just have the Way. *Capisce?*"

I said the word *"capisce"* in my gentle, albeit ironic voice; not in that harsh way most people say it to determine finality; but Grace had no idea what I meant by it until I explained the word to her: "*Capisce* is Italian. It simple means, do you understand?"

Grace smile, and then said, "I have the Way too, Oriano. I have it in Jesus. I live the life that Jesus wants me to live, and that's enough for me."

"Excellent," I replied. "As long as you find spiritual succor in the teachings of Jesus, what else could one ask for?"

"Nothing," she said, and smiled again; but she didn't pursue the subject. I was hoping she would, because I had opened the door for her to step into my private world; but she switched the subject to her daughter. "My Kathleen is straying, Oriano. I know she's a good girl, and I know she will never leave the Church; but I fear for her soul."

"Are you serious?" I said, with some astonishment.

"Yes. It's this feminist thing she's into. It's turning her head. She's started smoking, and I think she's experimenting with alcohol. I can't be sure, but the signs are there. And I'm fearful for her. It's genetic. Her birth mother is an alcoholic. And sex. I don't even want to talk about that. She says she's liberated. Liberated from what? I don't understand this young generation; and I don't know what more I can do for her. I pray for her every day, Oriano. I pray till my knees hurt."

"Maybe you're praying too much, Grace."

"One can never pray too much," Grace responded.

"What are you praying for?" I had to ask.

"That she stays on the right path."

"Which is?"

"The path of Jesus Christ."

"Jesus Christ's path, or Grace Kendal's path?"

"They're one and the same, I would hope."

"Maybe, maybe not. Do you remember me asking you not to pray for my salvation when you asked if you could pray for me?"

"Yes."

"And I told you that my spiritual destiny was my own?"

"Yes, I remember."

"Don't you think your daughter might have her own spiritual destiny?"

"Salvation is the spiritual destiny of all souls, Oriano. That's why Jesus died on the cross for us. That's why I pray for my daughter. I want her to keep Jesus in her life and in her heart. But Kathleen is head-strong. She can get so caught up in her own way of thinking that she loses touch with good sound reason."

"You mean she can be irrational?"

"You don't know the half of it. And it's all because of her illness."

"What illness?"

"Kathleen has ADD."

"Attention Deficit Disorder?"

"Yes. Hyper-attention Deficit Disorder. She was born that way. Her birth mother drank during her pregnancy, and it affected Kathleen. It's genetic, Oriano."

19

"What can you do but continue loving her," I said, bringing the unhappy subject to conclusion because I sensed that it wasn't appropriate to open up the subject of karma that I had spelled out in terms of one's own spiritual destiny. "Love is the final cure," I added, trying to put a gentle salve on Grace's perpetual sorrow.

"That's why I will never stop loving her. She is my cross, and I am destined to suffer for my child the rest of my life. But not my son Michael. I trust him implicitly."

Love. That's what made Grace Grace. She had learned the secret of the Merciful Heart of Jesus Christ; the gift of love. Cathy's mother had not learned the secret of love. That's why Cathy was so love-starved when I met her. I even told her deceased mother on the other side in a dream one night that her problem was that she did not know how to love. "Love gives," I said to Cathy's mother, who refused to hug her dying son because she was terrified of catching his cancer. "Love does not take. It gives," I repeated.

And Grace did give. In fact, she gave so much that I even poked fun at her totally unselfish commitment to her children. "You wait on them hand and foot, Grace," I said. I had been working in her home for two weeks and I had seen how Grace jumped whenever her son wanted something, like a mother answering a baby's cry; and all during her daughter's visit Grace spent hours on Kathleen's term paper that was already late.

"It's all bullshit," she said to me one morning when she came out of the computer room for a cup of tea.

I laughed. "Isn't that refreshing," I said.

"Well it is, Oriano. She's all over the map. She hasn't done her research. It's all bullshit," she repeated as she put the kettle on for tea.

I laughed again. It didn't surprise me to hear Grace use the word, because I knew she had it in her; but it threw me so early in the morning.

"*Bullshit,*" I said, and snickered.

"I know. But a spade is a spade; and her paper is all bullshit. I don't know what to do. That's why she came home, you know. She needs mother. She's a needy girl, Oriano. She's always been needy. You wouldn't believe what my phone bill was last month. She calls for everything. But what can I do? She is my daughter, and I have to stick by her."

"And what a lucky girls she is," I said.

I met Kathleen the day she arrived. I was downstairs painting the family room when Michael brought her home from the airport. She was a tall thin pretty girl with flaming red hair that shocked her mother.

"That's not the color of her hair, Oriano. Her hair is a beautiful blond," Grace said, shaking her head in disbelief. Obviously it came as a surprise to her.

"I like it," I said.

"Thank you. So do I," Kathleen said. "Mom doesn't want me to have it because she has red hair—"

"Oh Kathleen. You have beautiful hair. Why would you want to look like me?"

"I like red hair. Can't I have red hair if I want to? It is my hair, mother—"

"Yes, dear; it's beautiful. I just don't understand why you would want to change your hair color, that's all."

"Just for a change, mother. Change is good for a person, you know. Isn't that why you and dad moved to Ontario?"

"Do you see what I have to put up with, Oriano? She has a mind of her own, doesn't she?" Grace said, making light of her daughter's strong personality.

I laughed. "*Kathleen.* I love your name. It's one of my favorite names. And I love your hair, Kathleen. I've asked Cathy—my fiancé—to color her hair like yours; but the closest she came was strawberry blond."

"Oh, really? What did it look like?" Kathleen asked.

"It turned out nice. But I like yours better."

"Thank you. See, mom; why can't you be like him and just accept my choice?"

"I do appreciate the choice you made, dear. After all, it is your hair; and you can do whatever you want with it," Grace replied, in her motherly voice.

"I love you, mother," Kathleen said, and gave her mother a hug.

"And I love you too, dear," Grace said, and gave her daughter a kiss on the forehead.

"I have to get back to work. It was nice meeting you, Kathleen."

"It's a love-hate relationship, Oriano," Grace said to me the next morning in the family room while I painted the windows. "She loves me and hates me. And she does things to provoke me. Oh, she gets my Irish up. But I won't play her little mind games. I let her do her own thing. But it costs us, Oriano. You would not believe what we have put out for that girl. But she'll find her way eventually. I'm sure of it. It's in Jesus' hands."

I smiled. "How's the book I gave you?"

"I love it. It's my bedtime reading. I'm almost finished. I'll return it next week."

The book was *I Am with You Always: True Stories of Encounters with Jesus*, by G. Scott Sparrow; and I gave it to Grace the second day on my job. I also gave Grace two jars of Cathy's homemade jelly as a gesture of welcome to St. Jude—one blueberry, and the other wild cranberry and red wine which Cathy had never made before.

Brandon loved the cranberry and wine jelly. "I have a glow on when I go to school in the morning," he said to me, with a beaming smile. But the book inspired Grace to ask me if I had ever had a Jesus encounter.

I thought for a moment, wondering whether I should tell her or not; but I did. "Yes. Twice," I said, knowing very well that she would want details.

"Really?" Grace said, her voice imploring me.

"Yes. The first time when I knelt and prayed to Jesus for his help in a very desperate situation; and the second time in a dream experience."

"Oh, I would love to meet Jesus! How fortunate you are, Oriano! How blessed you must be—"

I thought it best to say nothing, so I just smiled.

"How? When?" Grace asked.

"Well, the first time was very personal. I was in a real pickle, Grace. My father was possessed by an unclean spirit that was

22

wreaking havoc in our home; so I turned to Jesus for help. And he came to me—"

"Oh, dear heart! Jesus came to you?"

"Yes. He gave me the strength to deal with my father's alcoholic demons—his unclean spirit; and I wrestled it to the ground. But I can't talk about it, Grace. It's the kind of stuff that novels are made of, so best leave it to fiction.

"And the second time?" she asked.

"On the other side," I replied.

"Pardon me?"

"In a dream. I met Jesus in a garden. I had a friend with me. A disgraced United Church minister. I wanted him to meet Jesus, so we met him in a dream."

Grace looked at me with a mixture of awe and wonder in her blue and brown eyes, which I could not get over because they gave me the impression that she was two separate people looking out of the same body. I smiled, because I knew that would shock her; but I felt it was time she saw a little more of me. I gave her a moment to digest what I said, and then added: "Dreams are a gateway to the other side, and it's not uncommon for people to meet Jesus in dreams. In fact, if memory serves me, some of the Jesus encounters in that book I gave you happened in the dream state, did they not?"

"Yes, they did; didn't they?" Grace said, finding her balance. "I would love to meet Jesus in my dreams."

"Just ask. Before going to sleep, ask Jesus if you can meet him in your dreams."

"Just like that?" Grace said, with some surprise.

"Yes. It might not happen the first night, or the second or third; but I'm sure you'll meet Jesus on the other side eventually. He's busy over here, Grace; so you might have to stand in line. Make an appointment. Imagine going into his office and asking his secretary to book you an appointment, and then just go to sleep with Jesus on your mind."

"You do have a writer's imagination, don't you?" Grace said, smiling at me. "Alright, I'll try it. What have I got to lose?"

"Good for you," I said, and laughed.

Try as she may, Grace couldn't quite read me; that's why I wanted to pursue my literary project. I wanted to record our talks because I felt that the symbolic implications of our two very different minds enjoined in Platonic discourse could prove not only fascinating from a literary perspective, but relevant to the whole spiritual movement that I saw taking place in society. In fact, I even brought up that very subject one day.

Once again we were in the dining room. It was my morning break, and we were having tea as usual. Herbal tea for myself this time because I had mentioned to Grace that I preferred herbal tea, so she surprised me one day with a package of mixed herbal teas. I was drinking peppermint tea that morning and somehow or other we found ourselves talking about the very sensitive subject of homosexuality.

"It's an unnatural act against God," Grace said, with a look of dogmatic severity on her Roman Catholic face. "I'm sorry, Oriano; but I cannot condone it. It's a sin."

"That's being judgmental, Grace. I neither condemn nor condone it; I simply try to understand it," I said, smiling at her sincerity.

But this threw her. She wasn't expecting such objectivity. And that's what puzzled her about me. Grace simply could not make me out. I knew that she liked whatever I had to say because it was so outside the box for her, but I threw her whole world view out of order with unexpected comments like my view on homosexuality.

"Then you believe it's genetic?" she said, after a moment's reflection.

"On the contrary, I don't. And I'll tell you why. When I took my vow of chastity (I had disclosed this to her in one of our talks) I was working for the summer in the town where one of my brothers lives, and in the evenings I tended to my brother's pool hall business. I had operated my own pool hall and vending machine business in St. Jude for a few years before I went to France to write my first novel, but that's another story waiting to be written. Anyway, having taken the vow of chastity yourself, you know very well that the libido can get pretty worked up; and unless one has a healthy, positive outlet for their sexual energies they're going to pervert their thoughts. Wouldn't you agree?"

"Yes, definitely," Grace said, without hesitation.

"Well, creative writing wasn't enough for me. I had too much sexual energy for reasons which I cannot disclose now because you wouldn't understand (I had accidentally awakened the "serpent fire," the kundalini energy lodged in the chakra at the base of the spine, while meditating one evening in Annecy, France), so it had to go somewhere; and where did my sexual energy go? Deeper into my mind, playing upon my imagination in ways that defy description. Eventually it latched onto the image of a young man who came into the pool hall every evening, a good-looking boy with slightly effeminate features; and wouldn't you know it, he began to excite me sexually. Grace, I kid you not; but I entertained the thought. Not because I secretly relished in sexual fantasies; I did not. I couldn't even fathom a sexual relationship with the same sex. I never have, and I still don't. I was simply infatuated with that young man. Not unlike Thomas Mann's protagonist in his novel *A Death in Venice*. Have you read it?"

"No. But I have read *The Magic Mountain*."

"Great novel. In any event, they made a movie of *A Death in Venice* starring Dirk Bogarde. He played the role of the dying Prussian writer Gustav von Aschenbach. The point being, he became infatuated with a beautiful young boy and became sexually aroused. So did I. I could not get him out of my mind. No; that's not true. Unlike Aschenback, I could get him out of my mind because I had developed the discipline from a teaching I was living at the time. But I consciously and deliberately entertained my secret infatuation for this young man because I wanted to see how much power it could have over me. However, when it got to the point where I could very easily have crossed the line into taking action I killed the infatuation. I had cultivated the inner discipline to do this. I had the moral strength and spiritual integrity to override any desire in my life; but I can't explain how I developed this trait. That's another novel. The point I want to make is that sexual desires aren't gender specific, because sexual energy isn't gender specific; it's just life energy, pure and simple. And it's up to us how we channel it. So if a person doesn't have the discipline to channel it, he or she can get caught up in sexual fantasies and behavior that go against the natural norm—like

25

homosexuality. So I don't believe it's genetic, Grace. I believe it's profoundly psychological. An archetypal play of energies, if you will. That's one explanation. There's another, much more esoteric; but I can't talk about that because I'm reserving that for a novel I'd like to write some day. I'm going to call it *Regression.*"

Awestruck, Grace didn't know what to say; so she just stared at me, her eyes probing my inscrutable soul. Finally she caught herself staring, and said, "Oriano, you never cease to amaze me!"

"Why?" I asked, smiling at her fascination with me.

"Because of the way you think. I've never met anyone who thinks like you. You're not afraid to take the bull by the horns, and I admire that. It shows character."

"Thank you. But it didn't come cheap," I said.

"It never does, does it?" she said, and smiled her warm, understanding smile. "So you wouldn't say that homosexuality is a sin, then?"

"Sin? What's that? When I was young I was terrified of missing Sunday Mass because it was a mortal sin; now they have Sunday Mass on Saturday night. I couldn't eat meat on Friday because it was a mortal sin, and now Catholics can eat meat any time they want. Sin? It's what the Church wants it to be. It's a state of mind, Grace. Like the immortal Bard said, 'there is nothing either good or bad but thinking makes it so.'"

"What about the Ten Commandments? Didn't God give them to Moses for man to live by?" Grace asked, her voice pleading with me to agree with her.

"Maybe he did, maybe he didn't; I don't know. Nor does anyone else for that matter. But no matter. I don't disagree with the discipline of the Ten Commandments, because man needs to harness his energies for his spiritual growth. But if you look up the etymology of the word sin you'll find that it comes from the Greek word *hamartia*, which means to miss the mark. So the question one has to ask is this: what is the mark? Do you know what the mark is, Grace?"

"Salvation," she quickly replied, her eyes wide open.

"I agree. But my understanding of salvation is slightly different from yours. Salvation for me means growth and enlightenment. It means spiritual self-realization and God consciousness. It means becoming one's true self. Salvation for you means—what?"

My question startled Grace. She sat back and thought for a moment or two. "It means going to heaven," she finally replied, nodding self-approval.

I laughed. "I'm sorry, Grace; but I can't help myself. That's so—what's the word? *Passé*? The belief of heaven and hell belongs to the past; which is why Christianity can't cut it in today's world. I know this offends your Catholic sensibilities, Grace; but the world is changing fast. Spiritual consciousness is awakening in every corner of the world today, and the old religious paradigms just can't contain the unfolding spirit of modern man. Heaven? Do you even know what that means? Is it a place, a concept, or a state of consciousness? What do you think?"

"I would think all of the above," Grace replied, with a nervous tremor in her otherwise confident voice. "I would think that heaven gives us something to strive for, and Jesus died on the cross to show us the way to into the kingdom of heaven; that's what I think," she added, with a finality in her voice that made me suspect I had gone too far.

I didn't want to leave our conversation on that note; so I had to restore my respect for the former Sister of Mercy's sacred faith—

"I agree with you. I believe Jesus showed us the way into the kingdom of heaven; but like I said, Jesus wasn't the only Wayshower. He showed us the Way according to his own understanding of the Way. From personal experience, I can tell you that there are many paths to the same place; and believe me Grace, the kingdom of heaven is a metaphor for the Way according to Jesus, a state of consciousness that one realizes as he lives the Way, and an actual place on the other side. But one doesn't have to die to go to heaven. One can go there anytime. Milton came close to this when he wrote in *Paradise Lost*, 'the mind is its own place, and it itself can make a heaven of hell, a hell of heaven.'"

Grace smiled a broad, approving smile that made me feel like one of her English lit students that had just scored an A-plus on his essay; and then she got up and went to the counter to plug in the kettle. "Some more hot water, Oriano?"

"Thank you, Grace; but I have to get back to work."

"We'll have to pick this up another time, then," she said, with some measure of satisfaction for my personal disclosure. "You do fascinate me, Oriano. Your views are so different from anything I have ever heard. You're so original that I don't know what to make of you. *I just don't know what to make of you!"*

"Well, Grace," I said, and then suddenly broke into laughter at the image that popped into my mind: I was a rare specimen that she had stumbled upon by pure chance. I had to tell her what I felt. "I see your life in St. Jude as another chapter in your quest for more meaning. You went into the convent to liberate your spiritual life from the materialism of the world; twenty years later you left the convent to liberate yourself from the confines of the cloistered life; and I suspect you left Newfoundland and moved to Ontario for the same spiritual need for more spiritual freedom, whether you were conscious of it or not. You did tell me that you see your whole life as a spiritual journey, didn't you?"

Grace laughed. *"As I said, you never cease to amaze me!"*

"Consciousness, Grace; that's what the spiritual journey is all about. Carl Jung wrote, 'My life is a story of the self-realization of the unconscious.' But that's true for all of us, isn't it? Some of us get there faster than others; that's all."

Grace smiled at me, and I felt her love as I went downstairs to take down the ugly brown imitation field stone wallboard so I could paint the walls the Dove White I had suggested to her and Brandon to open up their gloomy, depressing family room.

2. THAT HAPPY PLACE

Sometimes, though not very often these days, I get surprised when I get a call for a paint job, and Brandon Kendal surprised me. Actually, his secretary called. "Oriano, this is Jessie at St. Jude's. Our new principal would like an estimate to paint his new house."

"Oh, hi Jessie. Sure. Whose house did he buy?"

"Murray Benson's."

"The OPP?"

"Yes."

"Did Murray get transferred?"

"Yes. He's gone to Barrie."

"He wasn't here very long, was he?"

"Three years. His wife didn't like it here."

"Wasn't she the new physio at the hospital?"

"Yes. But she quit her job because she didn't get along with you-know-who."

I laughed. "Jessie, didn't they buy Tommy Ping's house?"

"Yes. And I hear it needs a paint job badly."

I laughed again. "What's your new principal's name?"

"Brandon Kendal. He can't come to the phone right now, but he can meet you at his house anytime after work."

"What time would be convenient for him?"

"He said anytime after four."

"Okay. Tell him I'll meet him at his place shortly after four. Oh, Jessie; do you know if the house is empty?"

"No. Their furniture came in the other day. Bummer, eh?"

"Oh, well; that's how it goes sometime. Make it four-thirty, would you please?"

"I'll tell him. Thanks Oriano," Jessie said; but when I drove up to the "executive house," as the self-important realtor Cora Maki grandiloquently described the split-level home to the Kendals, perched on McCrady Avenue overlooking our community of nineteen hundred people, the St. Jude River, the marina, and in the far distance the paper mill town of Rock Point on the shores of Lake Superior with smoke billowing out of its stacks, and which got the sun from sunrise to sunset—a breathtaking view that clinched the sale of the house for the Kendals—Brandon wasn't there yet; but his uncommonly friendly, smartly dressed, and very effusive wife with lovely red hair was though.

"I'm Grace Kendal," she said, giving me her hand to shake the moment I entered the back entrance. "Our home is a disaster," she quickly added. "We just got our furniture and I have nothing unpacked yet. I don't know where to start—"

"I'm Oriano Fellicci," I said, shaking her hand gently.

"Oh, Italian!" she said, with surprising enthusiasm. "I taught some Italian students when Brandon and I were living in Toronto. Brandon was working on his master's program. I love Italian culture. Brandon and I honeymooned in Italy. It was a belated honeymoon, mind you; but we loved Rome. We went to Naples and Venice also. I just love Italian culture. But you were born in Canada, weren't you?"

"No, Italy," I replied, with an irrepressible smile. I stepped inside and shut the door that I was still holding open.

"Isn't that wonderful? What part of Italy?"

"Calabria."

"Is that the north or south?"

"South."

"What part of the boot?"

"To tell you truth, I'm not quite sure right now. I think it's somewhere near the toe of the boot, but I'd have to check to make sure."

"No matter. Come in, come in. Brandon will be home any minute now. Please excuse the muddle. There's just not enough room in this house for all my furniture. But it was the only house on the market that could accommodate us. If you could only have seen my house in Newfoundland. I don't regret selling it, but I'm going to miss it. It's a beautiful home. I'm happy for the new owners. I'm sure they're going to love it. We did. Don't worry about your shoes, Oriano. We're going to be replacing the rug shortly. Please sit down. I'll just give Brandon a call—"

Grace sat on the love seat and used the phone on the end table. I sat down on the couch. My mind was busy processing all the information she had just given me.

I smiled to myself and glanced around the room. I had only been inside Tommy Ping's house once, when I gave him an estimate to paint it; but he never hired me. He had one of his employees from his store paint it.

Tommy Ping was the owner of the Canadian Tire in St. Jude, the only Canadian Tire store in the North Shore before they built one in Martin's Cove, so he could easily afford to hire a professional to paint his house; but not Tommy Ping. He always cut corners.

Tommy's old store on Front Street had burnt to the ground (word on the street was arson; or, to be more precise, "a Jewish fire" as Roy Hamilton called it), and he built his new store on the road coming into St. Jude from the Trans Canada Highway, three times the size of his old store which had no room for expansion (hence the lucky fire); but nine years later his new store with a three-bay service shop proved to be too small also. By that time however Tommy was ready to retire. He owned two apartment buildings in the city, one small strip mall, and a house in Vancouver where he originally came from.

"Brandon's on his way," Grace said, interrupting my thoughts. "That was Jessie, his secretary. A wonderful lady. Do you know her, Oriano?"

"Yes," I said, and smiled again. Grace's friendliness intrigued me.

"Well, we'll just wait until Brandon gets here. Tell me, Oriano; have you lived in St. Jude long?"

"Most of my life. I was only five when we immigrated. But I lived in France for a year. In the Alpine city of Annecy, in the *Haute-Savoie* region near the Swiss border."

"How wonderful! What did you do there?"

"I worked on my first novel. *This Petty Pace,* taken from Macbeth's famous soliloquy. 'Tomorrow and tomorrow and tomorrow creeps in this petty pace,'" I quoted. I don't know why on earth I revealed that. It just came out of my mouth.

"Yes, I heard that you were a writer. That young man, Gerry something-or-other, the plumber who hooked up the water for our fridge, told me that you were a writer. He said St. Jude is a very eclectic community. Would you agree?"

"Oh, I don't know. For me eclecticism implies the best of many sources, and I have trouble finding the best in St. Jude. Mediocrity would be more to the core," I replied, and broke into an ironic chuckle.

Grace smiled, staring at me; and that's when I noticed the color of her eyes.

She caught me. "Yes, they are a different color," she said, with a proud smile on her lightly freckled, fresh-looking very Irish face (despite the few lines). "This one's blue, and this one is what I like to call hazel chestnut; but everyone says it's brown. They go with my astrological sign, Oriano; I'm a Gemini."

"That's incredible," I said, still trying to process why she was so familiar with me.

"Isn't it?" she replied, with a restrained but proud smile. "And you? What sign are you, Oriano?"

"Leo," I replied.

"I should have guessed," she said, giving me another warm smile.

Grace had a beautiful smile. Her whole being seemed to be reflected in her smile, as though she had practiced the art of smiling and mastered its secret. I couldn't quite describe it at the time; but later, in the novel that she would inspire me to write, the word that I used to capture the essence of her smile was "beatific."

"Let me ask you something, Grace," I said, chuckling to myself at the thought that had just popped into my mind; "does this imply a paradoxical personality."

"Oh gracious, yes!" she exclaimed. "How perceptive!"

I laughed. I couldn't help myself. I had never experienced such instant rapport with a person before. Usually it takes two or three days of working in a person's home to be on such friendly terms. "In what way," I had to ask.

32

"I was a nun for twenty years, Oriano," she calmly replied in a much softer voice, instantly transforming before my eyes into a poised, demure nun.

Now I was really intrigued. *"No kidding?"* I said.

"Not at all. I belonged to the Sisters of Mercy. I took my vow of poverty, Oriano. I owned absolutely nothing. And I mean nothing. It's a very strict Order. And I was a woman of the world when I joined the Sisters. I was a secretary on an American military base in St. John's and I loved nice clothes and things. I had my own apartment and everything. But it wasn't enough for me, Oriano. I wasn't fulfilled. I needed more meaning in my life—"

Just then Brandon entered the house. He came into the living room. He had his suit jacket draped around his left arm, and his tie was loose.

I stood up and gave him my hand. "Oriano Fellicci," I said.

"Brandon Kendal," he said with a warm smile as he firmly shook my hand, his eyes sizing me up. "I'm pleased to meet you, Oriano. My secretary referred you to me."

"Yes, I've painted her house."

Grace took Brandon's jacket and hung it on one of the dining room chairs and returned to the love seat beside Brandon.

"Jessie has nothing but good to say about you, Oriano," Brandon said.

I smiled. Shortly after Jessie kicked her husband out of the house for having an affair with a young waitress at the North Star Restaurant and getting her pregnant she called me to paint her house."To change the atmosphere," she told me. I liked Jessie and felt sorry for her, so I painted her house for half the cost, throwing in a textured living room ceiling for free; so I wasn't surprised to hear that she spoke highly of me.

"That's always nice to hear," I said.

"We've just been having a nice chat," Grace said.

"Fascinating, actually," I added.

"Good. So you haven't shown him the house yet, Grace?"

"Not yet, dear. We were waiting for you."

"Very good. Well, Oriano; I think we want most of the house painted—"

"Oh yes, I should think so," Grace interjected. "I'll have to show you some photos of our house in St. John's, Oriano. It was supposed to be our retirement home, but—"

"You were too young to retire," I quickly offered.

"Exactly," Brandon said. "I was getting bored, Oriano. I needed a new challenge."

"You'll certainly have that in St. Jude," I said, with a wry smile. "After all, this is the town of hopeless causes."

Both husband and wife broke out. They could not help themselves. I knew that what I said was funny, but I didn't think it was that funny. I must have struck a private cord.

"How ironic!" Grace said, smiling at her husband. *"Oriano, if you only knew the story behind our move to St. Jude!"*

"I can imagine. You probably took it on as a spiritual cause, didn't you?"

Grace gave Brandon another look, and her face lit up with a radiant, loving smile. Brandon smiled back, with equal love and warmth in his smile. In that brief instant a whole lifetime of marriage passed between them. They turned to me, and Grace said, "Oriano, we're doing the Lord's work. We've always done the Lord's work."

"And what would the Lord like us to do with your house?" I said, and laughed.

They both laughed again, but with reverent restrain this time. Neither one expected such a comment. Then Grace replied in kind, *"We could certainly use the Lord's help for this house, Oriano!"*

I burst out. It was precious. I couldn't believe that a person could catch the capricious spirit of my sense of humor so quickly. "Well, Grace," I said, when I stopped laughing; "as immodest as this may sound, I've been known to work miracles with paint."

"I'm so glad. We do need one here, Oriano," she replied.

And she was right. As they showed me the house I spotted imperfections in every room they wanted painted, which was the whole house save Michael's workout room and a spare bedroom in the basement that Grace was going to use for storage.

The most glaring imperfections were in the workmanship to the stained baseboards and door and window casings and living room

34

ceiling corner moldings. The mitre cuts were atrocious, with some gaps standing out like little caverns.

I told Tommy Ping that I could caulk those cracks when I gave him my painting estimate, but obviously he didn't care; which didn't surprise me, because Tommy Ping didn't appear to me to have any aesthetic sensibilities.

And it didn't surprise me that the Benson's didn't do anything about the eyesores either, because I had worked for the OPP over the years and they were infamous for not putting anything into a house because they never stayed more than a few years—unless they purchased an older home, did some cheap cosmetic work (which they usually did themselves), and then dumped it on the market for a much higher price when they got transferred. It didn't matter to them because the government guaranteed the sale of their house; so either way, they came out winners. But they weren't my kind of winners, and I never liked working for them; and school teachers, for that matter.

So it didn't really surprise me that Brandon didn't want the trim in his house painted; just the ceilings and walls. "We don't know how long we're going to be here, Oriano," he justified. "We just want to spruce it up a bit. Wouldn't you say so, Grace?"

Grace didn't reply. She just sighed. I could tell that they had discussed this and that was the conclusion they had come to; but Grace wasn't satisfied. Finally, unable to contain herself, she said, "Oriano, what would you do?"

"To be honest with you, the trim in this house looks terrible. The workmanship leaves a lot to be desired. But I'll tell you what I can do. I'll work out an estimate for all the painting that you want done, and if you still have room in your budget to caulk and paint the trim then I'd go ahead with it."

"What about the doors?" Grace asked, staring at the front entrance mahogany door. "I cannot live with that, Oriano. I cannot."

"I've painted mahogany doors before, and it improved them considerably. There's not much more you can do with them."

"Okay. Include the doors in your estimate, Oriano; and we'll see about the trim later," Brandon said, making an executive decision;

but I knew that his wife would override him. It was only a matter of time, so I said nothing.

I worked out the estimate to paint all the rooms and doors, and then I said: "For the trim, if you decide to go ahead with it, it'll be twenty-five dollars an hour. That'll take me half a day for caulking and two more days for priming and painting, so that would be another five hundred dollars plus paint and GST."

"Let's go ahead with the painting and we can talk about the trim later," Brandon said, and gave me his hand to shake on my estimate.

"Fair enough," I said, happy to get the job. "I'll leave my color charts with you so you can think and sleep on the colors."

"Do you have any suggestions?" Grace asked.

"What was the theme color of your house back home?" I asked.

"An off-white," Grace replied.

"Why don't you be bold this time, Grace. I'm sure it's taken a lot of courage to make this move at this time in your life; be bold and choose some exciting new colors for this house. It could use some excitement."

They both laughed. "What color would you suggest for our living room?" Grace asked, as she glanced around the room.

I opened one of my Sherwin Williams charts and studied the colors. I knew which one I preferred, but I made out like I was thinking. "This one," I said, pointing my finger on it for them to see. "It's called Tempting Teal. Even the name of this color suggests the spirit of adventure," I added, and broke into gentle laughter at the synchronicity.

They both smiled at me, their eyes telling me that they saw much more than your everyday housepainter in me. "Will it go with our new rug, though?" Grace asked.

"What color is your new rug?" I asked.

"It has to go with my furniture, Oriano. Something like this," she said, pointing to the beige in the floral design of her sofa and love seat which had inspired my choice.

"Yes, it'll work," I said. "But why don't you sleep on it for a few days. I won't be able to start until I clean up my other job. I'll be done in about two weeks."

"Good. That should give me plenty of time to get my house in order," Grace said; and Brandon added, "Would you like some money now for the paint?"

"No. When the job's done," I said.

"Are you sure, Oriano?" Grace asked.

"Yes; but thank you all the same. I'll come up and see you before I start; okay?"

"Very good," Brandon said, giving me his hand to shake again.

When I left I couldn't get them out of my mind. Unlike all the school teachers I had worked for in over twenty years of contracting, Brandon surprised me because he didn't fit the mold; he accepted my estimate without quibbling.

I respected that. But more than that, I respected them for their courage to make such an audacious move at a time in their life when most people would gladly settle into early retirement; and I was determined to find out why they left St. John's, Newfoundland to move to St. Jude, a small, inconsequential town in northern Ontario named after the patron saint of hopeless causes...

I had one more week to complete the job I was on when I got a call from Grace early Saturday morning. She wanted me to come up to the house—"only if you're free," she very graciously said—to help her decide what color to paint her doors.

Brandon was in the city attending a district school board meeting. Grace would have joined him, but their son Michael was driving in from St. John's and would be arriving some time during the day.

We had decided on white for the doors, but Grace wasn't comfortable with white. "I painted all the doors at my house Dusty Rose," I offered, and opened the chart to show her the color. "But it only works at my place because all my trim is white. I don't think it would work here, Grace. All you're woodwork is stained brown—"

"I can't stand it," Grace said. "Why don't we just go ahead and paint the trim all white? Then we can paint the doors Dusty Rose. What do you think, Oriano?"

"That works for me," I said, smiling.

"Good. We'll do that, then," she said, with a sense of finality in her worldly voice.

"Would you like to run it by Brandon first?" I asked, just to give her a graceful way out in case her husband didn't approve.

"That won't be necessary," she said, with a hint of mischief in her smile. "We both trust your judgment, Oriano."

"Thank you," I said, and laughed. "Pardon me for laughing, Grace," I added; "but I was just thinking of the woman I'm currently painting for. She simply couldn't make up her mind what color to choose; and she still hasn't chosen the color for her family room yet. She says she's emotionally drained from a bad marriage, but I think she's stuck between a rock and a hard place."

Grace looked at me, her intriguing eyes beckoning me to explain. I smiled, and did so. "She told me her ex husband couldn't make any decisions. She had to make them all, and that drained her emotionally. That's why she has trouble making up her mind now. But from where I stand Grace, I think she's just justifying her inability to take responsibility for the choices she makes. That's why she can't make up her mind. A rock and a hard place."

"A rock and a hard place?" Grace repeated, imploringly.

"I'm sorry. I didn't make myself clear. This lady wants to be in control of her new relationship like she was in control of her marriage. Being in control means having to make decisions. But she doesn't want the responsibility for making wrong decisions in case she scares off the new man in her life; hence her paralyzing fear of making decisions."

"Oh, I see. A rock and a hard place. Good. That's very insightful, Oriano. And do you think I'm stuck between a rock and a hard place here?"

I laughed. "Not at all. I see you as a woman who knows exactly what she wants but who respects other people."

Grace smiled. "Thank you," she said.

38

"That's a happy combination, Grace," I added, in my philosophical voice. "Believing in oneself enough to know what one wants out of life, but at the same time being aware that other people are entitled to the same thing and respecting them for it. It's a tricky marriage, Grace; but if one can get personal choice and respect for others to work together, one will get along well with the world."

"That's very Socratic," Grace said, with a warm, approving smile. "That sounds like a marriage made in heaven."

I laughed. "Good one, Grace!"

Grace laughed too. Then, very seriously, she said, "How have you learned to reconcile the two, Oriano?"

"It hasn't been easy. On the whole people are blind to their own selfishness, and this always throws a monkey wrench into one's capacity for personal choice. The trick for me has been to draw the line in my relationships with people. One way or another, I let them know when they have crossed it and tell them to back off—"

"And respectfully back off yourself when you see that you are crossing another person's line," Grace firmly added.

"Exactly. That's why it's such a tricky marriage. It takes courage to stand your own ground, and a lot of wisdom to know when to back off. If you don't mind me asking, Grace; how did you come to such a happy marriage?"

"I love my husband," she said, with a twinkle in her eyes. "But to answer your question, it took time Oriano. We both had to iron out a lot of personal hang-ups before finding that happy place. Are you married?"

"No. But I am with a lady. Her name's Cathy Collingwood. We've been together for ten years now. And yes, you're right; it takes time to find that happy place."

"And have you found it?"

"Yes," I said, and smiled proudly.

"And how would you define your happy place, Oriano?"

I smiled again. "I'll define mine if you define yours."

"That's only fair," she said, with a playful twinkle.

"Well, I'd have to say that love is the main ingredient. Without love you can't have a happy place in a relationship. I love Cathy and she loves me. But that's a given. The trick to making a

39

relationship work—and I would think any romantic relationship—is knowing how to keep love alive; and that's where wisdom comes into play. Without wisdom every relationship is doomed to failure."

"And how have you kept your relationship alive, Oriano?"

"It wasn't easy, because Cathy came from a home where love didn't grow. As a matter of fact—and this is very personal, Grace—Cathy subverted our love many times without realizing what she was doing. It took a lot of wisdom and patience to nurture our love to the point where it could withstand the unconscious blows of our shadow."

"I beg your pardon?" Grace said.

"Are you familiar with the Jungian concept of the shadow self?"

"I'm afraid not. What is it?"

"The shadow is that part of the human personality that pulls us down into spiritual darkness. Love is Light, Grace; and the shadow does not like the Light. That's why it's so hard for people to keep love alive in their relationships. The dark side of the personality forever seeks to sabotage our love; so the trick to a happy place in one's life is, as Jesus put it, "to die to one's life." In other words, Grace; we have to kill the darkness to live in the Light. That's the metaphysics of a happy place," I added, with a wry smile.

Grace's face went serious, and I felt a sudden intensity of emotion. Tears began to trickle down her cheeks. I couldn't believe it. I didn't know what to say, or do; so I just let her cry. She didn't even seem to be aware of me.

Finally, she said, "Excuse me a moment, please," and went into the kitchen. She came back with Kleenex crumpled in her right hand. "I'm sorry for being so emotional."

"I must have struck a chord," I said, moved by her tears.

"Yes, you did. I do believe that there are forces of Darkness and forces of Light in the world. And I believe that we are forever at war with the forces of Darkness. But we have our Lord Jesus to protect us—"

"Yes, we do. Alright, Grace," I said, in my most cheerful, upbeat voice; "it's your turn now. How do you define your happy place?"

Grace's whole face lit up and her eyes sparkled with love. "Well, Oriano; I'd have to say that I love my husband first and foremost. But as you said, love must be kept alive; and we keep our love alive by respecting, supporting, and caring for each other. We're the best of friends, Oriano. We share everything. Absolutely everything. That comes from our religious training. Brandon was a monk before we met—"

"A monk?" I said, incredulously.

"Yes. For twenty-two years. He was going to take his vows for the priesthood, but he decided against it. Then like me he felt he wasn't getting as much out of his calling as he needed to be fulfilled as a person, so he left the Order. I left the convent and went to the same school where Brandon was teaching, and we fell in love and got married within the year. So we share the same spiritual values, Oriano. That's the secret to our happy place."

"Sharing the same spiritual values?"

"Yes."

"One couldn't ask for more. Happily, Cathy and I share the same spiritual values also; otherwise we wouldn't be together."

"Is she Catholic too?" Grace asked, with a radiant smile.

"No," I replied.

Grace's smile disappeared, but she didn't pursue the subject. "You're a fascinating man, Oriano," she said instead. "I don't think I've talked like this in years. You're so easy to talk to. Why is that, do you think?"

"I must have been a priest in a past life," I said, and laughed. I said that just to test the limits of her faith which denounced the idea of past lives.

Smiling, she said, "Maybe you should have become a priest."

"I did consider it when I was growing up. As a matter of fact, I tortured over it."

"If you had to torture over it, then it wasn't for you. You made the right decision, Oriano. I'm sure of it," she replied, with authority in her voice.

"I know I did," I said, smiling at her conviction.

"A decision to serve the Lord can only be made out of love, Oriano. It won't work any other way," she added, ending the subject;

41

but I saw an opening that I had to explore. I simply couldn't help myself—

"And what about leaving the Order? That couldn't have been an easy decision for you to make. Or was it, Grace?"

"No. I agonized over it for six years," she replied, with surprising candor.

I wanted to inquire further, but I didn't think I had earned the privilege yet; so I said, "And now you're happily married and all's well that ends well—"

She laughed. "You're so positive, Oriano. I'm looking forward to having you paint our house. I'm going to enjoy our conversations. When will you be able to start?"

"I have one more week to finish my current job, so I can start your house the following Monday. Do you want me to go ahead with the Dusty Rose, then?"

"Yes."

"And white for all the trim?"

"Yes."

"Are you sure?"

"Positive."

"Okay," I said, and got up to leave; but Grace didn't want me to leave just yet.

"Do you have to rush off?" she asked, her eyes imploring me to stay.

"Cathy and I are going into the city for groceries, but I won't pick up the paint for your house today; I'll pick it up next Saturday, so I'll just leave the color charts. That'll give you another week to sleep on the colors, just in case you decide to change your mind—"

"No, I've decided; but I was just going to offer you a cup of tea," she said, with the friendliest smile. I couldn't resist; so I sat back down.

"Sure, why not? I'd love to have a cup of tea with you, Grace."

"Oh good! I'll just go and put the kettle on…"

I couldn't get over Grace crying. Her tears said more to me about her as a person than all the impressions I had of her put together; and they were all good impressions.

Her tears were the same kind of tears that come to me whenever I watch a man or woman cross the finish line of a long distance race, especially a triathlon. It's not the victory as such that moves me to tears, but what it took for them to get there; that's what Grace's tears told me.

In that moment of instant emotional disclosure I saw the naked soul of what the author of my favorite poem and spiritual ideal called a "happy warrior." *"Who is the happy warrior?"* asks Wordsworth; and Grace answered the question for me with her tears.

"It is the generous Spirit," said the poet who touched the hem of God; and in Grace I saw a soul large enough to contain all of heaven, and my heart reached out to her in blissful sympathy. I knew from those few tears that whatever else she told me about herself she would never be as naked again, and I had to respect that because it was sacred ground. That, and not the love for her husband, was her happy place, because it was from that wellspring that all of her love flowed—the secret source of her spiritual life.

"Whosoever drinketh of the water that I shall give him shall never thirst," said Jesus. **"The water that I shall give him shall be in him a well springing up into everlasting life,"** and in Grace's tears I saw the water of a true believer; that's why she inspired respect in me from the moment I first set eyes on her.

I just *knew* that she was a kindred spirit. We had walked the same lonely path together. We were apart in time, distance, and faiths; but I had lived the same sayings of her Lord and Savior Jesus, and that made us kindred warriors.

It was instant recognition. A split second before her tears began to flow I was overwhelmed by the emotional energy of her whole spiritual life. It enveloped me and became one with my own life force, and I felt her godly sorrow in all of its carefulness, all of its clearing, all of its indignation, and all of its vehement desire, zeal, and revenge.

I knew that Grace was born in Christ; not in the way that TV evangelists talk of being born in Christ, but in the only way that Jesus

43

meant it—by dying to oneself, *"for whosoever will save his life shall lose it; and whosoever will lose his life for my sake shall find it,"* said Jesus. The tears that Grace shed in front of me told me that.

That excited me. I had never met another soul born of Christ's teaching. I had birthed myself with the help of other secret teachings, but in the transformative sayings of Jesus I found the extra strength I needed to extricate myself from the material consciousness of my mortal womb; and for that I was eternally grateful to Jesus.

That's why I kept my conversations with Grace within the Christian paradigm. But, I humbly confess, within my own spiritually enlightened understanding of the Christian paradigm and not within the dark and obfuscating paradigm that Christianity continues to offer the spiritually famished soul of man.

Our meeting was synchronistic. There was no other way to describe it. Nothing in life happens by chance. I had lived the spiritual life of the Way too long and experienced too many incredible coincidences to believe in random chance; and meeting Grace Kendal had symbolic implications that went well beyond our comprehension. It honestly felt like we were two characters in a novel that was yet to be written; and it terrified me.

But I went with it. I had no choice, for I too served God in my own way. And I opened myself up to the experience and let Holy Spirit do with me what it deemed. "And that," I said to Grace on the third day after I started painting her house, "was the passkey that opened the door to the mysteries of the Way. Let go and let God; that's the secret. But sadly, it's a paradox that very few people understand."

"How so?" Grace asked. "Jesus clearly tells us what the will of God is. Love your neighbor as yourself. Do unto others as you would have them do unto you—"

"I understand, Grace; the more we live the Way—be it according to Jesus Christ, the Buddha, Socrates, Lao Tzu, or whoever—the more we align our will with the will of God. I know this. You know this. But what do we do when we don't have a sign pointing us in the direction of God's will? What do we do then, Grace?"

"I don't follow you," she replied, furrowing her brow.

"Or when our deepest conviction goes against an express commandment of the Way as we understand it?" I added, to complete my thought. "What if I fall in love with a married woman, for example? I know that I'm told by one of the commandments to not pursue this love, but what if I can't help myself? I love her, and she loves me. Her marriage is no longer viable. She is unhappy and miserable in her marriage. What then? Do we suffer in silence rather than consummate this love as Cathy and I have done?"

"Jesus did say, 'Strait is the gait, and narrow is the way,' Oriano—"

I laughed. "Believe me; I know how straight and narrow the Way is, Grace. *Been there, done that!* But that's a naïve understanding of the Way. I know this may sound presumptuous, but the Way of Jesus Christ—or any spiritual teacher for that matter—is not a collection of moral guidelines, because the Way cannot be contained by any one set of rules to live by. The simple truth is that the Way is life itself; and learning how to live life with love is what God's will boils down to."

"I don't disagree with you, Oriano; but we do have to have moral guidelines to govern us," Grace responded, holding firm her precious ground.

"I'm not suggesting we throw them away, Grace. I'm saying that there's going to come a time in one's s journey through life when one can no longer be contained by the rules that he has chosen to live by. This doesn't mean that one can bend and break these rules to suit his fancy, not at all; it means that one has to transcend them if he wants to continue growing spiritually. And the only way to transcend a moral set of rules that constrain one's spiritual growth is to live by a higher spiritual law."

"But can there be a higher spiritual law than what Jesus set down for us to live by?" Grace asked, with the hint of a triumph in her smile.

"The difficulty with the teaching that Jesus brought to the world is that no one understands its essential purpose, which is the transformation of consciousness. The sayings of Jesus are the means by which one can transform the human self and give birth to his spiritual self. And when this miracle happens one becomes a spiritual

45

law unto himself. This is the meaning behind the puzzling saying that those born of the Spirit are unpredictable—because Spirit is not contained by any set of rules. *Capisce*, Grace?"

Grace *did* understand me, but she did not reply; she just stared at me and smiled. In her smile I saw her freedom, but Grace Kendal was devoutly Roman Catholic; and she could not go against her faith. And that's what attracted me to her.

It was a purely Platonic attraction, and I looked forward to every opportunity to talk with her; and there were many. In fact we had most of our conversations while I painted. I had to work, but I wasn't going to stop the flow of our talks just to work.

Something was going on between us. We both felt it, but it was difficult to put to words. Then one day Grace said something that began to shed light on our talks. "Oriano, my faith is my life. I've sacrificed everything for my love of Jesus. But I feel a stirring in my soul. That's why we moved to Ontario. I dread the thought, Oriano; but—"

"The boundaries of your faith are being tested, Grace; that's why we're dialoguing as we are," I replied, with a warm smile. I knew exactly where she was coming from.

"Do you think so?" she asked, with a puzzled look.

"It's providential," I said, with an ironic chuckle at how life worked.

"But my faith is my life, Oriano. I don't want my faith to be tested any more. As you said, I've been there and done that. I would simply like to live out the rest of my life in Christian peace—"

I chuckled at the thought of all the wars and massacres and atrocities committed in the name of Christianity. "I'm sorry, Grace; but I can't help myself. I find the concept oxymoronic. Christian peace? What's that?"

"Living as Jesus Christ would want us to live; that's my concept of Christian peace," Grace readily offered, as though answering a Catechism question.

"But you have a stirring in your soul—"

"Yes; and I'm very familiar with this stirring. I'm just going to have to pray for guidance. That's all I can do."

"I know the feeling well. I've had that same stirring in my soul so many times that I could smell it long before it wrapped its tentacles around me. I don't envy you, Grace. I know what you're in for. But as I've written in one of my books, *'there's only one way out of life, and that is through life.'* You've got no choice, Grace. You've taken the first step of another long journey by making this courageous move to St. Jude, so just go with it. If you resist it, it will only squeeze tighter; and the tighter it squeezes, the more you will suffer. It's axiomatic, Grace."

"I know, Oriano. I know…"

That's what I hated about Christianity. It kept the lid on the mysteries of the spiritual life. And it did this by obfuscating the mysteries of the Way with a mythology that has become so deeply rooted in the psyche of man that it has taken on its own shadow life; and it was this archetypal shadow that I had to wrestle with to transcend my suffocating Christian faith. And that was Grace's dilemma. She could not tell which Christ she was serving; the real Jesus, one of the greatest teachers of the Way that the world has ever known, or the Shadow Christ—an archetypal savior conjured up in the collective unconscious out of fear and lust for control of man's mind and soul.

I knew this going into every talk I had with Grace, but I dared not reveal myself. It wasn't my place to threaten her precious faith. I knew that, because I lived by a higher law than that of Christianity—the Spiritual Law of Non-interference.

No one has the right to interfere in another person's spiritual destiny; that's the Law of the Way. But Christianity doesn't recognize this law, because it does everything in its power to convert people to its faith. And in doing so Christianity subverts Soul and keeps society from transcending itself. I tried to point this out to Grace one day when she brought up the subject of suffering—

"Suffering is good for the soul, Oriano," she said, as though it was a cosmic law.

I chuckled. "I'm sorry, Grace," I apologized for my laughter; "but the conclusion that I've come to in my quest for answers to life's big questions is that suffering is for fools. I don't mean to disparage the spiritually liberating power of suffering; but how many times must a man be kicked in the head before he wakes up to how life works?"

"We learn through suffering, Oriano," Grace replied, holding her ground.

"I accept that. But once we have learned our lesson must we continue to suffer?"

"If that's what God wants of us, yes," she said, with an unexpected look of apprehension. *This was the first test of her faith in our Platonic relationship.*

I didn't want to pursue it, because I knew that suffering was central to Grace's faith; but I didn't want to let it go either, because I had paid too dear a price to free myself from the hold that the Shadow Christ had upon my psyche.

I had literally impaired my eyesight because of my blind faith in Christianity (by following the secret teachings of an offshoot Christian solar cult teaching), and although that was almost twenty years ago there was still enough anger in me to confront the lustful shadow of Christianity once again—

"Never again, Grace," I replied. "Never again will I forfeit my will to another. St. Paul tells us to work out our own salvation, but I didn't understand him at the time. I do now, though. I was a fool for believing many things that Christianity holds to be true, but I got kicked in the head once too often because of my blind faith; and I refuse to be kicked in the head ever again. Christianity is your faith, Grace; not mine."

"I hit a nerve, Oriano," Grace said, very softly in her Sister of Mercy's voice.

The softness of her voice threw me. It forced me to see my warrior self; and smiling at her, I said, "Yes, you did. It's a long story, Grace."

"Why the animus, Oriano?" she quietly asked.

"An offshoot Christian solar cult teaching called Somology," I replied. "A solar cult brought into the world by a so-called Child Christ. It impaired my eyesight, Grace; but I can't talk about that now. Not until I write about it first."

"I understand. But didn't Jesus tell us to look out for false prophets?"

48

"Oh Grace, the world according to the Roman Catholic Church—how simple it is!"

"But it is simple, Oriano. We don't have to look any further than Jesus Christ."

"This stirring in your soul, Grace; what do you think brought it on?"

"I don't know. I shouldn't even have mentioned it. I'm not sure it is even a stirring," Grace responded, with obvious regret in her voice.

She wasn't ready yet to step outside her paradigm. I smiled, and said, "The Way beckons you again, Grace. Listen to your heart. Just listen…"

When the Way beckons Soul must listen, because if it doesn't we suffer. That's the way life works, and no one is going to change that. I tried and failed, and so have many seekers. In the end, if we are wise, we will submit and play ball with God.

Learning the rules of life is what the Way is all about, and every time we break a rule we suffer. That's why I told Grace that suffering was for fools, because it's foolish to continue breaking the rules when it only leads to more suffering; but we do. Why?

"Consciousness, Grace; that's why," I revealed to her one Monday morning. I didn't expect our conversation to be so philosophical first thing in the morning. I had just started painting the computer room when Grace came in with something on her mind—

"Oriano, I've been thinking all weekend about something you said. You said that there are spiritual laws that govern life that we aren't aware of, didn't you?"

"Yes."

"And if we break these laws we will suffer one form of personal tragedy or another; isn't that what you said?"

"Depending upon the severity of our violation of the spiritual law that we break."

"I understand. But what I couldn't get out of my mind all weekend was your comment that suffering is for fools. Is that what you meant, that only fools break these spiritual laws that they can't see? Do you see my dilemma?"

49

"I know exactly how you feel, Grace. I anguished over this dilemma for years. How do we know that we are breaking a spiritual law if we don't know what it is? But that's how God plays the game of life with us. That's God throwing the ball into our court. Here, says God; here's the ball. Let me see you score now!"

Grace smiled at my metaphor; but she was so threatened by my comment about suffering that she had to get an explanation. "Oriano," she said, in her soft voice which I had by now come to recognize as her warrior's voice, "I took your comment about suffering very personally. I did not want to say anything to you on Friday because it took me by surprise. It literally threw me, Oriano. I have never heard of such a thing. I have always believed that suffering is good for the soul. This is central to my faith. After all, Jesus suffered and died on the cross for our sins. Suffering is the way of the cross. Through suffering we are born in Christ. That's the way of the Church of God, Oriano. That's what I have believed all of my life. But you tell me that suffering is for fools, and I am forced to conclude that you are calling me a fool."

"Not you personally, Grace."

"Yes, me. I know you didn't call me a fool intentionally; but it was implicit."

"You're right. I apologize. It was implicit. But only if you fall into that category."

"Apparently I do. But be that as it may; I want to know why you believe that suffering is for fools. I'm not sure I understand what you mean by this. It puzzled me all weekend, Oriano. I discussed it with Brandon, and we can't fathom your comment."

"Put some tea on, Grace. This is going to be a two-cup talk," I said, and laughed.

"Grace laughed also. "Okay, I'll do that," she said, and turned to leave.

When tea was ready Grace called me. "Jesus died on the cross," I began, very slowly. It was a steep ascent we had to climb, and I didn't want to scare her off. "You believe that he died for the sins of the world. I don't believe that. But whether he did or not we both agree that the concept of self-sacrifice is central to Christ's teaching, would we not?"

50

"Yes," she replied, very softly.

"When we talk of self-sacrifice we both mean that we have to die to that part of ourselves that keeps us from what Jesus calls the kingdom of heaven; yes or no?"

"Yes. *'Verily I say unto you, except you be converted, and become as little children, ye shall not enter into the kingdom of heaven.'* Mathew. 18: 3. That's what Jesus said."

"And what keeps us from being as little children?" I asked.

"Our adult capacity for sin," she replied, with conviction in her voice.

"Children are innocent, then?"

"Yes."

"Innocence then is what we are looking for in order to be saved—or enter into the kingdom of heaven, if you will?"

"Yes."

"Would you agree that innocence is a form of purity of soul? An unblemished inner self, if you will?"

"Yes, certainly. Only the pure of heart will enter the kingdom of heaven, Oriano. That I know for a fact."

"I know you do, Grace. Your smile tells me that. Okay; purity of heart. By heart we mean consciousness, though; don't we?"

"I guess we do. Well, maybe not. What does it mean to have a pure mind and a pure heart?" she asked, making sure that she was on solid footing.

"Can you have one without the other?" I asked.

"I'm not sure," she said.

"Look at yourself, Grace. If you have an impure thought does it not blemish your heart?" I asked, giving her a hand up the steep ascent of Plato's cave.

"I think you're right, Oriano. But what are you leading to? Are you saying that we have to sacrifice the impurity of our heart and mind?"

"Consciousness, Grace; we have to purify our consciousness in order to see the spiritual laws we are breaking that are responsible for our suffering. That's the essence of Christ's teaching. His sayings taken together are a complex spiritual methodology for the transformation—or purification, if you will—of our consciousness.

51

That's what Jesus meant by self-sacrifice. And whether you believe that his death upon the cross was an actual death or a symbolic death makes no difference to the central message of his teaching, because it works either way—if we live it, that is. You know it works, Grace; and I know it works. We just don't agree on why Jesus died on the cross, that's all. Are you following me?"

"Yes, I think so. By living our life as Jesus wants us to live it we sacrifice our impurities and become as little children, because only as little children can we enter into the kingdom of heaven. Is that what you are saying?"

"Yes. But the problem we have as adults is that we aren't aware of all the spiritual laws; so we can break them without realizing it. That's what makes the spiritual journey so damn frustrating—"

Grace laughed. "Jesus told us how to live, Oriano. What more could we want?"

"Do you remember what Jesus said to his disciples when they asked him why he spoke to the multitude in parables?"

"Yes. He said that it was not given to the public to know the mysteries of the kingdom of heaven, but to them it was," Grace replied, with an apprehensive smile.

"And he goes on to say, *'For whosoever hath, to him shall be given, and he shall have more in abundance; but whosoever hath not, from him shall be taken away even that he hath.'* Doesn't Jesus imply by this that the more we learn of the mysteries of the kingdom of heaven, the more of the mysteries we will become conscious of? In other words, Grace; through his sayings and parables Jesus gave the multitudes the means to transform their consciousness enough so they could open themselves to more of the mysteries of the kingdom of heaven which, if I may be so bold, is Christ's metaphor for the Way."

"What is? I don't follow you, Oriano."

"The kingdom of heaven is Christ's metaphor for the Way. Read the Gospels with that in mind Grace, and they will take on a whole new meaning. In any event, the point I want to make is that Jesus is telling us in his characteristically cryptic manner that the more we live the Way the more the Way will reveal itself to us. In other words, the more we live his teaching of self-sacrifice—you know, dying to one's life to save one's life—the more we become as

52

little children; and that's how we are saved. Now, we differ on what he meant by being saved. Christianity says that we go to heaven when we are saved; but I believe Jesus simply meant that our soul is liberated from the impure consciousness of our human self. Are you still with me, Grace?"

"I'm not sure," she replied, not knowing whether to be offended or not.

"Okay, let's go back. By living Christ's teaching we die to our false self. Can I express it this way?" I asked, looking for safer footing.

"Yes. I understand that. Go on," she said.

"Good. So the more we die to our false self the more real, or spiritual we become; wouldn't that follow?"

"I follow that. Go on," she said.

"And the more spiritual we become, the more aware we will be of the spiritual laws of life. That's what Jesus meant by saying, *'to them that hath more shall be given.'* In other words Grace, all I'm saying is that the more conscious we become the more consciousness we will have. It sounds like a tautology, I know; but it's not. It's like saying, it takes money to make money; or success breeds success. And conversely, misery loves company—to him that has not even what he has will be taken away. *Capisce* now?"

"I'm not quite sure. Go on, please."

"Okay. Now the tricky part. I said that suffering is for fools, and this bothers you; right?"

"Very much. I know that you have your reasons Oriano, and I very much want to understand them; so please, go on."

"Let me step this down, if I may. You know that smoking is bad for your health, do you not?" I asked, setting the next stage of our dialectic.

"Yes. That's what I keep telling Kathleen; but she won't listen to me. She's so head-strong, Oriano—"

I laughed. "Nevertheless, Grace; the point I want to make is that we know that smoking is bad for our health. But at one time we didn't know this. It took science a long time to make the connection between smoking and health. In other words, we weren't conscious of this connection. But now that we are conscious of this fact wouldn't you say that a person who continues to smoke consciously jeopardizes their health?"

"Yes."

"And would you call him wise or foolish?"

"Foolish, I would think," she was forced to reply.

"And if this person gets lung cancer from smoking, am I supposed to feel sorry for him for being a fool?"

Grace did not reply. She just looked deep into my eyes, her own blue and brown eyes full of wonder. A moment or two later, she smiled. "I understand, Oriano; but I wouldn't necessarily call him a fool."

"What would you call him, then?"

"A victim. Maybe he can't help himself. Cigarettes are addictive. I would still love him and pray for him," Grace replied, in her Sister of Mercy voice.

"I don't mean to sound callous, Grace. All I meant is that a person who consciously participates in his own demise is a fool. And by extension, anyone who breaks the spiritual laws that he is not aware of also participates in his own demise—be it what it may. That's all I'm trying to say."

"Can you give me an example, please?"

I sat back in my chair and thought before responding. I wasn't sure I should, because I knew that any example I gave would threaten her faith. "No," I replied.

"Why not?" she said, surprised by my answer.

"Because life is a game of one on one with God. Do you remember what Plotinus said? 'The journey home to God is a flight of the alone to the Alone.'"

"Oriano?" Grace pleaded.

"I'm sorry. As presumptuous as this may sound, to some it is given to know the mysteries of the Way, and to others it is not. We have to earn the secrets of God, Grace; because if we don't earn them we profane them. I'm sorry."

"Just one example," she pleaded again.

"Thank you for the tea, Grace," I said, and got up and went back to work; but a few minutes later Grace came to the computer room and said, "Oriano, I don't mean to pry; but how did you come to learn these spiritual laws?"

"With fear and trembling," I said, and laughed.

She laughed with me. "St. Paul, right?"

"Yes. He's my favorite Gospel writer. He's the one who helped me break the code."

"What code?"

"The code of the Way."

"I didn't know there was a code," she said.

"Grace, all of Christ's teaching is one big cryptic code!"

"You intrigue me more each day, Oriano."

"And you fascinate me, Grace," I said, smiling.

"I do?" she said, smiling demurely. "Why?"

"Because you too are born of the Spirit."

"I know I am, Oriano. But you puzzle me because you have so much Light, and—"

"Grace!" I exclaimed, startling her. "Christianity is not the only way to the Light of God. There are as many ways to God as there are souls of man. Why can't Christianity see that? God Almighty, you have no idea how that exasperates me!"

"I think I do," Grace very softly said, and then stepped over and put her hand on my shoulder. "I didn't mean to upset you, dear heart. We are all children of God…"

When I got home I immediately wrote everything I could remember about the day's conversation into my journal. Grace had opened the door to something I had been waiting years to talk about with a genuine Christian.

I knew that Christ's teaching worked, because I had initiated myself into the Sacred Life Stream of the Way with his sayings; and I knew that Grace had also. But the difference between us was that she was constrained by her faith and was feeling the pressure.

That's why she moved to St. Jude. The physical act of getting out of the small and homogenous Christian province of Newfoundland foreshadowed her longing for more spiritual freedom which she would find in multi-cultured Ontario; and it started with our synchronistic meeting.

True, the circumstances that led the Kendals to move to Ontario could be logically explained, like Brandon losing his position with the Catholic Board of Education in Newfoundland because the provincial government had passed legislation to eliminate the Separate School Board thereby forcing Brandon into an early retirement; but why did he refuse the position he was offered in the beautiful little city of Kelowna in the Okanagan Valley, British Columbia?

Kelowna certainly had much more to offer, especially for their son Michael who was an Olympic caliber skier who begged his father to take the position because he could ski Whistler; but it just didn't feel right for Brandon, and Grace supported his decision to decline the offer. But it was Grace who spotted the ad in St. John's daily paper for the position in St. Jude, Ontario. "I showed it to him, Oriano; but he wasn't too keen on it at first. I had to keep at him. I honestly don't know why; but the idea of moving to St. Jude Ontario preyed upon my mind—"

I laughed. "That's what gave Spirit the in to get you out of Newfoundland!"

"But it preyed on Brandon's mind also. The name St. Jude attracted both of us, Oriano. I had this same feeling twice before in my life, and I knew what was being asked of me. Nay, demanded of me—"

"When you were called to the nunnery?"

"Yes."

"And when you left the convent?"

"Yes."

"That stirring in your soul?"

"Yes."

"And now that you're in St. Jude, do you feel you made the right decision?"

"Oriano, I'm not going to deny that I didn't have doubts about leaving our beautiful home in Newfoundland; I had plenty of doubts. We're comfortable, Oriano. We could have stayed and enjoyed our retirement in St. John's; but I could see that Brandon wasn't himself. He was restless. That's why I prodded him to call about this position."

"It wasn't his idea?" I asked.

56

"We made the decision together. But he did have mixed feelings about it at first. It wasn't the position. Brandon welcomed the challenge of going back to his roots. He loves teaching, Oriano; and he's enjoying it very much. No; it wasn't that. It was the town's name, St. Jude; and the school's name, St. Jude Separate School. He felt that he was being called to a higher cause, and he didn't know if he was up to it; that's why I kept at him. I wanted what was best for my husband—"

I smiled at her love for Brandon. "I understand, Grace."

"We had to come, Oriano. We had no choice. St. Jude called us. Both of us heard the call, and here we are. It's God's will—"

"Well, Grace; all I can say is that you're both an asset to this community. You and Brandon have a lot to offer; and, believe me, St. Jude can use people like you!"

"Thank you. But tell me, Oriano; what kept you here?"

"Have you heard the expression, bloom where you have been planted?"

"Yes, certainly," she said, and then smiled. It was her beatific smile that always made me shiver, as though one of God's special angels was smiling upon me. *"And what a bloom you are, dear heart!"* she added, to confirm what I felt about her.

My face flushed red. "One of these evenings Grace," I said, without thinking, "I'm going to take you to the other side in a dream to that beautiful garden where I bloomed in the Sacred Heart of—" I stopped talking, realizing what I had just said.

Grace's eyes popped wide. *"What?"* she asked.

"Nothing. Forget it, Grace. I was just thinking out loud—"

But it was too late. The cat was out of the bag, and I knew that it would only be a matter of time before Grace built up the nerve to query me about it...

3. ON THE HORNS OF A DILEMMA

Grace Kendal was trapped by her faith. I was conscious of it, and she sensed it; but I couldn't tell her. She had to come to that realization on her own, because the Way is an individual path. That was why we fascinated each other. Despite herself, Grace needed me to liberate her from her constraining faith, and I needed her for what I felt were destined literary purposes; and our fascination grew even more exciting because neither of us could reveal why we needed each other, and the irony fueled our Platonic relationship.

For the first two weeks that I worked at her house there was such a powerful undercurrent of irony to every one of our talks that added so much intimacy to our conversations that sometimes we didn't even have to say a single word to convey what we felt or thought; a mere glance or smile was enough to make our point.

I'm sure Grace thanked God as I did that our attraction was purely Platonic. But that's what made it so exciting. She was so secure in her life and I in mine that neither of us was afraid to talk about our private life; and that didn't happen often in relationships. That's why I wanted to continue our talks. I wasn't sure what form my project would take, but I knew it would be a great story. After all, how often does one come across a story of Platonic love? I simply couldn't pass up the opportunity.

However, this posed an ethical problem. Knowing so early in our relationship that I wanted to exploit it for literary purposes, I had to be absolutely clear with Grace. I could not be disingenuous with her, because that went against the very fiber of my being; so the first opportunity I got I opened up the subject—

"Grace," I said, mustering my courage, "you taught English Lit long enough to know that the best stories are drawn from the writer's own life; Hemingway, for example. His first wife Hadley Richardson said that his first novel *The Sun Also Rises* read like it had all happened, and it mostly did, which is why he was sued by the people he based his story on; and, fortunately, they lost; and

Hemingway himself told us that his story *The Snows of Kilimanjaro*—which happens to be my favorite of all his short stories—was his most autobiographical; so I have to tell you up front that I see you as a model for a fascinating character that I may write about in a story one day—"

"Why?" Grace jumped in, with the biggest smile yet. "What is it about me that you think would make a good story?"

"Do I have to spell it out, Grace? You know damn well that your life is interesting, to say the very least!"

"Yes, I do Oriano. But I'm curious to know how your perceive me."

"Then it doesn't bother you that you interest me for a story?" I quickly asked, to deflect her question because I didn't want to disclose how I saw her.

"Not at all. I'm flattered. I only hope that you do me justice," she said, her eyes twinkling with unbounded curiosity.

"I hope so too," I said, and that cleared the air for me. And what a relief it was, too; because it was becoming unbearable supporting all of that irony.

But despite all the talks we had in the time I spent painting her house, it wasn't enough to do the story in my mind justice; so I had to continue our talks.

Grace was born in Christ. That's what made her so fascinating to me. I had never met a Christian born in Christ the way Jesus meant for us to be born with his teaching of spiritual rebirth; but what excited my imagination was Grace's dilemma.

I was so familiar with her dilemma that it pained me deeply to see her trapped on the horns of her spiritual freedom and constraining faith. That's why she felt a stirring in her soul. Her faith could no longer contain her, and she wanted out; but how?

I finished painting her house before we got to talk about the stirring in her soul, but I wanted to find out; that's why I wanted to continue our talks. I wanted her to open up to me about the most personal aspect of soul's journey home to God—the unbearable anguish of spiritual deliverance. I had told Grace of my personal anguish. Not the actual experience of my spiritual rebirth (which took half a dozen manuscripts to work out), but of the miraculous symbol that foretold my deliverance that appeared to me one night in my bedroom during my second year of philosophy studies at university.

When I returned from France I went to university to find an answer to the question that possessed my soul—*why did I do what I did that godforsaken night?* I was in my early twenties and running my pool hall business in St. Jude when I became possessed that fateful night by something—an entity, a force, an archetypal energy, I didn't know what—that compelled me to do something that so repulsed me that it shocked my conscience awake, and I could not live with myself; so I sold my business and fled to France.

But I could not run away from myself. I was stuck with that "thing" inside me, and I had to find out what it was and how it could have taken over my life the way it did that night; and thus began what I came to call "my journey to authenticity."

It was a long and painful journey wrought with so many twists and turns that I had enough material to write for the rest of my life; but I got tired of writing about it, and it was time to move on. That's why I wanted to take advantage of my relationship with Grace.

But I did find the answer I was looking for. I did solve the mystery of St. Paul's "selfsame thing" that Jesus had encoded in his teaching; and I wanted to share this with the only other person I had ever met who had taken Christ's teaching to its ultimate goal of spiritual rebirth—an ex nun and loving wife and mother, Grace Kendal.

Even her name excited my imagination. Grace embodied that special virtue born of love; and nothing she said or did in all the time that I spent working at her home proved me wrong. She was what I perceived her to be, a genuine Christian.

"A tiny dot of blue light appeared before my eyes," I revealed to her that afternoon when I told her the story of how Holy Spirit foretold my quest for my true self. "It was late at night, my bedroom was pitch black, and I lay on my bed in abject despair. Philosophy wasn't getting me anywhere, and I had no idea where to turn next for the answers I sought. Being a former nun, you may know what I'm talking about; but I doubt that anyone else would, because few people embark upon this journey. Then this dot of blue light expanded to form a perfect circle of blue light, about the size and shape of a three-foot donut suspended in mid air. Then a dot of yellow light appeared at the top and within the circumference of the blue circle; and a moment or two later the yellow light formed a straight line within the circumference of the blue light. And then it made a sharp ninety degree turn and formed another straight line; then another, and another until it formed a perfect square of yellow light within the circumference of blue light to create a symbolic squaring of the circle. I couldn't believe my eyes, Grace; and it took me years to understand what Holy Spirit was telling me with that symbol of the squared circle which told me that I would one day do the impossible and give birth to my spiritual self—"

A strange, almost fearful look came over Grace's face. I couldn't read it at first, but then I realized that I should not have disclosed my experience; it went to the very depths of my being and Christ's teaching, and it was too much for her Roman Catholic ears.

I had expanded the boundaries of our relationship with my revelation, and this made Grace instinctively uneasy; but being the woman that she was, she composed herself, smiled, and graciously said, "The Lord speaks to us in many ways, Oriano—"

"And what the Lord tells us in private should remain in private," I instinctively responded. "I'm sorry; I shouldn't have disclosed that experience. It's much too personal."

Again, she smiled. "How about a cup of tea?"

"I'd love one. But give me a few minutes to finish this wall first," I said, and picked up my paint roller and started painting.

Grace went into the kitchen and I rolled paint onto the wall that I had already cut in with my brush. I needed time to center myself. I had out-stepped my bounds and didn't feel right. I always felt that way whenever I revealed too much about my spiritual life, and I thought about the discipline of humility that Grace had cultivated as a Sister of Mercy which defined her character, and I berated myself. *"Damn!"* I said to myself. "When will I ever learn to keep my big mouth shut?"

I should have known better. The Law of Silence is one of the higher laws of the Way, and it demands that one not talk about one's relationship with Holy Spirit; but I still had too much vanity left in me, and that old familiar loathing for my blind egoism gripped me once again and I vowed to be more discerning in my conversations with Grace...

Gurdjieff, the "forest philosopher" as he was called by the literati in Paris, had a metaphor to describe the nature of man, a house with many levels, and the higher the level the more open and spacious the house; but man, being the blind and foolish creature that he is, lives in the basement, the darkest place in himself.

Gurdjieff's teaching, which he called "esoteric Christianity," opened the door for me to Christ's teaching of spiritual rebirth, and together (with the help of other teachings) I "squared the circle" and gave birth to my spiritual self in my mother's kitchen one summer day while she was kneading bread dough on the kitchen table; but fresh out of the womb, I needed spiritual nurture to survive—hence my foolish involvement with Somology, an off-shoot Christian solar cult teaching that promised me the spiritual energy I needed to nurture my newborn spiritual self—the "Logos" that was supposedly imbued with the rays of the sun that we ingested through the eyes with the solar techniques.

Somology did irreparable damage to my eyes. But that was part of the price that I had to pay to shed my blind Christian faith; so I knew the kind of hold that blind faith could have upon the psyche of a devout believer like Grace Kendal, and my heart went out to her because I felt her pain like it was my own.

By all appearances Grace was a happy woman, and in many ways she was; but deep within she hungered for more spiritual freedom. That's what the stirring in her soul was all about. It was time for her to move up to a more spacious room in her house; but her Roman Catholic faith stood between her and more spiritual freedom.

Ironically, she could see the wide-open rooms of the house that I occupied; that's why she was compelled to say to me, *"Oriano, you have so much Light!"* But it puzzled her, because she could not fathom how I had found my way to the upper levels of my house; and despite her abiding faith, she was attracted to me with such Platonic infatuation that I began to sense an uneasy comfort in her husband, and so I had to back off.

62

Grace shared the things we talked about during the day with her husband, and I sensed that her enthusiasm had begun to make him uneasy; so I had to indicate to Brandon that I did not pose a threat to their relationship—

"Brandon, you're wife has an exciting story to tell in your life together; and I think you should encourage her to sit down and write it."

"I've been telling her that for years, Oriano," Brandon said, with a cautious smile.

I laughed. "What's keeping you, then" I said, looking at Grace.

"You must have inspired her, Oriano," Brandon said.

"I have?"

"Yes. She's talking about it again; aren't you, dear?"

"I'd love to, dear; but I have to get my house in order first. Maybe this winter—"

"Grace, it's not that difficult," I said. "Start with a daily journal. And don't go back to the early days. Let your mind go back there gradually. Write about your thoughts and feelings today, and then let your mind go back slowly. You'll get there soon enough. Believe me, I'm familiar with journal writing; and it can be very rewarding."

"Have you ever thought of writing your memoirs, Oriano?" Brandon said. "They seem to be popular with the public today. Look at Frank McCourt. His *Angela's Ashes* has sold millions of copies. And if I'm not mistaken, he's got a second volume out now. I don't know the title, though—"

"*'Tis,*" I said. "And yes, I have written the story of my own odyssey; but I haven't sent any of my memoirs out. I'm going to leave them for posterity."

"Why?" he asked.

"Mine's a peculiar story, Brandon. I'm sure you're familiar with Robert Frost's poem *The Road Not Taken*—"

"Indeed we are," Brandon said, and looked at Grace and smiled. She smiled back, her beautiful lightly freckled face radiant with love.

"You're on it now, aren't you?" I said, smiling at their love for each other.

"We certainly are," Brandon said, with excitement written all over his round, happy face that for some reason brought to mind the Trappist monk Thomas Merton.

"Good. I admire and respect people who dare to take the road less travelled. But to be honest with you, Brandon; I took a road that very few souls travel. And it's not a road that many people can identify with; so there's no point trying to get it published. What I'm trying to do is tell my story in other ways, primarily through fiction."

"Don't give up. You'll get there one day," Brandon said.

"Thank you. I appreciate it," I said.

"It took Joyce a long time to be accepted. You've read Joyce, haven't you?"

"'Welcome, O life! I go to encounter for the millionth time the reality of experience and to forge in the smithy of my soul the uncreated conscience of my race,' said Stephen Dedalus in *Portrait of the Artist as a Young Man.* I loved that book. And I loved *Dubliners;* but not *Ulysses.* I couldn't finish *Ulysses.* And I couldn't even start *Finnigan's Wake.* I hate to say it, Brandon; but the late Joyce is much too pedantic and abstruse for me—"

"And me," Grace admitted without hesitation.

"Me too," Brandon confessed, with a little smirk on his round face. "But what a writer all the same. He never gave up, Oriano. And neither must you—"

Happily, I had won Brandon's confidence back; but now I had to be careful how much Light I let his wife see during the day as I worked, because it finally dawned upon me that too much Light had a way of throwing their happy life together out of balance; so I had to step down the voltage of our conversations.

It was difficult at first, and almost painful because once I opened the spigot I just had to let the creative juices flow; but after I caught myself two or three times I began to see that it was much more effective to always try to make my point within the context of Christianity, because Grace could identify with that.

But I knew that should we continue our conversations after I finished painting her house I would have to stray from her safe

Christian paradigm, because it was much too small to contain the infinite consciousness of the Way; so I had to let her know one way or another that she had a way out of her spiritual dilemma—

"What do you think the goal of the spiritual life is, Grace?" I asked her one day, which came out of the context of our conversation on individual rights and freedom.

"Salvation," she quickly answered.

"That's too pat, Grace. Let's see if we can break it down a bit. Would you say that salvation is spiritual freedom?"

"Yes, I would. As Jesus said, the truth will set us free."

"I agree. But free from what, Grace?"

"From the untruth of the world, Oriano. And there is so much of it these days."

"I agree; but can you tell the truth from a lie, Grace?"

"I think I can," she replied, but with some suspicion in her voice.

"Is it true that Jesus was born of a virgin; or is that a myth?" I asked.

"It's a matter of faith, Oriano," she replied.

"Faith isn't truth, Grace; it's blind belief—"

"One must have faith, Oriano. Jesus said, *'If you have faith as a grain of mustard seed, ye shall say unto this mountain, Remove hence to yonder place; and it shall remove; and nothing shall be impossible unto you.'* St. Mathew, Chapter 17, Verse 20."

I smiled, because Grace had made reference to the grain of mustard seed several times in our talks; but it did not dawn upon me until just then that it was the symbol that best reflected her blind Christian faith, and I had to tread very carefully.

"Grace, would you agree with me when I say that a person is only as free as the philosophy that he or she lives by will allow them to be?" I asked.

Grace thought for a moment, and then replied, "Yes, I would."

"Suppose for example that a person lives by a very materialistic philosophy of life; he or she would have very little spiritual freedom, wouldn't you say?"

"Yes, I would agree. Definitely."

"This is why there's such spiritual hunger in the world today, Grace. We've become a consumer society hell bent on getting more stuff, as the phrase goes. In any event, for a materialist to grow spiritually he or she would have to expand the boundaries of their philosophy; *n'est ce pas?*"

"That goes without saying, Oriano," she replied, smiling at me.

"Good. We're on the same page. Now, how does one expand a philosophy of materialism," I asked, taking a bold leap upward.

"It's much easier for a camel to pass through the eye of a needle than it is for a rich man to enter into the kingdom of heaven. You can't expand it, Oriano. I think we have to learn how to live our life without being possessed by our material possessions."

"Excellent. Your vow of poverty gave birth to that wisdom, didn't it?"

"Yes, it did," Grace replied, and smiled demurely.

"But isn't it possible that Jesus meant more than material possessions with his camel and needle metaphor? Christ's words have many levels of meaning; and by rich man he also implied a personality rich in material consciousness. Since Christ's whole teaching has to do with dying to that part of ourselves that keeps us from being as innocent children, don't you think his rich man metaphor implies the death of man's desire to possess material things? In other words, Grace; a rich man can also enter the kingdom of heaven if he is spiritually detached from his possessions—"

"Yes, I agree with you Oriano. There are many rich people in the world who are good Christians. I don't doubt that for a moment. But Jesus was making a point about serving two masters—"

"Precisely. No man can serve two masters. He must serve God or mammon. I agree. All I'm saying is that we have to learn how to be in the world but not of the world; and we do that by adopting a philosophy that will give us spiritual freedom."

"Jesus Christ gives us that, Oriano."

"I know he does, Grace; but there's a world of difference between what Jesus taught and what Christianity wants us to believe."

"I don't believe there is," Grace replied, stepping back nervously.

"That's where your faith comes into the picture, Grace. You believe what Christianity wants you to believe, and that's asking too much of me."

"The grain of mustard seed, Oriano—"

"I have faith, Grace; but my faith is not blind," I replied.

My comment took her by surprise. She did not give me a quick response. She just smiled, and softly said, "You will come back to Jesus one day, Oriano. I believe it."

"I've never left him, Grace. It was my Roman Catholic faith that I outgrew."

She did not respond. She just smiled her Sister of Mercy smile at me, which could be quite disarming, and I never got to make the point that I wanted to make about the spiritual life that day, nor any other day while I painted the rest of her house; but I hoped that we would pick up that exciting topic another time...

Can a person be authentic and still live a lie? The short answer is yes. The long answer is what the spiritual journey is all about, and few people go far enough on this journey to learn that spiritual growth is directly proportional to one's authenticity; hence my reason for leaving Christianity to find my true self.

My life was a lie, but I did not know that it was a lie; that's why I suffered spiritual anguish growing up. I could always sense my life-lie, but never pinpoint it. Like an elusive shadow, it would come out at the most inopportune times; almost as though it had a mind of its own, like it did the night that it shocked my conscience awake.

Grace was right when she said that the truth will set us free; but what truth? Christianity's? Was Jesus the Son of God? Was he conceived by the Holy Ghost in the womb of a virgin? Did he die upon the cross for the sins of the world? And did he rise up from the dead after his crucifixion?

As a young and innocent Roman Catholic, I believed it all. I believed in mortal sin and eternal damnation in hell. I believed in the forgiveness of sin and everlasting life in heaven. I believed in Original Sin, and I believed that we only live one life that Jesus came into the world to save. I was a believer like Grace Kendal.

I wasn't independent enough in my thinking to question the veracity of what millions of Christians took for granted; but that changed one night in the twenty-third year of my life when my conscience was brutally assaulted by a sexual experience that so repulsed me that it compelled me to extricate myself from the unconscious lie of my life.

My journey to authenticity began one day on the breakwater to the little island in the St. Jude River where I asked the most important question of my life—*what price truth?*

My philosophy studies at university had taken me as far as they could, and I did not know where to turn next. I looked up, and with a lump in my throat said, "Dear God; I know that we have to pay for everything we get in life; I know that we get nothing for nothing, so please tell me, what price truth?" And thus began my spiritual quest for my true self.

Years later, having forged my own path out of dozens of teachings and countless encounters with my life-lie, I wrote in my journal: *"The shortest way to God is through hell!"* I found God. Not that God was ever lost, I was; and to find my way to God I had to authenticate my life by dying daily to my false consciousness because, as I was forced to realize with every little excruciating death, the less false we are the more conscious we become of God. That's why I lived in the spacious rooms of my house.

So when Grace quoted scripture telling me that truth would set us free, I knew that to be true; but ironically that stirring in her soul was her spiritual need to deliver herself from the unconscious falseness of her blind Roman Catholic faith. And that's why she fascinated me. I knew that she was authentic; but I also knew that she lived her life within the confines of the seductive lie of Christianity; and I felt the anguish of her soul.

Grace was real, but her reality was constrained; and it didn't matter how long she knelt and prayed to her Lord and Savior Jesus Christ, she was destined to suffer spiritual anguish until the day she delivered herself by expanding the fixed boundaries of her faith. I had no choice in my spiritual quest, and neither did Grace.

But I also knew in my heart that she would never do that. She had too much invested in her faith. The first day that she arrived to St.

Jude she drove down to the Catholic Church to thank God for a safe journey and asked Jesus to welcome her to her new home."In my new parish of lost causes," she confessed to me, with a devilish twinkle in her eyes.

I laughed. "So you're on a mission, are you?" I said.

"Yes, I am. My whole life is a mission. We came to St. Jude because God needs us here to save souls. I think we were destined to meet, Oriano. I believe that with all my heart now. My life is a spiritual journey—"

"Whose isn't? We're all on this journey, Grace; only some of us are more conscious of it than others," I replied, embracing her challenge to save me.

"True. And I believe my mission in life is to help those who aren't conscious of it. If I could Oriano, I would go to the remotest regions of Africa to spread the Word of God. I've thought of it often, but my family comes first."

"Oh Grace," I said, with a heavy sigh, "I admire your Christian zeal; but I'm afraid I can't share your conviction that the world needs to be saved."

"It's going to hell in a hand basket, Oriano. Secularism is spreading like cancer, and we need people to spread the Word of God. That's why I have decided to join the committee dedicated to recruiting new members to the Church. Pauline asked me. Do you know Pauline Kaminsky?"

"Yes," I said, "I know her—"

"That sounds ominous," Grace said, frowning.

"Let's just say she's one of the reasons why I could never go back to the Church."

"*Ohhh?* Is there something I should know?"

"Not really. Suffice to say that I would rather face ten starving lions in the arena of life than one angry Christian like Pauline Kaminsky."

"You've had dealings with her, then?"

"You could say that," I said, with a wry smile.

"I won't pry, Oriano," Grace said, with a smile that told me that she too had similar experiences with fellow Christians.

We understood each other. We didn't have to explain ourselves to know what we were talking about. But how was I going to introduce Grace to the freedom that awaited her outside her blind faith when she saw me as a lost soul? How?

I had outgrown my desire to save the world, so I had no compulsion to liberate Grace Kendal from herself. Besides, I knew the price one would have to pay for interfering in another person's karma; so all I could do, as I had learned to do so well since I became aware of the Law of Non-interference, was to let the chips fall where they may...

When I stepped onto the breakwater to the little island in the St. Jude River I had no idea that when I stepped back onto the mainland my entire life would change by the revelation that had come to me. "If that's the price you want me to pay for truth, then so be it," I said to God; and thus began my lonely quest to the headwaters of my life.

My answer came to me on the rocky breakwater. I stopped walking, and like my hero Socrates who apparently did that often, I stood dead still in deep thought.

I don't know how long I stood on the jagged rocks of the breakwater, the St. Jude River flowing furiously on one side and the calm bay of the St. Jude marina on the other; but in my mind I saw Oedipus Rex, the tragic King of Thebes who gouged out his own eyes to expiate himself of the heinous sins of patricide and incest, walking blindly to his fate, and in a sudden flash of fateful inspiration I knew what I had to do to find the answer to the question that preoccupied me night and day—*why did I do what I did that godforsaken night?* Oedipus exiled himself out of his own kingdom of Thebes, and so too would I exile myself out of the kingdom of my own senses by dying to all of my desires. That was the lonely path that I chose to take that day.

I had stepped onto the breakwater lost and directionless because philosophy had taken me as far as it could in my quest for my true self, but when I stepped back onto the mainland I had a sense of purpose that would take over my whole life like a raging forest fire, not unlike Jung's daemon-driven purpose to find his lost soul when he dared to confront his unconscious which he recorded in *The Red Book.*

"I took a vow of chastity too, Grace," I said to her one day over a cup of tea in her living room. Our theme that day was on the virtue of moral self-discipline, and we had begun our talk as I painted the closet door in the front entrance.

While I painted the door I discovered a spring-loaded switch to the light in the closet. Opening the door released the switch and turned on the light, and closing the door shut off the light; but the light bulb in the closet was burnt out, so I asked Grace to get me a new bulb. I screwed in the new bulb and the light went on because the door was open.

Grace smiled. "Well, I'll be!" she said, fascinated by the ingenious devise.

I had never seen one before either, but as I played with the switch opening and shutting the door a light went on in my mind: *"Grace, this whole thing is a waking dream!"*I exclaimed, and broke into laughter. "Do you see the symbolic implications?"

Grace stared at me, puzzled. "I'm afraid I don't. What do you mean?"

"What were we talking about before you went to get a new bulb?"

"The vow of chastity," she replied.

"The virtue of moral self-discipline. That's what your vow of chastity and poverty and obedience gave birth to—the noble virtue of purity of mind and heart; *n'est ce pas?*"

Grace smiled. I could tell that she enjoyed it when I used that French phrase, and especially when I ended a comment with the Italian word *capisce*. They added something special to that *je ne sais quoi* of our spontaneous talks.

"Yes, I would agree with you Oriano," she said. "Purity of mind and heart, indeed; that's what we strive for."

Smiling at her, I said, "Wouldn't you say that purity of mind and heart is a form of spiritual light?"

She looked at me, her captivating blue and brown eyes a little less puzzled because she was on very familiar ground now, but still intrigued. "Yes, Oriano; but—"

71

"The door to the closet of our life, Grace," I said, and shut the closet door. "The light was burnt out. We couldn't see too well inside the closet. Now I open the door and the light goes on and we can see clearly inside the closet. In like manner, the illuminating virtue of moral self-discipline lights up the dark closet of our soul—"

Grace's face lit up at the revelation, and she burst into laughter. *"Oh, Oriano!"*

I laughed also. "That's what's called a waking dream, Grace."

"A waking dream?" she said, once again puzzled.

"Yes. A waking dream is one way that Holy Spirit speaks to us in our daily life. God is always speaking to us, Grace. Holy Spirit is the Voice of God and Light of the Way, and it speaks to us in all kinds of ways, like coincidences, signs and symbols, synchronicities, which I believe we're in the middle of right now by the way, and night dreams that help solve our problems and point the Way to us, and so on. A waking dream is an experience provided by Holy Spirit to point out a spiritual truth that we are in need of, like this closet door experience here that sheds light on our discourse. Let me explain this, because I can see that you're confused—"

"I am. Please, tell me," she said, her eyes begging.

"Okay," I said, smiling at her curiosity. "Carl Jung said in his memoir *Memories, Dreams, Reflections*, "The sole purpose of human existence is to kindle a light in the darkness of mere being." The closet here is symbolic of our inner life, which most people aren't aware of because it's a dark and lonely place inside our personal closet—our inner being if you will; but we can light up the closet of our inner life with the illuminating virtue of moral self-discipline like your vow of chastity, poverty, and obedience—"

"My God, you're right!" she exclaimed, throwing her hands into the air. "I know exactly what you mean! *You are a Light-bringer, Oriano!"*

I laughed at Grace's show of emotion. "Good. You see my point. You've just had your first conscious waking dream experience!"

Grace stared at me as if seeing me for the first time. "How you fascinate me," she finally said, her eyes boring into my soul. "The more we talk, the more I learn about you; what next, pray tell?" she added, mystified by her fascination with me.

"Why don't you put on some tea and we can talk some more about the illuminating virtue of moral self-discipline," I said, smiling at her predicament.

"I'll do that," she said, and went into the kitchen while I finished painting the closet door that was responsible for our first intimate Platonic experience together.

Memories of my *Royal Dictum* days surfaced as we talked over tea. Oedipus Rex had inspired my dictum of self-denial that I penned into my pocket notebook as I stood on the breakwater that fateful day; a daily reminder to exile myself out of the kingdom of my own senses and go against the natural currents of the pleasures of life. That was the price that I chose to pay for the truth I sought: *"I am like Oedipus Rex. I embrace my becoming blindly and I leave all of my sins behind me. I am going to go against the natural course of evolution, and each obstacle that I encounter I will consume. I will that this be so."*

"I made my vow for life, but it only lasted for three and a half years because it had served its purpose," I revealed to Grace over tea that day. "But you know what? As difficult as it was for me to make my vow and keep it faithfully (I stopped smoking, having sex, eating meat, and so on), it was just as difficult to break my vow when I realized that it had served its purpose; but I had to get on with my life—"

Grace smiled her understanding smile. I liked this smile the best, next to her beatific smile that lit up the whole room. "It took me six years, Oriano. I couldn't move for indecision. I felt like I was swimming in a sea of molasses—"

"It's hard, isn't it?"

"Would you like to know what did it for me?"

"Please," I said, delighted to be so privileged.

"My brother's death. My young brother Darren got cancer in his right eye. Then it spread to his brain. I prayed for him, Oriano. I prayed to God to take my life instead of his. He had two beautiful children who needed him. Oh God, how I prayed. I would have gladly sacrificed my life for my baby brother; but God had other plans for us."

"You didn't leave the Order out of spite, did you Grace?"

"No. But I was very disappointed. It took me a long time to get over my brother's death; but I realized that I could better serve God out in the world, so I left."

"Out of curiosity, Grace; did you feel vulnerable when you took your first step outside your Order?" I had to ask, hoping she would honor me.

"You have no idea how vulnerable I felt."

"That's just it; I do. That's why I asked."

She smiled. "Of course you do, dear heart. But that was only the half of it. I had to cultivate new skills to survive in the world. But then I met Brandon who, as you say, had been there and done that; and he helped me to adjust to the cruel world—"

"And what, if I may ask, is your best survival skill?"

"Love. It's the cure of the world," she replied in a soft, gentle voice; but not her warrior's voice. It was a different voice; much softer, kinder, a voice with such profound confidence that it made her warrior voice sound puny and weak.

Her answer conveyed all the heavenly powers of love, and it showed itself in her very life. From the day I met her, despite all her nervous talk, I sensed an inner strength that I couldn't put my finger on; but now I knew. I smiled, and said, "Grace, you've discovered the secret of God; haven't you?"

She did not reply verbally. She just stared at me smiling. Then she got up and got the kettle and poured more hot water into my cup first and then hers. I placed my tea bag back into my cup and let it sit for a bit and then took it out and placed it back onto the saucer that she had provided for our tea bags, and she did the same.

As she stirred milk into her tea she looked up from her cup into my eyes, and with a serious look on her face said, "How did you discover the secret of God, Oriano?"

"When I looked into the Face of God," I replied without hesitation, because she had earned the privilege of knowing my most precious secret.

She did not say anything. She stared at me a moment or two, and then smiled my favorite smile that enveloped me with a divine love…

Pauline Kaminsky came to pick Grace up the day I was taking down the depressing imitation field stone wallboard in the family room; they were going into the city for a district meeting on how to bring new people into the Church.

Grace called me upstairs for tea. "Pauline won't be here for another half hour, so I'll have tea with you Oriano," she said, and put the kettle on. Taking out a bag of tea from the box of mixed herbal teas she said, "How about raspberry?"

"Excellent. I often have raspberry tea when I go to the Husky House."

"I had tea at the Husky House yesterday. It's a nice little restaurant, isn't it?"

"For a fast food restaurant, it's not too bad," I said, smiling at Grace. I was smiling because she was all dressed up and she looked— "I don't know what word I would use to describe how you look today, Grace," I said.

"Oh," she said, smiling demurely.

"You look lovely. But that's not the right word," I said, studying her ensemble, a priest-like black blazer over a black turtle neck and black and white and grey plaid scarf around her upturned blazer collar, and smartly matched black and white and grey plaid skirt.

"And what word would you use, Oriano?" she asked.

"Daunting. You look like you mean business today, Grace."

"Well, this is kind of official business. After all, we're going on a mission of God."

"Don't mess with Grace today," I said, and laughed.

"Do you like it, Oriano? It's not too formal, is it?"

"It's casual-formal. And that reflects your whole personality very well, I might add."

"How? In what way?" she eagerly asked, her eyes wide as saucers.

"It's dressy; but there's an air of casualness about the ensemble," I replied, studying her outfit. "The black gives you a very dignified and formal look; but the plaid softens the look. It's you, Grace; and I like it very much."

"Thank you. I like it too. It's one of my favorite outfits."

"Who else is going with you?" I asked.

"Just Pauline Kaminsky and myself. Cora Maki and Cora's sister-in-law, I don't remember her name, can't make it today. I think there are two or three others from the Catholic Woman's League in the committee, but I haven't met them yet."

"And the purpose of this meeting?"

"We're going to brainstorm. We're going to see if we can come up with new ideas on how to bring new people into the Church. You wouldn't happen to have a good idea, would you Oriano?"

"Yes, I do; but you wouldn't be interested," I said.

"Why not?" Grace said, surprised by my answer.

"Because it would be paradigm-shifting."

"In what way?"

"Well," I said, choosing my words carefully, "the reason Christianity is losing people left and right is because it hasn't kept abreast of the unfolding spiritual consciousness of the times. You haven't read *Why Christianity Must Change or Die* by Bishop John Shelby Spong, have you?"

"No, I haven't. Is he a Catholic Bishop?"

"No. Anglican."

"Oh. And what does he have to say?"

"The gist of his book is that society has outgrown Christianity's theism, and I agree. The God of Christianity is too small for today's consciousness, Grace; and if you want to attract new people to the Church you have to expand your Christian paradigm."

"How?" she asked, her eyes telling me that she was taking mental notes.

I didn't reply, even though I wanted to. "That's your problem, Grace; not mine."

"Let me phrase it differently. What would it take to get you back to the Church?"

"You wouldn't want to know," I said, and laughed.

"Why not? Tell me, Oriano; I most definitely want to know."

"You're not ready to know," I said; but I caught myself and quickly added, "I'm sorry, Grace. That's presumptuous of me. Why don't I just say that some things are better left unsaid? Can you live with that?"

"No, I cannot. I'm sorry, Oriano; but you've piqued my curiosity and I very much would like to know why—"

The doorbell rang. *"Saved by the bell!"* I exclaimed.

"You!" Grace said. "I don't know how you keep getting away with it!"

"With what?" I said, still laughing at the timing of the bell.

"You know very well what I'm talking about," she said, and got up to answer the front door. I got up too. As I headed downstairs Grace was letting Pauline into the house. "You know Pauline Kaminsky, don't you Oriano?" she called to me on purpose.

"Yes, very well. And how are you today Pauline?"

"Very well, thank you," she replied stiffly.

"You ladies have a nice day today," I said, and turned to leave.

"You too, Oriano," Grace said. "You know where the kettle is if you want tea. Just help yourself."

"Thank you," I said, and went back downstairs to work.

The next morning Grace was surprisingly reticent. When she called me for tea (I was still doing prep work on the walls where the wallboard used to be) I asked how the day in the city went. "Very well, thank you," she said.

"Did you come up with any interesting ideas?" I asked.

"Some," she said. Then, nervously, she said, "I'd like to ask you something Oriano. If it's too personal, please pardon my curiosity—"

"Feel free," I said, anticipating her.

"Pauline has a very strong opinion of you. I'm not sure how to take her. Why does she have it in for you?"

I laughed. "Not me personally, Grace; my energy."

"I beg your pardon?" she said, with a puzzled look.

"Pauline can't stand my energy. It's much too honest for her. She's hollow at the core, Grace; and hollow people can't stand real people," I said, and smiled.

I knew that this would intrigue Grace, but there was no point skirting around it. She did not reply for a moment or two, and then said, "*The Wasteland.* T. S. Elliot?"

"I wasn't thinking of Elliot, but if the shoe fits."

"Has Pauline always been like this?" she asked, her eyes imploring me.

"People aren't born hollow, Grace; they become that way by the values they live by. Pauline is a spurned, self-centered, willfully woman. Ask her daughter. She ran away from home twice. Her mother is a church-goer and a busybody when it comes to other people's spiritual beliefs, but Pauline doesn't have a clue what the spiritual life is all about."

"I gathered as much. But what does she have against you, Oriano. She said some pretty strong things about you."

"Like what?" I asked, feeling Grace's discomfort.

"She said that you're involved in some kind of evil new age cult. The Devil's work, she said. I had to come to your defense, Oriano. I couldn't listen to that—"

"Thank you," I said, and chuckled. "The Devil's work? I didn't think she would go that far. But that doesn't surprise me, Grace. What Christians don't understand they ascribe to the Devil. It's always been this way—"

"Pauline does come on strong with her religion. I saw that immediately. What's her history, Oriano? Was she always so passionate about her religion?"

"No, I don't think so. I think she poured all her energy into her religion after she left her second husband. He was a wife-beater, Grace. I don't know if you know this, but Pauline had her own business here that she inherited from her father; the North Star Restaurant. Her father owned half the town. Anyway, Pauline's husband owned a trucking business; but he got killed one winter hauling pulpwood from one of the bush camps. Not long after she started dating her young Polish chef. Joe Kaminsky was a good fifteen years younger than her. But Pauline needed a man, and he sweet-talked her into marrying him. Then a year or so later he started beating her. She ended up in the hospital once; but he was a real smooth talker. I knew Joe. He's a strong Catholic. In fact, if I'm not

78

mistaken he told me he was in the seminary for a year or two. I'd see him walking to Sunday Mass with his leather-bound Bible in one hand and his wife's hand in the other, and the following week he would beat Pauline's face in and then bring her roses—"

"No?"

"Yes. Then Pauline sold the North Star and moved to Joe's hometown. Joe had his heart on owning his own farm, so Pauline bought a farm in rural Saskatchewan. But less than a year later she came crawling back to St. Jude with terror in her eyes."

"No?"

"Yes. He must have scared the daylights out of her out there in the middle of nowhere. What was she thinking moving to a farm with a wife-beater? But she left him, I'll give her that. But then she found Jesus and she became what she is today—a devout but mindless believer in her Lord and Savior Jesus Christ."

"But what does she have against you, Oriano. She's almost afraid of you. It's like—"

I laughed again. "It's my energy, Grace. Some people can't stand my energy. It's not just her. There are a number of people in St. Jude that can't stand me; but they don't have the temerity to tell me to my face. Like Pauline. We've never talked."

"I don't understand," Grace said, genuinely perplexed.

"I don't know if I can explain it, Grace; but I'll try just for you."

"Please. I'd really like to know—"

"Okay. A person's energy field reflects their inner life. No one can hide what they really are. Their energy field betrays them. This energy field reveals itself in colors, which is called a person's aura. Some people can see auras. I can sense them. A person's aura reveals their true colors, pun intended. So as good a Roman Catholic as Pauline thinks she is, she's inauthentic in her spirituality; and this falseness is reflected in her energy field. And when she comes into contact with someone who is authentic her whole sense of self is threatened. That's why she can't stand me. I threaten what she thinks she is."

"I gathered that. But what does she think she is, Oriano?"

"A good Christian," I said, and laughed.

"Ohhh," Grace sighed. "Yes, I think I understand what you're saying."

"She may mean well, Grace; but she's dangerous. There's no room in her heart for any other religion but Christianity, and that's not healthy."

Grace laughed. "She does come on strong, I'll say that. But dangerous?"

"It's Christians like her that give Christianity a bad name. Pauline refuses to see that God has provided a spiritual path for all types, including philosophical housepainters. It's arrogance, Grace. But a lot of Roman Catholics are guilty of that."

"Not me, I hope—"

I smiled. "Grace, you're a sight for sore eyes!"

She laughed. "Tell me, have you ever had any business dealings with Pauline?"

"Why do you ask?"

"She told me she can't afford to hire you because you're too expensive. I mentioned this to my husband, and he said your rates are market value. Why would Pauline say that about you, Oriano? Is it animus?"

"How intuitive you are, Grace. Pauline has a skunk on her conscience, and rather than deal with it she projects her guilt by maligning people who threaten her self-image; hence her animus. I did a job for her twenty years ago. I was just starting out in the painting business, and I wasn't very confident in my trade because I was just learning. Pauline asked me to paint her North Star Restaurant sign. It had neon tubes. I told her I didn't know much about sign painting, but she said all I had to do was scrape the loose paint and outline the lettering; so I took it on. I had no idea what to charge her, and not wanting to overcharge her I gave her a price of two hundred dollars. I had to rent scaffolds and pay a friend of mine who did sign painting on the side, but when I scraped off the old paint I accidently broke a neon tube. It cost me seventy-five dollars to replace; so by the time I paid for the scaffolds and my sign painter friend it cost me twenty dollars of my own money. Then, as coincidence would have it, two or three years later I happened to meet a sign painter in the city and we started talking and he told me about Pauline. He said that he

80

had given her a price to paint her sign two or three times, but she felt his price was too high. He dropped his price from twelve hundred to nine hundred dollars and he wasn't going to go any lower because he felt it wasn't worth it; but she still felt it was too high. I couldn't see it then because I was too green, but I can see it now. Pauline screwed me good, Grace. She knows that she took advantage of me; that's why she has a skunk on her conscience. It took me a long time to find my happy place in this world of self-serving people, Grace; but honesty is important to me. I couldn't live with myself if I were unethical. So I try to be fair with all my customers. I've blown it a few times, but on the whole I'm a pretty fair guy. But Pauline came by her self-serving business ethics honestly. Her father was a shrewd businessman. He never paid the going rate for anything if he could help it, but he always charged what he could get away with; and Pauline's the same way. She's always wanted her cake and eat it too, and people like that have a long way to go before they understand the essence of Christ's teaching. She may be a nice lady in many ways, but Pauline's a hypocrite; and hypocrites and I just don't see eye to eye."

"You do have a long memory, don't you Oriano?" Grace said, and then smiled her understanding smile. "But then, you are a writer. Have you ever written about this?"

"What? About Pauline?"

"Yes."

"Not specifically. I may have used her type in a story, but not the details of her life. I wouldn't give her the satisfaction of appearing in one of my stories. But who knows? When my Muse calls, I have to obey; and perhaps someday I may write a novel about the dark side of St. Jude. I would call it *Jude the Obscure* if that title hadn't already been taken—"

Grace broke into laughter. "Thomas Hardy. I taught that novel to my grade twelve class. It's one of my favorite novels. Well, Oriano; what am I supposed to tell her? Pauline is a very active member of the Church—"

"Don't say anything. Just let the chips fall where they may," I said.

"Live and let live. I respect that, Oriano," she said, with an approving smile.

"To make my point, Grace; Pauline hired a moonlighter to paint the exterior of her house last summer. The man makes over fifty grand a year at the paper mill, so he can afford to do paint jobs on the side for half the going rate; but what do I care? As long as I'm making a living, that's all that matters to me. I love my work, Grace; but I also love writing, and my work gives me time to write during our long winter months."

Grace wrinkled her brow. "Pauline hired a moonlighter?"

"Yes. He's a mill painter. He's been stealing jobs from me for years."

"Can't you report him?"

"For what? Not declaring his extra income? Not charging GST? I could, Grace; but I'm not a snitch. There's a spiritual law that takes care of things like this."

"What law?" she was quick to ask.

I smiled because I didn't want to go there; but I had opened that door and I had to do some quick thinking to keep the Law of Karma within Grace's sin-forgiving Christian paradigm. My mind raced frantically, and finally I found the right context—

"Be not deceived, God is not mocked; for whatsoever a man soweth, that shall he also reap. For he that soweth to his flesh shall of the flesh reap corruption; but he that soweth to the Spirit shall of the Spirit reap life everlasting." I believe that's from St. Paul's letter to the Galatians. It all comes down to the values we live by, Grace. Are they spiritual or material? If they're material, we can expect to reap spiritual corruption as St. Paul said; and if they're spiritual, we will reap everlasting life—"

"YES!" Grace exclaimed, throwing her hands into the air.

I laughed at her outburst. I didn't expect it. "I take it you agree, then?"

"I most certainly do! Twenty years of poverty has taught me to see through the emptiness of the material life. What does it get us in the end, Oriano? No one has figured out yet how to take it with them, have they?"

I broke out. *"Good one, Grace!"*

"Well, no one has; have they?"

82

"No. And no one ever will. That's what Shelly tells us in his iconic poem *Ozymandias*. But that's always been the problem with society. We're blind to our own mortality. People can't see beyond the immediacy of their daily life"

"Exactly. I like nice things, Oriano. I'll be the first to admit that. I like my house to look nice. I couldn't live in a house that didn't look nice. I like nice furniture and nice paintings and nice clothes; but I could drop everything and do with nothing. I could very easily, Oriano. Been there done that—"

I burst into laughter. "You just love that expression, don't you?"

"I never heard it before I met you. But it's a part of my vocabulary now."

"Oh Grace, how refreshing you are!"

"Thank you. Now please tell me what I should say if your name comes up again with Pauline, because I may just say something that—"

"I can't tell you what to say. Trust your own judgment, Grace. You know me well enough now to know what kind of person I am. Or are you suspicious of me?"

"No, I'm not suspicious of you. But I will be honest with you, Oriano. I think you're a very wise man who knows how to tell people what they need to hear."

"And you're a very humble woman who likes to hear what wise men have to say," I said, and burst into another fit of laughter.

"You! You little devil, you!"

Without thought, out of my lips flew the words of St. Paul to the Corinthians, *"And no marvel, for Satan himself is transformed into an angel of light!"*

Grace had no comeback. She just stared at me, dumbfounded. Smiling, I got up and quietly went back to work…

4. IF NOT US, WHO?

It was only a matter of time before the subject of spiritual equanimity came up. Grace had it, to a large degree; that's why she was Platonically attracted to me. "Like attracts like," I said to her, with a welcoming smile.

She had been hinting at it all morning, wondering what I possessed that attracted her to me. She couldn't come right out and ask me, because that was out of the question; but she had to know why she found herself always talking to me while I worked.

"I thought that opposites attracted, Oriano," she said, with a look of hesitant curiosity in her mixed blue and brown eyes that I was very familiar with now.

She couldn't help herself, she had to enter my world to find out what the attraction was; but she was hesitant to venture into strange and unfamiliar territory.

"In the material world, perhaps; but in the spiritual world like attracts like. Birds of a feather, and all that," I replied, as I skimmed the taping compound off the joint.

"*Ohhh?* So, tell me Oriano; what feathers do we have in common?"

Finally she asked the question that she had been longing to ask me for the last couple of days, and she had done it without compromising her delicate sense of decorum.

I smiled as I put more drywall compound onto my hawk. "Would you like a short simple answer, or a thought-provoking philosophical answer?"

She thought for a moment. "Both. Give me the simple answer first, and then I'll put on the kettle and you can give me the philosophical answer."

"Alright," I said, as I spread the mud onto the joint I was filling. "The feather that you and I have in common is moral self-discipline. That's the mystery of our Platonic fascination with each other—"

"That's it!" she burst out. "I knew there was something about you that I liked from the day I met you; but I couldn't put my finger on it. *That's it, isn't it?"*

I laughed at her epiphany. "There's only one way to smelt the spiritual gold of life, Grace; and that's by transforming the dross of our material life with moral self-discipline," I explained, and laughed again at the expression on her face.

Grace hadn't quite adjusted to my sense of humor yet, because she had never met anyone like me before; but she was warming up to it very quickly. Her eyes told me.

"You're getting into your philosophical answer now, aren't you?"

"Yes."

"I'll go and put the kettle on, then," she said, and went to the kitchen.

I was working in the back stairwell. I had already done her living room, two coats of Tempting Teal, which excited both Grace and her husband because it was such a bold change of color for them; but she had misgivings about leaving the wallboard wainscoting and wallpaper in her hallway which extended into one living room wall.

I knew it would only be a matter of time before she asked me to take down the wainscoting and wallpaper and paint the walls the same color, which I suggested she do to maintain thematic consistency; but I didn't push it. That had to be her choice.

"Oriano, tea's on," she called from the kitchen.

"In a minute," I yelled back. I had one more joint to fill, and when I finished I cleaned my two "blades" (tapers tools for joint filling) and my hawk and went upstairs.

"I'm so glad you're fixing up that eyesore," she said, referring to the piece of drywall that was put up in the entranceway, but instead of taping it they (probably Tommy Ping) had covered the joints with molding which was entirely out of keeping because it made the piece of drywall look like a fake bulletin board stuck in the wrong place.

"Can you fix that?" she asked me when we were choosing the color for the stairwell. "I can't stand to look at that every time I come into the house."

"No problem," I said.

"Would you, please? It looks so—"

"Tacky," I said, smiling at the grimace on her face.

"That's the word," she said, and smiled her teacher's smile of approval.

"I'll take care of it," I said, and laughed. I couldn't help myself. Grace's aesthetic sensibilities were shocked by imperfections, and that amused me.

"I've never seen a house with so many—I don't know what to call them."

"Deficiencies," I said, and laughed again.

"Exactly. But this was the only house on the market that could accommodate our furniture. We had no choice, Oriano—"

"You don't have to apologize for the house, Grace. It's not a bad house, all things considered. And look at the view you have—"

"Yes; it is breathtaking, isn't it? It almost makes up for the rest of the house," she said, and laughed. It was a quiet, dignified laugh that added to her charm.

She didn't know it, but her comment placed her refined sense of taste above the breathtaking view, which said a lot about her character and touched me deeply; and I joined in her laughter. She was catching the spirit that would soon pervade every one of our daily talks, some days moving us both to tears of joyful laughter.

We were alike in many ways; but most obvious was her need to tell her story, an irrepressible need that also possessed me for over twenty years and compelled me to write every morning for two and three hours before going to work my trade.

Not everyone has this compulsive need to tell their story, only certain people; and Grace was one. Whatever it was that made her what she was, she had to share it with someone because in her heart she knew it was worth sharing.

But it wasn't simply a matter of wanting to share one's story because it was worth sharing; something about one's life compelled one to share it, as though one had a special message that the world had to hear; and Grace and I had a special message.

That's what attracted me to anyone who had a story to tell, and Grace's story captivated me from the moment she told me that she was a nun for twenty years; and so I listened patiently without interrupting her until she had completely exhausted whatever aspect of her story that she would be talking about that day.

And it always left her feeling good, as though she had finally gotten it out to someone who appreciated her story, however trivial it appeared to be on the surface; and just as Doctor Jung came to see that his patients healed in the telling of their stories, so could I feel the deep wound in Grace's soul heal just by listening to her story.

Being a short story writer, I knew that no detail of a story stands alone in a person's life; they are all part of a whole. And one's story can never be told to complete satisfaction until the whole story of one's life can be seen in all of its individual purpose.

That's what characterizes every person's story, their sense of purpose. People that don't have a sense of purpose don't have a story to tell; and Grace's story had to be told to someone who understood what her purpose was, despite the fact that she herself didn't quite understand it. That's why she gravitated to me like a moth to a flame.

She sensed that I would understand her story, and she was compelled to talk to me every day that I worked in her house; and as I listened I heard such a unique story that I knew I would have to write her story one day. It was destined.

Ironically, Grace knew this also; but she didn't censor her thoughts with me. And this intrigued me for the longest time until it dawned on me that she was so secure in her own life that it didn't matter whether I appropriated her life story or not. In fact I'm certain that she secretly hoped I would write her story one day, that's what encouraged the idea to ask if she would like to continue our talks after I painted her house. But I had to work that idea long and hard before I shared it with her, because of what I saw in her that she was blind to; and just in case I didn't ask her, or if I did and she declined for propriety's sake, I paid careful attention to her story because I didn't want to miss any details of her life. I wanted the whole picture. I knew I would never get it short of recording her story; but being a synoptic writer who can see the essential story in one glance, it wasn't all that important to me. I just had to get the details right for narrative integrity.

That's what made our relationship so fascinating. It wasn't merely Platonic—which in itself excited my intellectual nerve-endings; there was a mystical dimension to our relationship that added up to so much more than the sum of its parts that it made me light-headed, like being drunk on Holy Spirit; and by all indications, Grace as well.

That's why we enjoyed so much laughter, and why Cathy and Brandon felt uneasy about the fascination that Grace and I displayed for each other. They could not fathom the profound implications of Grace's need to tell her story and my need to listen, so I had to tread very carefully with both Cathy and Brandon.

I hoped that Grace would as well, but I couldn't be sure; and every so often I dropped little reminders in our conversations that despite our Platonic fascination with each other we had to maintain a respectful decorum to ensure the integrity of our separate relationships, hers with her husband, and mine with Cathy.

"You were saying something about smelting spiritual gold," she said as she poured tea into my cup. "I made it strong today, Oriano. I'm not sure how you like it."

"It'll be fine," I said, not wanting to tell her that strong tea left a lingering tannic aftertaste; but that was only because I didn't drink tea with milk like Grace.

I spooned in half a teaspoon of sugar, stirred the tea, and said, "Smelting spiritual gold is the *sine qua non* of all spiritual paths. Some paths are more conscious of this than others, but essentially they all lead to the same place—"

"Which is?" Grace jumped in, eager to start the ascension.

"I could say God, but that would be too pat," I replied, smiling at her eagerness to explore the ethereal forms of the higher worlds of thought. "Besides, it wouldn't explain anything, because who can understand what God is all about?"

Grace's eyes sparkled. I loved watching her eyes, not for the uniqueness of their color, but for the window that they provided onto her beautiful soul.

"I agree. God is too big for us to understand. But we can know God, Oriano—"

"We can?" I jumped in, to ensure her confidence in our dialectic.

"We can know God through love. By learning to love, we get closer to God."

"Wonderful!" I exclaimed, startling Grace. "God is love, and the more love we give to the world the closer we will be to God. *You're absolutely right, Grace!"*

She smiled at my excited response, her eyes alight with appreciation. I heard *her*, and the goodness that she felt filled the room with a presence of the Holy.

"Unconditional love," she amplified, in a quiet, reverential voice. "Love without any strings attached, Oriano. The purest love of all—"

This was the first time I heard her warrior's voice, and it intrigued me because it added a new dimension to our relationship; a certain understanding that went beyond words, as though the vibratory frequency of her new voice conveyed much more than the mere meaning of her words, an irrefutable gnostic knowing.

"Love without strings. I like that," I said, surprising myself by the softness of my own voice. "I call it selfless love. I agree with you, Grace; that's the way to know God. But the trick to loving selflessly is to know when, where, and how to love; otherwise life will tear you apart so fast it'll make your head spin—"

Grace burst into laughter. "I've never met anyone quite like you in my whole life!"

I smiled, trying not to blush. "I've been told I'm different."

"You certainly are. *You're so full of Light!"*

"Like attracts like, Grace," I said, and then a quote suddenly popped into my mind. **'Let your light so shine before men,'** said Jesus—

"You're right! We shouldn't hide our light under a bushel, should we?"

"We couldn't even if we tried, Grace; and do you know why?"

"Why?" she asked, with the spontaneous eagerness of a curious child.

"Because you and I have been bought with a price, that's why. That's the feather that we have in common. **'The light of the body is the eye,'** said Jesus. **'If therefore thine eye be single, thy whole body will be full of light.'** Your eye was made single through your love of

Jesus, and mine through conscious effort and voluntary suffering; but regardless how we got here, Grace, the fact is that you and I share something very special."

"What? I know we do, but I can't for the life of me put my finger on it!"

I sat back in my chair, looking at her. I thought for a moment or two, and then I said, "You don't have to answer me, Grace; but I'd like to ask you something. It's very personal, I know; but I'd like to confirm something for myself."

"What?" she asked, eager to share her story with me.

"You say you've never met anyone quite like me before; well, I've never met anyone quite like you before either. I suspect I know what it is that fascinates me about you, but I'd like to confirm it for myself; so, if you'll pardon my presumption, I'd like to know why you went into the convent. What compelled you, Grace?"

Grace expected something far more personal (though I couldn't guess what), and her face lit up like a beacon of light. "I wanted to serve God, Oriano. I wanted to dedicate my life to Jesus. I heard the call, and I answered. It was as simple as that."

"And by dedicating your life to Jesus you made your eye single," I said.

"I'm not quite sure what that means. I've always been puzzled by that. Do you know what Jesus meant, Oriano?" she asked, furrowing her brow.

"It's all part of Christ's code. His whole gospel teaching is a cryptic code for the transformation of self-consciousness. Actually, to be more precise, Christ's teaching is a technique; or a long and difficult process if you will, for spiritual self-realization. By dedicating your life to Jesus you made your eye single; meaning, you saw the world through Christ's teaching. In other words, Grace; you gave your life spiritual purpose by dedicating it to Jesus. And this spiritual purpose is the single eye that Jesus refers to."

"I'm still not quite sure I get it. Can you simplify it for me, please?"

"I can try. Okay; Jesus uses the eye as a metaphor for seeing the world in a certain way. If we see the world through the eye of moral self-discipline, such as Christ's teaching, then we make our eye single. We concentrate our energies into a single focus. But if we see the world through what Jesus calls an evil eye, then we can't concentrate our energies into a single focus. That's why Jesus said that we can't serve two masters. If we serve God our eye is made single because we have one goal, which is to serve God; but if we serve mammon our focus will be scattered all over the place because of our many desires. *Capisce?"*

"I believe I do," Grace said, but as she stared at me with wonder in her eyes the thought occurred to me to reveal something much deeper about Christ's metaphor that would add a whole new dimension to her understanding of the Way of Christ.

"Grace, let me share a little discovery I made about this mystifying saying," I began, very thoughtfully. "Try something for me, if you would. Substitute the personal pronoun 'I' for the physically seeing eye in Christ's saying. When you read what Jesus said with the pronoun 'I' it will take on a whole new meaning. It speaks to the heart of Christ's teaching, which is to make our two selves into one self. In other words, by focusing on Christ's teaching of love and moral self-discipline our lower and higher self will become one single 'I', and we will be made whole. As Jesus said in the Gospel of Thomas. *'When the two will be as one, and the outer like the inner, and the male with the female neither male nor female.'* Meaning, one is made whole; a single self, the pronoun 'I' that I substituted for the seeing eye. When the two selves, the spiritual 'I' and evil 'I', are made into one 'I' we're made whole. This is the secret meaning of Christ's teaching that Bible scholars like Elaine Pagels have been trying to decode for years. *Capisce* now, Grace."

Grace stared at me in awe. I had by this time told her that I was no longer a Christian, but there I was decoding Christ's teaching, and this mystified her.

"Oriano, why did you leave the Church?" she was forced to ask. "You seem to understand Christ's teaching so well; why would you leave the Church?"

I couldn't help but smile at her conundrum. "I'll be as honest with you as you have been with me, Grace," I said. "I didn't leave voluntarily. I was pulled and dragged and severed from my Christian faith with such brutal force that I still bear the scars."

91

"But how? Why? I don't understand—"

Again, I smiled at her conundrum. "What can I say? It's not something I can put into a few words. I told you that I was a seeker. But I'm one of the lucky ones; I found what I was looking for. Like you, Grace; I found myself. You found yourself in the convent, and I found myself out here in the cold, cruel world. But what does it matter how we find ourselves? You identify with Jesus Christ because he helped you to find yourself, and I don't. Which doesn't mean that I don't love Jesus; I do, Grace. But what you don't seem to grasp—and not only you, but Christianity—is that there is more than one way to find yourself. Christ's teaching is one path, but not the only path; and it wasn't enough for me. I needed a conscious understanding of the Way, not blind faith; so I was forced to drop my Christian faith in search of a more conscious way home to God. I had no choice, Grace. I too was called to my path. Like I told you, life is an individual journey."

Grace shook her head in wonder, her eyes trying to read my soul. She couldn't fathom the sacred mystery outside her own Christian faith, and it bothered her. But she couldn't deny her feelings about me, and her experience of me contradicted her Christian understanding; and this contributed to her fascination with me.

"Oriano, if I may; I'd like to ask you something very personal."

"By all means," I said.

"Do you believe in the afterlife?"

I laughed. "Certainly."

"Then you believe in heaven and hell?"

"Yes and no," I replied.

"What do you mean?" she said, furrowing her brow.

"Not in the traditional Christian sense, Grace. *"In my father's house are many mansions,"* said Jesus. "But we're getting into metaphysics here, and I should be getting back to work—"

She looked at me with disappointment in her eyes, but she did not insist. "I understand," she said.

"I'll tell you what. We'll talk about Christ's metaphor of many mansions another time. I promise—"

But the subject never came up again; leaving one more topic that I wanted to explore with her should I have the nerve to ask her to continue our Platonic relationship…

I didn't realize it for several days, but by forcing myself to keep my conversations with Grace within the confines of the Christian paradigm I began to have a growing sense of awareness of just how small the Christian perspective on life really was; and I found this amusing in a sad kind of way. Fortunately I was familiar enough with Christ's teaching to always make my point, because Christ's teaching speaks the Way, and the Way cannot be contained by any one spiritual perspective on life; but every so often I wanted to scream because I felt so constrained by the inflexible Christian paradigm.

But I didn't scream. I thought first, and then spoke; but my deliberate thoughtfulness did not escape Grace, and she made a comment one day that led to one of the most fascinating and moving dialogues that we had while I worked for her—

"You're very thoughtful," she said, in her own thoughtful voice. "You never speak without thinking first. That's an admirable quality. If you will pardon my curiosity, were you always like this; or did you have to cultivate this—what can I call it, Oriano?"

"Attitude?" I said.

"I'm not quite sure that's the right word. I see it more as a character trait."

I thought for a moment. "I agree," I said, nodding my head.

"I've only met one other person who spoke like you do, Oriano. No; that didn't come out right. I meant to say that he spoke thoughtfully like you do. But I understood why he was so thoughtful. Brother Thomas understood the power of silence. He never quite found the inner peace that he was looking for; but he was a brilliant man and insightful writer, and he gave me advice that I will never forget—"

Grace fell silent. I smiled, but said nothing. I waited for her to tell me, but she didn't; and the silence was beginning to get pressing. "Was he in a monastery?" I asked.

"Yes. He died a few years ago. What a great soul. He was the most genuine man I have ever met. But you—"

I couldn't get over the tenor of our conversation that morning. Grace had just returned from morning Mass. I was taking down the wainscoting and wallpaper in the hallway because, as she put it the day before, "It didn't work with our new color. Brandon and I talked it over, and we decided to paint the hallway too. I hope you don't mind."

"Of course not. Now the room will look finished."

"Yes, it didn't look finished; did it?"

"Tommy Ping must have put up this wallpaper, Grace," I said, as I stripped off another piece.

"Do you think so? Why?"

"Because it looks like slapped-on class," I said, and laughed. "Tommy Ping didn't have class, Grace. The wallboard downstairs told me that loud and clear. Houses speak to me, and this house shouted artificiality."

Grace smiled at my comment. "I felt that too, Oriano. And if there is one thing that I cannot stand, it's artificiality."

I burst into laughter. "Well, Grace; after we chase all of Tommy Ping's ghosts out of here your house will take on some real character, not this phony class."

"Good. And when we're all done we'll have you and Cathy up for a nice home-cooked Newfie dinner—"

But when Grace came back from Mass in the morning she was different. She had something on her mind. "In what way do I intrigue you?" I asked.

"I couldn't put my finger on it," she replied, in a tone of voice completely alien to our conversations, a very serious, almost distant voice, "but it came to me this morning while listening to Father say Mass—"

Grace fell silent again. I waited. The silence lasted. It was getting pressing again. "Do I remind you of your monastic friend?" I had to ask.

"Yes," she said, still distant. "Would you like to know what he told me, Oriano?"

"Only if you feel free to tell me," I said.

"How thoughtful of you. Now that's something Brother Thomas would have said—"

Grace fell silent again. This was most unusual, and it began to make me feel slightly uncomfortable. "Grace," I said, to snap her out of her reverie, "what Order did Brother Thomas belong to?"

"The Trappists," she replied.

"Thomas Merton was a Trappist," I said.

"That's who I'm talking about, Oriano."

"You mean you met Thomas Merton?" I asked.

"Yes. I thought of him this morning during Mass—"

"No kidding? You met Thomas Merton?"

"Yes. I looked him up. I read everything he had written, and I wanted to meet him—"

Grace fell into reverie again. I waited for a minute or two, and then said, "What was he like in person, Grace?"

Either she didn't hear me, or she simply didn't want to answer my question; she went right into Thomas Merton—"'*God created man with a soul that was made not to bring itself to perfection in its own order, but to be perfected by Him in an order infinitely beyond the reach of human power,'*" she said, quoting Thomas Merton. "And how does God do that, Oriano? How does God bring soul to perfection?"

Grace had a far-away look in her eyes, as though transfixed on something beyond human thought; something mystical. "How?" I asked.

"With the gift of sanctifying grace," she replied, and then she smiled and lit up the whole room with the incredible light of her love; and my heart filled with goodness.

Her smile was angelic; beatific. It was as though she had been imbued with the love of the Holy Ghost. It was as palpable as the air I breathed. I didn't want the moment to end, but I felt compelled to say to her, "You do your name justice, Grace."

"Thank you," she said, as naturally as if to say that it was raining outside, which it was; a cold, freezing rain.

"He affected you deeply, didn't he?"

"Who?"

"Thomas Merton."

"Yes. He was a great influence on my life. And in many ways you remind me of him. That's what I was thinking of this morning during Mass—"

"How?" I asked to keep her from slipping away again.

"I'm not quite sure. Brother Merton told me that he had not yet found the inner peace that he was looking for; but he told me he had met such a person in a Buddhist monk. He asked him for the secret of inner peace, and would you like to know what he was told?"

"Please," I said.

"Joyful selflessness," Grace replied, in her reverential voice.

My face lit up in a bright smile. "That's exactly the same conclusion that I came to, Grace. In fact, I even worked it out into a working formula that captures the heart and soul of Christ's whole teaching of self-sacrifice. Would you like to hear it?"

"Yes, please."

I paused for a moment or two, smiling to myself at where the spirit of our relationship had taken us so early in the day. *"The more you give of yourself, the more of yourself you will have to give"* I replied, and paused again "And conversely, *the less you give of yourself, the less of yourself you will have to give.* Inner peace, Grace; it comes only when you have completely shifted your center of gravity from your ego to your spiritual self; and that, I'm sorry to say, is why Thomas Merton could not find the inner peace that he was looking for. He was still too much of the world."

"Do you think so?" Grace said, with a mystified look on her face. "Have you read Thomas Merton, Oriano?"

"I wouldn't presume to say what I did about him if I hadn't read him," I said, and broke into a gentle laugh at the absurdity of the thought.

"Of course," she said. "How foolish of me. But would you please explain what you mean, Oriano? I'm not quite sure I understand you."

"Well," I said, resting my elbow on the step ladder, "I'm not quite sure I should get into this now. It might be a bit too early in our relationship—"

"You fascinate me intellectually, Oriano. But more than that, you excite me in a way that Brother Thomas Merton's books excited me; and I can't understand why—"

"I suppose that's because we're both radical individuals who happen to write about the spiritual life; only Merton did it from within his Christian paradigm, and I'm doing so from my own singular perspective—"

"Which is?"

"Spiritually eclectic," I replied, with an ironic smile.

"That's not good enough, Oriano," Grace said, to my surprise. She sounded annoyed. "You're keeping something from me that you don't want to disclose, aren't you?"

She saw through me, and I chuckled. "Yes and no, Grace. I could tell you what it is specifically; but the irony is that I am telling you with every word that I speak, because I understand that life itself is the Way. Everything that we say and do speaks the Way. Like painting your house, for example. I can see it, but you can't. Your new house is symbolic of your whole life; and the changes that you're making to your house foreshadow the changes that you are being called upon to make in your new life here in St. Jude."

Grace fell silent again. Then she began to cry. Tears flowed down her cheeks. Unembarrassed by her tears, she looked at me and said, "Please tell me, Oriano."

I looked into her eyes, and very softly said, "Grace, in your heart you know what I'm talking about. It's your own faith that's blinding you—"

"My faith?" she said, wiping the tears with her hand. "I don't understand."

"Do you remember the conversation we had about personal freedom? We're only as free as the philosophy that we live by will allow us to be? Well, that goes for our faith as well. We're only as free as our faith will allow us to be; and your faith—like Thomas Merton's—will not allow you to see what's before your very eyes."

"I just don't understand that, Oriano," she said, with tears in her voice.

I took a deep breath. "Alright, let me see if I can approach this from a different angle. When you see a solution to a problem, you understand the problem; but how can you see what I'm talking about when you're looking at what I'm saying through a glass darkly?"

"My faith, you mean?"

"Unfortunately, yes."

"Oriano—" she said, in a voice that implored me not to go there; but she had opened that door, not me. Nonetheless—

"Alright, Grace," I said, and smiled. I felt her uneasiness, and I had to restore the comfort level of our relationship. "The spiritual life is all about making conscious the unconscious, and this applies to our faith as well," I began, very thoughtfully." We begin our journey home to God with blind faith because we just don't know where to go, but as we progress on our individual journey to God—and it is an individual journey, Grace—we have to make conscious what we live by unconsciously; and that's what intrigues you about me, because I don't live by blind faith. I am conscious of the Way, and I live the Way consciously. And just to satisfy your undying curiosity about me, my spiritual path is known to the world generically as the Way of Total Awareness. It's the most ancient of all spiritual paths and the origin of all spiritual teachings. Even Jesus drew from this path."

Grace took a deep breath, and then exhaled. She looked at me long and hard, and quietly said, "What do you think of Thomas Merton?"

"I think he was a wonderful writer, but he was also exquisitely unresolved. That's why he appeals to a lot of readers. His book *The Seven Story Mountain* is a great starting place for anyone setting out on the spiritual journey."

Grace gave me her Mona Lisa smile. She understood exactly what I meant, but she could not pursue it; her faith would not allow her…

Once again, we never got to complete our conversation on the free gift of sanctifying grace, which I wanted very much to explore before moving on; but she wasn't ready yet to hear what I had to say on the subject, and so she backed off. She sensed that she was putting her faith at risk and chose once again to play it safe.

But how long could she play it safe? She had moved from St. John's Newfoundland to St. Jude Ontario to heed the Call of Soul to expand her spiritual horizons; but she had no idea that it might be outside the context of her faith.

That's why she always backed off whenever I brought her to the edge of her faith, as I did with our dialogue on Brother Thomas. But I understood that, and I never forced the issue with her. And that also added to the fascinating dynamic of our relationship, because I had no desire whatsoever to impose my personal views on her.

That was the most difficult lesson that I had to learn on my spiritual quest for my true self, the realization that everyone must come to a conscious awareness of the Way on their own. One must live the Way to understand the Way, and Grace was doing that; but her experience of the Way was limited to the confines of her faith, and this posed a problem for her that had finally begun to surface, and she was suffering.

Ironically, from the day that Grace arrived to St. Jude she became involved with her new parish Church. She inquired if they had a choir, which they didn't; so she set about right away to form one, and this brought new life to the parish.

Grace had a beautiful voice, and she always belonged to a choir from the time she was a young girl; so she was looking forward to having her house completed so she could have choir practice in her home.

"I prefer to have them at home, Oriano," she said one day as she played the piano for me. I had asked her to play a song or two and she was only too willing. Then she began to sing, and I had to stop working to listen because she had such an angelic voice. I couldn't believe how beautifully she sang, and I told her so—

"Grace, you sing like a bird of paradise."

"Thank you. I've been blessed."

"*I'll say!* Good God, it won't take long to chase Tommy Ping's ghosts out of this house with a voice like that!"

Grace keeled over with laughter. She couldn't help herself and laughed for a good minute. When she stopped she said, "Oriano, God's going to punish us for that!"

"Why? All I'm talking about is the change of energy in this house, that's all. God understands that."

"Change of energy?" she said, and turned to look at me. I was sitting on the sofa. She put down the lid on her piano keys, "I think I understand; but all the same, I'd still like to hear your explanation—"

"Sure," I said, happy for the opportunity to dip into the well again. "I've painted houses for over twenty years now, Grace; and I can tell you that houses are imbued with the energy of their owners. That's a given. Any ghost-busting parapsychologist can tell you that. So if I make fun of Tommy Ping's ghosts, I'm not speaking in jest; I'm being serious in a sardonic way. Energy is vibrations, and music changes the vibrations of a house; so if a house has negative energy— like the inauthentic energy that Tommy Ping left in this house with his slapped-on class—then the way to change it is to imbue the house with positive energy, as we're doing now; me with the virtue of excellence that I leave behind in my work, and you with music and your sensibilities for aesthetic beauty."

Grace shook her head in wonder. *"Where do you get all this from, Oriano?"*

"Certainly not from within the Christian paradigm," I said, and broke into laughter; but I shouldn't have said that. It was an assault upon her faith, and I felt an instant pang of guilt; so I quickly added, "It's all a matter of perspective, Grace; and my perspective on life includes much more than what Christianity has to offer."

"Is that why you won't come back to the Church?"

"Yes."

"Well, it's enough for me Oriano," she said, but her voice was a bit nervous. Realizing it, she added, "In Jesus I have all I need to complete my life."

"Indeed you do," I said, and got up. I went back to work; but an hour later Grace called me for tea. As she poured the tea she said, "Oriano, do you think I made the right decision to come to St. Jude?"

"Grace, how can I possibly answer that?"

"I know. It was foolish of me, wasn't it? I just feel so alone sometimes. No, that's not what I meant to say. I feel so helpless sometimes. I trust that God will provide for me, Oriano; but you know what I mean, don't you?"

"Your stars are in alignment. You can't see it yet, but everything is falling into place for you. I know it—"

"Do you really? How do you know, Oriano? Please tell me."

"I just do. It's like Frost's poem *The Road Not Taken*—'and way leads on to way.' Do you remember?"

"I know the poem well. It was our inspiration for leaving St. John's. It wasn't an easy decision for us, Oriano; but we had to make it. Brandon was getting restless. He had too much to give to be retired, so I pushed him to apply for this job. I did it gently, mind you; but he needed prodding. We both needed a change. We were growing stale in St. John's. We needed a new challenge in our life; that's why we decided to sell the house and move here. It wasn't an easy decision to make, but we prayed to God and He answered."

"How?" I asked.

"He got Brandon the job. If it's meant to be, we said, God will provide."

"Good. I like that. I admire and respect you both, Grace. It's a courageous move to make any time, but in your time of life especially—"

"That's what all our friends told us."

"That doesn't surprise me. People love security, Grace; and very few people have the courage to risk—"

"Exactly. That's why we had to leave. We had grown too complacent in our spiritual life, and we had to put it all on the line again."

"So that's why you came to our little town of hopeless causes?" I said, and laughed; but to Grace it was no laughing matter—

"Yes. Now you know," she said, and sat back with a great sense of relief.

I smiled, not knowing what to say; but I had to respond to Grace's very personal confession. "I'm sure the Catholic community of this town is going to appreciate you moving here, Grace; it needed some new blood."

"I heard. But I also heard that Father Louis is doing wonders for the parish."

"Yes, he is. My mother just loves him."

"She would, wouldn't she? Your mother can speak to him in Italian, can't she?"

"Yes."

"Oh good. He's such a wonderful priest, Oriano. You know him, don't you?"

"No. I've never met him," I said, hoping she wouldn't go there.

"Why don't you come to the Church sometime and meet him?"

"Grace—"

"I know, mind my own business; right?"

"I know you mean well, but I do have my own spiritual destiny."

"Can I pray for you, Oriano?"

"You can pray for my good health, you can pray for my writing career, but please don't pray for the salvation of my soul because that's my responsibility; okay?"

"Are you sure? Remember what Brother Thomas said—"

"Yes, I do; but do you remember what St. Paul said?"

"'Work out your own salvation with fear and trembling.' Philippians 2, Chapter 2, Verse 12. I wish he would never have said that."

I laughed. "Well?"

"Jesus is still our savior, Oriano. I don't doubt that for a moment."

"I love Jesus, Grace; but like I said, he's not my savior."

"Aren't you afraid of going—"

"Don't say it! Please don't. I'm way beyond that understanding of the afterlife."

Realizing that she had gone too far, Grace smiled. "I'm sorry, Oriano. I'm starting to sound like Pauline, aren't I?"

"You can't bludgeon people into submission with guilt anymore, Grace. The world has changed. If you want people to come back to Jesus you have to win them over with an enlightened understanding of the Way; otherwise you will fail. And that, I'm afraid to tell you dear heart, is your personal conundrum."

"My conundrum?" she said, puzzled.

"Yes," I replied, and stood up. "I'd love to sit here and discuss it with you, Grace; but I have to get back to work or your husband will begin to wonder what the hell I'm doing here all day—

I had to remove all the door trim and baseboards to take down the panel wainscoting and wallpaper in the hallway that extended into the living room wall, and the back wall of the hallway was all panel board with no backing, so I had to hang a sheet of drywall and tape it after I took down the wallboard.

There were five doors in the hallway, including a linen closet door, and the trim around these doors was so tacky—the joints weren't mitered; they had an engraved square piece of wood at each corner—that Grace asked her husband if it was possible to put on new trim and baseboards, and Brandon consented with little persuasion; but I only had a mitre box and hand saw, so I borrowed a carpenter friend's electric chop saw to do a more professional job and speed up my work; and by Sunday morning I was finished.

But I didn't return to work on Grace's house for two weeks because I had to squeeze in another job. Grace understood and let me off the hook. "By all means. Oriano," she said, happy to oblige; "do your other job. The carpet will be installed by the time you get back and then you can put on the new baseboards."

She had decided to paint all her trim white, which worked well with the Tempting Teal of the living room and hallway and entranceway; but this was all extra work which I had to run by Brandon first.

"Oriano, better we do it now than later," he said, and he was right because he knew that Grace would never live with stained baseboards that did nothing for the exciting new color that they had selected for the walls.

So slowly, in her own quiet way, Grace was getting all the work on the house that she wanted done (like most women that I have worked for). They were only going to paint the walls first and change the living room rug because they were only planning to stay in St. Jude for three years and didn't want to invest too much into the house; but it wasn't long before they decided that they might be staying five years, so why not have the house look the way they wanted? That was Grace's thinking, anyway.

"And way leads on to way, I kept saying to her whenever she had a change of heart. "Who knows, Grace; you may even retire in this town—"

She smiled. She didn't want to admit it, but she had to leave herself open to the possibility. "Who knows?" she said. "It's in God's hands, Oriano."

"That's an interesting concept, Grace," I said, unable to stop my Socratic mind from working. "It took me years to come to terms with it—"

"What?" she asked, intrigued by my comment.

"Destiny and free will," I replied.

"It was free will that caused Adam and Eve to eat the forbidden fruit, Oriano," she quickly offered, little realizing what she had just done.

I laughed. I wasn't sure if she meant it seriously or just to provoke a dialogue; but it didn't matter to me because she had just opened the door to something that I very much wanted to talk about with the former Sister of Mercy—the concept of Original Sin.

"Do you believe in it, Grace?" I asked.

"What?" she asked.

It was my first day back. I had been away for exactly fifteen days. I didn't know if that high energy level between us would still be there or not. I was psychically drained from all the negative energy of the house I had just taped and painted—in two years the homeowner's step-daughter got killed in an ATV accident, his teenage son committed suicide out of guilt for letting his step-sister take the ATV out alone, his wife died of cancer, and he lost his job to his boss's sister—so I wasn't at my dynamic best when I returned to Grace's house; but within the first hour it felt like slipping on an old philosophical glove, and I was anxious to dialogue with Grace.

"Do you believe that Adam and Eve passed on the stain of Original Sin by the act of procreation?" I asked, wondering whether she would step into the dialectic with me.

Grace thought for a moment, and then said, "At one time I would have said yes, Oriano; but today I have to say that I believe the story of Adam and Eve is a myth."

"Then from whence Original Sin?" I asked, with a chuckle.

"I think we're born with it," she replied, with that nervous hesitancy that I had become familiar with whenever she wasn't sure of her belief. "The story of Adam and Eve was created to help us understand the concept of Original Sin."

"So according to Christianity our immortal soul is created at the moment of human conception with the stain of Original Sin which Jesus died on the cross to cleanse?"

"Yes," she replied, without hesitation.

I wanted to laugh, but I couldn't. I had to see how far Grace would take this logic before it collapsed under the weight of its own absurdity. "Where does Original Sin come from then if the story of Adam and Eve is a myth?"

"When soul is created it is alienated from God, Oriano. This alienation from God is the stain of Original Sin."

"And you accept this upon faith alone?"

"Yes."

"So soul is born with Original Sin and Jesus died on the cross to wash away the stain of Original Sin and baptism into the Church ensures soul's entry into the kingdom of heaven?" I asked, pushing the envelope as far as I could.

"Essentially, yes," she said. "It's all a matter of divine faith, Oriano."

Once again, I wanted to laugh; but I held myself back. "Let me see if I have this straight. Christianity would have us believe that at the moment of our human conception our immortal soul is co-created with our mortal physical body and it is blemished with the stain of Original Sin which God had his only begotten son Jesus sacrifice his life on the cross to remove for us to prepare our way into the kingdom of heaven?"

"Yes," she simply said.

"Would you like to know how I see this, Grace?"

"Please," she said.

"Christianity injects us with a virus called damnation, and then offers us a serum called salvation. I'm sorry, Grace; but that's too much for me to swallow."

"It's a question of faith, Oriano. We have to believe."

Still laden with the angry, depressing energy of the house of grief and disappointment that I had just completed I wanted to shout. I wanted to scream. I wanted to pull my hair out. I wanted to run as far away as I could from that mindless Christian nonsense; but I could not because I liked Grace, and I had to give the former Bride of Christ her due.

I knew from experience that the Way of Christ did work to liberate soul from the confines of our ego self, but not in the way that Christianity would have the world believe; and that was the tragic irony of the Christian religion. And Grace was living proof.

"Well," Grace," I said, with a heavy sigh; "as long as it works for you, what can I say? Life is, after all, an individual journey."

"You don't believe in Original Sin, then?"

"Original Sin has a different meaning for me."

"Ohhh?" Grace said, seeing an opening to save me. "What?"

Without realizing it, I had boxed myself into a corner; and I couldn't do anything about it. How could I tell Grace that I did not believe in the Christian concept of one life born in sin? How could I explain to her the Spiritual Laws of Karma and Reincarnation within the rigid paradigm of her faith?

"How can I put this?" I began, as I frantically scratched for solid ground. "I believe the story of Adam and Eve is a metaphor for the positive and negative aspects of the creative life force; or Holy Spirit, if you will. Whether soul is created at the moment of human conception or not doesn't really matter to me—"

"Do you believe it is," she interjected.

"That's neither here nor there, Grace. The argument I'm trying to present is that the concept of Original Sin lies in the negative aspect of the creative life force."

"I don't understand what that means," she said, with a puzzled look.

"The logic is simple," I said, with a big smile because I finally saw light at the end of the dark tunnel of Christianity's self-serving logic. "What creates soul if not the creative life force, which is Holy Spirit? And we know that the life force is both creative and destructive, don't we?"

"In what way, Oriano?" she asked, again with a puzzled look.

106

"Out of death comes new life," I replied, as I worked my way towards the Light outside the cave of spiritual ignorance. "All of nature tells us that. Science tells us that energy can neither be created nor destroyed; so where does the life force go when a living thing dies?"

"Don't tell me you're an atheist, Oriano?" Grace said, shocked by my reference to science. *"Please don't tell me that—"*

I laughed. "Don't be silly, Grace. Atheism is the final refuge for lost souls. I'm not lost. I found my way out of Plato's cave. All I'm saying is that Holy Spirit is the creative life force, and the life force has two aspects to it; a positive and a negative aspect. And I'm saying that since Holy Spirit is responsible for all creation, then it must be responsible for the creation of our soul; ergo, soul is born with the positive and negative aspects of the creative life force. And my inner voice tells me that the negative or destructive aspect of the creative life force is what the author of the Adam and Eve story called Original Sin. That's what separates us from God. *Capice?*"

Grace did not know what to say. She stood in the doorway to Brandon's office, whose walls she had decided to paint in Tempting Teal also because they both had grown to love the color, and she just stared at me with a befuddled look on her face.

"Pretty heavy stuff for Monday morning, eh Grace?" I said, and laughed.

"Yes, very heavy," she said, completely nonplussed.

Thank goodness for my hearty laugh that cut through the heavy air. "Grace, the bottom line is that I believe in the concept of Original Sin also; but just not as you do," I said, and broke into another chuckle. "As I said, life is an individual journey."

Still not satisfied, she said, "Do you believe in Jesus Christ, Oriano?"

"As I said, I believe that Jesus was a teacher of the Way."

"But do you believe that his death upon the cross washes away the stain of Original Sin?" she asked, wanting to know exactly where I stood.

"No. I believe that by living the Way as Jesus meant for us to live it we can transform our consciousness and transcend our human self, which is the carrier of Original Sin. I'm afraid to say this, Grace;

107

but I believe St. Paul was right when he said that we have to work out our own salvation with fear and trembling."

"Well, Oriano; I don't know what to say. I believe in Jesus Christ, and I believe that St. Paul had his reasons for saying what he did; but I can't fathom them—"

I burst into laughter. Grace smiled, and then laughed too. She had to let out the pressure of her dilemma somehow. "Oriano, what do you say to a cup of tea?"

"Splendid idea," I said...

The fifteen days that I was away from Grace gave me time to think about our relationship. It was definitely Platonic, and absolutely fascinating; and what a difference in consciousness from the unresolved woman living with the man whose wife had died of cancer and whose house I had just taped and painted.

But then, Grace was not just any woman; and the more I compared the two women the more convinced I was that I should ask Grace if she wanted to continue our conversations after I painted her house. I even went so far as to broach the subject over tea my first day back; but I did so very cautiously—

"Grace, did you see the movie on TV Sunday night; *Tuesdays with Morrie,* starring Jack Lemon?"

"Yes. Wasn't that a wonderful movie? Brandon and I cried our hearts out."

"Cathy and I cried too," I said, smiling at the coincidence.

"Did you really?" she asked.

"Yes. It touched us. Wasn't that a wonderful thing the young journalist did, recording his talks with Morrie so he could have a record of his old professor's life wisdom?"

Grace smiled again. I couldn't read her smile this time, and I wasn't quite sure if she was onto me or not. "Morrie certainly had a lot of life wisdom to offer him, didn't he?" she replied. "Do you know which one of Morrie's sayings I liked the best, Oriano?"

"Which one?"

"He said that we have to learn how to die to know how to live our life fully. I agree one hundred percent with that. It's a paradox, Oriano. But that's what Jesus Christ's teaching is all about, isn't it?

We have to die to our life to find our life. Morrie was Jewish, so he wasn't referring to Jesus. He came to that place of wisdom on his own."

"I agree with that too, Grace. As a matter of fact, I'd go so far as to say that the more we die to life the more passion we have for life. It's incredible how it works, but that's just the way it is—"

Grace smiled. It was her understanding smile. I knew it was, because her eyes seemed to tear up whenever she smiled her understanding smile. *"'Strait is the gate, and narrow is the way which leadeth unto life, and few there be that find it.'* Mathew, Chapter 7, Verse 14," she quoted with a very deep, thoughtful look on her face. "That's what made me sad about Morrie Schwartz."

"Oh? In what way, Grace?"

"He didn't go far enough, Oriano."

I wasn't quite sure what she was getting at, but I had a good idea; and I welcomed the opportunity. "He didn't go far enough on the narrow way, you mean?" I said.

"Yes. Morrie was a good soul. You could see that. But he was still afraid of death."

I smiled at her spiritual equanimity. That's what attracted me to her, her inner resolve; that same inner sense of certainty of our immortal nature that I experienced when I gave birth to my spiritual self.

"Morrie wasn't quite resolved, was he Grace?" I said, to confirm my insight.

"No, he wasn't. That's why he was still afraid of dying. He hadn't come to that point in himself, Oriano; that special place—"

Grace often left her thoughts uncompleted, as though she didn't want to say more than she should for fear of betraying herself; and I had to complete them for her. "I think I know what you're saying, Grace. Morrie hadn't died in the sense that you and I understand Christ's saying about dying to one's life to save one's life—"

"Yes. Exactly," she said, and smiled. "That's what Jesus meant when he said that the way is narrow that leadeth unto life and few there be that find it."

"I don't disagree with you in principle, Grace; but I think Morrie was one of the lucky ones. I think he did find the Way near the end. He may not have walked the Way as far as you have, Grace; but he embraced his death with the same courage that he embraced life, if not more. I know what you mean; but we can't all die the way Jesus meant for us to die—consciously, that is. Morrie's death was forced upon him by his fatal illness, but he grew spiritually in his dying; and I love and admire him for his courage."

Grace stared at me, not knowing exactly what I meant by my insight into the two kinds of dying—the conscious death of the Way, and the unconscious death of life; but she wanted to confirm her suspicion. "Have you died in Christ, Oriano?" she asked.

"I really don't know what that means, Grace; but I can tell you in all sincerity that I took Christ's teaching as far as it could take me. Yes, I did die to my life; and in dying I found my true self. If that's dying in Christ, then I did so; but not everyone is bought with a price, Grace," I said, hoping she would pick up on my reference.

"St. Paul?" she said, with a sweet smile.

I chuckled to myself. "Yes."

"You have been bought with a price too, then?"

"Yes."

"You like St. Paul, don't you Oriano?"

"He's my favorite Gospel writer."

"Mine's St. John. So, tell me; how did you come to be bought with a price? Or am I being too personal?"

"Grace, you can't expect me to reveal that to you over a cup of tea; do you?"

"Why not?" she very boldly asked.

"Because that's the stuff that novels are made of," I replied, and laughed. I loved her boldness, and hoped that she would persist.

"I had to ask, didn't I?" she said, with a sweet smile.

"I know you did; but that's like me asking you to tell me about how your life of austerity in the convent that led you to die the final death—"

"Oh, dear heart; what a story I have to tell!"

"Then tell it, Find yourself a quiet corner of the house and sit down and write it!"

"I keep putting it off, Oriano. But you do keep giving me inspiration."

"And you me," I said, and just then the title of my book came to me as it often does in one synoptic flash of creative illumination— *"Tea with Grace!"*

"Pardon me?" she said, wrinkling her brow.

"Tea with Grace," I repeated. That's what I would call the story of our Platonic relationship if I ever get to write it. What do you think, Grace? Do you have something to pass on to posterity like Mitch Albom's old professor Morrie?"

"Much more," she replied, with a bright twinkle in her beautiful eyes. "But we are being presumptuous; aren't we?" she added, just to play it safe.

That was my opening, as indefinite as it was, and I thought carefully about what I was about to say. My mind raced. It came to me—

"On the other hand, to add a fourth question to the famous three questions that Bob Rae quoted for his last book—*If not us, who?"* I said, with a twinkle in my own eyes.

Grace stared at me, curiosity written all over her face. "What famous three questions, Oriano?" she asked, her finger circling the rim of her tea cup in nervous anticipation.

"Bob Rae, the former NDP Premier of Ontario, used them as his premise for his new book. You probably haven't heard of it. It's called *The Three Questions.*"

"No, I haven't. What are these three questions?"

"They're attributed to a wise man that lived in Babylon more than two thousand years ago. Rabbi Hillel. The three questions are: *If I am not for myself, who is for me? But if I am only for myself, what am I?* And, *If not now, when?* And as presumptuous as this may appear to be, Grace, I've added a fourth question—*If not us, who?"*

"I'm afraid you've lost me, Oriano," she said, feigning a puzzled look.

I laughed. "Grace, it's not every day that two souls that have been bought with a price meet in the same town and in the same house and talk about life and literature and Jesus and salvation and Newfie cooking—"

111

She burst into laughter. "I'm going to cook you and Cathy a nice traditional cod dinner, Oriano; but I have to get my house in order first. As soon as the dust settles—"

Then she went on about Newfie cooking and we never got back onto the topic that I wanted desperately to talk about…

5. THE GREAT DIVIDE

I didn't dare think about it, but the thought kept finding its way into my mind and wouldn't leave me. "It's not possible," I said, trying to convince myself; but in the back of my mind I knew that it was not only possible, but that it was actually happening, and there was not a damn thing I could do about it.

The feeling first came to me on the Saturday morning that Grace called me to pick up the color charts. We were in her living room. Grace was sitting on the sofa and I was kneeling on the rug in front of the coffee table. We were looking at the new colors that she had finally chosen, and she wanted my professional opinion; again—

"Ultimately you have to live with it, Grace; so it's up to you."

"I realize that, Oriano; but that doesn't help me, does it?"

I laughed. Grace saw through my caution and demanded my professional advice again. "Okay," I said. "To tell you the truth, I think you're playing it too safe."

"After tossing and turning all week long, Grace finally decided on a creamy white for her living room, hallway, and kitchen and adjoining dining room, which disappointed me because I was tired of my customers forever playing it safe with colors.

"I've made some very difficult decisions in my life, Oriano; why should I be afraid of something as simple as choosing colors for my house?"

"You tell me," I said, smiling at her quandary.

"Why is it so difficult, Oriano?" she asked again, throwing the ball right back into my court. "You must encounter this all the time, don't you?"

"I do; and I attribute it to the propriety factor," I replied.

I couldn't read her smile, but I did see a twinkle in her eyes. "Oriano, have you ever made a decision that changed your whole life?" she asked.

I had no idea where that came from, and it took me by surprise. I smiled, and then recklessly jumped right into the opening that had been provided for us—

"Yes; many times. As a matter of fact, at one time in my life I dared to make life-changing decisions at the toss of a coin."

Grace stared at me wide-eyed, with the most curious expression on her face. Obviously she hadn't expected me to answer her question. "At the toss of a coin?" she said, with a mystified look. "You actually tossed a coin to make decisions for you?"

"Yes. It was an experiment. I'm sure you've heard of the expression, let go and let God," I said, opening a door to one of my most private corners of my soul.

"Yes, of course," she said, with a bemused look.

"Well, I let go and let God," I said.

"With the toss of a coin?" she said, with a startled look.

"Yes. I even altered the course of my romantic life with the toss of a coin."

Grace stared at me. Realizing that she had opened the door to something she wasn't really expecting, she decided to see what was on the other side.

"Are you telling me that you made a decision to be with someone or not by tossing a coin?" she asked, incredulously.

"Yes. And I really liked that woman, Grace; but my coin said no, so I never pursued the relationship. That's pretty bold, don't you think?"

Grace's face lit up. Her smile approved of my boldness. But I had piqued her curiosity. "Did you regret making that decision?" she asked.

"I didn't make it," I said, and broke into laughter.

Startled for a moment, Grace said, *"Oh yes; you tossed the coin—"*

"It was crazy, I know; but I did it for one reason only—to learn to trust myself. I was on a quest, Grace; and I had run out of options. So I had nothing to lose."

"I'm afraid I don't understand," she said, now completely taken by me.

114

"There's nothing to understand. I was a seeker, and I had run out of road; so I made my own road," I replied, and broke into another hearty laugh.

Grace didn't know what to say, so she just stared at me. I smiled at her. She smiled back, nervously. "You were a seeker?"

"Yes."

"What were you seeking?"

"My true self."

"And did you find your true self?"

"Yes."

"Where?"

"Where I least expected."

"And where was that, may I ask?"

"Let me answer that with a poem that I wrote in high school," I said, and shifted my position on the floor for comfort. I don't know why I decided to share the inspired experience that foretold my quest for my true self, but as I used to say in one of past lives, "in for a penny, in for a pound." I smiled, and continued, "In all sincerity, Grace; this poem came to me out of the blue. My daemon has never again possessed me as completely as it did when I wrote my high school poem *Noman*. This poem was as real to me as you and I talking. I was Noman, and I was summoned to God by the Angel of Death. God said to me, 'Noman, hast thou my fish's scale?' I replied, 'No.' Then God said to me, 'Thou hast three days and three nights to find my fish's scale,' and I was sent to search the four corners of the world to find this fish's scale that God demanded of me. But because there were four corners to the world—North, South, East, and West—and it would take one whole day to search each corner, it meant that I could fail to find the fish's scale because I only had three days to search. Well, to make a long story short, I failed to find God's fish's scale because I ran out of time; and would you like to know what God did to me, Grace?"

"What?" she asked, now totally entranced by my bizarre story.

"God banished me from heaven. He banished me to the fourth corner of the world, the corner that I had no time to search for God's fish's scale. And would you like to know where this corner of the world was, Grace?"

Grace was speechless, and she just nodded.

"St. Jude," I said, trying to keep a straight face. "Right here, in this town of hopeless causes. This was the fourth corner of hell that God banished me to to find His fish's scale. "And I did find it, Grace. I found it right here," I said, pointing to my heart. "The fish's scale that God wanted me to find was my lost soul. It was locked up tight in my heart, and the only way to free my lost soul was to pry open my heart—"

Grace's face lit up, like she had just had a divine insight; which she did: *she had just been touched by the illuminating spirit of our nascent Platonic relationship!*

Catching herself staring at me, she smiled and said, "And how did you do that, Oriano? How did you pry open your heart, pray tell? I'm very curious."

"There are two ways to pry open the human heart, Grace," I answered, smiling. "Most people open their heart with love; but I opened my heart with consciousness."

"With consciousness?" she said, again with a puzzled frown.

"Yes. Love will free one's soul much more easily and quickly than consciousness, but I couldn't take the path of love because I didn't know how to love. I was a natural born egoist; and egoists can't love anyone because all their love is self-centered. So I had no choice but to transform my ego consciousness to find my true self."

Grace was mesmerized. "And how did you do that?"

"By learning how to let go and let God," I replied, and burst into laughter.

Nonplussed, Grace just stared at me. She didn't know what to make of me. My heart went out to her. She saw the look on my face, and in an instant her whole physiognomy changed. In a firm, steely voice she said, *"I took the path of love, Oriano!"*

"Of course you did. Now, about these colors?"

Again taken by surprise, she stared at me for the longest moment; and then she smiled. "Just like that?" she said. "I don't know if I can choose colors after all of that?"

"After what?" I said, trying to keep a straight face.

She stared at me blank-faced, and then she smiled a half smile to let me know that she knew what could not be said out loud about the secrets of the soul; a mystic Mona Lisa smile that revealed the secret without revealing it—*our first Platonic flirtation.*

We chose the original colors that we had agreed on, and from that day on I got the strangest feeling that whenever I walked into her house I was walking into a Platonic world of unmanifest reality, not unlike working on a new novel and not knowing what to expect from the characters in my story; and I couldn't wait to see what would happen.

I could never put my finger on it, but it always felt like Grace and I were engaging on two levels—one physical, down-to-earth, and very ordinary; and the other free and ethereal, like two archetypal spirits mingling in a strange new kind of love-making that satisfied a profound longing in our soul to simply be ourselves.

And we never knew when the Platonic spirit of our relationship would take over our conversations. That's what made our relationship so mesmerizing. We could be talking about the most mundane thing one minute, and the next minute we would find ourselves soaring to the heavens with a thought set free by the easy flow of our conversation.

This happened to me many times before, but not as intensely as with the former Sister of Mercy. I knew what would happen whenever I met a person Soul to Soul, so it didn't surprise me that our conversation would take off into the heavens; but what made my relationship with Grace so remarkable was the distinct nature of our two spirits co-mingling in a dialectical discourse of spiritual inquiry. That was totally new to me.

Grace had realized her spiritual identity through love, and I had realized mine through consciousness; and whenever we began a conversation we engaged in a sweetly satisfying dialectic of love and consciousness. We didn't understand it, but we both knew that it was happening every time the spirit of our relationship possessed us; and we couldn't resist engaging in Platonic love-making just to see where it would take us.

"It's been a long time since anyone has engaged my mind like you have, Grace," I said to her over tea in the dining room. "It has to be your spiritual training as a Sister of Mercy. I can't think of any other reason—"

Grace smiled her Mona Lisa smile. "Life without God just doesn't have the same flavor, does it Oriano?"

"Not at all. And for the life of me, I cannot imagine how anyone can live without God in their life—"

"But people do. *They do, Oriano!*"

"I know they do, Grace. God is a convenience for most people. They pull out their belief in God whenever they need God for one thing or another; but they don't have a clue what it means to be conscious of God in their daily life—"

"Exactly! God is central to our lives, Oriano. Brandon and I have dedicated our life to God, and we hope and pray that our children will do the same one day."

I smiled at the thought that popped into my mind. "Grace, the irony is that people can have their cake and eat it too if they only knew how."

"You're absolutely right. I learned more about how to serve God raising my two children than in all my years in the convent!"

"Good for you! That's exactly how I feel about the spiritual life. I don't think one should have to live in a convent or a monastery or an ashram to find God. I think the spiritual life should be lived out here, in the real world of honest-to-goodness everyday struggle; the world of common decency and heartache—"

"That's precisely how Brandon and I feel! That's why we moved to St. Jude, Oriano. We left our beautiful home in St. John's to serve God in our new mission!"

"And I'm sure you're going to love it here," I said, and got up to leave. "I like our conversations, Grace; and I'm looking forward to working for you."

"Me too," she said, with the biggest smile; and that day, before leaving for the city with Cathy to pick up groceries and paint for Grace's house, I began recording our talks in my new 360 page Hilroy Notebooks which I titled "Conversations with Grace."

It was happening again, but this time I was much more conscious of it happening to me. The last time it happened I had no control at all. Not that I had control this time, but I wanted to have control; that's what inspired me to ask Grace if she would like to continue our Platonic relationship after I finished painting her house.

I wanted to bring the mystical aspect of our relationship out into the open. I wanted to capture our dialectical discourses with a tape recorder, just like Mitch Albom had done with his old professor dying of Lou Gehrig's disease and which he worked into his best-selling book *Tuesdays with Morrie* that was made into a movie starring Jack Lemon who, ironically, was himself dying of cancer. It was the best role of his life.

But this was different. Grace was very much alive and well and sensitive and quickly becoming a vital part of the Catholic community in St. Jude; how could I ask her to dialogue with me on her faith which I knew to be the source of her spiritual unease? And yet, as much as I resisted the thought, I knew that it was meant to be. I knew deep in my soul that we had been brought together for one reason only, and that was to resolve the symbolic nature of our unique relationship—her trying to save my soul by bringing me back to the Church, and me expanding the parameters of her rigid faith.

Very much like my novel *The Other Side* that I had just written. I had no intention of writing it. It was forced upon me by my Muse, and the coincidence blew my mind when the title of my novel was serendipitously confirmed for me by the sign hanging on the gift shop in Richard's Landing on St. Joseph Island where Cathy and I had gone for our leafing holiday shortly after I painted Grace's house; the sign read THE OTHER SIDE.

On our drive down to St. Joseph Island I asked God to give me a sign to confirm that "The Other Side" was the better title for my novel (my working title was "Crossing the Border"); and when I saw the sign above the gift shop in Richard's Landing I knew that it was meant to be. And now I was being shanghaied again, and I couldn't do a thing about it. My Muse called the shots. I was already well into my book of short stories when Brandon's secretary called me; but when Grace and I met I heard the call so loud and clear that I had to suspend my book of stories and use my allotted daily writing time to edit my novel *The Other Side* and record my unbelievable conversations with Grace.

It wasn't enough, though. As thoroughly as I recorded our daily talks (and thoughts and associated memories and ideas that would transform the reality of our relationship into a creative work of fiction), they were never resolved. For one reason or another, our talks were always left hanging, and I had to see them through; but would Grace comply? Would she be willing to participate in the making of a novel?

I honestly didn't know, and I didn't have the courage to ask her. I had dropped hints during the course of our talks, but she never picked up on them—and if she did, she refused to let me know; so I had to make the decision on my own and suffer the rejection should she refuse. And she had good reason to refuse. She saw where our conversations were headed, and we both knew that she feared the consequences—

"With consciousness comes responsibility, Grace," I said to her one day, in oblique reference to her dilemma. "That's why people prefer to stay asleep."

"Asleep?" she queried.

"'*Wake up!*' said Jesus to his disciples. That's what his whole teaching is about, Grace—waking up from the sleep of life; waking up to our spiritual self. That's what all spiritual paths are about—"

"I don't disagree with you, Oriano; but Jesus Christ is the Son of God. His teaching is different from all other teachings. He suffered and died on the cross for our sins—"

"Grace—" I quickly interrupted her. "You should read the book *Why Christianity Must Change or Die*, by Bishop John Shelby Spong. It offers a much more conscious perspective on Christianity. As much as I respect your Roman Catholic faith, I have to tell you in all honesty that it's much too constraining for the spiritual consciousness of the world today, and it's choking the spiritual life out of society."

With a shocked look, Grace said, *"Why would you say that?"*

"I don't know if I can answer that. It's so obvious to me now that I honestly don't think I can put it to words—"

"Please try," she said, with a frightened look in her eyes.

"How can I possibly make you see what your faith won't allow you to see? I had to leave the Church, Grace. I couldn't breathe.

I honestly couldn't breathe. I had to get out and find some air. How can I explain what that means? Why did you leave the convent? Maybe you felt the same thing I did—"

Grace was forced to smile, but she did not say anything for the longest time. She thought very carefully before speaking—

"I wasn't fulfilled, Oriano. That's why I left. I got the call to motherhood."

I understood exactly what she was talking about. I knew that she was a woman who listened to her inner voice, and her inner voice had told her to move on; but why was she being so stubborn about moving on now?

"Grace, may I ask you a personal question? It goes to the very heart of your faith."

"What?" she asked, with a twinge of fear in her voice.

Suddenly coming to my senses, I sat back in the beautifully crafted dining room oak chair and smiled apologetically. I couldn't ask her that question outright; I had to go about it in a roundabout way—

"Let me phrase my question in terms of an analogy," I said, with an ironic smile. I had been waiting years to try this analogy out on a genuine Christian, and I couldn't have found a more suitable candidate than an ex nun who was married to an ex monk whom she loved dearly and who both continued to serve their Lord and Savior Jesus Christ by being faithful to their Holy Mother Church. "Suppose a man is married to a woman for twenty years. They have children and he loves his wife and family dearly. And in twenty years of marriage he has never strayed or questioned his love for his wife. Now further suppose that in the twenty years that this man has been married to this woman she has been having an affair with his best friend. It isn't out of the question, Grace; because I've known marriages very much like this. Now further suppose that this man finds out one day. Someone informs him, but he refuses to believe it. That can't be, he says. He knows his wife; she wouldn't do that to him. I know a man here in town that went into denial when he was told that his wife had a fatal attraction to their new United Church minister. So this man in my analogy goes into denial too. He simply refuses to believe that his wife would be having an affair with his best

121

friend; and for twenty years, yet. But further suppose that this man gets incontrovertible proof that his wife is having an affair with his best friend. He catches them at their rendezvous motel in the city and they confess to their affair. He gets angry, of course. This would be a normal reaction. But when all the dust settles he has several choices. He can leave his wife or he can stay. It all depends upon his wife, of course. Suppose that she wants him to stay. Suppose she says to him that even though she has never really loved him, she finds him a good man and a good father and a good provider. Why should she leave him at this time of life? So she gives him the option. He can stay or leave. But she refuses to give up her affair with the man she loves. Of course, he's married too. They usually are in these situations. I know it sounds like I'm taxing my analogy, Grace; but human nature being what it is, I don't think so. I think there are real life examples everywhere. So the point I want to make is this: does the man stay or leave? What do you think he should do?"

"You say he loves his wife?"

"Yes."

"Even after he finds out that she doesn't love him?"

"You can't turn love off and on, Grace. Yes, even after he finds out that she doesn't really love him. He's totally disgusted with her and his best friend, but he can't help himself; he still loves her. He may not speak to his friend again, but that's expected."

"But why would he stay if she doesn't love him?" Grace asked.

"Maybe he believes in the sanctity of marriage. Maybe he's a good Roman Catholic who believes that marriage is for life. Maybe he loves his wife's cooking, or the way she makes love to him, or the way she irons his shirts and looks after all his needs; I don't know, Grace. It could be any number of reasons. Many people stay married for different reasons. I've painted houses where the husband and wife sleep in separate rooms, and not because one's an insomniac, but because they just don't love each other anymore. I even know of a marriage here in St. Jude where the man has his own apartment in the basement while his wife lives upstairs. She was having an affair with the former mill manager in town. The whole town knew about the affair, but her husband wouldn't leave the house. He couldn't afford to go anywhere; so he stayed home and played the cuckold. I don't know why a person would want to stay in a marriage that has lost its love, but it happens all the time; so what do you think our man should do, Grace?"

"I believe in the sanctity of marriage too, Oriano; so I would think he should stay. Is there a chance that his wife might change her mind and stop her affair?"

"Not in my analogy. Just like the lady who had the affair with the former mill manager; she refused to stop her affair despite the fact that the whole town found it morally repugnant considering that she was the principal of the public school at the time—"

"No? The principal of the public school?"

"Yes," I said, laughing.

"And the whole town knew about it?"

"Yes. They flaunted it, Grace. They went out in public and on holidays and everything. He left his wife, of course; but her husband wouldn't leave his house. It was a real scandal, but they didn't care. They loved each other."

"Oh goodness. That poor man—"

"The cuckolded husband, you mean?"

"Yes. What an indignity."

I smiled. Should I, or shouldn't I? I asked myself. I had the perfect opportunity to make my point about blind Christian faith, but could I open Grace up to a much more ignominious indignity?

"I wouldn't even have to think about it, Grace," I said. "I'd pack up and leave if it were me. I could never suffer such humiliation. As a matter of fact," I said, chuckling at the memory that had just surfaced, "I wrote a short story about a friend who was cuckolded by his best friend. I couldn't stand to see him being made a fool of in town, so I took my friend out for a drink one night and told him about his wife's affair with his best friend. It ruined our friendship, Grace; but I had to tell him. He packed up and left his wife and now he's happily remarried and living in southern Ontario. So, what do you think the man in my analogy should do? Should he stay or leave his wife?"

"I honestly don't know, Oriano. I think he would have to kneel down and pray to God for guidance—"

"And if it were you, Grace; what would you do?"

"I don't know. I honestly don't know—"

"With consciousness comes responsibility," I repeated, and smiled; but Grace did not make the connection, and we left that conversation unresolved also. And it was one that I wanted to resolve badly; because of all the talks that we had it was the one that had opened the door for Grace the widest...

I could not stay. I could not suffer the indignity of being a Christian cuckold. I loved and respected Jesus as a God-realized Way-shower, but Christianity's affair with Power so affronted my sense of moral consciousness that I had to leave the Church; I had no choice. I simply could not play the fool having found out what I did about Christianity. And it all started when I was twelve years old.

I shared this formative experience with Grace two days after I returned from the house that had psychically exhausted me. "I was walking home," I began, as my memory brought me back to my experience. "It was Saturday morning, and I had just come from my weekly confession. Don't ask me why or how, but I was in a very acute state of moral awareness that day; and as I walked home the feeling came to me that something wasn't quite right with the concept of mortal sin and eternal punishment in hell-fire. I remember holding up my two hands like this, like two scales of justice, and thinking: in this hand I have one mortal sin committed in a moment of time; and in my other hand I have eternal damnation. 'That's not fair,' I said to myself. And it occurred to me that a mortal sin committed in a moment of time could not possibly be equal to eternal damnation in hell; it could not. Something was not right, Grace; and I sensed it that day."

"But you could redeem yourself, Oriano. All it would take would be a perfect act of contrition—"

"I realize that; but the equation itself was out of balance for me. It just did not make sense that God would condemn me for eternity in hell-fire for one mortal sin like eating meat on Friday. I could not believe that God could be so unfair—"

"But God isn't unfair, Oriano. God loves us. That's why he sent his only Begotten Son to die for us—"

"You miss my point," I interrupted, annoyed by the empty old arguments that I used to have the patience to suffer before but chose not to that day. "It's that Christian damnation-virus and serum-salvation thing that I became aware of as I walked home from confession that day. I was twelve years old, Grace; and the idea of God punishing me for eternity in hell-fire for one measly mortal sin committed in a finite moment of time was beyond my capacity to fathom. 'It's not fair,' I said to myself. *'It's just not fair!'"*

Grace did not respond. She could tell by my voice that I wasn't going to be won over by empty persuasion, so she smiled and said, "What did you do, Oriano?"

"Nothing. But the idea was firmly planted in my mind."

"What idea?"

"That maybe it wasn't God that was unfair."

"What do you mean? God is eminently fair, Oriano."

I chuckled. "Come on, Grace; it doesn't take a rocket scientist to figure this out."

"I never studied rocket science, Oriano. I studied the scriptures. I studied the life of Jesus Christ. I studied the teachings of the Holy Mother Church—"

"And you find the two compatible?" I asked.

"What?"

"Scripture and Church dogma."

"Yes, of course."

"What do you mean, of course? That's been a source of contention since I don't-know-when. That's what the Jesus Society and scholars like Elaine Pagels have been trying to resolve. What do you mean, of course?"

"There's no contention, Oriano. It's all a matter of divine faith—"

"Or blind acceptance," I said, and picked up my paint can and stepped onto my step ladder and started cutting in along the ceiling of the master bedroom.

I worked for several minutes before Grace said anything; she just stood in the doorway waiting. The silence was heavy; but I was determined not to break it.

"You like to think for yourself, don't you Oriano?" she finally said, in a nervous voice. "You say you were twelve years old—"

"Grace, let me tell you something that happened to me when I made my decision to pay for the truth I sought by exiling myself out of the kingdom of my own senses," I said, in a tone of voice I had never used before with her. "I didn't come to my decision lightly. It began to dawn on me at university that all the great philosophers that I was studying didn't know any more than I did about God and truth and life's meaning; they were all just as lost as I was. It dawned on me that day that my own thoughts were just as valid as their thoughts were; but I couldn't trust my own thoughts, Grace. And that was the tragic irony!"

"I think I understand you, Oriano," she replied, very softly.

"No, I don't think you do. Let me explain myself. I came to my decision to exile myself out of the kingdom of my own senses because it finally dawned on me that I could not reason my way to God; I had to earn my way to God. How I knew this, I'll never know; but it just came to me that we get nothing for nothing in this world, so I had to pay a price for the answers I was looking for. And that's when the play *Oedipus Rex* popped into my mind. That's when I saw what I had to do to find my way home to God. I had to exile myself out of the kingdom of my own senses. I paid for the little bit of truth that I have. I paid for it by denying myself mountains of personal pleasure. I died a millions deaths, Grace. I paid for my truth with my life's blood—"

"Believe you me, Oriano; that I understand!" Grace responded, with all the conviction in her voice of one who had been initiated into the sacred mystery.

"I know you do, Grace; and that's what puzzles me."

"Puzzles you? Why?"

"It puzzles me that you—" I stopped in mid sentence. "Oh, I understand," I sighed. "I understand why you embrace your faith without question—"

"What do you mean?" she asked, genuinely perplexed.

"Your vow of obedience, Grace. I never took a vow of obedience. I know what chastity is, and I know that the vow of poverty is just another path to detachment, which I understand only

126

too well; but obedience? No; I left university in my third year because I came to the conclusion on the breakwater that fateful day that the only thing I could build my life upon with any certainty would be the truth of my own experiences; and that's what I did. I built my life upon the truth that I extracted from life with my own experiences; and that's why I think for myself, Grace I trust myself more than Christianity—"

Grace did not reply. She just smiled. Then, summoning her courage, she said, "Maybe it's pride, Oriano—"

"Pride be damned!" I exploded. "Don't throw that in my face! I've paid too dear a price for my spiritual freedom to have it mocked by some tired old cliché! I'm not like Milton's Fallen Angel who boasted 'Better to reign in hell than to serve in heaven!' I've been bought with a price, Grace; and my pride was the biggest part of that price. I burnt three holes in the retina of my eyes because of my stupid blind faith in an offshoot Christian solar cult teaching, so don't mock me with clichés. All I'm telling you is this: I could not build my life upon blind faith. I had to *know*. I simply had to *know*. Is that so difficult to understand? I could not trust my life to blind faith; *I simply had to know!*"

Grace took a deep breath. Then, very quietly, almost in a whisper, said, "I want to understand you, Oriano. I honestly do. Why don't I let you work?"

She turned and left quietly. I continued painting, still fuming. About thirty minutes later I finished cutting in the corners and I was ready to roll the walls, so I went to the basement to get my tray and extension pole; but as I walked by Brandon's office on the way to the basement I saw Grace kneeling with her elbows on the arm of the recliner chair with her head in her hands. She was praying.

When I walked by with my tray and extension pole she was still kneeling with her head in her hands. I went upstairs and started rolling the walls. About an hour later I heard Grace's voice from the bottom of the stairs, "Oriano, tea's on!"

"I'll be right down!" I yelled back.

Before sitting down for tea I went up to Grace, who was standing at the counter, and very softly said, "Grace, I owe you an apology—"

"No," she interrupted me, "I owe you an apology.

"Me first," I insisted. "I don't know what came over me, but I had no business talking to you the way I did—"

"I understand, Oriano—"

"Please, let me finish. Our conversation awakened old memories, and I wasn't myself. What you saw was—how can I put this? I'd like to say that it was my happy warrior self that you saw, but it wasn't. No; what you witnessed upstairs was my seeker self that shouted more than once—nay, ten thousand times—'*Awake! Arise! And let us to battle!*' Mine was not an easy path to God, and I still bear all the scars. I'm terribly sorry that you had to see that part of me, Grace. It's completely and utterly merciless."

Grace smiled. Then she put her arms around me and gave me a hug and whispered into my ear, "I prayed for both of us, Oriano. I hope you don't mind."

I smiled. "Thank you," I said; "but you needn't have bothered. This ship has set sail, Grace, and no one's going to turn it around. Not even God."

"*Not even God?*" she said, astonished by my comment.

I laughed. "Don't take me literally, Grace. That's just my way of saying that my spiritual course in life has been set and there's nothing that anyone can do about it."

"*Not even God, Oriano?*" she repeated, still astonished.

I laughed again. Grace couldn't fathom my humor, and her eyes betrayed her. "Don't be shocked, Grace," I said. "It was God that set my course."

"*Oriano,*" she said, with a sigh of relief, "*I just don't know what I'm going to do with you. You're something else—*"

"Don't do anything. That's the whole point, Grace. It's my life, and I'd like to be master of my own fate. Are you familiar with the poem *Invictus*, by Henley?"

Grace smiled her Mona Lisa smile, and then slowly her smile left her face and a serious, thoughtful look possessed her, and in a steely voice that spoke her own indomitable spirit, she quoted Henley's *Invictus*—

"It matters not how straight the gate

128

How charged with punishment the scroll,
I am the master of my fate;
   I am the captain of my soul.'"

"That's the one," I said, delightfully surprised. "Give me a moment, please," I added, and then delved into my own memory bank... 'Beyond the place of wrath and tears /Looms but the horror of the shade, /And yet the menace of the years /Finds, and shall find me unafraid.' Now can you understand where I'm coming from, Grace?"

Grace smiled, and then she laughed. It was a gentle, soul-felt, approving laugh. "I think I do, Oriano; but I honestly struggle with it."

"Why?"

"I don't know. I can see that you're a man of God, but you puzzle me."

"Would you like to know why I puzzle you?"

"Yes, please. But first, let's pour our tea before it gets too strong."

Grace poured our tea and then I said, "I puzzle you because you can't see my God. God is God, Grace; but God has many faces, and the God that you see is not the face that I have seen. That's the great divide between us—"

"I don't understand. I only know of one God, and that's our savior Jesus Christ."

"Exactly my point, Grace."

"You don't believe that Jesus Christ is God?"

"The short answer is no, I don't; but I do believe that Jesus realized God consciousness."

"God consciousness? What do you mean by that?"

"When Jesus said *'My Father and I are one,'* that has been interpreted to mean that he was God and God was him; but it could also mean that Jesus had realized the conscious of God in himself. Soul, our spiritual self, is a part of God; and Jesus Christ's whole teaching has to do with waking us up to our own divine nature. Jesus had awakened to his divine nature. That's why he said that whatever he could do so could we all. *'For whosoever shall do the will of my Father which is in heaven,'* said Jesus, *'the same is my brother, and*

129

sister, and mother.' And all I'm trying to point out to you Grace is that we do the will of our Father by being true to our own divine nature; and it is the uniqueness of each divine self that makes God such a wonder to behold."

"I don't understand you, Oriano; but I have no doubt that you believe what you are saying," Grace replied, with a mixed look of love and wonder in her eyes.

"No less than you believe in your faith, Grace," I said, smiling at her confusion. "And therein lies the crux of our great divide..."

I left the Church, but I stayed with Jesus Christ. Grace left the convent, but she stayed with the Church; and it was this divide between Jesus Christ and the religion of Christianity born of his life and teaching that destiny had brought us together to bridge.

For the life of me, I could not figure out what it was about our attraction that so thoroughly possessed us that we both floated on air for hours after my work day was done; but that night, as I recorded our conversation when I told Grace that I was the captain of my soul, it finally dawned on me what the symbolic nature of our relationship implied, and it disturbed me profoundly."Why me?" I wrote in my journal in brackets after I had recorded everything I could remember. "And why now?"

But I needn't have done that, because I knew why. Deep inside I knew that one day it was going to happen; and when all was said and done, I could not have been more blessed. And upon reflection I added, in new brackets, *"If not us, who?"*

Like the man in my analogy, I left my marriage to the Church because I could not stand to be made a fool of by the unconscious falseness of Christianity; but Grace stayed in her marriage to the Church and turned a blind eye to the lies of Christianity because of her love for Jesus. That was our great divide.

I could not fault Grace, though. She loved Jesus, the man who introduced the world to the Way with such messianic conviction that it has become a pathway home to God for a countless number of people. But the tragic irony of Christianity is that along the way it perverted Christ's teaching of spiritual liberation into a doctrine of spiritual enslavement, and that was the divide that Spirit had brought us together to bridge.

Christianity loves Power, and it has been having an illicit affair with Power for centuries—ever since it made Jesus Christ the sole savior of the world. Ironically some Christians like Grace Kendal manage to liberate their spiritual self from their ego with Christ's teaching, but they continued to stay in the Church out of love for Jesus and thereby implicitly condoned the lie of Christianity that Jesus is the savior of the world.

And this was the providential nature of our dialectical relationship—to bridge the divide by preserving the integrity of Christ's teaching while exposing the lie that Jesus died on the cross to wash away the stain of Original Sin that has alienated Soul from God; the seductively lie that only through Jesus Christ can the world be saved.

Soul does not need to be saved. Soul needs to be awakened from its primordial slumber. The only alienation that Soul has from God is its own lack of consciousness; and this is why Soul must go through the life-process—to awaken to its God nature through many, often painful life-experiences.

Jesus knew this, and his whole teaching was designed to wake Soul up from the sleep of life. But to awaken Soul with Christ's teaching takes more than what most people are willing to pay, because it demands a commitment of enormous self-sacrifice; hence the tragic irony of Christianity.

This self-sacrifice that is central to Christ's teaching of spiritual liberation has been completely perverted by the idea that sins can be forgiven. One doesn't have to sacrifice his sinful self as Christ's teaching taught; one just asks God for forgiveness, and the priests of the Holy Mother Church have been empowered to forgive sins.

"Oh, Grace," I said to her one day when the theme of our talks on sin had evolved to the point where I was almost forced out of the Christian paradigm to make my point; "it's in the Gospels. Jesus himself said, *'and if thy right eye offend thee, pluck it out and cast it from thee...And if the right hand offend thee, cut it off, and cast it from thee.'* He was telling us that we have to transform our inner self

131

in order to be saved; we can't just kneel and ask God to forgive our sins—"

"After the fact, Oriano," she quickly responded. "When we sin we can ask Jesus for forgiveness. Of course we have to change our sinful ways. That's what Jesus wants us to do. We have to live a pure life to be saved. We have to learn what sin is and how not to commit sin. This is what it means to be a Christian. We cannot repeat our sinful ways, Oriano. But our Lord Jesus will forgive us our sins should we be tempted back into our sinful ways. This is what makes Christianity such a beautiful religion—"

I burst into a fit of laughter that took Grace by surprise. I had to explain myself or risk damaging the delicate balance of our relationship—

"Why do you think I left the Church, Grace? Do you think I'm too lazy to live the Christian life? I know what it means to live the life that Jesus wants us to live. I took his sayings out into the marketplace, and believe me I know what it means to pluck out my lustful eye and cut off my offending hand and pull the mote out of my own eye and walk the extra mile and not tell my left hand what my right hand is doing and not vaunt my charity—I know, Grace; but life has taught me that the sins we commit don't simply disappear into thin air with Holy Confession or an act of perfect contrition. The stain of our sins stays with us, Grace. And not only does this stain stay with us; it is passed onto our children and children's children. That's why I had to leave Christianity—because my whole personality became blemished by the archetypal stain of my ancestral sins, and I had to find a way to rid myself of this dark and disturbing presence, this shadow specter that can take over our life if we aren't careful. Believe me when I tell you this; I didn't leave the Church because I didn't believe in Jesus Christ. The irony is that I did and still do believe in Jesus. I just don't believe what Christianity has done with his teaching—"

"Are you saying that you don't believe in the forgiveness of sin? Is that what you're saying Oriano?" Grace asked, trying very hard to understand me.

132

"That's exactly what I'm saying. Once a sin has been committed it has to be resolved by an equal but opposite act of goodness. This redresses the balance in the universe."

"I don't understand," she said, genuinely perplexed.

I smiled, and then chuckled to myself. "I guess it's hard to see, Grace. Maybe if I explain it in terms of energy. Suppose that I do you a negative deed. I commit the sin of theft by gouging you in my work. I have stolen something from you that I haven't earned. Would you consider gouging a sin?"

"Yes, I would; and I have been sinned against by gouging many times, Oriano," Grace said, and laughed.

I laughed with her. "Good. You see where I'm coming from, then. Now suppose that this sin of gouging could be transformed into the energy of personal freedom. That's not too difficult to imagine, is it? If I steal money from you that I haven't earned I have stolen a certain amount of your freedom, because money represents freedom; *n'est ce pas*?"

She smiled. "Yes," she said; "but only a certain kind of freedom, Oriano. Money doesn't buy the kind of freedom that Jesus has to give us—"

"Of course not. And that's my point, Grace. Christ's teaching gives us spiritual freedom if we are faithful to his teaching; right?"

She smiled again. "Yes," she said.

"Good. So the point I want to make is that sin deprives us of this spiritual freedom; or, to be perfectly accurate, sin makes it more difficult for us to realize this freedom that Christ's teaching offers us. In other words, when we sin we stand between ourselves and our own spiritual freedom. When we sin we blemish our soul with the impurity of sin-consciousness; and by living Christ's teaching—his sayings, to be precise—we not only purify our impure sin-consciousness, but we redress the people we have sinned against. So if I were a true Christian I would have to make restitution for gouging you. In short, I would have to return to you the freedom-energy or money that I stole from you. *Capisce*?"

"I'm not quite sure. I believe in the power of forgiveness, Oriano. I have forgiven the workmen who gouged us when we had work done on our home in St. John's—"

133

"I don't doubt that you forgave them, Grace; but does your act of forgiveness wipe away the sin-consciousness of their theft from you? Those men gouged you and they are accountable to a higher spiritual law than Grace Kendal's Christian law of forgiveness. You can ask God to forgive them, but they are still accountable for their theft because they are responsible for their own salvation—not you, Grace. Do you see my point now?"

"I'm trying to, Oriano. I'm honestly trying —"

"Okay, let me put this into a larger framework. Maybe if you see the big picture it will make sense to you. Do you remember our talk about how Christ's teaching purifies our consciousness so that we become as innocent children? Jesus said, *'Except ye be converted, and become as little children, ye shall not enter into the kingdom of heaven.'* Jesus is telling us in code that we have to transform the impurity of our sin-consciousness in order to enter heaven; and he tells us how to do this when he says, *'Whosoever heareth these sayings of mine, and doeth them, I will liken him unto a wise man, which built his house upon a rock.'* House is Christ's code word for soul, and rock is his code word for the eternal truth of the Word of God. So by living the Word of God that is encoded in Christ's sayings we transform the impurity of our sin-consciousness and liberate our spiritual self from the confines of our material human consciousness. That's what Jesus meant by being born again. We give birth to our spiritual self through the conscious effort of living the Word of God. Now do you see what I mean when I tell you that I don't believe in the forgiveness of sin? Sins cannot be forgiven for the asking. The impure consciousness of one's sins has to be transformed, or purified by one's own conscious efforts by living the Word of God. Do you understand me now, Grace?"

She looked at me with the most peculiar expression on her face, and the look of sudden horror in her eyes told me that I had gone too far; that I had taken her way beyond her spiritual ken—

"Only by the grace of God are we saved, Oriano," she said, and smiled. It was not her beatific smile. It looked like it, but it was empty; and it gave me the shivers.

I knew instantly what I was up against, but I had to be very careful how I responded. I had inadvertently summoned the Shadow

Christ in Grace—the archetypal falseness of Christian consciousness; and I had to see if I could bring Grace back—

"You're right," I agreed with her. "Ultimately God is our savior, Grace. God made us, and God saves us—"

She smiled, her eyes lighting up again. "Yes, God made us; and God saves us. I agree with you, Oriano. Our Lord Jesus died on the cross to save us…"

I smiled to myself, and then I got up from the table. "I'd love to continue this, Grace; but duty calls—"

This was the first time it happened, but I was expecting it. I knew that one day the inherently self-transcending spirit of our dialectic would take us beyond Grace's capacity for Platonic flight; that's why the archetypal Shadow Christ appeared.

I sensed its presence immediately. I had seen it before, many times; and it looks so much like the real thing that people mistake it for the real thing. That's why people like Grace can never break away from Christianity. They have no idea of the hold that the archetypal lie of Christianity has upon their psyche.

But I was thankful for our talk all the same, because now Grace had been brought to the outermost edges of her faith, and she had caught a glimpse of the freedom that awaited her on the other side of the great divide. That's why the Shadow Christ surfaced from her unconscious to take her back to the security of her blind Christian faith.

It happens all the time. It happened to me. But I was so pathological in my need for authenticity that I dared to go where angels feared to tread. That's why I was able to write in my journal when I finally made the connection between the Christian Devil and Jung's concept of the Archetypal Shadow—*"Satan, you are so crafty that I know not which is you and which is me!"*

Strangely enough however, I had brought up the subject of the shadow one day with Grace's daughter in the dining room. Kathleen was having breakfast (she never got up before ten o'clock in all the time that she was there), and Grace and I were having tea.

Kathleen had fried herself two eggs and bologna. I began the conversation by saying, "That smells familiar. What is it, Kathleen; fried bologna?"

"Yes," she replied. "It's a Newfie thing."

"No it's not. Cathy loves fried bologna too. She told me she grew up on it."

"Well it started in Newfoundland!" Kathleen said.

"All good things come from Newfoundland; right?" I said.

"Right!" Kathleen said, and put her plate down on the table and poured ketchup on her bologna and began eating her breakfast. I watched her. She swallowed a bite-full, and then said, "You ever been to Newfoundland?"

"No; but I'd love to go there someday."

"You'll love it. It's the best place in Canada. And you won't find friendlier people than us Newfies!"

"You're quite the ambassador, aren't you Kathleen? Tell me, what would you do if you had to leave Newfoundland?"

"I'm not going to," she replied.

"But what if you can't get a job there?"

"I will."

"Your mom tells me you're into social work. Do you like the work you do?"

"I'm taking courses too. In fact I have a paper I have to write while I'm here. So it's not a holiday, mom—"

"I know, dear. Have you started you paper yet?"

"I've got a draft going. I'll let you read it after I get it finished."

"What's your paper on?" I asked.

"About the criminal aspect of human nature."

"Wow. That's a big topic."

"Well, it's not the criminal aspect really. It's about aberrant behavior."

"That sounds exciting. You shouldn't have any problem getting research material," I said, with a mirthful chuckle.

"What do you mean?" Kathleen asked, puzzled.

Grace smiled. "Oh, Kathleen; he's just pulling your leg. He means that society is full of people that don't behave in a normal way. Isn't that so, Oriano?"

"Especially in a town of hopeless causes," I added, with another burst of laughter. "So, Kathleen; tell me about your paper. What's your premise?"

"What do you mean?"

"What's the central idea of your paper? It has to have a central idea, doesn't it?"

"I don't have one," she said, almost defiantly. "I don't think I need one. I'm just writing about what I think causes aberrant behavior."

"And what do you think causes aberrant behavior?"

"I think it's environment. I think the way children are brought up determines how they will behave. If a child is abused then they won't grow up to be normal adults. That's been proven. They become abusers themselves."

"The cycle can be broken, Kathleen," her mother said.

"Yes, I know it can mother. That's what I'm going to write about in my paper."

"And how does one break the cycle, Kathleen?" I asked.

"By not doing it, obviously. I don't know the details. I haven't researched my paper yet. That's why I have to go into the city tomorrow. I have to go to the university library to check out some books. I brought a list with me."

"What time are you planning to go?" her mother asked.

"Early. I have a lot of research to do. I want to do some shopping too. I need a new sweat suite, mom. I forgot to pack mine, and I need it to do my workouts. So, mom—"

"Yes dear," Grace said, and smiled.

"So, Kathleen," I said; "tell me, what do you think is the psychological cause for aberrant behavior? It goes beyond the scope of child abuse, surely. Many people become aberrant in their behavior without having been abused as children."

"Do you think so?" she replied, wide-eyed.

"I know so. I've been aberrant in my behavior a few times in my life and I wasn't abused as a child. There are people in this town that believe I'm aberrant right now," I added, giving Grace a wink that Kathleen couldn't see.

"Really?" Kathleen said. "Like what? I can't tell. What?"

"It's all a matter of perspective, Kathleen. But that's neither here nor there. The point is that aberrant behavior is open to other determining factors."

"Such as?"

"Such as the dark side of the personality."

"What does that mean?"

"Have you read C.G. Jung in your courses?"

"No. Who's he?"

"One of the founders of modern psychiatry. He was a contemporary of Sigmund Freud. In fact, he was a student of Freud; but he left Freud to start his own school of therapy. Jungian therapy today is very popular. If I were to become a therapist, I'd be a Jungian because of its focus on dreams."

"I can see you doing that, Oriano," Grace said, with a warm smile.

"I love Jung, Grace. He goes a long way to explaining the dual nature of man."

"Dual nature?" Kathleen said. "What do you mean?"

"The two sides of the personality. The conscious and the unconscious side. Jung calls the conscious side of our personality the ego, and the unconscious side the shadow. The shadow is the repressed, hidden side of our personality; and it's this dark side of our personality that's responsible for aberrant behavior. Are you sure you've never hear of Carl Gustav Jung?"

"No, I haven't," she replied.

"Jung is spelled with a J, Kathleen. J-U-N-G," her mother said, spelling it out.

"Oh! I know him! Yeah, I read some of his stuff!"

"It would be too much to look into for your paper, dear," Grace said, in her caring mother's voice. "But it might be worth your while to read Jung for your own understanding of human behavior. Don't you think so, Oriano?"

"It certainly wouldn't hurt," I said, very much enjoying our morning tea.

"Yeah, maybe I will," Kathleen said. "So what's this shadow thing all about, then?"

"Like I said, the shadow is the dark side of our personality. It's that part of our personality that we don't want to deal with, like some things we do that we don't want to remember or want the world to know about; like lying, cheating, stealing, or doing something humiliating. We don't want to think about these things, so we repress them and they become the dark side of our personality. We try to suppress all this stuff, but sometimes we can't keep it suppressed; and our shadow comes out and takes over our personality. And that can be cause for some pretty aberrant behavior, Kathleen."

"Wow! I didn't know that. So how do you know if it comes out or not?"

"That's the whole problem. When it—and by it I'm talking about the shadow side of our personality; when it comes out one can't see it himself, like Dr. Jekyll couldn't see his Mr. Hyde when he came out because Mr. Hyde took over Dr. Jekyll's personality. In other words Kathleen, we can't see our own shadow because we're too close to see it; but other people can see it. The problem with the shadow is that it thinks its normal, but it's not and we don't know it. A normal person has a rational view on life, but the shadow is irrational because it's made up of all our contradictions and dark desires and sexual fantasies and personal humiliations and broken promises and unfulfilled dreams—"

"Wow! That's heavy stuff going on down there!"

I broke into laughter. "Well, put Kathleen!"

"Maybe I should read up on this for my paper?"

"You won't have time, dear," her mother said, with a concerned look. "Oriano's synopsis of Jung's psychology must have taken him years to arrive at. You don't have time for that. Just concentrate on what you know; that's all you have to do."

"Okay; so if this shadow thing got all this stuff going on down there how come we don't know about it?" Kathleen asked, genuinely perplexed.

"Writers have known about it for centuries," I said, with an ironic chuckle. "Where do you think psychology gets its best ideas from? Nonetheless, Jung tells us that we can't see our shadow without moral self-discipline, and I agree. But that's only our own shadow. We can often see the shadow side of another person's personality. That's the peculiar nature of the shadow; it can't see itself. But that's too confusing for you, Kathleen. Let's just say that we can see the dark side of a person's personality by their behavior."

"Like aberrant behavior, you mean?"

"That's one way. Keep in mind that our shadow is not our real self. It's our false self. So every time we see someone behaving falsely without them realizing that they are behaving falsely we know that their shadow has taken over their personality. It's fascinating, and one could make a career out of studying the shadow. As a matter of fact, Jungian therapists have done just that. They call this kind of therapy 'shadow work,' and 'romancing the shadow'—"

"Wow! So you're saying that this shadow is responsible for things that people do that aren't normal?" Kathleen said, her eyes alight with newfound wisdom.

"Yes and no. The shadow has found a way to walk among men without anyone spotting it. It takes a man like Jesus to see the shadow side of life. Do you remember what Jesus said to one of his disciples? *'Get thee behind me, Satan,'* said Jesus. I think it was the Apostle Peter. Well, he was addressing Peter's shadow—"

"No shit?" Kathleen said, all excited; but the look on her mother's face told me I had gone much too far, so I quickly backed off—

"But that's too deep for your paper, Kathleen. Suffice to say that Jesus saw the shadow as the evil part of man's nature and he wanted to rid us of this evil with his teaching of love and kindness and compassion and good works; right, Grace?"

"Absolutely. You have to stick with what you know, dear—"

"I know, mother. You keep telling me that. But I don't know what I want to write about yet—"

"You mean you haven't even started?" her mother said, with a sudden change of tone in her voice. "What have you been doing all this time?"

"I'd better leave," I said, and got up.

"Yes, you better; because I think mom and I are going to get into it again."

"She's just looking after your best interests, Kathleen."

"I know. But you don't know my mom. She can be pretty stubborn sometimes."

Grace smiled. She wanted to respond, but didn't. She was much too proper to have me witness a family scene, so she just said, "I love you, dear."

"I know you do! That's the whole problem, mother. You love me too much. *You smother me with love!"*

"Excuse me," I said, and walked away smiling; but then I turned around and said, "Kathleen, let me read your paper if you get it done before you leave; would you?"

"After mom types it up for me!" she yelled back.

Chuckling, I went back to painting the cupboards in the family room kitchenette; but as I worked I couldn't stop smiling. "What a handful," I said to myself.

6. WORK IS ITS OWN REWARD

I asked Jesus in a dream one night whether he thought the world would have been a better place had he not brought out his teaching of spiritual rebirth, but Jesus turned the question back on me, "Do you think it would have?"

I replied, "From what I know about Christianity, I would have to say yes." Then Jesus surprised me and said, "There are days when I would have to agree with you."

I laughed. Even Jesus had to admit to the great divide that existed between his teaching and the religion that grew out of it; but we never discussed it any further. Jesus had another appointment to go to. He had been summoned by the Lords of Karma.

"Come again, O," he said, before leaving. "We have much to talk about."

But I got too involved in my own life to look him up again. Besides, I was on a different path, so I had no reason to look him up again (Jesus is stationed on the Mental Plane of Consciousness, or what St. Paul would have called the Fourth Heaven); but then I met the former Sister of Mercy and became so passionately involved in a dialectical relationship with her that I wanted to look Jesus up again to ask him what he thought of my idea of creatively bridging the great divide in my new novel—

"All you can do is try," he said. We were in his office. I had made an appointment with his private secretary just before going to sleep one night (this was an imaginative technique that I employed whenever I wanted to speak with an Ascended Master, which only worked now and then), and I didn't know if Jesus would see me; but I found myself sitting in his office in my dream, so I asked what he thought of my idea. "Just keep in mind that the Way is always an individual path," he added, which was his way of telling me that his teaching was not the only path back home to God.

"How could I possibly forget that?" I said, with a chuckle.

"It's much easier than you realize, O," he replied, addressing me by my nickname which I had picked up when I operated my pool hall business in St. Jude before going to France to begin my quest for my true self. "After all, look at what happened to me!"

I burst into laughter. "Yes, you did take yourself a bit too seriously; didn't you?"

"A bit?" replied Jesus, feigning shock. "Good God, had I taken myself any more seriously I would have returned as they promised I would!"

"Trailing clouds of glory, no doubt," I said, and laughed. "So, do you think I should go ahead with it? It's awfully presumptuous."

"But if not you, who?" said Jesus.

"Maybe Neale Donald Walsh," I said, with another chuckle.

"No. Neale has his own mission. He was chosen to broaden the scope of man's spiritual horizons with his conversations with God; or, to be precise, with Soul, his higher self. Your mission, should you choose to accept it, is to bridge the great divide—"

I laughed at his reference to the TV show *Mission Impossible*, and catching the spirit of his humor, I replied, *"For Christ's sake, why me?"*

"Not for my sake," Jesus replied, with the biggest smile on his face; "for all those poor souls trapped by their faith."

"I know; I know..."

I woke up from my dream and got out of bed and recorded it immediately before I forgot the details; but I wasn't very comfortable with what Jesus had told me.

I really had no desire to be a bridge builder. When I left the Church I did so on such bad terms that it took years to get over my anger at Christianity; but then I met the former Sister of Mercy from St. John's Newfoundland and something changed.

I couldn't explain it, but I knew that something was happening to me. It felt like I had been preparing my whole life to meet her. But it wasn't just Grace Kendal that I met when I painted her house; that's what made the whole experience so fascinating.

Grace lived her life according to Christ's teaching and what her Roman Catholic Church wanted her to believe, but what set her apart was the fact that she had awakened to her own spirituality and was denied further spiritual growth by the limitations of her inflexible faith; and for some reason we were destined to meet.

"Do you believe in fate, Grace?" I came right out and asked her one day when I could no longer support the feeling that we had met for reasons other than the obvious.

"I believe in Divine Providence," she replied.

"And by that you mean that God destines our life?" I said, opening the door.

"I'm not so sure about that," she said, very thoughtfully. "We do have free will. Like Adam and Eve, we don't have to eat the forbidden fruit."

"So we have a choice for good or evil, is that what you're saying?"

As though testing the ground before stepping, she said, "I would think so."

"And where does Divine Providence come into it, then?"

"When God wants us to find Him," she replied, full of recovered confidence. "God loves us, Oriano. And He will do everything He can to save us from ourselves."

"So God sets up conditions for us to find Him, and these conditions are what you call Divine Providence?" I said, setting the premise for the dialectic.

"Yes," she said.

"I don't disagree with that. I know that God—or, to be precise, Holy Spirit, the Voice of God and Light of the Way—speaks to us through the language of life—signs, symbols, coincidences and what have you; but that's not what I'm talking about here. I'm talking about destiny. I'm talking about two people meeting for reasons that neither one can comprehend—"

Grace knew that I was referring to us; but she was much too modest or afraid to take the thought where I wanted her to take it.

"Some people are destined to meet, Oriano. Brandon and I were destined to meet and fall in love," she replied, and smiled demurely.

I smiled back to acknowledge her implied answer and dropped the subject because there was no point going someplace that she wasn't ready to go to yet; but the more we talked, the more this magical place manifested in our conversations.

We were two self-realized souls that had gained entrance into the Shambhala of our mind every time we took flight on the wings of Platonic inquiry, and try as she may to keep it at bay, Grace could not; and she even went so far as to admit it one day—

"Oriano, I don't know what it is about you and these talks that we're having every day; but they make me so light-headed that I'm beginning to imagine things—"

"What things?" I eagerly jumped in.

"I don't know if I should tell you. I remember what happened to Sister Ann in the convent—"

Grace stopped in mid thought. She just stared at me, and tears began to form in the corner of her eyes. I waited for her to continue, but the tears trickled down her cheeks and she continued to stare at me. But it wasn't me she was staring at.

"Grace, are you alright?" I asked.

"Yes. Fine. I was just thinking about Sister Ann. Such a beautiful soul—"

"What happened to her?"

"She had a breakdown, and she never recovered."

"I'm sorry to hear that," I said, feeling Grace's sorrow.

"One day Sister Ann called Mother Katherine and asked her to call an assembly because she had something she wanted to tell everyone," Grace continued, her eyes now wet with fresh tears. "We stood in the great hall and we all wondered what could be so important. Then Sister Ann told us that Jesus had come to her and told her that he had chosen her to be his special messenger to the world—"

She stopped again in mid thought. I waited for her to continue, but she didn't; so I broke the pregnant silence. "Where is she now?" I asked.

"In a home."

"Oh, I see," I said, making the connection. "And you're afraid that what happened to Sister Ann may be happening to you?"

"Yes."

"Why? What are you seeing that frightens you, Grace?"

"I'm not frightened, Oriano. I just think I might be having a slight breakdown. I haven't stopped since we decided to move to St. Jude. While Brandon was settling into his new position, I haven't stopped—"

"You think you're getting a little frayed at the edges, is that it Grace?"

"Yes," she said, with a worried look on her face.

"Well, you can take a nice little break when I go to my job in Nesbit—"

"But I have the carpet layers coming next week," she quickly responded, as if jolted by a fresh shot of adrenalin. "I can't stop, Oriano. I have to get my house in order before Christmas. I have my choir and midnight Mass to prepare for; and Brandon wants to have the Christmas staff party here. That's why we've decided to put the living room rug downstairs. Do you think it will work there?"

She made me smile. "I see no reason why not," I assured her. "We're painting the walls Dove White. That's a pretty neutral color. It won't clash with the rug, and it will certainly brighten up that dingy room. As a matter of fact, since we're going to do the kitchenette doors in Dusty Rose this rug should look good there. I think it'll work out very nicely, Grace. You have nothing to worry about."

"Oh good," she said, as though a big load had just been lifted off her shoulders.

"So, Grace; what were you imagining?" I asked, before we got sidetracked.

"Promise me that you will never mention this to anyone," Grace said; and then she caught herself and smiled. "I know you're a writer, so you can't make such a promise; but please don't use my name should you write about it someday."

"Of course not, Grace. Fiction may be drawn from real life, but it's still fiction."

"I know. But this is very personal. I don't know what it is I keep seeing, but ever since I met you I've been getting visions of a magical city. It just appears before my eyes. It's not in front of me now. It is and it isn't. It must be in my mind. And I hear music. I've never heard such beautiful music in my entire life—"

"Oh Grace, you lucky woman!" I burst out, to her astonishment.

"Lucky woman?" she repeated, her eyes begging for an explanation.

"Yes. You're probably having visions of a spiritual city on the inner planes. Maybe Shambhala. And the music you're hearing, that's the Sound Current!"

"Sound Current?" she said, with a mystified look; and instantly I regretted revealing what I did because it was too far outside her Christian paradigm, so I had to do some quick talking to bring her back—

"Holy Spirit sometimes speaks to us with music," I said, and laughed to lighten the gravity of her experience. "It's no mystery, Grace. Mozart heard the Sound Current all the time. How do you think he could produce such heavenly music at such an early age?"

"I've always believed that, Oriano. I think music is the Voice of God speaking to us."

"And it is," I said, delighted that I had brought her back. "And your visions of this magical city, there's a book that just came out called *The Secret of Shambhala,* by James Redfield. You might have heard of him. He wrote the bestselling novel *The Celestine Prophecy*—"

"My daughter read that book. Kathleen's looking into all this New Age stuff."

"Oh oh," I said to myself. *"I shouldn't have gone there. What the hell am I going to do now?"* I took a breath, and said, "Well anyway, his new book is about a mystical city called Shambhala. It's believed to be a city of enlightened beings. A place of peace, happiness, and tranquility. Have you ever seen the movie *Lost Horizon*? It's supposed to be inspired by the mystical city of Shangrila—"

"What a coincidence!" Grace interjected, unable to contain herself. "Brandon and I just saw it on TV a couple of nights ago! It's a fascinating story, Oriano. We enjoyed it very much. But it's all allegory, isn't it?"

"Allegories are sometimes more real than the real thing, Grace," I said, and laughed because something more real than real was happing to us.

"Do you mean that there is such a city as Shangrila?"

"Some people think so."

"Do you?"

"Yes."

"Have you seen this city?"

"I've dreamt about it several times."

"Dreams aren't real, Oriano," she replied, feigning a serious look.

"On the contrary, Grace. Dreams are the gateway to the inner worlds. My mother dreams of her dead relatives all the time. At least once a week my mother dreams of somebody she used to know in Italy who passed over to the other side. No, Grace; you've got it wrong to believe that this is the real world. Reality is relative to consciousness, and the inner worlds do exist on another level of consciousness; so if you think that dreams are just dreams you're missing out on a whole new world of possibilities—"

"I've had some very interesting dreams, Oriano," she quickly replied, consenting to my perspective much more readily than I expected. "I still can't explain some of the dreams that I've had. They were out of this world—"

"Just like your visions of this magical city; they're out of this world. Your visions are waking dreams, Grace; that's all they are. You're just seeing this city with your spiritual eye. There's absolutely nothing to worry about."

"Do you really think so? I haven't even told Brandon yet."

"Tell him when you're ready. That's a beautiful experience, Grace."

"I'm not so sure I can. I don't know what's happening to me, Oriano; but something's going on in my life. I prayed for an answer, but—"

"Grace, I don't know how to say this to you; but we've set something into motion that's bigger than the both of us. There's something symbolic going on here."

"What do you mean?" she asked, with a concerned look.

148

"I don't know what I mean. That's the whole problem. I think we were destined to meet for reasons that neither of us wants to fathom—"

Grace stared at me for what seemed like forever, and then her face slowly metamorphosed into a warm, loving smile that told me she knew exactly what I was referring to; but her smile also told me that it wasn't something we could talk about, so we dropped the subject and moved on to something else...

I was curious about Kathleen. From our first meeting I could tell that she had a love bond with her mother that she didn't want to break but which kept her from living her own life; and this was responsible for the tension between them.

Kathleen was looking into this "New Age stuff", as Grace called it, which meant that she was questioning her Christian faith; and that didn't bode well for her very Roman Catholic mother whose whole life centered around the Church.

Curious about Kathleen's interest in New Age literature, I waited for an opportunity to talk with her in private; and I got my chance the same day that she came home from the city and her mother was going out with Pauline Kaminsky.

Actually, Kathleen had spent the night in the city. She went to the university first to do her research, then she went shopping, and then she spent the evening in Coyote's where by happy coincidence a band from Newfoundland was playing.

"I felt right at home," she said. "Can you believe it? I come all the way to Ontario to hear a band from back home! *Far out!*"

"So you had a good time?"

"Yeah. I had a great time!"

"Did you make it to the university library?"

"Yeah. I went there first thing. I got some research done. I didn't finish it though. I have to go back."

"You just want an excuse to spend another night in the city," I said, and laughed.

"Yeah. What's wrong with that?"

"Nothing. It's your life, Kathleen."

"Exactly. That's what I've been trying to tell my mom for years. But she won't listen to me. She thinks because she pays my rent I should do what she wants."

"And your schooling, and your clothes, and your car—"

"I know. I'm just peeved. Mom gets on my back because I don't live up to her expectations. I'm different than my mom. I'm adopted, you know. I don't have my mom's genes. My biological mother is an alcoholic. That's why mom is after me all the time. She doesn't want me to end up like my birth mother. But I won't. Just because my birth mother's an alcoholic doesn't mean I'm going to become an alcoholic. It doesn't, you know. I like to drink for a good time, but that doesn't mean I'm an alcoholic waiting to happen. I've seen what alcoholism can do to people. Newfies like to drink, you know. It's a way of life down home. That's what I'm going to school for. I like doing social work—"

"Maybe you don't have your mother's genes, but you sure love to talk like your mother," I said, and laughed.

"I know. Mom and I are alike in a lot of ways. I like nice clothes just like mom. She's got great taste in clothes. And mom's a great cook too. She taught me how to cook and bake and everything. I love my mom, Oriano; but we don't see eye to eye on a lot of things."

"Like what?"

"Religion," she whispered.

"Are you kidding me?" I said, feigning shock.

"No. I'm a feminist. I believe in the rights of women. I believe in free choice—"

"Oh God, you don't?"

"Yes, I do. I think a woman should have the right to be in charge of her own body."

"And what does your mother have to say about that?"

"Mom's a pro-lifer. What else could she be? She takes her religion way too seriously for me. I can't be like that. I'm a free spirit—"

I laughed. I couldn't help myself. "What does that mean, Kathleen? You're completely dependent upon your parents for everything; don't you think you're stretching the concept a little?"

"No, I'm not. My parents have an obligation to see me through school, so that shouldn't change the way I feel about things. I have a right to my own life, don't I?"

"I can't disagree with that."

"You can't?"

"Nope."

"That's nice to hear. Why don't you tell mom for me. She has a real high opinion of you, you know."

"Really?"

"Yeah. She says you're a deep thinker. She really likes talking with you."

"And I with her. So, tell me Kathleen; I hear you're reading some New Age literature. What books are you reading?"

"I just finished *Conversations with God,* Book 3, by Neale Donald Walsh. Have you heard of him? He's fantastic!"

"As a matter of fact, I just picked up his new book in Chapters last weekend. *Friendship with God.* Do you have that one?"

"No. I haven't seen that one yet. What's it about?"

"I haven't had a chance to get into it yet, but from what I skim-read it's about the effect that the publication of his books have had on his life and about his concept of God when he was growing up, and so on. It sounds interesting."

"Do you believe Jesus is God?"

"No."

"Me neither. I think Jesus was just a man. I think Jesus got caught up in some kind of political thing of his time and got crucified for being an agitator. I think he had a lot of good things to say, but I don't think he was God. What do you think, Oriano? Do you agree with me. Mom doesn't of course. She was a nun, you know."

"Yes, I know. But you know what, Kathleen? I agree with everybody."

"You can't agree with everybody. *Come on!"*

"There's a grain of truth in every opinion, Kathleen. The trick is not to make a mountain of sand out of it because you can't climb a mountain of sand."

She laughed. *"Right on!"*

I smiled. "So, Kathleen; how do you reconcile your New Age belief with your mother's Catholicism?"

"I don't. We don't see eye to eye on anything religious. But I go to church just to please her."

"How did you diverge so radically from your mother?"

"Pardon me?"

"How did you come to see life so differently from your mother? How did you arrive at your belief that Jesus Christ is not God?"

"I don't know. I just don't. I think God is bigger than Jesus. I think God is something that we can't know. I believe in God, Oriano; don't get me wrong. I just don't believe we can know God, that's all. I call myself a New Age agnostic. And a feminist!"

"A New Age agnostic feminist who believes in God. That's quite a handle. I can't imagine what your mother must feel—"

"I know what she feels. She doesn't like it one bit. Mom hates feminism. She thinks we're all a bunch of shit-disturbers."

I couldn't help myself and laughed. "Well, don't be too hard on her. Your mother is a very special lady, and one of the nicest people I've ever met. I know you have a right to your own life, but don't break your mother's heart. You have to find a way to diverge from her beliefs without damaging your love for each other—"

Suddenly, just like her mother, Kathleen broke into tears. It took me completely by surprise. I waited, and through gushing tears she said, "Oriano, I'm pregnant. I'm going to have an abortion, but I don't know how to tell my mother—"

"*Wow!* What a bombshell! Is that why you came home?"

"Yes," she sobbed. "I have to tell her, but I honestly don't know how—"

I took a deep breath. I didn't know what to say. I knew instantly that it would break Grace's heart, but what could Kathleen do? She had a right to her own life. "Kathleen," I said, as softly as I could, "don't tell your mother. What she doesn't know won't hurt her."

"I have to tell her, Oriano," she said, now sobbing uncontrollably.

152

I put my arms around her and held her slender body close to mine. She was trembling with tears. I held her tight as she cried into my shoulder.

"What am I going to do?" she sobbed.

"Talk to your dad. Tell him first. He might be a little more understanding."

"I thought of that, but I have to tell mom eventually. I have to tell her before I go back home. I have to—"

And she did. I was working downstairs in the family room the day Michael was to drive her to the airport. She had an afternoon flight to Toronto where she was going to be staying with a friend who had arranged for her abortion; then she was going back to St. John's. She had told her father the night before leaving, but she made him promise not to tell her mother. She had to do that herself; but she waited until an hour before leaving with her brother for the airport. They were standing in the back stairs landing.

"Kathleen," I heard Grace, through tears, "you will break my heart if you do—"

I stopped painting and listened intently. I had already said goodbye to Kathleen, so I didn't go to the door. I heard Kathleen crying—

"I love you, mom. I love you so much—"

"Please Kathleen, I beg you in the name of our precious Mother, don't do it," Grace pleaded with her daughter. *"You cannot take that poor child's life—"*

"Mother—"

I couldn't listen. It was too painful. I shut the basement door and went back to work. I didn't go up for my afternoon tea break. I worked downstairs all afternoon and washed up in the laundry sink and quietly slipped out and went home.

The next morning Grace met me at the back door with a big smile. "Good morning, Oriano. Come in, come in—"

I bid her good morning and went downstairs to the laundry room where I had all my paint and working material, but Grace followed me down. She had laundry in the washer. As I selected my paint and wiped my oil paint brush that was soaking in varsol Grace

153

took laundry out of the washer and put it into the dryer. I didn't know what to say, so I said nothing. But Grace wanted to talk, so she began—

"Oriano, you don't have children so you can't possibly know what it's like for a mother these days. It's a test, Oriano; a real test—"

"I can imagine," I said.

"I wonder if you can," she said.

I smiled. "There's no imagining the real thing, Grace; but if a person is empathetic enough, I'm sure he can come close. That's what creative writing is all about."

"Perhaps you're right. I'm sorry, Oriano. I didn't mean to doubt you. I just think sometimes only a mother can understand what another mother has to go through with her children—"

Grace wanted to broach the subject of her daughter's pregnancy, but she wasn't quite sure that I knew; and I wasn't going to tell her. She had to bring it up, not me.

"I think you're right, Grace. Only another mother can know what mothering is all about," I said, as I stirred my paint can.

"Have you ever thought of having children, Oriano?"

"No. Believe it or not, Grace; from an early age I've had the strangest feeling that I'm the last of my own line. Don't ask me what that means, but that's how I've always felt. In other words, I don't have a need for progeny."

"That's strange. Most men do," she said, a little mystified.

"I know, but I'm not like most men," I said, with a chuckle. I picked up my paint can and brush and went to work on the family room windows. I was putting on the second coat. A minute or so later Grace came out of the laundry room and stood by the kitchenette counter and watched me paint.

"Oriano, what do you think of my daughter? Isn't she something?" she said, trying her hardest to sound casual.

"She's very much like you, Grace," I said, as I dipped my brush into the can.

"Oh? In what way?" she asked, again trying to sound casual.

"Strong-willed," I replied, and smiled.

"She is that. I pray for her, Oriano. I pray every day—"

I did not reply. I did not know what to say. The silence became pressing. Grace couldn't help herself. "Oriano," she said, in a nervous voice, "Kathleen's a very emotional girl. You heard her yesterday, didn't you?"

"When?"

"When she was leaving."

"I heard something, but I couldn't make it out. The door was closed."

"Oh? You didn't hear Kathleen crying?"

"No," I lied again.

"Well she was. She's very emotional. It was difficult for her to say goodbye. It was difficult for me—"

Grace stopped in mid sentence. I continued painting as if nothing was wrong. "Parting is such sweet sorrow," I said, quoting Shakespeare.

"Bitter-sweet," she said, with tears in her voice. "Well, I'd better let you work. I have to go down to the church for a bit, and then we'll have tea when I get back."

"That's fine," I said; but when Grace came back from church she opened up the subject again, her voice much more confident now.

"May I ask you something, Oriano?" she said, as she poured the tea. I could tell that she was trying to be as casual as ever, but knowing what I did I could sense her nervousness. "Something personal," she said.

"Sure," I said.

"You don't go to church anymore, do you?"

"No."

"May I ask why?"

"You know why, Grace. I've outgrown my Christian faith."

"But you still believe in Jesus, don't you?"

"As I told you, I believe Jesus was a teacher of the Way; but I don't believe that he was the Son of God, or God."

"Kathleen doesn't believe Jesus is God. She believes Jesus was just a man. I don't know how she came to believe that, Oriano; but she does. How did you come to your belief, if you don't mind my asking?"

"It wasn't easy, I assure you. I had to pay a very dear price to divest myself of my Christian faith—"

"But why would you want to divest yourself? I don't understand that—"

By the look on her face and the sound of her voice I could see that she was genuinely perplexed. She simply could not fathom why Christians would want to divest themselves of their faith. It was inconceivable to her, and it pained her deeply.

I didn't want to, but I felt compelled to tell her; so I took a deep breath, and said, "Grace, I'll tell you what you're so desperate to know. Let me see if I can find the right context first…Life is a school for Soul. We're born into this world to learn and grow spiritually. Some of us learn the easy way, and some of us learn the hard way. Jesus came into the world to teach us the Way. The Way is the spiritual path back home to God. Christ's teaching is a difficult path to live by, because it speeds up the lessons that we have to learn to grow and become spiritually conscious. I believe in Jesus Christ, Grace. I believe in Jesus because I took his teaching out into the marketplace and put it to the test; and it worked for me. It worked just as Jesus promised it would. I died to my life to find my life; and now I'm free of the need for spiritual salvation. Once I became free of this need I could go my merry way, as it were. I was free to live my life without being driven by my inherent need to be saved. It's this need to be saved that's the root cause of man's anxiety in life. But this need to be saved is merely Soul's desire to return back home to God; so it doesn't matter how we define it, we won't be happy until we find the Way. But the irony about life is that the Way is everywhere to be found. The Way is not limited to Christ's teaching alone, Grace. That's what's so beautiful about the Way. Now, what you have difficulty grasping is that you have been brought up to believe that Jesus Christ is the sole savior of the world. That's wrong. It's dead wrong, and tragic—"

"But Oriano—"

"Let me finish. You have no right whatsoever to impose your belief about Jesus Christ upon me or anyone else, and that includes your daughter—"

"But I'm her mother—"

"Let me finish, please. This belief you Christians have that Jesus died on the cross to save the world has warped the psyche of the world, and it's time you people woke up and smelled the coffee. I'm sorry for coming on so strong, Grace; but I'm getting sick and tired of Christianity's in-your-face bullshit. If you want to believe that Jesus is God, that's fine; but don't presume that God is going to deny salvation to any soul that does not come to God by way of Jesus Christ; that's just not so. Like your daughter said to me, God is bigger than Jesus Christ—"

"Kathleen said that to you?"

"Yes."

"Did you have a long talk with her?"

"Not long; but it was a good talk."

"Well, I don't know what to do with her. I brought her up to believe in Jesus Christ, but she's going her own way and I'm afraid for her soul—"

"Grace, haven't you heard a word I said? Kathleen is a fine young lady. She has her own spiritual destiny to work out. Can't you just let her find her own path in life?"

Grace looked at me and smiled. "What else can I do, Oriano? This is what I believe."

"I understand. But the bottom line is that the Way is an individual path home to God, and it cannot be contained by any one teaching; especially Christianity."

"So much seems to be happening to me lately," Grace replied, in a strange, far-away voice. "So much—"

I could feel her fighting back tears. "Grace, you need a break. Not from what you're doing; but from yourself."

"Myself? I don't understand," she said, her eyes bleary with tears.

"You're a good person, Grace. Even a blind man can see that. But I'm a good person too. I know I am, because I made it a top priority in my life to be a good person. But being a good person doesn't give me the right to tell other people how to be good. You asked me why I divested myself of my Christian faith, and now I'll tell you. It's too difficult to be a Christian and a good person. Christianity is fraught with so many contradictions that one is forever

157

at odds with himself; and I couldn't take that any longer. I had to leave the Church to find an easier way to be a good person. I know that the only way into the kingdom of heaven is by being a good person, but Christianity sets us up for failure by the outrageous demands it makes upon us. No person can be a Christian and not suffer the anxiety of failing. Take yourself, Grace. You believe your daughter may fail to meet the demands of your faith; but is that fair? Who set up these demands, Grace? And are they real?"

"I believe they are," she quickly replied.

"I know you do, and that's the whole problem. I don't believe they're real. I believe they were set up to keep people enslaved to the Church. I believe Christianity has been having an affair with Power for so long now that it expects the world to condone it. But I can't condone it. And neither can your daughter. Kathleen is waking up to her own destiny, and if she chooses a different path from yours you have to respect her."

"But I fear for her soul, Oriano—"

"Oh for God's sake, Grace! Is there any point talking to you Christians?" I said, and stood up from the table. I couldn't suffer that logic any longer.

I shocked Grace. She stared at me. "Please tell me one thing, Oriano. How do you know if you're right?"

"Experience is the ultimate litmus test of life. I've walked the walk, Grace; and I don't talk about the Way unless I've been there myself. Now if you'll excuse me, I have to get back to work. Thank you for the tea…"

It happens often in my work. I run over the time I have allotted for a job because the home owners get me to do extra work, and in Grace's case I was about to overlap a small taping job that I had booked in the city; so I asked her if she wouldn't mind if I went and did it and then return to paint the main floor washroom and her son's bedroom.

"By all means," she said.

"Thank you. I appreciate it," I said.

Kathleen had left for Toronto, and I had three more days of work before my job in the city; and in those three days I could not get

Kathleen out of my mind. I kept asking myself, why would she tell me that she was going to have an abortion?

The more I thought about it, the more I felt that it too was meant for synchronistic reasons that I did not want to fathom; but try as I may, I could not push it to the back of my mind. It kept popping up as I worked until I got tired of fighting it.

Why did she tell her mother? That question kept forcing itself upon me. I did tell her that what her mother didn't know wouldn't hurt her, but Kathleen had to tell her mother; why? She knew it was going to break her mother's heart, that's why she broke out in tears when I told her that she had to find a nice way to tell her mother that she did not want to live the life her mother wanted her to live. Her need to live her own life conflicted with her mother's wishes, but she loved her mother and did not want to disappoint her; that's why she broke into tears. The pressure of her conflict was unbearable.

Kathleen knew how deeply her mother felt about abortion; it was murder and a grievous mortal sin. And she also knew that she could respect her mother's faith and have her baby, which her mother would raise herself if she had to just to preserve the integrity of her faith, or she could give her baby up for adoption as she had been given up by her birth mother—she knew all of this; but she chose instead to have an abortion. Why?

And why did Kathleen have to tell her mother about her abortion anyway? She could have had it and kept quiet. She loved her mother deeply, that was obvious; so what in heaven's name possessed her to break her mother's heart?

The more I thought about Kathleen, the more I thought about my own life and why I had to break the hold that Christianity had upon me; and it all came back to me in a rush of painful memories: Christianity demanded something of me that I could no longer give— blind, subservient obedience. I had no right to question my faith. But the older I got, the more curious I was about the spiritual life; and the more I sought to satisfy my curiosity, the more it conflicted with my faith; and my break from the Church was as inevitable as Kathleen's break from her mother's hold upon her. That's why she had to tell her mother about her abortion; she had to make her mother realize in no uncertain terms that she differed in her beliefs from her mother's.

Kathleen's belief in a woman's right to choose overrode her mother's belief, and possibly even her own belief that abortion was murder and an abominable sin against God; but she was willing to risk her mother's love and eternal damnation just to have the freedom to live her own life. That's why she was compelled to tell her mother.

When I made my decision to break away from one teaching and then another, starting with Christianity, I made it because if I did not I would be lying to myself; and I could not live with myself knowing that my life was a lie. Not after I had taken my vow to find my true self or die trying. It went against the *raison d'être* of my life.

And neither could Kathleen live with herself if she did not live up to what she believed. By telling her mother that she was going to have an abortion she was liberating herself from the hold that her mother's faith still had upon her, and she knew that this was going to break her mother's heart; but as painful as it was going to be, she had to tell her mother. She had no choice.

"I love you mom. I love you so much—" I heard Kathleen crying as she was about to leave for Toronto; and I heard what her mother said to her, *"You will break my heart if you take your child's life—"* But it was so painful to hear Grace and her daughter crying as they each held onto their own beliefs that I had to close the basement door and go to the far end of the family room where even the muffled sound of their voices could not reach me.

It was guilt and fear and anger and anxiety and disappointment and doubt and dread and desperation that I heard in their crying voices; but what came through the loudest was the deep love that they had for each other.

Grace feared for her daughter's soul. She could not possibly do otherwise, believing what she did about abortion; and Kathleen feared for her soul as well, because her belief in a woman's right to abortion could not possibly have overridden years of going to confession every Saturday and asking God to forgive her sins so she would be pure enough to receive the Blessed Sacrament Sunday morning. Confession and the Holy Eucharist were her life growing up; how could she not suffer repressed guilt for having an abortion?

That's what made their parting so painful. I could hear years of emotion rising to the surface in mother and daughter. It was symbolic. I heard all the forces of Christianity rush out to hold onto one poor soul that wanted to break free of the faith, and it brought tears to my eyes at the memory of my own break from the Church.

It was more painful than a Greek tragedy, because I knew how difficult it was to break away from a belief that one has outgrown; but I had no idea that Christianity's hold upon the psyche could be so insidious until the death of my parish priest whom I served as an altar boy and to whom I had confessed all my sins right up until I stopped going to Mass—my most private sexual thoughts that I had to relieve onanistically.

Father Meyer was killed in a motor vehicle accident. I read his obituary in the city paper one day, and suddenly I felt a letting go of something that I can only describe as an invisible hand that clutched the most private part of my soul; and the relief that I felt was so consciously palpable that it forced me to see just how much power Christianity has over its blind, faithful believers—*even long after they have left the Church!*

I thought I was free of Christianity, but my parish priest's death liberated me from a hold that I did not even know was there, and that sent a chill up my spine; so I knew exactly what Kathleen was up against when she chose to tell her mother that she was going to have an abortion. She was up against the very source of the Roman Catholic Church's control over its followers—*the awesome salvific power to forgive sins!*

With her decision to have an abortion Kathleen defied Christianity's power to forgive sins; but she knew in her heart that by having an abortion she would break the hold that Christianity had upon her—*but at the risk of her own possible damnation!*

That's why I was moved to tears. Like Kathleen, I wasn't sure of eternal damnation either, and the fear was always with me until I learned otherwise; but Kathleen hadn't reached that point of enlightenment in her own spiritual journey yet, and I heard the silent horror of eternal damnation in her voice; and especially in her mother's voice.

Grace did not want to see her daughter's soul put in jeopardy by murdering her unborn child. That's why she said to me the following day, "I fear for her soul." I didn't want to tell her where I stood on the issue, because that was not the time to talk about it; but I felt Grace's pain, because I knew the power of her belief in the Church.

I wanted to laugh. I honestly did, because all that pain was unnecessary. It was, to use Jean Paul Sartre's phrase, "useless passion." That's what I meant when I told Grace that suffering was for fools. But she could not grasp that concept. It was beyond her.

As much as I respected and admired her, Grace was a fool for letting her faith affect her the way it did; and it was a subject that I wanted very much to discuss with her should I have the courage to ask her to continue our Platonic relationship…

The day after Kathleen arrived from St. John's she had a mind-splitting headache. It hit her the night before, and she hardly slept at all; so she looked stressed out when she came into the kitchen-dining room in the morning.

"Mom, maybe I should see a doctor," she said, still in her nightgown.

"Oriano, they do have an emergency ward in the hospital here, don't they?" Grace asked, in an even tone of voice that told me she had been through this before.

"Yes," I said.

"Kathleen, should I take you to emergency?" she asked.

"I don't know mom. Maybe I'll take another Tylenol. Are there any left?"

Grace went to the washroom and came back with a small bottle. "There's still some left. Take one more, and if your headache doesn't abate in the next hour I'll take you down to emergency; okay dear?"

"Okay mom," Kathleen said, and took the Tylenol that Grace handed her. Then Grace got a glass of water from the refrigerator tap and Kathleen swallowed the tablet.

"When did you get your headache?" I asked.

"Last night," she said.

"Would you like me to take it away from you?" I said, not really knowing why I volunteered; it just leapt out of my mouth without thought.

"How?" Kathleen asked, with a blank look on her face.

"Yes or no?" I curtly said, which surprised me.

"Yeah, sure. I don't want this headache. It's killing me."

Grace stared at me, wondering what I was up to.

I gave them both a big smile. "Kathleen, do you have something small that I can hold for a few minutes? A watch or something?"

"Yeah, sure; why?" she asked.

"I need it to make the connection," I said.

"What connection?" Grace asked, with a hint of alarm in her voice.

"Don't get anxious, Grace," I said, smiling to reassure her. "It's an old folk remedy that my mother passed on to me. I don't do this often. I've only done it for one or two other people besides Cathy, but it works; so I thought I'd try it on Kathleen."

"Try what?" Grace asked.

"The folk remedy, mom. So you want my watch to hold onto?"

"Yes, that'll do," I said, and Kathleen went to her bedroom and came back with her watch. She handed it to me and I got up. "I'll give it back to you in a few minutes."

"Okay," she said, wondering what I was up to.

Grace looked at me, and by the look in her eyes I could tell that her level of alarm had risen. I had to dispel her fear before I left the room.

"Grace, it's not voodoo or black magic or anything like that. As a matter of fact, I say a few prayers that my mother taught me one Christmas Eve. I can't explain it to you, because it's a secret folk thing passed on orally; but I know it works because my mother did it to us whenever we had been charmed for one reason or another—"

"Charmed?" Grace queried.

"It's called *la fascino* in Italian; but don't ask me to explain, Grace. Like I said, it's a folk thing that you might think superstitious, but it's nothing to be afraid of. It's just a few secret prayers that were passed on from one generation to the next."

"Christian prayers?" Grace asked.

"Of course," I said, and laughed; which eased her mind somewhat.

"Oriano, do what you have to do," Kathleen said. "I don't care if it's superstition or not. As long as it takes away my headache who cares how it works?"

I smiled at her simple honesty and went into the living room and did a short contemplation using my secret word (I received my power word during my initiation into a higher order of my spiritual path) to establish a direct link-up with Holy Spirit; then I squeezed Kathleen's watch in my hand, and under my breath said, "Divine Spirit, please pass Kathleen's headache energy through me into the Life Stream. I'm doing this for the good of the whole." Then I waited for it to happen, and within a minute or two I started to yawn non-stop; deep, lung-filling, wide-mouthed yawns, and I knew that it was working.

I smiled to myself and waited another minute and then went back to the dining room. Grace and Kathleen were waiting for me with a look on their face.

"Here, Kathleen," I said, handing her watch back.

She took it and said, "What do I do with it?"

"Tell the time," I said, and laughed. "Nothing. Just put it on. I needed it to establish a link-up with your energy field, that's all."

"I've still got my headache," she said.

I yawned deeply, and said, "It'll go away shortly."

"Really?" Kathleen said.

"Yes," I said, and yawned once more.

"How come you're yawning so much?" Kathleen asked.

"I'm just replenishing my life force," I said.

"Life force?" she said.

"Yes. The *élan vital*, or vital life force that's in the air we breathe. Yawning takes in large quantities of the life force, and I'm just replacing what I passed through me with your headache energy. You were loaded, Kathleen."

"Really?" she said, with a mystified look on her pretty young face.

"Yes," I said, and yawned again; an extra long, deep yawn. I held my hand to my mouth as I yawned, and then I chuckled. "Good gosh, you were loaded! You must have picked it up yesterday from the people around you."

"Picked what up, Oriano?" Grace asked, her eyes wide with alarming curiosity.

"Psychic energy," I replied, and yawned again; another, deep-lunged yawn. It felt good to replenish my life force, and I smiled.

"Why do you keep yawning," Kathleen asked.

"As I passed your headache energy through me into the Life Stream it took some of my life force with it; and when I yawn I replenish my vital life force. But I shouldn't have told you this, Kathleen. It's part of an ancient body of secret knowledge."

"Can you pass on these prayers to me?" Grace asked.

I didn't want to take Grace out of her element, so I lied. "I'm sorry, Grace; but it's a family thing. It's passed on from one family member to another. I'm the only one in the family who wanted to know how to do this thing for *la fascino*, so mom passed on the prayers to me one Christmas Eve. I do it for Cathy whenever she comes home from work zapped of her energy. It'll work for you, Kathleen. Just give it a few minutes."

"Do I have to do anything?" she asked.

"No. Just go about your day," I said, and then excused myself and went back to work; but a short while later Kathleen came downstairs to tell me that her headache was completely gone. "How did you do it?" she asked, with a mystified look.

"I told you. I passed your headache energy through me into the Life Stream."

"I know you said that, but how did you do it?"

"I just did it," I said, and laughed.

"Well I don't understand how it works, but my splitting headache's gone and that's all that counts," she said, still in her nightgown.

"Good. Now can I get back to work?"

"Yeah, sure. Thanks Oriano. I appreciate it," she said, and left.

I didn't think about this until days later, but I must have made a very strong impression for her to tell me about her pregnancy. She trusted me. Grace, on the other hand, still had suspicions the day after I took Kathleen's headache away—

"Oriano, was that a coincidence yesterday or did you really take Kathleen's headache away?" she asked as I rolled paint onto the basement bedroom walls that Grace was now using for her ironing and sewing room.

"Coincidence?" I said.

"Yes. Kathleen did take a Tylenol just before you did what you did."

"Oh, right. Maybe it was a coincidence, Grace; I don't know. I think the folk thing worked though because I only yawn like that when it works. If I wouldn't have yawned like that I would've known it didn't work and that it had to be something else."

"That's not very scientific, is it?"

"Oh, Grace; don't worry about it. If it works it works. If it doesn't it doesn't. What's the big deal?" I said, as I loaded my roller sleeve up with the paint in my tray.

"You intrigue me, Oriano. I don't know how to take you sometimes. Do you have some kind of psychic gift?"

"I don't see it as a psychic gift."

"Are you a healer?"

"I don't think so."

"What are you, then?"

"A housepainter," I said, and laughed.

Grace shook her head. My laughter was much too genuine for her to harbor suspicion, so she dropped the subject and said, "Oriano, what am I to do with you?"

"Enjoy my company while it lasts, Grace. It's not every day you get to meet a person like me," I said, and broke into fresh laughter.

"You're absolutely right. I've never met anyone quite like you before. You're a fascinating man, Oriano. But you're not telling me everything; and before you leave this house I'm going to find out what it is that you're holding back—"

I smiled. "Those born of the Spirit are unpredictable, Grace. You'll never get a fix on me, because like Padre Pio used to say, 'I'm a mystery unto myself'—"

Grace smiled her mystic smile at the mention of Italy's favorite saint who suffered the Holy Wounds of Jesus for fifty years, but without the ironic twinkle in her eye; and then she left because she was taking her daughter out to show her the town and her father's school and then they were all going out for lunch at the St. Jude Cafe…

After Kathleen's departure my talks with Grace took on another layer of irony. It was enough that I had to keep our conversations within her Christian paradigm, but not telling her that I knew about Kathleen's plans for an abortion added a dimension of irony that sometimes made me want to laugh; but I couldn't for Grace's sake.

It was amusing watching Grace maintain her poise whenever Kathleen's name came up in our talks, and it was a joy to see that her love for Kathleen had not diminished one iota since her daughter dropped the bombshell on her; but I couldn't help but feel sorry for her also every time she fought back her tears—

"Hate the sin but not the sinner," she said to me one day when the theme of our talk came around again to sin and the forgiveness of sin.

"It would be even better if we could transcend our hate altogether and just be," I replied, and laughed at the thought.

"Yes, that would be lovely," Grace responded, in her thoughtful Sister of Mercy voice. "But that's not a state that we can realize, can we?"

"Why not?" I asked.

"Because we will always be subject to temptations as long as we occupy this body of flesh and blood. The best we can hope for is to try to be in the world but not of the world. Like our Lord Jesus, Oriano; he took on a body of flesh and blood to show us the Way. But the way of the cross is difficult; so difficult—"

I could always hear sorrow in Grace's voice, like a subtext to everything she said, and knowing what I did about her daughter added an extra layer of anguish; but I wanted to explore the subject of self-sacrifice with her—

"The way of the cross is not for everyone, Grace," I said. "There are easier ways to spiritual self-realization consciousnesses."

"There is only one way, Oriano; and that is to die to the life of the flesh like our savior Jesus," she responded, in her disciplined, self-sacrificing voice of steel.

I knew that voice well. I too had died to the flesh like Grace. I too had sacrificed my life on the cross of my *Royal Dictum* (my edict of self-denial). I too had been bought with a price; and I put my paint roller down and turned to her, and said—

"You're wrong, Grace. There is more than one way to be born again. Rather than die daily one can learn to live daily; and by this I don't mean to go out and gorge oneself on life. I mean living one's life with virtue—"

"Virtue?" Grace said, with a sudden burst of new curiosity.

"Yes, virtue. Let's take my work here. I'm painting your house, and you're not unhappy with my work. Am I correct in assuming this?"

"Yes, of course. You're doing an excellent job, Oriano. Very professional. Brandon and I were just talking about your work last night over dinner, and he said that you're making a silk purse out of a sow's ear—"

I laughed. "Well, I am doing my very best with what I have; but the point I want to make is that I put virtue into my work. I didn't apprentice under anyone, Grace; I learned my trade through trial and error. And the most important lesson that I learned for my trade is that you cannot take integrity out of your work, because if you do you rob your work of all its virtue. And if a person doesn't have virtue in his life, what does he have?"

"What do you mean by virtue?" she asked.

"Virtue is by definition inherent excellence. Now follow the thought, if you will. Would you agree that our soul is part of God?"

"Yes. Our soul belongs to God, Oriano. That's why it's so painful to be apart from God," she said, as though reciting her catechism.

"Alright. Let's take it from there. So our soul longs to be with God, then?"

"I would say so," she said, and smiled. Grace could feel that we were about to take Platonic flight, and it excited her. I could almost feel her goose bumps. "That's why God sent his only Begotten Son into the world to harvest lost souls," she added.

I smiled to myself. I didn't want to lose my train of thought by digressing into a discussion on the question of Christ's divinity, so I continued—

"You would agree then that souls long to be back with God; that our longing for God is born of our alienation from God, and the way of the cross is one way for us to return home to God? Would you agree with that or not?"

"Yes. That's why Jesus died on the cross. He died to show us the way to God."

"Fair enough. I agree with that also. But what I have to point out to you Grace is that there is another way back to God besides the way of the cross, and that's by realizing the inherent goodness of our spiritual nature—i. e., virtue. Do you see where I'm going with this now?" I asked, hoping she would grasp my point.

Grace looked puzzled. "I think so. You're saying that by being good we realize virtue; is that what you're saying?"

"Yes."

"I see. But I don't understand what this has to do with your trade. Virtue is a moral quality, isn't it?"

"Yes, it is. But wouldn't it be immoral if I didn't do a good job here?" I said, and broke into laughter. I couldn't resist the temptation to play upon the thought.

"I wouldn't be happy if you didn't do a good job," she replied, smiling at my quick wit. "But I wouldn't see it as being immoral, Oriano."

"That's where we differ. I believe that the inherent goodness of work is intrinsically moral. What does moral mean if not upright, noble, principled, truthful, scrupulous, exemplary, and sincere? In a word, the virtue of work implies a certain kind of spiritual excellence; and I believe that the more virtue we put into our work, the closer we will be to God. This is what makes work ennobling, Grace."

"I agree with you there, Oriano. I learned that in my twenty years of being a nun. Work ennobles the soul. I don't doubt that for one moment—"

169

"Yes, but only when one puts virtue into one's work. One has to work with integrity, honesty, and sincerity. One has to work with a sense of pride in what one is doing. One cannot cheat or cut corners or play fast and loose with the rules. I know this for a fact, Grace. I've been down this road a million times. You've heard the expression 'work is its own reward,' haven't you?"

"Yes, of course."

"Why is work its own reward if not for the virtue that one can realize from one's work? But only if one does one's work with integrity. And by integrity I mean that one has to do one's work for one reason only; and can you guess what that reason would be?"

"To do good work, I would think," Grace replied.

"Exactly. Doing good work implies excellence. Every job has its own intrinsic level of excellence, and it's up to the worker to realize this excellence. That's what it means to make a silk purse out of sow's ear. But I've learned through my trade over many years of trial and error that to realize virtue in one's work takes more than excellence; it takes a certain kind of moral probity. Don't ask me why or how, Grace; but without this moral probity one just does not realize the virtue of goodness that comes from excellence. So by doing my work to the best of my professional ability I realize the intrinsic excellence of my work; but when I add moral probity to my work I realize more than the intrinsic excellence of my work. I realize a certain goodness that makes my work virtuous. That's why they say that work is its own reward; because work done with moral probity can be a natural way back home to God. In other words, Grace; the more virtue that we get from the work we do, the closer we will be to God. It's *ipso facto,*" I added with a hearty chuckle.

Grace's face lit up like a florescent bulb. "I was told at the convent that work is good for the soul, and now I know why. *You do continue to amaze me, Oriano!*

I tried not to blush. "I've been studying the Way for years, Grace; and since I had to make a living somehow I decided to get as much benefit from my trade as I could. And believe me, what a joy it was to discover that when you add moral probity to your work you can forge your own path back home to God!"

Grace smiled, her eyes as big as saucers; and then she laughed. *"Oriano, why did you have to leave the Church? You're such a good Christian!"*

"It's ironic, isn't it?" I said, and broke into a mirthful chuckle.

"Then why don't you come back? You would be such an asset to our little flock of Catholics here in St. Jude—"

"Are you kidding me?" I said, in all seriousness. "After what it cost me to break free of the hold that Christianity had upon me?"

"What hold?" she quickly asked, her eyes alight with fresh interest.

"Grace, I can't begin to tell you what price I paid to extricate myself from the hold that my blind Christian faith had upon me. The spiritual life is a conscious life, and consciousness is never ending. I can't go back. If I did I would have to go back to sleep; and I can't do that. I like being awake now, Grace. *I like it too much!"*

"I don't understand you, Oriano. I honestly don't. But I will pray for you. I would love nothing better than to see you in Church one day taking Holy Communion."

"Don't hold your breath, dear heart," I said, and laughed.

7. THE FAR COUNTRY

I thought about Grace while I did my small job in the city. It was a basement renovation. The young couple who purchased the house had saved up to convert the basement into a family room with a fireplace. They had two children, a five year old boy and a three month old daughter.

I had taped, painted, and textured the ceiling of the basement bedroom for them the year before, and now they wanted a room for the children to play in and have family gatherings, so they called me back because they liked the work I did.

I enjoyed working for them, but I never saw them. Not like working for Grace. She seemed to be attracted to me for whatever reason, and I to her; and as I worked alone in the young couple's basement I thought about our attraction.

Why the gravitational pull? I knew it wasn't sexual. Although in her early sixties, Grace was still a beautiful woman; but despite the fact that I have always had a fascination for older women, Grace did nothing for me in that way. Besides, had she attracted me in that way I would not have violated the sanctity of her love for Brandon nor my love for Cathy by teasing myself with the attraction. No; it was something else entirely, and I thought about it long and hard as I worked in the quiet of the young couple's newly renovated family room with the newly installed gas fireplace.

It was quite because I could not pick up the CBC on my radio. The reception in the basement was terrible, so I shut my radio off and occupied my mind with thoughts of Grace and our incredible conversations that seemed to find their own direction.

And, of course, I thought about Kathleen's abortion and how Grace was dealing with it. I knew that when push came to shove Grace's objection would be tempered by her love for her daughter; and that, I chuckled mirthfully, would be good for her. "That's the way life works," I remember saying to her one day.

"I know, Oriano," she replied. "And the tests don't get any easier, do they? They get harder every time."

"How else can we grow spiritually?" I said.

"But there seems to be no end to the lessons we have to learn," she said, sounding almost but not quite annoyed with God. "I'll never understand it. Do you?"

"There's no end to perfection, Grace. But the irony of the spiritual life is that with every lesson that we're forced to learn we become a little more perfect."

Grace smiled. Then she laughed. "I think you're right, Oriano. God is infinitely perfect, and with each lesson we learn to become a little more God-like."

"By Jove, I think she's got it!" I exclaimed.

Grace burst into laughter. "Oriano, what is it about you that I can't put my finger on? Can you tell me?"

"I don't know. I've been trying to figure out why we get into these fascinating conversations. What do you think it is?"

"I asked you first," Grace responded, playfully.

"Well," I said, opening the door a crack, "I think it has to do with your separateness and my aloneness. You have that Newfie way of being familiar with people. You call people by their first name, and often, which I don't mind; and I sense in you the separateness of the nun's life. You're close but distant at one and the same time."

"But so are you!" she exclaimed, surprising me with her outburst. "You too are close but distant. Why is that? You were never in a monastery, were you?"

"Not a monastery, but I've been to sanctuary many times; and, believe me, that was much more cloistered than a monk's life can ever be!"

"In what way? I don't understand, Oriano—"

"In the convent you were separate but together with your fellow sisters. You turned your back on the world and became the Bride of Jesus Christ, but you did this within an organized religious context. You did it with the support of your Order. When I turned my back on the world I did it alone. I did not have the support of any religious Order to sustain me in my time of loneliness and fear and temptation; but my aloneness became the source of my strength, and ultimately my sanctuary."

"But why did you turn your back on the world. Did you do it to find God?"

"Not at first. I did it to find myself."

"I don't understand," Grace said, genuinely mystified.

"Like I told you, I exiled myself out of the kingdom of my own senses because that was the price I had to pay to find myself. So I know what it's like to be separate from the world. You nuns don't have anything on me when it comes to the life of abstinence," I said, and laughed. "That was my sanctuary, Grace. I did it alone. And that special space of total aloneness is with me always now. It's my sanctuary."

"And that's where you get your strength?"

"Yes. Just as you get your strength from your separateness."

"I get my strength from Jesus," Grace quickly replied.

"You were his bride once, Grace; but not anymore. Now you belong to the world like the rest of us. Jesus Christ may be your inspiration, but you get your strength from the consciousness of your separateness. You can take the nun out of the convent, but you can't take the convent out of the nun—"

And that's when it hit me. It was my second day in the city. I was texturing the ceiling—the bulkhead, to be precise; the boxed in section of the furnace air duct—and I was thinking of that conversation when it came to me why we had this incredible fascination for each other—*"Apartness!"* I burst out.

The young home-owner couldn't hear me upstairs because my compressor made too much noise, so I didn't feel bad about my outburst. *"We have the same soul space!"* I added, and broke into laughter at my revelation.

I had to stop spraying because I was too excited. I put my hopper and texture gun down and shut off the compressor and made a note in my notebook which I always carried with me on my jobs, except for Grace's house because I didn't want to make it that obvious to her that I was taking notes on our daily conversations.

I wrote down three words: *separateness*, *aloneness*, and *apartness* to remind me when I expanded upon the thought later at home. I went back to spraying, but as I sprayed the bulkhead I thought about our attraction and slowly it all began to make sense.

People who live the secular life are different from people who live the cloistered life. Grace knew that. If not consciously, after twenty years of marriage to Brandon she knew it subconsciously. And her husband, who had also lived the cloistered life for twenty-two years, shared Grace's consciousness of separateness. But then Grace met me.

I never lived the cloistered life. But I did live the interior life of abstinence. It was in many ways similar to Grace's way of the cross; but she could not fathom the consciousness of my aloneness. I was a housepainter very much of the world, and yet she could sense that I was different, despite the fact that I was a writer and all writers are different.

She could not put her finger on what it was about me that differentiated me from the secular world that she knew so well and was a part of but still separate from. She could see that I was very much a part of the natural flow of the material world by the way I talked and behaved, but she could also see that the material world did not mean to me what it meant to the secular public; and this not only attracted her to me, it frustrated and annoyed her immensely; but she was much too polite to pry into my private life.

Grace had to wait for me to reveal myself. That's why her eyes would pop wide open whenever I revealed something personal about my life; and, I confess, I also paid close attention to her whenever she spoke of her private life.

That was the fascination of our attraction. We were both interested in each other's private life. I wanted to know how she had cultivated her consciousness of separateness, and she wanted to know how I had cultivated my consciousness of aloneness. But because I knew so much more about her consciousness than she did of mine, she would get frustrated with me and say, *"I don't know what it is about you, Oriano—"*

And I would laugh, because I did take some measure of pleasure in not being seen. I attributed this aspect of my personality to Gurdjieff's "way of the sly man," which I had pretty well mastered by the time I met Grace; and as much as it annoyed her, it was my

175

protection against an incredulous and judgmental world. But Grace took no less pleasure in the security that she got from her Sister of Mercy consciousness of separateness; so we also had that in common, whether she was aware of it or not.

Grace prided herself in her knowledge of the secular world—the shallow, materialistic, and hypocritical life of vanity and desire; but it puzzled her to see someone who had cultivated a consciousness so separate but indistinguishable from the secular public that it forced her to stop and do a double take every time we talked; and that was why our conversations were so measured. She did not know where to tread with me…

For the three days that I worked at the young couple's home, starting with my hour long drive to the city, I thought of Grace and whether I should ask her to continue our Platonic relationship. "I'll never get another opportunity like this," I said to myself as I drove home in the late afternoon of my third day; "so why not go for it?"

There were many good reasons why I shouldn't, and only one good reason why I should. I had jumped the gun too soon several times in my life with literary ideas that possessed me, and I paid a price for my over-zealousness; that's why I had dropped a number of hints in my talks with Grace just to see if I should proceed or not.

As I drove home I thought about the courage it always took to begin a new book. I thought of Ernest Hemingway and how he wrote his novels. He said that he never sat down to write a novel; he always began by writing a short story, and if the story took off on him it would become a novel because he trusted the creative process.

I understood that. I had just written the third story of my second volume of short stories when I stopped working on my book to record my daily talks with Grace, so I had a good feel for how a short story could easily grow into a novel if that's where it had to go; and I could tell that there was much more than a short story in my relationship with Grace, especially since Kathleen dropped the bombshell on her unsuspecting mother.

Why, I don't know; but I felt that Brandon would take the news of her abortion a lot better than his wife, and I had to find out if

I was going to go ahead with my idea for a novel. But more importantly, I wanted to get Grace's feelings on the subject.

I knew where she stood because the question of sin had come up in our talks, but not enough to explore how we both really felt about the contentious issue of abortion; and now that Grace's own daughter was going to have one I felt almost compelled to pursue my talks with her just to see how Kathleen's abortion was going to affect Grace's life.

It was a curious coincidence that I was thinking about courage as I drove home—the courage that I needed to ask Grace to continue our conversations, Kathleen's courage to have her abortion, and Grace's courage to put her faith to the test again—when I drove by the Terry Fox monument overlooking Lake Superior and the courage it took that young man who had lost his leg to cancer to run across Canada to raise money for cancer research but who had to stop his run at the halfway point where they erected a monument to his memory because his cancer had returned and he had to be hospitalized. That's what was on the record, anyway; but in reality he had to stop his run at the outskirts of the town of hopeless causes that Grace and her husband had embraced to do God's work for the next five years of their life. I smiled at the irony of that young man hitting the wall of despair in St. Jude which ended his ultra marathon run; but I had to admire his indomitable courage.

"What's life without courage?" I heard myself asking.

"Bland!" I exclaimed, and broke into laughter. And I put on my Beethoven's Ninth Symphony tape to listen to for the rest of my drive home.

The insipidity of life without courage made me sad. I was so familiar with courage that I couldn't help but laugh at some of the things that I had done in my life—abandoning a promising entrepreneurial life in St. Jude and going to France to begin my impossible quest for my true self; building a triplex with no mortgage (the bank wouldn't give me one because I was self-employed) and only nineteen dollars in my bank account, with hardly any tools, very limited carpentry skills, and in the nadir of an economic recession that had all but wiped out my contracting business; making major decisions in my life at the toss of a coin to hone my instincts and trust my own intuition; but of all the courageous decisions that I had to make in my life, the most courageous was to stare down the lie of my life—my lustful shadow that compelled me to go on my quest for my true self.

"Anyone can run across Canada, artificial leg or not," I mused as I drove past the Terry Fox monument, *"but not everyone can stare down their life-lie!"*

I had just witnessed this tragic capitulation in my family a couple of months before I started painting Grace's house, the power of one's life-lie to take over their whole life, in my older brother Faust in whom I had awakened his shadow with a letter I had written him that so threatened his life-lie that he not only severed our twenty year correspondence relationship, but who stopped talking to me altogether except for the odd civility when he flew home to visit mother during her illness.

That's the kind of power that one's life-lie can have over one's life; and that's what frightened me about asking Grace to continue our relationship—the fear of waking her up to her life-lie with our talks. I knew only too well that a Platonic relationship—which is what my brother Faust and I enjoyed in our long and discursive twenty-year correspondence—cannot help but force one to confront the lie of his life, because the very nature of dialectical inquiry is to seek out the truth; so was I willing to risk waking Grace up to the lie upon which her entire Roman Catholic life was founded?

It didn't matter that Grace had awakened spiritually by living the way of the cross for twenty years as a Sister of Mercy and continued to live in her married life, she still believed that Jesus was the Son of God who had died for the sins of the world; and as long as she continued to believe what her faith asked her to believe—that man's immortal soul is created at the moment of his mortal human conception, the forgiveness of sins, and eternal damnation in hell— she would remain trapped by the lie of her faith.

In this way Grace was the same as people who are blind to the lie of their life, which Jung called the shadow side of our personality; but what made Grace different from everyone I had met in my life was that she had awakened spiritually by living the way of the cross—a life of self-sacrifice that had transformed the consciousness

178

of her ego enough to awaken her to her spiritual nature. That's what made her so fascinating to me.

Being awake myself, I could spot another spiritually awakened soul; and that did not happen often in my life. But it was painfully obvious to me that Grace could not take flight because her faith would not let her; that's why she was so Platonically attracted to me.

She saw my spiritual freedom in our conversations and was so excited by this freedom (which she referred to as the Light that she saw in me) that it inspired me to start taking extensive notes for a possible novel; but did I have the courage to ask her to continue our relationship knowing what the risk would be?

That's what I thought about as I drove home from the city that day. It was Friday, and I wouldn't be going back to Grace's house until Monday morning; so I still had all weekend to think about it. And I still had a few days of work at Grace's house, so I really didn't know what was going to happen. I had to trust the process.

But I was sure of one thing though after thinking about it for three days in the quiet of the Engler's family room; I would write my story one way or the other, because it wasn't every day that one met a person like Grace Kendal. And if I passed up the opportunity I knew that my Muse would condemn me to a life of eternal repetition like so many best-selling contemporary authors—*Conversations with God, Book 18;* and *The Twenty-Seventh Insight*; and yes, of course, *Chicken Soup for the Compromised Soul*...

Being an English teacher for most of her post-nunnery life, Grace Kendal knew something about the art of creative writing; but she never quite fathomed the mystery of the creative process. Few people do, for that matter; including writers.

"It's a mystery to me how the writer's imagination works, Oriano. I've experienced it myself. Many times, in fact. But I write letters mostly. I enjoy letter writing. It airs out the soul. Letter writing is a lost art form, you know. I keep telling myself that I'm going to write the story of my own interior castle one day, but I keep putting it off. Maybe I will now. All of these wonderful talks we've been having have given me new inspiration—"

"*Good!* Find yourself a nice quiet corner of the house and just sit down and do it. There's no other way, Grace. No ifs, ands, or buts. Just do it!"

"I'd like to, Oriano; I really would. I do have a story to tell, I assure you. Nothing like St. Teresa of Avila, mind you. But then, we all have a story to tell; don't we?"

We had talked about St. Teresa's books, which I had explored when I was studying the Christian mystics, and I had to laugh at Grace's ready modesty.

Modesty was a spiritual skill that she had acquired living the way of the cross. I was familiar with that skill. I had acquired it living Gurdjieff's Work. Primarily with the techniques of *self-remembering* and *non-identification*; two of the most difficult techniques of any spiritual path in the world to master.

Working on one's self was not unlike Christ's way of the cross; a deliberate, conscious effort to transform the consciousness of one's ego. But like most people that lived the spiritual life, Grace didn't understand the logic of self-transformation. For her it was simply a matter of mortifying the flesh to check the ego and do God's will.

"Not at all, Grace," I said to her, with an ironic chuckle. "Most people don't have a story to tell because they haven't really lived their life. They've just put in time. They live to exist, not exist to live. You live your life, Grace. You don't just exist. That's why you have a story to tell. You take control of your life. Most people don't. But nature will only take us so far, and then we have to take evolution into our own hands. That's why you were called to the convent. As the ancient alchemists would say, you were called to complete what nature left unfinished. You were also called to leave the convent; and now here you are in St. Jude taking control of your life again. That's why you have a story to tell."

"Do you really think so?" Grace replied, smiling demurely.

"I know so," I said, with a chuckle at her ready modesty.

"But how do you know, Oriano? You don't really know anything about me. Pardon me. I stand corrected. You know something about me; but how can you be sure that I have a story to tell. Everyone has a story if you dig deep enough, don't they?"

180

"Grace, no one can be a nun for twenty years and not have a story to tell. I'm very familiar with the way of the cross. No one can live that kind of interior life and not be a walking story. Did you ever see the movie *The Nun's Story*, starring Audrey Hepburn?"

"Yes," she replied, with an instant frown. "And I didn't care for it."

"You didn't care for it?" I repeated, incredulously.

"No, I didn't," Grace replied, rather curtly.

"Why not? That story moved me to tears. I loved it!"

Grace did not respond to my excited appreciation of the movie. She just stared at me, and smiled. I couldn't quite read her smile, but I saw sadness in her eyes; and I had to find out what it was about *The Nun's Story* that she did not like.

"What is it that you didn't like? Audrey Hepburn's acting, or the nun's story itself? Didn't you agree with her reasons for leaving the convent? What, Grace? I'm curious."

Grace snapped out of her reverie and said, "Oh, I just don't care for Audrey Hepburn; that's all. Not in that role, anyway."

I sensed that she wasn't being totally honest with me, but I couldn't pry. I had to work my way very carefully into the interior castle of her very private Sister of Mercy soul. "I thought she played an extraordinary role. In all honesty, Grace; she moved me to tears many times," I said, hoping to appeal to her sensitive emotional nature.

"Not me," she curtly responded, again to my surprise.

I wanted to say something, but I couldn't; something stopped me. What was it about Audrey Hepburn that Grace didn't like? I knew very well that what we don't like in other people we refuse to see in ourselves; but that wasn't what I saw in the former Sister of Mercy. It wasn't the mote in Audrey Hepburn's eye that annoyed her; it was something much deeper. The way she reacted to my appreciation of Audrey Hepburn spoke volumes; but what? My mind made a million computations, but in the end it was Grace's voice that revealed her private soul to me: *she was envious of Audrey Hepburn, or the nun that Audrey Hepburn played; or both.* But to verify my insight, I said—

181

"Audrey Hepburn was in a class all of her own, Grace. I don't know what it was—yes, I do know. I know exactly what she had that made her what she was; and it was this quality that shone in her role in *The Nun's Story*."

"What quality?" Grace was quick to ask.

"You have it too, Grace. But not to the degree that Audrey Hepburn had it," I replied, knowing that this would excite her curiosity.

"What quality, Oriano?" she asked again, with a puzzled look.

"I don't know how to explain it, Grace. I can see it, but it's indefinable. It's that indescribable *je ne sais quoi* quality that's born of one's spirit."

"I don't understand," she said, furrowing her brow.

"Neither do I. But I know it when I see it."

"How do you know?" she asked.

"Because I have it too," I said, and laughed.

"You've piqued my curiosity, Oriano—"

"I know. Have you read the book *The Nun's Story*?"

"Yes; and it was much better than the movie—"

She made me laugh. "Have you read anything else by Kathryn Hulme?"

"No. Have you?" she quickly asked, with a defensive edge to her voice.

"As a matter of fact, I have. Kathryn Hulme studied the same teaching that I studied and lived for many years. We were on the same path, Grace."

"Ohhh?" Grace said, her ears all perked up. "What path, Oriano?"

"An esoteric teaching based on the same principles as Christ's way of the cross," I said, with a private chuckle at Grace's newly awakened interest.

But catching herself, she responded with absolute conviction, "There is only one way of the cross, Oriano; and that's the way of our Lord Jesus Christ!"

"Not so, Grace. That's why Gurdjieff called his teaching 'esoteric Christianity.' It's a variation on Christ's way of the cross, only more adapted to the modern world. But it doesn't matter what we call it; a rose is a rose by whatever name. Which reminds me of what Gurdjieff said about his teaching. 'At first roses, roses; then thorns, thorns.' That's because the way of the cross is the way of self-sacrifice, and the teaching that Kathryn Hulme lived was called 'work on oneself,' and if I'm not mistaken she met the ex nun who inspired *The Nun's Story* while she was studying the Work in Paris with Gurdjieff. The ex nun—I think her name was Sister Luke, but I'll have to look it up when I get home; she was also living the Work after she left the convent. She belonged to a special group of women that Gurdjieff had formed. Margaret Anderson, the founder and editor of *The Little Review* magazine that introduced Ernest Hemingway, James Joyce, and T. S. Elliot to the world, was also a member of this special group of women that studied Gurdjieff's system; and by special, I mean women who preferred women—"

"What system? You've really piqued my curiosity, Oriano," Grace eagerly asked, completely bypassing my comment about the special group of lesbian seekers and going straight to the teaching that had awakened me to the sayings of Jesus and the Way.

"Work on oneself, Grace," I said, with a big smile. "A system of self-transformation no different than the way of the cross. But only if it is *lived*. That's the key. Without this key it won't do a damn thing for you. And neither will the way of the cross. *Unless a man doeth these sayings of mine he shall not inherit eternal life*, to paraphrase Jesus; but only the Work is lived out in the cold world, not in a convent. That's the difference—"

"The way of the cross is lived out in the world also," Grace quickly responded, her voice betraying all the toil and hardship of her post-nunnery life.

"I know, Grace; but you lived the way of the cross within the context of your religious Order—"

"I'm still living it today, Oriano. There is no end to the way of the cross. Not if you're a believer. You should know that. You were brought up Catholic."

I smiled. There was no point going there, so I said, "I know; but the point I want to make was that Kathryn Hulme wrote another book called *Undiscovered Country*. This is a metaphor used by some writers to describe that certain geography of the soul where one goes whenever they live the way of the cross—"

"Geography of the soul," Grace said, excitedly. "I like that phrase, Oriano. It says so much—"

"I know. It's the undiscovered country of God. And that's why I love Audrey Hepburn so much. Like the nun whose life she played, Audrey Hepburn was a citizen of this undiscovered country. She seemed to me to be just here visiting. She had an aura of such incredible innocence and charm and dignity, a certain aristocracy of the soul—"

"Oh come on now!" Grace exclaimed, shocked by my excited description.

"What? You don't agree?" I said, playing dumb to her envious shadow personality.

"No, I don't. She may have been a good actress, Oriano; but aristocracy of the soul? Come on! I think you're exaggerating."

"Grace, I'm seldom wrong in my perception of people. Audrey Hepburn was an old soul who came into this world to lift our spirits with her inherent dignity and nobility of character in the roles that she played, like *Roman Holiday* and *The Nun's Story*; that's why she became the Goodwill Ambassador for UNICEF. She was a great humanitarian blessed with the Light of God. She was a Keeper of the Flame, Grace; and she passed on the Holy Flame of God to the world through her films. That's what made her special."

Grace had the most curious expression on her face. *"Keeper of the Flame?"*

"Yes. She was imbued with the Holy Flame, Grace."

"What do you mean by that?"

"She had that special quality that defines those who have been to the Far Country, like Sister Luke in *The Nun's Story*. Audrey Hepburn was a perfect cast for that role."

"What Far Country?" Grace asked, now more mystified than ever.

I could feel her goose bumps. "The undiscovered country of the soul. That place Jesus called the kingdom of heaven which you can only get to through the narrow gate—"

"You mean by way of the cross?"

"Yes. But art can open up this narrow gate too. That's why artists can be so full of Light. This Holy Light of God is the Way that artists call inspiration; but the sad thing about artists—and I'm including writers in this special category of Keepers of the Flame—is that once they compromise their talent they stop shining the Holy Light of the Way. They're kicked out of the Far Country of God, as it were; and they have to draw upon their own impoverished mind for the inspiration of their art."

Grace was mystified. "I love your metaphors, Oriano; but how do writers compromise their talent? Do they sell out for material gain? Are you talking about a Faustian bargain with the Devil? Is that what you mean?"

I smiled at her reference to Goethe's *Faust*. It was so appropriate. But I sensed a Freudian foreshadowing, and I had to be very careful. "It's a tricky thing, Grace. It can creep up on you without realizing it. In fact, that's usually the way it happens. Take Hemingway, for example. His one battle in life was with himself. Specifically, between his shadow and creative self. Hemingway fought all his life to not compromise his natural talent for writing, but he revealed himself in *The Snows of Kilimanjaro*, which I consider to be his best story. That's why he drank so much. And that's why he became so depressed and paranoid late in life that his fourth wife Mary had to take him to the Mayo Clinic for electro shock treatment. He couldn't hold back his demons of compromise. He couldn't live with himself, Grace. That's why he took his own life with one of his hunting rifles."

"Demons of compromise?" Grace repeated, with a look of horror in her eyes.

"That's much too complex to get into now," I replied, suddenly realizing that our dialectic had focused the Holy Flame of God much too intensely upon the dark regions of her unconscious personality. "I don't think I could even explain it to you if I tried. It has to do with a deep understanding of the shadow self. Suffice to say that a writer who compromises his talent has nothing new to say because he's been kicked out of the Far Country of God where he got his best thoughts, ideas, and inspiration; that certain geography of the soul where the Light of God shines brightest. I've followed the career

185

path of many contemporary artists—actors, writers, painters, and especially singers like Leonard Cohen whom I call the 'guru of angst'—and it amuses me to see how their success has robbed them of the precious flame of their individual talent—"

"Success will never rob you, Oriano; I'm sure of that," Grace jumped in, with that faith-imbued Sister of Mercy certainty in her voice that made me smile.

"Probably not," I replied…

Over the weekend I read over my notes on all my conversations with Grace and I was amazed at what emerged. I could not believe it, but before I put down my notebook Sunday morning an image of a bridge began to form in my mind.

I shut my eyes. On one side of the bridge I saw Grace standing, looking at me. I was standing in the middle of the bridge shouting at her to cross over, but she could barely hear me. I had to walk closer so she could hear me. *"Damn!"* I exclaimed.

"What's the matter?" Cathy asked me. She was in the kitchen making blueberry muffins. I was reading my notes in the adjoining living room.

"Nothing," I replied.

"Something's the matter. Tell me," she said.

"It's happening again," I said.

"What? Another story?" Cathy said. She knew I hated it when my Muse interrupted the flow of my writing with an "intrusive" insight.

"Yes," I said.

"Don't fight it. Just go with it," she said, stirring her batter.

"I don't have much choice, do I?"

"You always have a choice," Cathy said, to reassure me.

"No, I don't. Because if I don't go with it I'll regret it; and I hate regret."

"Then just do it," she replied, and poured her batter into the muffin pan.

"I will," I said, and shut my eyes again and let my mind go blank.

186

Slowly the image returned. The bridge in my mind's eye spanned a huge gorge, and a gushing river flowed below. Over time the force of the water had deepened the gorge, and it made me dizzy looking down; so I didn't. I focused my attention on Grace standing on the other side of the gorge, but she wasn't alone now. She was pushing a wheelchair onto the bridge. I couldn't make out the man in the wheelchair, but he had a neck brace to hold his head up and a white tube attached to his throat. I strained to see what was on that side of the bridge, but I couldn't make it out; so I took a few deep breaths and relaxed my attention. Slowly an image began to materialize. Church steeples, domes, cathedrals—many in ruins and some that were being restored by hundreds of men, women, and children scurrying about like busy ants. I stared in awe. And then the thought came to me to turn around and look behind me, and I saw the same image except for one thing—the buildings weren't in ruins, and a bright light shone from each and every one. I turned back to Grace's side of the gorge to check, and the image was exactly the same except that the people over there were busily working on all the temples of worship. I opened my eyes, reflected for a moment or two, and then I broke into laughter. *"I understand!"* I exclaimed.

"What do you understand?" Cathy asked. She was used to my spontaneous outbursts, and wasn't startled by them. She rather enjoyed my creative process.

"My story," I replied.

"What's this one about?" she asked.

"A bridge," I replied, and laughed.

"A bridge?" she said, puzzled. "What kind of bridge?"

"A bridge that spans two worlds," I replied, smiling at the image that my Muse had just given me to capture the archetypal essence of my Platonic relationship with Grace.

"I don't understand," Cathy said.

"I didn't either at first, but I do now. The story has to do with the concept of spiritual revitalization through imagery. The creative mind, if you will; or Platonic ideal, to be exact. Do you remember the spiritual law, as above so below?"

"Yes."

"Well, I've just been given an image of what I have to do with this story. But to be perfectly honest with you, sweetheart; I'm not looking forward to writing it."

"Why not?" she asked, surprised by my comment.

"Because this story is about Grace Kendal."

"Oh," Cathy said, and instantly fell silent.

"What do you think I should do?" I asked, with trepidation.

"It's your story," she curtly replied.

"Of course it is; but what do you think of the idea?"

"I thought you had given up on that idea," Cathy replied in her cold, unresolved personality voice which, as much as she hated to admit it, was her mother's voice.

"I didn't give up on it," I said, knowing very well what was coming; but I had to get it out into the open. "I just kept it to myself, that's all."

"Well if you're not going to share it with me what can I tell you? It's your story; do what you want with it," she said, and began cleaning up the kitchen.

"Why are you so threatened by Grace Kendal?" I asked.

"I'm not threatened," she replied, again in her mother's voice.

"Don't bullshit me. You're whole personality changes whenever I bring up her name. What's the matter with you women, anyway? Must you all be so damn territorial?"

"Don't get angry with me. I said I don't care what you write about. If you want to write about Grace Kendal, then write about her. It's no skin off my nose."

"Your whole face is peeling," I responded, and quickly burst into laughter.

"Funny!" she shot back, her voice dripping with resentment.

"Look Cathy, my fascination for Grace Kendal isn't personal; it's literary. To be precise, it's Platonic. And I'm hoping to translate this Platonic fascination into a novel. That's what that bridge image is all about."

"What do you mean by Platonic fascination? What kind of fascination is that?"

"It's an attraction of the mind, Cathy. That's all it is."

"So you're attracted to her mind now?"

188

"What do you mean by now?

"Just what I said."

"There is no now. For God's sake, Cathy; it's not romantic. It's Platonic. Grace fascinates me because she was a nun for twenty years. She's excited my literary curiosity and I've excited her imagination; that's all. I have a story in her that's shouting to be written. What do you think I am, anyway?"

"I don't know what you are."

"What does that mean? How long have we been together?"

"Ten years."

"And in ten years have my eyes ever wandered?"

"I don't know. Have they?"

"Don't get smart. You know damn well they haven't. I've told you a hundred times that you're a little girl inside that's never had a chance to grow up. I don't want to sound cruel, sweetheart; but this jealousy thing you have is childish. You have absolutely nothing to worry about. I love you, so please do something about this thing you have whenever you feel threatened by people that excite my curiosity—"

"You mean people like Grace Kendal?"

"Grace Kendal today, tomorrow Joanne Henderson!"

"Who's Joanne Henderson?"

"Nobody. And that's my point!"

"Well I just don't think you should ask Grace Kendal to continue your conversations, that's all. I don't think that's right!"

"Well if it's going to make my life easier with you, I won't ask her. But don't you dare expect me to do this again. I'll sacrifice my writing for you this time, but I won't in the future just to accommodate your petty jealousy—"

"It's not petty!" Cathy exploded.

"Oh yes it is! Besides, who knows if she would have even gone for it? But I won't find out now, will I? You have no idea what kind of life this woman has lived. She's not just any woman, Cathy. She was a nun for twenty years, for God's sake! Do you have any idea what kind of life that is? It'll scour your soul. I've read St. Teresa of Avila, so I know something about the nun's life. That's why she fascinates me. It's not every day that I come across a nun who leaves the convent and marries an ex monk and adopts two kids. Writers would give their right arm for this kind of material. Can't you see that?"

"I don't care. I just don't think it's right."

"What, my story?"

"No. I just don't think you should continue your talks with her."

"But I just told you I'm not going to."

"Good. So let's drop it then."

"No. Not until we clear the air first."

"There's no air to clear."

"Oh yes there is. You have to come to terms with this thing you have for other women that threaten you, because if you don't we're in for a bumpy ride."

"Why? Do you plan to make a habit of this?"

"For God's sake, I don't know what kind of people I'm going to meet in my life! You know damn well that if someone interests me I'm going to pay attention because that's what writers do. Do you think we just pluck our characters out of thin air? It doesn't work like that, Cathy. Not for me, anyway. You should know that by now. So you have no need whatsoever to feel threatened—"

"Well I'm sorry for being protective!"

"But I've never given you cause to worry. Why are you so threatened?"

"Because I'm a woman, that's why!" Cathy screamed.

I burst into laughter. I couldn't help myself. It was finally out. Cathy couldn't help herself either and started to laugh too. I got up and put my arms around her and hugged her close to my body and held her tight until all of our anger was gone.

"I love you, sweetheart," I whispered into her ear.

"And I love you, darling," she said, squeezing my body.

"I'm sorry, Cathy."

"Me too."

We kissed, and then I said, "Can we have breakfast now?"

"What would you like?"

"How about blueberry pancakes?"

"And sausages?"

"Sure," I said, and went to get another bag of blueberries that we had picked in the summer and a package of pork sausages from the spare little freezer in her office.

8. A SOUL MOMENT

So my mind was made up for me before I had a chance to ask Grace. I wasn't happy about that because I would never know if she would have said yes or no, and I really wanted to know one way or the other; but I shouldn't have been surprised that it turned out this way, because it was consistent with the unresolved nature of our conversations.

There were many things that I wanted to find out from Grace before I completed my paint job, but I knew it would be impossible to force a conversation with her because the very nature of our dialectical relationship was unpredictable.

I couldn't reveal myself to Grace, despite our shared understanding that there was a possible novel in our relationship; so I had no choice but to place all of my trust in the capricious spirit of our dialectical discourses.

It must have been meant to be this way, I reasoned as I thought about the unexpected turn of events. I had been working myself up to ask Grace for the better part of two weeks, and I was ready; but when I learned just how threatened Cathy would be I had no choice but to preserve the integrity of our love; so I took on the cross and sacrificed myself yet again for the greater good. On the other hand, to be perfectly honest with myself, I may have used Cathy as an excuse to not ask Grace, which was probably the greater truth.

"Grace," I said to her shortly after I began working on the main floor washroom Monday morning (I was cutting in the corners with my brush and Grace was standing in the doorway; she wanted to see what the color looked like), "when I exiled myself out of the kingdom of my own senses to find my true self, I made a commitment for life; but after three and a half years I realized that I had to go back into the world, and, believe me, that was just as hard to do as it was for me to walk away from the world. Did you feel the same way when you decided to leave the convent?"

"Oriano, I don't think anyone can understand what it means to turn your back on the world. The way of the cross is a very special kind of life—"

She fell silent. I had almost forgotten about her moments of unexpected silence, and I was just about to say something when I caught myself; so I waited.

Grace was staring into empty space, and it didn't surprise me to see tears in her eyes. She saw me staring at her, but it didn't register. Then, just as suddenly as she had slipped into her private world, she came out—

"Pardon me, Oriano; what were you saying?"

"I think what I was trying to say is that the spiritual life is unpredictable. We can never know for sure what God has in store for us—"

"Exactly," she said. "I was just saying to Brandon this morning that our life in St. Jude isn't going to be easy. Don't misunderstand me, Oriano. We like it here. We expect to be here for five years before we officially retire; but things are different for us now."

"Oh? In what way, Grace?"

"That's just it, we don't know. Brandon and I had a long talk this past weekend, and neither of us could understand what was happening to us; but we both agreed that something is definitely happening."

"What do you mean by something?" I asked.

"I can't put my finger on it, and neither can Brandon. St. Jude is exactly what we expected, but it's more than that; and we can't seem to understand what God is asking of us. We sold our beautiful home in St. John's and left our family and friends to serve God in St. Jude, and we're doing that; but it feels different this time. It's like we're standing on the edge of a mystery, and we just can't fathom what God has in store for us."

"I know the feeling very well, Grace."

"You do?" she said, with surprise in her voice.

"Yes. I've stood on the edge of mystery so often in my life that I've grown used to it. Let me ask you something, if I may. Do you feel alone?"

"What do you mean?"

"You know what I mean. I know you have a great marriage, Grace; and I know you love your children more than anything, but you feel alone now, don't you? You feel like your whole life has been brought into question, and you feel vulnerable—"

"Oriano, how could you possibly know that? It's like you've just read my soul!"

"It's familiar ground for me, Grace. It's that special place that lies between here and there. It's the no-man's land of the soul—"

Grace smiled at my metaphor, but instantly her face turned into a serious frown and she said, *"No-man's land of the soul?"*

"Yes. The *here* of our life now, and the *there* of our life-to-be. You're on the cusp of change, Grace. You came to St. Jude to serve God, and God is thanking you by offering you a chance for more spiritual growth—"

"But how? Through more pain and suffering? Oh my poor Kathleen. *My poor, poor child—"*

Grace burst into tears. She tried with all her might to stop herself from crying, but emotion overwhelmed her and she wept unselfconsciously.

I wanted to put my arms around her and comfort her, but I couldn't; Grace's personal space did not invite hugs, so I just waited for her to cry herself out.

I didn't have to wait long. Just as suddenly as she had started crying, she stopped. I rolled out several tissues of toilet paper and handed them to her. She wiped her face and then smiled at me. "I'm sorry, Oriano. What must you think of me?"

"I think the world of you, Grace. I think you're one of a kind, and you have absolutely nothing to be sorry for. I can feel your pain, and you bear it well."

"You can't possibly know what I'm feeling, Oriano. I'm a mother going through a very difficult period—"

I smiled at the irony, and as much as I wanted to tell her that I knew about Kathleen, I couldn't; so I just said, "Grace, I did a job for a mother of a Down's baby a few years ago. He was in his late twenties when I did that job, but she confessed to me in private that had she the choice today she would never bring a Down's baby into the world. She's a very good mother; a devout Christian who sacrificed her life for her child. I don't know the particulars, but I'm intimately acquainted with self-sacrifice; so I understood what this mother was telling me about raising a mentally challenged child. And believe it or not Grace, I'm pretty sure I understand where you're coming from too; and in all honesty, I think God brought you to St. Jude for your spiritual growth—"

"How? In what way, Oriano? I don't understand. I just don't understand why God would test me this way—"

"Grace, what's the purpose of a life test, anyway?"

"To open our hearts to more of God's love, that's why I think God tests us. With ever test that we are given we are asked to go a little further on the path to God; but I'm afraid I just can't seem to go any further—"

"Why not?" I asked, hoping she would not withdraw into silence.

"Because I don't know where to go, that's why. I honestly don't know. I have doubts now that I have never had before in my life. I'm not sure of my faith. I'm—"

She stopped in mid thought, but it was too late. I smiled, and said, "God's given you a chance to expand your faith, Grace; that's all. It doesn't mean that you have to abandon it to go further on your path. If I've learned anything about the spiritual life, it's this: one path leads to the next, but when we take the next path it doesn't mean that it invalidates the path we were on; so your faith is not in jeopardy, Grace. Believe me, I know. I'm an eclectic, and I've drawn the best from all the spiritual paths that I have studied and lived by—"

"But I doubt my faith, Oriano. *Oh my precious Jesus; please forgive me—*"

Grace turned and walked away. She went into the living room and sat down on the sofa and put her head in her hands to hide her shame.

"Grace," I said, following her into the living room. "I didn't mean to upset you. I can see you're overwrought. I'm sorry—"

"No," she said, taking her hands away from her face; "I'm just upset, Oriano. I'm going through a very difficult time, that's all. It has nothing to do with what you said. I've been avoiding it for some time now. I thought our move to St. Jude would help me get over it, but it's not helping. I have doubts, Oriano; very serious doubts. I left my Order because I thought I could better serve God in the world, and I have given my all to serve God in the world; my all! I just don't know what more I can give—"

"Your faith," I heard myself say, to my surprise.

"My faith?" she repeated, incredulously.

"Not all of it. Just that part that's keeping you from growing spiritually."

"My faith is my life, Oriano. I can't separate my faith into parts. I believe in Jesus Christ, the Son of God who sacrificed his life upon the cross to wash away the sins of the world; and I believe in our Holy Mother Church, the one true Apostolic Church of God which represents our Lord Jesus Christ on earth. That's my faith, Oriano. It has made me who I am. When I took my vows I gave myself to Jesus in poverty, chastity, and obedience; but most of all, I gave myself to Jesus in service. Oriano, you may not know this; but the Sisters of Mercy is a special Order. It was founded by our Venerable Mother Catherine McAuley in Ireland in 1831 to serve the needs of homeless and abused women and children; so we took a fourth vow besides poverty, chastity, and obedience. Our fourth vow is to serve the poor, the sick, and the ignorant to help them live a full and dignified life; and although I am no longer a Sister of Mercy I am faithful to my vow of service. That's why I left the convent, because in my heart I knew that I could better serve our Lord Jesus in the secular world. How can I separate my faith from my life, Oriano? It's who I am."

"I see you got your hair cut over the weekend," I said, with a smile.

Grace smiled involuntarily. "Do you like it?"

"Very much. Tell me; wasn't that hair you left in the hairdresser's shop also who you were? I know my analogy may be a bit vexing, but I want to make a point. Our physical body goes through changes, and so does our inner body. And we can make these changes voluntarily and go gracefully into the night; or they can be forced upon us."

"By whom? Life? Is that what you're trying to say, that life forces us to change?"

"Life is the Way, Grace; and if we don't go with it we will suffer the pain of resistance. There's an old Stoic poem by Cleanthes that puts this into perspective: *'Lead me, o Zeus, /And thou o destiny, /The way I am bid by thee to go. /To follow I am willing, /For were I recusant, /I do but make myself a slave /And still must follow.'* In short, Grace; we can walk alongside our destiny, or we can be dragged by it."

"But my faith is my life, Oriano; and if I have any doubts about my faith I have doubts about my life—"

"Grace, don't make a mountain out of a molehill. You Christians are good at that. It isn't as complicated as you make it out to be. Your faith is your life, I understand that; but obviously your faith is causing you some anxiety right now. So what does that tell you?"

"I don't know. That's my problem. I'm not sure any more. If only Kathleen—"

Grace caught herself and stopped in mid sentence. I smiled and said, "Kathleen has her own destiny, Grace. She's a beautiful young lady who simply wants to live her own life. I can understand that—"

"But to abandon her faith? I simply cannot fathom that!"

"Maybe she has to abandon her faith to appreciate it. I had to. I had to walk away from my Christian faith to see it for what it really was. It wasn't easy for me, Grace; and it can't be any easier for Kathleen. Believe me, it tore me apart to drop my faith; but I have no regrets today. It took a long time to get over my anger at Christianity; but I have no more animus today. Christianity is a wonderful path to God, but it can also be an obstacle to God. Why did you leave the Sisters of Mercy, Grace? You tell me that you could better serve Jesus out in the secular world; wasn't that abandoning your faith? Did you not take a vow to be a nun for life?"

"Yes, I did; but I felt it was time to go. It wasn't an easy decision to make, Oriano. I agonized over it for years."

"I have no doubt. So why can't you give your daughter the same benefit of the doubt? I'm sure she didn't come to her decision lightly."

"Because she's so young. She doesn't know what she's doing with her life."

"How old were you when you entered the convent?"

Grace smiled. "Yes, I was the same age. But Kathleen has these ideas about life that I just can't accept—"

"Why not? Just because her ideas about life don't fit into your paradigm doesn't mean they're invalid. You can't fit my ideas about life into your paradigm either; but that doesn't mean you're more right than I am, or that I'm more right than you are. It just means that we're on our own path back home to God, that's all—"

"But there's only one path to God, Oriano; and that's through Jesus Christ—"

"*O please!* I'm not your daughter, Grace; and you have no authority over me whatsoever. I'm my own man. And I became my own man because I took my own path to God, which is precisely what Kathleen wants to do. And for you to restrict her path to Jesus Christ alone is to do your daughter a great disservice."

"I love my daughter, Oriano; and I only want what's right for her."

"Then let her go. You know damn well that the only real love is unconditional, so why can't you just let her find her own path? Christianity doesn't have a monopoly on the Way, you know. If Kathleen doesn't agree with some aspects of Christian dogma, that doesn't mean her soul is in danger of eternal damnation. That's a bugaboo that you had better get out of your mind if you want to hold onto your daughter's love. Trust your love, Grace. Trust your love more than your faith. When all is said and done, love is the Way. Love is the place that all spiritual paths lead to; so why fight it? Why fight your love for your daughter? Why pit your faith with your love for Kathleen? That's why you're hurting so much Grace. That's why you're in doubt. And would you like to know how you can stop hurting, Grace?"

"Please. Please tell me, Oriano—"

"Expand your faith voluntarily. Because if you don't expand it voluntarily life will stretch it for you until you can no longer stand the pain and do something as drastic as you did when you left the Sisters of Mercy."

By the look on Grace's face I knew I had struck a chord, and she just stared at me in awe; but she caught herself and said, "How? How can I expand my faith, Oriano. I don't quite know what you mean by that. My faith is complete. It's who I am—"

I smiled at her quandary. "As you said, Grace; you're standing on the edge of a mystery. Why not step into it and find out what this mystery is all about?"

"How? Where do I go? What do I do, Oriano? Do you know?"

"You don't have to go anywhere or do anything, because the Way is everywhere. Just let go and let God. Trust your love, Grace. Don't fetter your love to your faith. If you truly want to serve God, then trust God. Let God lead soul back home. Don't impose conditions on God with your faith. Trust your love in God, Grace. That's all you have to do. Love God by trusting God. Do you remember my analogy of the married man?"

"Yes."

"Well, it's obvious that your love for Jesus won't let you leave your marriage to the Church, so you have two choices. You can stay blind to the lie of Christianity and suffer spiritual anguish; or you can learn to love consciously. It's all a question of choices—"

"What lie? I'm not following you, Oriano."

"The lie that's standing between you and your daughter," I said, and smiled. "Now I'd better get back to work before the paint in my tray skims up on me. Give Kathleen my best when you talk with her, will you please?"

"Yes, of course," Grace said, with a look of guilt in her watery eyes. "You certainly have given me plenty to think about, Oriano. What am I going to do when you leave?"

"Where am I going to go, Grace? I still live in St. Jude."

"I know. But it won't be the same, will it?"

"No, it won't. But we'll see each other off and on, I'm sure."

"I certainly hope so. I promised you and Cathy a nice home-cooked Newfie dinner. Probably cod—"

Grace made tea and called me. I had one more wall to roll in the washroom. When I rolled the wall I went into the dining room and sat down. Grace had two tea cups, on saucers (her best china, for some reason), but the tea was not poured yet; and a plate of assorted cookies.

"I'm going to be supply teaching, Oriano," she said, as she poured my tea. "I'll be starting in the new year."

"Are you looking forward to it?" I asked.

"Yes and no. I would like to get a gas fireplace for the family room and a new patio deck, plus a few other things that I would like to do with the house, and it really is a burden on Brandon; so I've decided to supply."

"Well, just with what you've done so far Grace the house looks wonderful. There may be a few more Tommy Ping ghosts hiding somewhere, but I think we chased most of them out—"

Grace laughed. "Yes, good old Tommy Ping. What kind of man was he, Oriano?"

"A small man who made money his god," I replied, smiling.

"Yes, the world seems to be coming to that, isn't it?" Grace said, with a noticeable sadness in her voice. "Everyone wants more—"

I burst into laughter. She stared at me, wondering what I was laughing at. "Grace, don't call the kettle black," I said, with another chuckle.

"I beg your pardon?" she said, puzzled.

"You're going back teaching. Why? To get a gas fireplace for the family room and a new patio deck—"

She started to laugh. "What a hypocrite I am, aren't I? Here I am pointing my finger at the world and I'm no different! I need to go on a retreat, Oriano. I need to go for a whole month and scour my materialistic soul!"

I chuckled. "Do you go on retreats, Grace?"

"Yes. Every year Brandon and I go on separate retreats. It does the soul good. Have you ever gone on a spiritual retreat, Oriano?"

"Yes. Cathy and I have gone to Villa Loyola in Sudbury several times. Villa Loyola is a home for retired Catholic priests, but they've turned it into a spiritual retreat center for the public to help defray the cost of maintaining the building. Cathy and I get away at least once a year, even if only for a weekend. It helps to maintain balance in our relationship."

"How do you do that, Oriano?"

"What? Maintain balance in our relationship?"

"Yes."

"By getting away from the familiar. By being with like-minded people who re-enforce our spiritual values—"

"What are your spiritual values, if you don't mind my asking?"

I sat back and thought for a moment. I took a sip of tea, and then said, "Freedom and responsibility are the two fundamental spiritual values that I hold dear. We can't have freedom without responsibility, Grace; so my whole life is founded upon the premise of responsible freedom. In short, I believe that there are no free rides in this world; and my philosophy of life is born of my understanding of goodness."

"Goodness?" Grace said, with some surprise. "What do you mean by that?"

"It's a simple philosophy. Just being a good person is where it's at for me. That's the sum total of my truth. But it's not easy in today's world, because everywhere we turn we're expected to compromise ourselves—"

"Isn't that the truth?" Grace jumped in, and smiled at me. It was a smile of satisfaction, because she was given a deeper glimpse into my private life. She took a sip of tea, and in a serious voice said, "Oriano, may I ask you something personal?"

"If you like," I said, anticipating her question.

"What do you mean when you say that you have outgrown your faith? I don't understand what that means, and I would very much like to understand."

I felt urgency in her voice. I also wanted to ask her things that I might not get another chance to ask, and my heart beat faster than normal. I admired her courage—

"Like you said, Grace; your faith is your life," I answered, wondering if I should go there. "I didn't like my life. I didn't like it because it wasn't who I was. My life and I were two different entities—"

201

"I beg your pardon? Two different entities? What does that mean? I am my faith. My faith and I are one—"

"And are you happy being who you are?"

"Yes. Reasonably happy. Why?"

"Why are you questioning your faith then, Grace?"

"I shouldn't have told you that. I'm sorry, Oriano. I wasn't myself—"

To my horror, I heard myself saying, "Take your head out of the sand, Grace. You can't stay in denial for the rest of your life."

"Denial?" she said, startled. "I'm not in denial. I don't question my faith, Oriano. I believe in Jesus Christ and our Holy Mother Church. My whole life is centered upon my faith. I'm not in denial. What makes you think I'm in denial?"

"Do you remember my marriage analogy, Grace? Well, all I can tell you is that I sense that you're becoming aware of the—what can I call it? The infidelity, or unconscious lie of your religion. It's there, but you just don't want to see it—"

"What infidelity? What unconscious lie? I don't understand what you mean. I believe in the divinity of our Lord Jesus Christ; and I believe that he died for our sins; and I believe that he rose up on the third day; and I believe—"

"I know. But like the husband in my analogy who believed his wife was faithful to him didn't make it true; and just because you believe in your faith doesn't make it all true. Your belief has restricted your spiritual freedom, Grace—"

"What do you mean by that?" she jumped on me, in a fearfully defensive voice that I had never heard before. "My belief in Jesus is my freedom, Oriano. Without Jesus I would have no spiritual freedom in my life—"

"I understand that, Grace. All I'm trying to say is that our beliefs are the medium of our spiritual freedom. Did you know that if you put goldfish into a larger tank they grow bigger? The size of their environment, or medium if you will, determines how big they will grow."

Grace looked at me with the most peculiar expression on her face, as if she had just been found out. I smiled. She frowned, and then said, "Is that a metaphor?"

"Yes."

"I'm sorry; I don't follow your meaning."

"Let me express my point another way then. You've heard the expression—and probably used it yourself many times, I'm sure—that small people do small things. What does this refer to, Grace? Doesn't smallness here refer to character?"

Her face lit up. "Yes, it does. Small people do small things. I know that. It takes a great soul to do great things, and life is a struggle to overcome our smallness. Would you like to know how Mother Katherine taught me this simple truth, Oriano?"

"Yes, please," I said.

"Fidelity in little things. That was Mother Katherine's motto. I made it my motto, Oriano. She used to say, 'No task too menial in the service of our Lord.' Grace's eyes faded out, and within seconds she was staring into empty space again. I chuckled. She heard me, and said, "What's so funny?"

"You remind me of Brother Lawrence," I said.

"Ohhh? You've read Brother Lawrence, Oriano?"

"Yes," I said, smiling. "And I also practiced the presence of God."

Grace was beside herself. "You did? Brother Lawrence is my ideal, Oriano; my absolute ideal! I modeled my life on him!"

"I can see that. And that's what I love about you, Grace. You've got the noblest virtue of all—humility."

"Oh, dear heart; if only that were true—"

"I shant argue the point, Grace," I said, smiling at her disciplined modesty. "Suffice to say that smallness of character is the result of smallness of soul, which is determined by our values. The more selfish the values, the smaller the character; and the values that we live by are born of the beliefs we hold. So it follows that to be as free as we can possibly be our beliefs have to be expandable; and the only way to expand our beliefs is to become more conscious of life, and truth, and God—"

"You're doing it again, Oriano," she interrupted me. "Whenever you start talking like that I get goose bumps—"

"I know. This happen sometimes. But it only happens with certain people. I don't do this intentionally, Grace; it just happens—"

"Do what?" she asked, dying to know my secret.

"Letting Soul speak," I replied, smiling at the direction our talk had taken. "Or, to use your words, Grace; letting my Light shine. You needed to hear something; that's why you got goose bumps. It's Soul to Soul communication; that's what it is. But let me bring this point home before we lose it altogether. To grow spiritually we need more freedom, and the freedom we have is determined by the beliefs we live by; so it follows that if we're feeling constrained, if we're feeling boxed in, if we're feeling anxious about this or that, it means that something is holding us back, something is restricting us; and the way to liberate ourselves is to step outside the box, as it were. There's an expression that's becoming popular today. It goes like this: think outside the box. Have you heard it?"

"Yes, I have. But how does that apply to me?"

"If you're questioning your faith—and I think you are, whether you want to admit this to me or not; but not necessarily the fundamentals of your faith, just some aspects—then you're feeling boxed in; and this feeling of being boxed in is nothing more than your spiritual need to grow. It happens to everyone, Grace. Whenever you feel boxed in, it simply means that you need more personal space; and the only way to get it is to expand your consciousness—"

"How, Oriano? How?" Grace blurted out. She caught herself and apologized. "I'm sorry. I didn't mean to butt in like that. I don't understand what came over me."

"That's just you, Grace. Just you," I said, smiling.

"Just me?" she said, with a puzzled look.

"Yes. The inner you. Okay; to answer your question. It's obvious, Grace. We expand our consciousness by stepping outside the box. Our faith, our philosophy, our personal beliefs are our box; and to expand our consciousness we have to expand our spiritual medium. It's that simple, but not simple to do. That's our conundrum."

"Explain that, please."

"What? Our conundrum? Our spiritual medium?"

"Our spiritual medium. What do you mean by that?"

"By spiritual medium I mean the things we live by. As I said, Grace; we're only as free as the things we live by allow us to be. Now, the tricky part—and this is what separates the men from the boys. If one's beliefs are founded upon false premises, then one severely limits their spiritual freedom because one's soul is only as free as one's medium will allow it to be, and inauthenticity inhibits soul's growth. Don't ask me to prove this, because this can't be proven. It has to be experienced to be proven. In other words, Grace; spiritual growth is determined by one's personal medium. So if you feel boxed in it means that you've outgrown your spiritual medium. And that's what I mean when I tell you that I've outgrown my Christian faith. I stepped outside the Christian box; and I don't regret it for a moment because I have never experienced so much freedom in my life."

"I could never do that, Oriano," Grace said, with a look of horror in her eyes. "I belong to Jesus. He's my whole life—"

"Oh Grace, how charming you are!"

"Charming?" she repeated, with a puzzled frown.

"Yes, charming. No one's asking you to deny Jesus. Jesus is the way, the truth, and the life for you; I understand that. Good. Stay with Jesus. He's your salvation. But keep in mind that everything you believe about Jesus may not be true; and it's the inauthentic part of your faith that's inhibiting your spiritual freedom."

"My faith is founded upon the Word of God, Oriano. I have to accept that."

"Then accept it. No one's asking you to give it up. All I'm saying is that there is more spiritual freedom outside the Christian paradigm than you realize. You don't have to believe me. Live and let live. It's your choice, Grace," I said, and got up. "I think we should empty out Michael's room after lunch. I might be able to get the first coat on today…"

Michael's bedroom reflected his personality. Everything was in its place. It wasn't overly neat (I doubt any young man's bedroom can be); but what separated Michael's room from any young man's bedroom that I had painted in twenty years of contracting was the absence of posters on the wall. In fact, the only picture Michael had on his dresser wall was a family photo; and on the dresser were two framed photos of girls. Grace told me that Michael had gone out with them both at the same time, and that he liked having their picture in his bedroom. And on his night stand beside his bed stood a framed photo of his girlfriend with whom he had just broken up before leaving Newfoundland to drive his little Mazda sports car to Ontario.

"I guess he must be brokenhearted," I said to Grace as we began taking the clothes out of his closet and placing them onto the bed in the adjacent bedroom.

"Oh he's young, Oriano. He'll get over it soon enough, if he hasn't already. There are plenty of nice Catholic girls here. He's already met one. He had her here the other night. They shared a pizza watching a late movie together. You might know her. Her name is Connie Theriault."

"Yes, I know her. She's my sister-in-law's niece. She's a nice looking girl. Michael's got great taste, Grace," I said, and laughed.

Grace smiled. "He's a good boy, Oriano. He's never given us one ounce of trouble. Kathleen, on the other hand—well, what can I tell you? She's my reason for leaving the Order—"

I laughed. "And you love her!"

"She's my daughter; what else can I do but love her? Especially now. I have to give her all my love and support until she's mature enough to deal with life on her own. I only hope I'm still around when she does—"

I laughed again, on purpose. Grace smiled, and then laughed too. "Do you think she might drive you to an early grave?" I said, pushing the humor.

Grace did not respond. She just smiled. I felt her anguish. I carried the last of Michael's clothes into the other room and then began taking stuff off the dresser.

"Here, Oriano; I'll do that," she said, and picked up the statue of St. Michael with a rosary draped around one wing and three or four of Michael's skiing medals draped on the other wing. She was about to carry it into the spare bedroom when for no apparent reason she tripped and the statue hit the corner of the small wooden stool that Michael used to reach up into the top shelf of his clothes closet and St. Michael's head came flying off and rolled outside the bedroom and into the hallway.

"Oh goodness," I said, and rushed to help Grace.

She wasn't hurt, but she was devastated that she had broken Michael's statue. *"Oh dear,"* she moaned. *"What have I done?"*

I went out into the hallway and picked up St. Michael's head and the strangest thing happened—a sudden fright possessed me. A cold, instant fright.

"Oriano, what's wrong?" Grace said, alarmed by the look on my face. "You're as white as a ghost."

"I don't know. I just had the strangest feeling. I don't know what it is. Here, Grace; I think you can glue the head back on. It looks like a clean break."

Grace took St. Michael's head and tried it on the statue and saw that it was a clean break and with a bit of glue it would look as good as new; but she was worried about me. "Are you sure you're alright?" she asked me, with a concerned look.

"I think so. I can't explain it, Grace. I just had the strangest feeling—"

"What kind of feeling?"

"I don't know. I can't explain it. I sure hope this isn't some kind of omen—"

"What do you mean, Oriano?" she said, alarmed.

"St. Michael's head," I said, with a nervous chuckle. "I held it in my hand and I felt an instant fright. Like something horrible is going to happen—"

"To you?" Grace said, with a horror in her eyes.

"I don't know. I honestly don't know. But I do know one thing, Grace—"

"What? What, Oriano?" she pressed me, fearing for her son.

"Whenever something out of the ordinary happens, it's for a very good reason. I've experienced this before, Grace; many times—"

"What do you mean?" I don't understand—"

"Whenever something out of the ordinary happens it means that Spirit is trying to tell us something. It's a sign, Grace; but I don't know what it means."

"But I tripped and fell, Oriano. I broke the head off St. Michael. *Oh my precious Jesus, please protect my son; please protect my Michael—"*

207

"Grace, Grace; don't panic. It was me who felt the fright, not you. It's me that the sign was directed to—"

"Do you think so?" she asked, with alarm all over her face.

"Yes. I felt the fright, not you. Don't concern yourself. With a little glue you can put St. Michael's head right back onto his shoulders. Don't fret, Grace—"

"But what about you? Don't you feel concerned? You must have felt something—"

"I did; but I don't know what it means. *But hey, my life's in God's hands!"*

Grace's face lit up. Composing herself, she smiled and said, "I think I have some crazy glue in Brandon's office. Let me check."

I cleaned off Michael's dresser and then moved it away from the wall. Grace came back. "Did you have any?" I asked.

"Yes. Let's put St. Michael's head back on," she said, with her Sister of Mercy voice of confident assurance. She even looked taller.

I smiled at how quickly Grace had composed herself. She held St. Michael's head and squeezed crazy glue onto the neck and then squeezed some onto the broken neck of the body and waited before fitting the two together.

"There," she said, a minute or so later; "a perfect fit." And then she carried the statue into Brandon's office and placed it onto his desk with a scotch-taped note attached to St. Michael's chest that said "Do not remove."

When she came back into the room Grace stripped the bed and I pulled it away from the wall. "I'll just go and put these in the laundry room," she said.

I followed her downstairs to get my roll of poly that I used for drop sheets. In the laundry room Grace turned to me and said, "Oriano, what do you think it means?"

"I wish I knew, Grace."

"You were white as a ghost."

"Was I?"

"Yes."

"Who is St. Michael, anyway? Isn't he the Archangel who slew the dragon?"

208

"Yes. St. Michael slew Satan in the battle of heaven. He's the patron saint of our Holy Mother Church. He defends us against evil. Do you know what St. Michael's name means, Oriano?"

"No."

"It means 'Who is like God.'"

"Is that why you called your son Michael?"

"Yes."

"Did you give your son the statue, Grace?"

"Yes, when we adopted him. We wanted St. Michael to protect our son."

"Against the dragon?" I asked, hoping to draw her out.

"Yes, the evil of the world. We gave it to our son so St. Michael can protect him from paternal evil. His biological father—"

Grace stopped in mid sentence. I waited, but I sensed that she regretted saying what she did. "You believe there's evil out there, Grace?" I said, to break the silence.

"Yes. Don't you?"

"I don't know what to call it, really. Maybe it's evil, maybe it's something else. Maybe it's just man's own negative energy that we see as evil. If anything, I'm inclined to lean in that direction—"

"What direction?" she asked.

"That we create our own evil in the world."

"You don't believe in the Devil, Oriano?"

"Yes and no. I think the Devil exists because we created him. I don't think he exists in his own right, as such. I think the story of the Devil tempting Adam and Eve in the Garden of Eden is a myth. A teaching fable of some sort—"

"I don't believe that for a second. I have witnessed the Devil at work in life—" Grace stopped abruptly, and once again faded into that far-away place.

A minute or so later she came back and smiled as though picking up from where she had left off with no awareness of her absence. I smiled back and said, "I've witnessed the Devil at work in life too, Grace. My father was possessed by an unclean spirit; but then I discovered Jungian psychology and my perspective on evil was modified—"

"Modified?" she said, shocked by my comment. "How can you modify evil? Evil is evil, regardless whether we see it through Christian or Jungian eyes. I don't think psychology can enlighten us on evil, Oriano. *I don't think that for one minute!"*

"Maybe modify was the wrong word. I just meant that I began to see evil differently, that's all," I replied, feeling that I was treading on very sensitive ground.

"Evil is evil, Oriano; and it doesn't matter how we see it, it's still the Devil's work."

I smiled at her conviction. "Are you afraid of evil, Grace?"

"I'm afraid of the Devil, and I won't hesitate to admit it; but Jesus protects me. What do you think is responsible for all the evil in the world? Why would a man rape a woman, Oriano? *Why, if he wasn't driven by the Devil?"*

Her question hit me in the chest like a rubber bullet, and I felt stunned. I stared at her, and for the first time in all our talks I saw her for who she really was, a devout Roman Catholic to the very core of her being for whom Satan was a living reality and evil an ever present danger to the soul of man. I had to step back to center myself. I took a deep breath, and very calmly said, "What drives a man to create a billion dollar empire, Grace; the god of mammon, or his own insatiable ego? Do you remember Shelly's poem *Ozymandias*? His mighty empire didn't amount to much over time, did it? Just a bunch of rubble in the sands of time. Was it all vanity, as the Preacher tells us in *Ecclesiastes*? Who knows what drives a man to rape a woman? Psychiatry tells us that these men are so lacking in self-esteem that they have to confirm their identity by subjugating women to their will. Is that evil, or an aberrant psychological condition? Maybe it's both; I don't know. That's all I'm saying."

"I forgot; you're an eclectic, and you look at every possible angle, don't you?"

"I try," I said, and smiled to allay her fears of my perspective on evil.

"Well, what can I say? I've been a Roman Catholic my whole life; how else can I look at the world? I see evil out there, and I see the Devil at work in people's lives. But I also see God at work in life too; so I will not despair. *I will not, Oriano!"*

Grace had found her center, but she also revealed something about herself that told me I had definitely made the right decision to not pursue our relationship.

We finished cleaning out Michael's room and I went back to painting the washroom, and as I worked I thought of St. Michael slaying the dragon and Grace's deep-seated fear of evil possessing her son because his biological father had raped his mother...

We both felt it, but neither of us could talk about it—our Platonic relationship was coming to an end; and a sense of urgency could be detected in each other's voice.

Grace was still perplexed by our relationship. She still had not come to terms with the symbolic implications of our dialogues; but I did. I knew that fate had brought us together to bridge the great divide that existed between Christianity and Christ's original message; and I tried to bring this up after lunch that day.

I was applying the finishing coat to the washroom and Grace was once again standing in the doorway. It was like she had to get as much of me as she could before I left; that's why she cancelled her coffee date with Pauline—

"Grace, do you feel we were brought together for a reason?" I asked.

"Yes, I do Oriano; but what? Can you tell me?"

I stopped painting and turned to her. I was standing on my two-step stepladder and I stepped down to be on equal footing; I didn't want the symbol of me standing higher than her to affect our talk. "Do you believe in the divine law of synchronicity?" I asked.

"What do you mean?" she asked, her eyes as big as two moons.

"You know what synchronicity means, don't you?"

"Yes, of course. It means coincidence, does it not?"

"Meaningful coincidence. Synchronicity points to a mysterious order in the universe; an omniscient guiding presence. Have you read Hermann Hesse?"

"Yes. I taught him. His novel *Steppenwolf* and some of his poetry."

"Good. Well, Hesse believed that there is no such thing as accidents in the circle of synchronicity. He believed that destiny plays a part in man's life; and so do I. I think that our meeting was destined—"

"But why, Oriano?" she jumped in excitedly, her eyes on fire with unquenchable curiosity. "I think so too, but I don't know why. *Can you tell me why?"*

I had to chuckle. "I think we met to precipitate the individuation process."

"Pardon me? I don't understand that. What do you mean by individuation process?"

"Synchronicity has interested me for a long time, Grace; so I read everything I could on the subject, starting with Jung's seminal essay on synchronicity. And everyone who has studied synchronicity seems to agree that meaningful coincidences happen in a person's life for their spiritual growth, or what Jung calls the individuation process; and as presumptuous as this may sound, I suspect that we were brought together to help you step outside the box that's keeping you from taking the next step in your spiritual journey—"

"What box?" Grace interjected, with a twinge of fear in her voice.

"Your faith," I replied, with matter-of-fact frankness. "But before you defend yourself—which I know you feel compelled to do, Grace—let me share something with you. This is why I believe synchronicity brought us together. Saturday Cathy and I went into the city to do our grocery shopping. Of course, I had to have my Chapters' fix; so she dropped me off at Chapters while she did Wally-World—"

"Wally-World?" Grace asked, puzzled.

"Wal-Mart," I explained, and laughed.

"Oh, yes. I've been to Wal-Mart. It's a very busy store, Oriano."

"The busiest in town. In any event, I was browsing one of the bargain book aisles when for no apparent reason a book fell off a shelf directly in front of me and landed at my feet. Some people attribute this kind of thing to book angels, or library fairies; but however it happened, I picked up the book and read the cover and then burst into laughter."

"Why? What was the title of the book?" Grace asked.

"*Soul Moments*, by Phil Cousineau," I replied. "It's a collection of stories on meaningful coincidences. And then by pure chance, which I believe was divinely choreographed also, I opened the book at random and read something that Jung said. I can't quote exactly what the line was, but basically it had to do with Jung's belief that individuation has to do with finding meaning in one's life; that when we need more meaning in our life and don't know where to find it, the divine law of synchronicity comes into play in our life—"

"But isn't that Divine Providence? Isn't that what God does all the time, intervene in our life to show us the way?" Grace responded, all excited.

Grace made me laugh. "Yes, God does that. I prefer to call it Divine Spirit. Jung calls it meaningful coincidence, and the Chinese call it the Tao; but whatever name we call it, it happened to me at Chapters last Saturday. I wasn't quite sure how to define our relationship, Grace. I knew it was Platonic, but I didn't know why exactly. I sensed the symbolic implications of our daily talks, but I couldn't fathom why they were so—"

"Meaningful?" Grace burst out, and I could feel the goose bumps on her skin.

"Yes, meaningful," I replied, with the biggest smile. "But more than that, really. You see, Grace; they weren't all that meaningful to me because I don't have this need to be better connected to the universe of meaning, as it were; but you do. And the book that fell off the shelf explained the puzzle for me. I sat down and began reading it in the store, and by the time Cathy came to pick me up I had my answer—"

"What Oriano? What did you find out?" she asked, unable to restrain herself.

"Synchronicity happens for a reason, Grace; and I think we met to help you see that one can live the spiritual life outside Christianity. I know this may be an affront to your faith, because deep down inside I know that you honestly believe that the only way to

God is through Jesus Christ; but it's this conceit that's stifling your spiritual growth—"

"Do you think so?" she asked, with a look of horrified guilt on her face.

"Yes, I do. I think that being a Bride of Jesus Christ for twenty years had prejudiced you, Grace," I said, and burst into laughter. I couldn't help myself.

To my dumbfoundment, Grace saw my humor and laughed too. "Maybe you're right, Oriano. I can't be sure of anything anymore, can I?"

"That's why I think we met, Grace. I think the gods of fate brought us together for you to see that there's room in God's heart for everyone, regardless of their faith. Jesus may be your savior, Grace; but he's not the only savior that God sent into the world. But what astonished me most about the book was the author's description of synchronicity. Would you like to know what he calls a synchronistic experience?"

"What?" she asked, her eyes hungry for all she could get.

"A *soul moment.* That's what he calls an experience of synchronicity. He describes it as an electrifying experience; a visitation by a god; a palpable inrush of grace and power and meaning; an inexplicable conviction that one is moving beyond fate and into destiny; a *soul moment.* Now tell me the truth, Grace; doesn't that describe some of the incredible conversations that we've been having from the first day we met?"

Grace folded her hands as in prayer and put them to her chest, and shutting her eyes she softly said, *"Oh my precious, sweet Jesus—*"

She had a look of rapture on her face, and I felt a sudden inrush of energy. "Don't you feel it right now, Grace?" I said, incredulously.

"Yes," she responded, in a soft whisper. *"Yes, dear heart; I can feel the presence of our Lord Jesus. I can feel him—"*

I felt the presence of the Holy also, and it gave me goose bumps; but I didn't feel the presence as Jesus Christ, as such. I had experienced the presence of the Holy before, especially when writing, and every time that I let go and let Soul speak as I had done so many times with Grace; but I still had work to do—

"Excuse me, Grace," I said (she had gravitated closer to me in the washroom and was standing by the sink); "I have to paint around the sink—"

"Oh!" she said, startled. "I'm sorry, Oriano—"

"It's alright. I have to brush in around the sink before I roll the wall."

"Yes, of course," she said, apologetically.

I smiled, and then chuckled. "To make a long story short, Grace; I think meeting you was divinely choreographed. I only wish we could continue these incredible conversations after my work here is done, but I'm afraid that's not in the cards."

Grace gave me her Mona Lisa smile. Then she looked deep into my eyes, and in a sad but firm voice said, "I'm afraid you're right, Oriano."

"But it's been grand, hasn't it?" I said, and burst into a hearty laugh.

She couldn't help herself and broke into laughter also to relieve the pressure of the most satisfying *soul moment* of our relationship, which I knew instantly that I would describe in my novel as the spiritual climax of our Platonic love...

9. THE PARADOX OF CHRISTIANITY

Something strange happened. It may have happened to me before, but I never noticed it because I had never experienced a *soul moment* for so long. The longest I had experienced a *soul moment* was for an hour or so; but with Grace it lasted well over a month.

When I went back to Grace's house the next day to finish painting Michael's room I noticed something distinctly different about Grace. I couldn't put my finger on it right away, but over our morning cup of tea (in her old china) it came to me—*the magic between us was gone!*

The puzzled look in Grace's eyes told me that she was questioning the whole nature of our relationship. Her body language betrayed her. She looked and acted as though she had just been caught with another man, and Grace had trouble looking me in the eye.

Having been there myself (literally), I could read the signs clearly; and Grace was ashamed. Her shame was so palpable that I could cut it with a knife. Grace had gotten involved with me Platonically, and for whatever reason she now felt guilt and shame for her infidelity to Jesus Christ, her Lord and Savior. I just knew that.

But why? What happened overnight? What had she done to feel that way? There was no denying what I sensed. I trusted my intuition completely, and Grace exhibited all the signs of the guilt and shame of infidelity; but why?

I had to find out; but how? From the moment I walked into her house our conversation felt strained, as though she wanted to avoid me. I went straight to Michael's room and began rolling the white paint onto the ceiling, but Grace didn't come around once; and this puzzled me, given the extraordinary experience that we had shared the previous day. But she did call me for tea.

I sat down, smiled, and said, "Didn't you sleep well last night, Grace?"

"As a matter of fact, no. I tossed and turned all night long."

"Oh," I said, hoping she would elaborate; but she didn't. She just stirred her tea, round and round. I had to break the tension. "What's the matter, Grace?"

"Nothing," she replied, forcing herself to smile.

"It's not my place to say this, Grace; but I can't help but sense that something's changed." I waited for her to reply, but she didn't. She continued stirring her tea and avoiding my eyes. I had to break the silence. "Nothing's happened, Grace. Nothing at all. What you're feeling is born of your own imagination—"

"I beg your pardon," she said, coming alive. "What do you mean, what I'm feeling? How could you possibly know what I'm feeling? How?"

"I have a sense for these things," I said, wanting very much to smile; but I didn't.

Grace looked at me, but she could not hold her gaze for very long. "I don't know what it is, Oriano. I just feel that I'm on the verge of some catastrophic change—"

She burst into tears. She got up and walked out of the room and didn't come back. I left my tea and went back to Michael's room and began cutting in the corners with my brush. I rolled on the first coat of paint, and then I went home for lunch.

After lunch I did the second coat and began cleaning up. I took off all my masking tape and then went out to see Grace. She was in the kitchen, making a meatloaf for dinner. It was well past tea time, and she hadn't called me for tea.

"I'm all done, Grace," I said. "You said you wanted to re-arrange the furniture. How would you like it?"

"Oh," she said, sounding surprised; but I could still feel the strain in her voice. "Don't bother, Oriano. I can take care of that."

"It's no bother," I said.

"I'd like to vacuum first. Please, don't bother. Sit down and I'll make us tea."

"Okay. Put the kettle on. I'll just go and put my stuff downstairs."

When I sat down for tea Grace forced herself to look at me. "I did have a difficult night, Oriano. I'm not myself today. Please forgive me."

"There's nothing to forgive, Grace. You're plate's been full for quite some time now. I understand."

"But do you, Oriano? Do you?"

"Yes, I do," I said, with a warm, commiserating smile.

"I don't think so," she curtly replied, in a new and quite different tone of voice that I had been expecting. "You can't possibly know what I'm going through—"

"Probably the same thing you went through when you decided you no longer wanted to be a Bride of Jesus Christ; a sense of guilt and shame—"

"I beg your pardon," she said, astonished by my comment. "How could you possibly know what I felt when I left my Order? I find that to be terribly impertinent, Oriano. As a matter of fact, I find many things that you have said to me terribly impertinent—"

I chuckled. Finally, it was out. I was right. I had read her correctly. Her shadow had been forced out by the intensity of our *soul moment* the day before. It was too much for her unconscious falseness, and now her inauthentic self had taken over her personality to protect itself from the scorching, soul-cleansing Holy Flame of God; and poor Grace had no idea whatsoever and was completely beside herself.

"Wherein lies my impertinence?" I said, challenging her unconscious Christian falseness. "What did you do, Grace; examine your conscience last night? Is that it? Do you think I'm a threat to your faith? Is that why you think I'm impertinent?"

"Yes," she briskly replied.

"Why? I haven't asked anything of you. You've taken a stroll with me into a meadow of wild flowers in the Far Country of God, and you enjoyed the beauty and fragrance of these wild flowers while I worked for you; and now you've decided that you don't like these flowers any more. Why?"

"Wild flowers? What flowers?"

"The flowers that are growing in the far country of your undiscovered soul, Grace. But I can see that you have no memory of these flowers now. But that's okay. In a week or two, perhaps a month, or five years from now you'll hear the haunting call again."

"Call? What call? What are you talking about, Oriano?"

I smiled and stood up. Looking down into Grace's eyes, with tears in my voice, I said, "The call you heard when you entered the convent; and the call you heard when you left your Order; and the call you heard when you fell in love with your husband; and the call you heard for motherhood; and the call you heard to come to St. Jude. The call from the Far Country of God, Grace," I added, for clarity's sake; and then I turned and walked away from the table with the certain knowledge that our Platonic relationship—that unbelievably exciting, spiritually uplifting, enrapturing *soul moment*—was over.

I felt Grace's eyes following me out the dining room. I walked downstairs with a heavy step, broken-hearted that our relationship had to end that way.

Sadly, I cleaned up and marked the left-over cans of paint for touch-ups and loaded my van and left. I didn't have the heart to say good-bye.

I mailed Grace my invoice so I wouldn't have to see her again; but she surprised me and dropped off her cheque at the hospital office where Cathy worked. Cathy brought the sealed envelope home and gave it to me. It was a thank-you card with my cheque.

The card said: "Oriano, thank you for a job well done. And thank you for the wonderful conversations. Grace."

I was well into another job by the time I got the card from Grace, but by coincidence Patty Malone, a young mother of four whose house I was painting and a graduate of the Royal Conservatory of Music in Toronto, was a devout Roman Catholic who played the piano and sang in Grace's choir, initiated a conversation about Grace.

"Grace Kendal says that you're a fascinating man, Oriano," Patty said, within hours of my job. I had started with her living room which she wanted textured and painted. It was two weeks before Christmas and the rush was on. "She said you're one of the best-read people she's ever met. But you know what? I told her that didn't surprise me. My girlfriend's husband in Parry Sound is a housepainter and he's a voracious reader too. He has his master's degree in psychology and taught school for two or three years, then he quit and got into house painting. He says he likes it because it frees his mind to think—"

"*Quelle coincidence!*" I said, and laughed.

"So, tell me Oriano; did Grace ask you to join the choir? You're Catholic, aren't you?" Patty asked, fishing to find out what took Grace weeks to get out of me.

"No, and no," I said, and laughed again.

"No, she didn't ask you; and no, you're not Catholic?"

"Yes to both. Grace heard me whistling and singing to myself several times while I painted her house, but she never asked me to join her choir. She knew I didn't go to Church anymore."

"That's true. I've never seen you in Church. Aren't you Catholic? You're Italian, aren't you?"

"Born in Italy, but no less Canadian than Pierre Burton," I said, and laughed.

"How come?" Patty asked, innocently.

"How come what?"

"You don't go to Church?"

"I don't need religion in my life, Patty. I threw away my crutches long ago," I said, with another chuckle, very much enjoying how she probed me.

To my surprise, Patty laughed too. "I can understand that," she said, with a big smile on her face. "My father was a strict Catholic. He's old Irish, and he ruled by the book. We couldn't get away with anything—"

Within the week I learned that Patty's strict Roman Catholic father who raised his children to be good little Catholics had divorced her mother after having an affair with her mother's best friend. He had his marriage annulled and married his lover; but after seven years of marriage to the woman who broke up his family he left her too, and now he was so racked with guilt that he suffered from chronic bouts of depression that Patty had trouble dealing with—

"He calls me up every two or three weeks to tell me his troubles," Patty revealed to me. "I'm the only one in the family who has anything to do with him. But I don't know what to tell him. The last time he called he asked me what I thought he should do. He's in love with a woman thirty years younger than him—probably more, knowing my father; and he wants to know if I think it's okay to marry her. What was I supposed to say to him? I told him that he always did what he wanted, so why bother asking me? I don't think he wanted to hear that because I haven't heard from him for two months. I didn't know what else to tell him. And then I got a call from Iris—my

220

mother's best friend who stole her husband—and she wanted me to talk some sense into my father. What do they think I am, anyway?"

"And I suppose they're all good Catholics? Please tell me they are, Patty!"

"They are. My father doesn't believe in mixed relationships. I told you, Oriano; he's a strict Roman Catholic—"

"O man, thy name is contradiction!" I said, and burst into laughter.

Patty laughed too, more at my spontaneous response than the absurdity of her father's situation. "It was okay for him to break the rules, but it wasn't okay for us," Patty said, very soberly with spent anger in her voice. "But that's okay. He's paying for it now. He's not a happy man, Oriano. He's lonely and miserable, and I don't feel sorry for him."

"How's your mother these days?" I asked.

"She's fine now. But she's not the same. He broke her heart. She gave up everything to raise her family, and then he does that to her. How would any woman feel after that?"

"Betrayed," I said.

"Exactly. But mom's okay now. It took her a few years to get her life together, but she did. She's a strong woman, and we love her very much. She's coming here for Christmas and I can't wait. We're very close."

"Wonderful," I said. "Tell me, Patty; how come you still go to Church after what your father did? Didn't he give you cause to question your faith?"

"At first I did. But I don't anymore. I know that there are a lot of Catholics who pay lip service, but I don't care what they do. I go to Church because I love the music. I've been the Church organist for five years now. That's why I'm glad Grace started the choir. I wanted to start one, but I had my hands full with my children and piano lessons. But they're all in school now and I can contribute. We're putting on a Christmas concert, you know."

"Really?"

"Yes. Grace is on us like butter to bread."

I laughed. "She's quite the lady, isn't she?"

"She's steel, Oriano. Pure steel."

"That's her nun's training. She's made of a precious alloy, Patty."

"Alloy?" Patty queried.

"Yes, alloy. When a person lives the way of the cross their secular life is broken down and then smelted into a precious alloy. That's what separates the true Christian from phonies like your father. It's not an easy path, Patty."

"What path?"

"Christianity. Being a good Christian is hard. Very hard. Do you know why?"

"Why?"

"Because it asks too much of us, that's why. It imposes conditions upon us that few of us can live up to. That's why I admire Grace so much. She's true to the conditions. But she's hurting now because she's outgrown her conditions."

"Do you think so? I sensed that, you know."

"Did you really?" I said, amazed by Patty's intuition.

"Yes. I didn't know what it was until just now. I think you're right. I think she's—I don't know what. What did you say it was?"

"I'd better not say, Patty. I like Grace. She's one of the nicest people I have ever met, and one of the most genuine Christians. I just hope she works it all out."

"Work what out?"

"Her dilemma."

"What dilemma?" Patty asked, genuinely perplexed.

"The dilemma that all Christians have to face at one time or another in their life—the spiritual limitations of their faith. You see, Patty; soul—the inner you—needs freedom as our body needs air. Our soul breathes freedom as our body breathes air, and if our soul doesn't get the freedom it needs to grow then we will suffer what existentialists call angst. But I think this kind of suffering is stupid. In fact, I think it's pure idiocy."

"I don't believe everything I'm told. I know better. I saw what religion did to my father, and I don't agree with a lot of things the Church says; but I still got to Mass every Sunday. That's not going to stop me. I think it's good to raise children in a religious environment. I think they need a sense of morality in their life. I think it's good for

222

them to believe in God. They can make up their own mind about religion when they grow up; but where would we be in society without the moral guidelines of religion?"

"I love your attitude, Patty," I said, surprised by her uncommon wisdom. "You don't have to live the way of the cross to appreciate Christ's message to the world. That's Grace's dilemma. She can't see beyond her rigid faith. That's why she's hurting so much."

"Do you think so? I wondered about that, you know. I got the feeling that something wasn't right with her. But she has a fantastic voice. Have you heard her sing?"

"Yes. She sang for me one day. Patty, I didn't mean to disclose what I did about Grace. I'm just so impressed by her that I've given her dilemma a lot of thought."

"I understand. You don't have to elaborate. My father's in the same boat. Do you know what his parish priest told him to do? He told him to talk to someone in the family who would understand him. He said it would be good for him to get it off his chest. So guess who he called?"

I laughed. "And you told him what you thought?"

"I didn't want to, but he pushed me; and now he hasn't called for two months. I wonder if he's going to call for Christmas. He probably won't, you know. My father's really stubborn. Everything has to be on his terms."

"Why is that? That seems to be a Christian thing, you know; everything on its terms. That's one reason why I had to leave the Church. I couldn't take the pressure."

"Do you miss it at all?" Patty asked, in all innocence.

"At first I did, but not anymore. I live in a different world now, Patty. I breathe a different air. It's a little more rarified, but I love the freedom."

"Do you like music, Oriano?"

"Very much. In fact, I was going to ask if you'd play a tune or two."

"What did you have in mind?"

"Do you know The Last Rose of Summer?"

"Do you like that?" she asked, with a look of surprise.

"It's one of my favorite," I said.

"That's the piece I chose for my finals at the Royal Conservatory," Patty said, with the biggest smile at the amazing coincidence.

I burst into laughter. I shouldn't have been surprised by the coincidence, but coincidences always surprise me; and this one was a little too poignant. "You wouldn't by any chance be taking any more piano students, would you?" I asked, pushing my luck.

"Yes. In the New Year. Why, are you interested?"

"Not for me. Cathy," I said, still glowing from the coincidence. "Can I buy a year's piano lessons? I want to surprise Cathy for Christmas. The piano's just sitting in our living room, and she's been meaning to take lessons again; so why not?"

"That would make a wonderful Christmas gift. But you know what? If you do, I think I'll hold onto your money just in case she doesn't want to take piano lessons. Okay?"

I smiled at Patty's thoughtfulness. No wonder her father cried on her shoulder, I thought to myself. "Where do you get your wisdom from, Patty?" I asked.

"My music," she replied, without hesitation. "My music keeps me sane, Oriano."

"There's much more truth to that than you think, Patty. Have you heard of the Mozart effect?"

"Yes, I have. I haven't followed up on it yet, but I want to try it out on my kids. Why, do you like Mozart?"

"Beethoven's my favorite composer, but Mozart's a close second. In any event, I want to share a dream with you that I had a couple of nights ago. I'm big into dreams, Patty. I'm very Jungian. A couple of nights ago I dreamt of Grace's husband, Brandon. I went to his school in my dream and explained the Mozart effect to him. I told him he should play Mozart in his classrooms as background music, because it would help the kids to concentrate and learn. Quiet background music to awaken the soul, as it were. I often put on Beethoven when I'm writing—"

"Isn't that interesting," Patty said, her face alight with excitement. "Do you know that Mr. Kendal just asked me the other day to teach music at his school?"

"Quelle coincidence!" I burst out, and laughed again. I couldn't help myself. The coincidences just kept mounting, and the excitement was becoming too much. "And you said yes, of course?"

"I'm seriously thinking about it," she said, with a radiant smile of astonishment on her uncommonly wise and loving face…

It was curious, all the little coincidences that I experienced during and after my work at Grace's house; but I knew the reason. I knew that when I got into the "zone," as I referred to *soul moments*, the stars aligned themselves to make my life flow that much more smoothly; but what I didn't expect was for my relationship with Grace to continue on the inner planes in the world of my dreams.

My first dream happened several days before Christmas. I met Grace at her house in my dream (the dream worlds are parallel realities), and although nervous and embarrassed from the way we parted company, I said to her, "Grace, I'm sorry for leaving the way I did; but you weren't yourself."

"I know. I was in a state, Oriano. I do get like that every so often. I don't know how Brandon puts up with it. My children learned to keep their distance when I fall into that state. Mother Katherine called this state 'black moods.' We all have them, she said. I do apologize, Oriano—"

"Whenever Ernest Hemingway got into this state he called it 'black ass,' I said, smiling at Grace's revelation. "But the problem with the great writer was that he couldn't get himself out of his dark moods and finally his 'black ass' destroyed him. That's the danger of giving in to the shadow side of our personality—"

"But how do we stop it?" Grace blurted out. "In the convent we were told that prayer was the answer, but it didn't work all the time; just sometimes. I can't pray myself out of my black moods anymore, Oriano. I cannot—"

"What is a black mood, Grace? What causes these moments of darkness to possess us? What are they? Do you know?"

"No. I wish I did, but I don't. Do you?"

"Yes, I do. Do you know that Soul is a happy entity? It is, Grace. I can't prove it, but I know this from personal experience. The more spiritually centered one is, the happier he will be; so it follows logically that these black moods that possess a person point to a spiritual imbalance in one's life—"

"I'm not imbalanced, Oriano. My whole life is centered in Jesus Christ. The first thing I do when I get up in the morning is ask Jesus to bless my day; so I'm not spiritually imbalanced. Whatever gave you that idea?"

"Then why the black moods, Grace?" I asked.

"I don't know. I honestly don't know," she replied.

Grace did not know that we were on the other side, in the parallel world of dreams; she thought that we were in her house on the physical plane having another one of our fascinating conversations. But I knew.

I was conscious in my dream, and I smiled at Grace's quandary. "Grace, have you ever tried centering prayer?" I asked.

"Yes, but it doesn't help anymore. The only thing I can do is wait until it passes. That's all I can do. I don't like it, but prayer doesn't help anymore. It just doesn't help—"

"Have you tried Prozac?" I said, and laughed.

Grace looked at me, and then smiled. "You do have a wonderful sense of humor, Oriano. It never fails to lighten my spirits. Are you always so buoyant?"

"I told you Grace, Soul is a happy entity," I said, and woke up laughing. I got up and recorded my dream in my notebook because I knew that our relationship was still going on in the inner worlds and that this dream was just the first of many more to come; but I didn't know when they would come, or even if I would remember them.

That's what puzzled me about my dream travel experiences to the other side. I didn't have the control that I wanted to have. It worked sometimes, but not all the time; so I knew that I could meet Grace in my dreams any time, and I did see her again briefly on the eve of the new millennium—

"Happy millennium!" I shouted to her, waving. She was standing by herself staring at the fireworks. We were in her hometown of St. John's, Newfoundland.

Why she was standing all alone, I did not know; nor did it occur to me for it to be out of the ordinary. Grace waved back.

226

"Happy millennium!" she shouted. *"I'm going to have you over for dinner soon! I promise!"*

"Can I bring Cathy along?" I shouted back.

"Of course!" she replied, and turned her face to the sky to catch the fireworks; and then my dream shifted scenes which had no relevance to my relationship with Grace; but as brief as my encounter with her was, I knew that she still had serious issues with her faith, and I also knew that I would be there for her in the multiverse of dreams...

Grace Kendal, a good, honest, caring wife and mother and conscientious church-going Roman Catholic personified the living paradox of Christianity. In Grace I saw everything that was good and bad about Christianity that fate had brought us together to reconcile; and as much as I avoided thinking about it, it was forced upon me.

I knew I had a one-of-a-kind story in Grace Kendal, but I had no idea what form it would take. I just kept notes on our relationship because that's what writers do when they meet people that excite their literary interest (Joyce used to sneak off to the washroom in pubs to record bits of conversation, but Hemingway boasted that he never kept notes), and I knew that somewhere down the road a story would eventually jell; but it began to jell sooner than I expected with a letter that I received from Kathleen.

Cathy came home with the mail one day and said, "You have a letter here from someone in Newfoundland."

"Newfoundland?" I said, surprised.

"That's what the return address says," Cathy said, handing me the letter. "Who do you know in Newfoundland?"

"The only person I know is Grace Kendal's daughter. She lives in St. John's. I wonder—"

I didn't open the letter immediately. I held it in my hands for a few minutes, with Cathy waiting impatiently for me to open it but trying not to show it as she scurried about the kitchen preparing something for dinner.

I shut my eyes and tried to sense what was in the letter, and the feeling that I got was one of desperation. I felt a wave of anxiety wash over me.

227

I opened the letter and read:

Mr. Oriano Fellicci,
St. Jude, Ontario
Sunday, Jan. 9, 2000

Dear Oriano,

I am writing you this letter because I enjoyed talking with you and I feel I can trust you. Besides my girlfriend you are the only other person I told about my pregnancy and my plans to get an abortion. Then I told my father next. I know I hurt my father, but dad took it much better than mom did. I knew I was going to break mom's heart, but I had to tell her. I hope you can understand that. But that's not why I am writing you this letter.

I need your help Oriano. Now that I had my abortion I'm scared of going to hell. I went to confession, but I'm not sorry for what I did; and until I repent for what I did God will not forgive me. But I can't repent because I believe a woman has a right to her own body, and I'm really scared. I don't want to go to hell. What can I do?

Please help me. Please please please help me!

Sincerely,
Kathleen Kendal

P. S. You took my headache away. Can you take my heartache away? Please. I know you can help me. Thank you. KK

"Well?" Cathy said, seeing that I had finished reading the letter and was just sitting there absorbing Kathleen's anguish.

"Well what?" I said.

"Was it from Grace's daughter?"

"Yes."

"And?"

"She just wants some advice on a question of faith."

"Faith?" Cathy said.

"Yes. Her Roman Catholic faith."

228

"Are you going to reply?"

"Yes."

"What question of faith?"

"Kathleen's in conflict. She's reached a point in her spiritual life where she has to fish or cut bait. It's not an easy place to be, sweetheart."

"What conflict?" Cathy asked.

"Cathy—"

"You can't tell me?"

"Of course not. It's personal. I can't violate Kathleen's trust in me."

"I'm sorry I asked," Cathy replied, in a tone of voice that elicited a response.

"How would you feel if I talked about some of your inner conflicts?" I responded, in the same touchy tone of voice.

"What conflicts?" she said, defensively.

"Things that you haven't come to terms with yet," I replied.

"Such as?" she challenged.

"Let's not go there, okay? Kathleen has a serious problem with her faith, and she asked for my help. I have to respond."

"Then do so," Cathy said, in her dismissive voice that always got to me because it gave her the last word by default.

"Look lady," I instinctively responded in my no-nonsense voice, "I came to your rescue when you were lost in the wilderness, so don't get haughty with me now. I don't have the patience for this kind of pettiness—"

A cold chill swept through the room. Cathy knew that tone of voice well, and she knew better than to reply. She made dinner, and we ate in silence as we always did whenever the beast of our relationship reared its ugly head.

I needed time to think about Kathleen's letter before responding; but as I thought about what I would write the central idea of my story began to jell...

Kathleen's letter was destined to fulfill the symbolic implications of my Platonic relationship with her mother, which was to bridge the great divide that existed between the central message of

Christ's teaching and Christianity; and it took less than a day to convince myself that the great divide that I saw in Christianity was playing itself out in the lives of Grace Kendal and her daughter.

Grace did not believe in abortion because it went against her faith, and her daughter had to have an abortion because her need for more spiritual freedom was greater than her Christian faith; hence the great divide.

"So my story will be about a mother and daughter," I thought to myself one day on my first job of the new millennium; "an ex nun and mother whose faith in Jesus Christ and his Church is central to her life, and her daughter who has outgrown her faith and suffers from post-Christian guilt." I burst into laughter. *"Post-Christian guilt,"* I repeated, under my breath. "That's it, isn't it? That's what Kathleen's suffering from!"

I hadn't worked out how I was going to respond to her letter, but I knew that whatever I said would have to be powerful enough to absolve her false sense of guilt. "But I have no idea what to say," I said, answering my own thought.

For three days while I worked at our local plywood mill manager's residence washroom—painting first, and then laying ceramic floor tiles which I did occasionally—I thought about Kathleen's crisis of faith; and the more I thought about it, the more the theme of my story emerged.

"The paradox of Christianity," I summed up under my breath on the third day as I was wiping the tiles of excess grout. That's what my theme will be, I thought; the natural conflict that arises out of one's Christian faith and one's need for greater spiritual freedom that one's faith cannot give them. *"Eureka!"* I shouted.

"What was that?" Nikkie, the mill manager's wife shouted up to me from downstairs. "Did one of the cats mess up your work?" she asked, when she came upstairs.

I laughed. "No. I was just thinking out loud."

"Oh. It must have been a really good thought," Nikkie said, and laughed.

I liked Nikkie, She had a bubbly personality and took life pretty much as it came, which pleased me. I had done a lot of work on her house before I went to the Kendal's, but I had to return to do the washroom that Nikkie wanted done in the New Year.

"It was a great thought," I replied. "I just got the central idea for my new novel; that's why I'm so excited."

Nikkie, who knew I wrote because I had disclosed the entire storyline of my last novel *The Other Side* to her while I painted her house, was delighted. "Oh good! What's this one about?" she asked.

"I can't tell you yet, Nikkie. I have to write it before I can talk about it. Like my mentor Hemingway said, talking about a story before writing it is like taking the dust off a butterfly's wings. It loses its magic."

"Give me a hint," she said.

"A hint? I guess I can," I said, smiling at Nikkie's irresistible charm. "It's about a mother and daughter and the conflict that arises out of a difference in their beliefs. I can't say any more than that."

"That doesn't tell me anything," Nikkie said. "Mothers and daughters always have conflicts. My mother and I don't see eye to eye on a lot of things. My mother still can't accept my brother's gay life style, but I do. It was hard at first, but he's my brother. I had no choice—"

"Similar conflict, Nikkie. My story has to do with an issue no less contentious than homosexuality and Christianity—"

"Well tell me!" she shouted, and then laughed. "You can't keep me in suspense now. It's not fair, Oriano!"

"One word, okay?"

"As long as it tells me."

"Abortion," I said, and smiled.

"You don't have to say another word. Can I read it when you finish it?"

"I haven't even started yet! Give me a break, will you—"

I enjoyed my relationship with Nikkie, as well as her husband Kenny who for some reason admired me for my independence and literary aspirations.

"I envy you," he said to me when I did my first painting job for him at the mill two months after he took over as the new manager. "I wish I could do what I wanted."

"It's not all it's cut out to be," I said. "I get up every day at four to write, and then I have to go to my day job for eight hours or more to feed the wolf. Do you know what Cathy calls me, Kenny?"

"What?"

"She's given me an Indian name. She calls me Oriano-half-a-day because I put in half a day's work before she gets up in the morning."

Kenny laughed. "Oriano-half-a-day. I like that. We should get together sometime. Maybe for dinner or something."

"Sure. I'd like for Cathy to meet you and Nikkie. Give us a shout after we get your house in order."

I had interrupted my work on his company residence to do some quick cosmetic painting at the mill office because Kenny had some top executives coming in from British Columbia and he wanted to make a good impression.

"Okay," he said. "Looking forward to it." And we did get together. The four of us went cross-country skiing and then we went to Kenny's house where we all sat around the fireplace sipping "Blueberry Heaven" (blueberry cordial that I had made from the plentiful summer crop of wild blueberries), and eating Nikkie's home-made veggie pizza.

But I couldn't get my letter to Kathleen out of my mind, and I thought about it all afternoon skiing and at Kenny's house. Cathy could tell that I was in two worlds, and she even commented—

"Oriano, what story are you working on now?" she asked, and laughed.

"I haven't started it yet," with a big smile.

"Well you're working on something," she said. "He does that, you know."

"What?" Nikkie asked. "Are you thinking about your writing now?"

"Not really. Let me ask you guys something, if I may. If you were faced with a situation where your principles were put on the line—and by principles I mean what you stand for; what would you do? Would you stick to your guns, or would you capitulate and compromise your principles?"

"I'd stick to my principles," Cathy was first to reply.

"I know you would, dear. I've been there when you were put to the test; but do you think you're strong enough to pass the big test?"

"What big test?" Nikkie asked.

"I can't explain it, Nikkie; but life seems to be like that. We get tested every day, but we don't realize it. And then out of the clear blue the big test comes—"

"What big test? You didn't explain that," Nikkie said.

"He's talking about an ethical test," Kenny offered.

"Basically, yes. A situation which asks of us to do the right thing. We know what the right thing is, but if we do the right thing we pay a great price; so what I'm asking is this: can we pass the big test when it comes?"

"What big test!" Nikkie shouted, and laughed.

We all laughed too. Then I said, "The test that puts you at odds with the rest of the world. The test that separates you from your family, friends, and co-workers. The test that stigmatizes you for the rest of your life—like Al Pacino's movie *The Insider*. Did you see that movie?"

"We saw it," Nikkie said. "We saw it at Silver City. Have you guys been to Silver City yet?"

"Once. And that was enough for us," Cathy said. "We saw a Gulf war movie with some friends and we all walked out. It was so loud we couldn't stand it."

"It was *Three Kings*," I said. "George Clooney starred in it. God it was loud."

"That's what we thought too," Nikkie said. "We're not going back there again."

"Big screen, big sound, big headache," I said, and laughed. "I don't know how those kids can stand it."

Kenny laughed. "Anyway, about this big test. You're talking about something as big as blowing the whistle on the tobacco industry like Al Pacino did in *The Insider*?"

"It's all relative, Kenny," I said, thoughtfully. "What may be a big test for me may not be so big for you. Just as long as the test questions our basic sense of who we are; that's what I mean by a big test. So what I want to know is this: what do you think you would do if you were put to the test?"

"I don't know," Kenny replied, with simple honesty.

"You wouldn't sell out, Kenny," Nikkie said, looking at her husband. "How many times have you been there?"

Kenny smiled self-consciously. "I know. But I think I understand what Oriano's saying. I think he's referring to the mother of all tests; aren't you?"

I laughed, and so did everyone else. "Exactly," I said. "We don't know when it's going to come, but you can rest assured that it will come when we're most vulnerable."

"What would you do, Oriano?" Kenny asked.

"It's come and gone for me, Kenny," I said, with an inexpressible sense of satisfaction. "It came a number of years ago. But that doesn't mean I'm home free now. As long as we're in this world we're going to be tested; but if we pass the big one life doesn't have as much power over us. Then we can enjoy life a lot more."

"But how do you know if you passed or not?" Nikkie asked, in all seriousness.

"Sometimes you don't. And that's when it really hurts. That's what I was thinking about earlier. I know someone who was put to the test, and she passed; but now she's paying a terrible price for making the right decision. But don't ask me to explain, because it wouldn't be fair to her. I just wanted to know what you guys thought about what it means to hold onto your principles—"

"But sometimes your principles can be wrong. What happens then?" Nikkie said.

"If you stick to your guns and you're wrong?" I queried.

"Yes," Nikkie said. "What happens then?"

"That's a good one," Cathy replied. "Now just watch how Oriano gets out of it."

I laughed. So did Kenny. Nikkie wasn't sure why we were laughing, and she just smiled and waited for me to work my way out of that conundrum.

"Well," I said, chuckling, "life is self-correcting. If we are wrong in our principles and stick by them, life is going to grab us by the balls and squeeze tighter!"

Everyone laughed. We all had a good time; but still, in the back of my mind, I thought of poor Kathleen…

It may have been a vulgar metaphor, but it made my point about the uncompromising nature of life; it just keeps on squeezing until we break or cry uncle. Either way, we suffer; and it was the nature of this suffering that I spent my life questioning.

Finally however I did work out the logic of man's relationship with life; and what amazed me was how simple it really was. Life is a one way trip to reality, and like it or not we're all going to get there eventually; so learning how to make our journey as easy as possible is what our fundamental purpose in life should be. And the best way to do that, I reasoned after years of insufferable anguish, was to live life as honestly as possible because the authentic life does not create the kind of karma that causes suffering.

That was Kathleen's dilemma. She was being honest with herself when she decided to have an abortion. She believed it was a woman's right to have control over her own body, and to make her point she aborted her fetus; but now she was suffering from the Christian guilt of having sinned against God, and how I was going to do it I didn't know, but I had to convince her that abortion was not a sin against God.

Shakespeare came to mind as we skied that cold sunny afternoon. *"There is nothing either good or bad but thinking makes it so,"* said the playwright; and that, I decided, would be the working premise of my letter to Kathleen…

10. LETTER TO KATHLEEN

87 Springleaf Drive
St. Jude, Ontario
Friday, Jan. 28, 2000

Dear Kathleen,

Your letter came as a delightful surprise. Yes, I will help you because I know what it means to stand alone against the mighty forces of Christianity.

Before I take your heartache away, let me tell you this: God loves you no matter what. In the eyes of God we are untried souls that have to go through life to grow until we become conscious of God's love; so it does not matter what we do in life, it's all part of the learning experience that we have to go through to help expand the consciousness of God, and God does not frown upon whatever we do to learn what we have to learn.

Yes, Kathleen; we are all a part of God, and although God may appear to us to be complete unto itself God needs us to fulfill itself also. And God fulfills itself through the slow and grinding perfection of each and every soul.

This is why God sent Jesus into the world. I agree with you in believing that Jesus was not God; but he was a very special man who had a profound knowledge of the Way, and his spiritual duty as a God-conscious man was to introduce the Way to the world to help us grow in spirit so we can become God-conscious beings like him.

Now, the most important thing that we have to know about Jesus is this: he was not the only person to be initiated into the mysteries of the Way and mandated to bring it to the world. Christianity would have us believe that Jesus was exclusively "the way, the truth, and the life," but that is simply not true; **and that is the first lie of Christianity.**

Christianity has told many lies since this first lie, and it is these lies that keep souls trapped in a state of false consciousness responsible for so much of the spiritual doubt, dread, and anguish of the world. This is what's responsible for your heartache, is it not Kathleen—doubt, dread, and anguish? You are in dread of going to hell because you doubt God's forgiveness for a sin that you despaired committing; is that not so?

But what is sin, Kathleen? Christianity would have us believe that sin is a transgression against God. God gave Moses the Ten Commandments to keep souls on the straight and narrow—on the spiritual path to God, if you will; and any violation of these commandments is said to be a sin.

I don't disagree with the intent of the Ten Commandments— which is to keep souls on the spiritual path; but the problem I had growing up Roman Catholic was that I could not believe God would send me to everlasting punishment in hell for committing a mortal sin. I simply could not believe that, Kathleen; and I dreaded going to hell so much that I made it my life's quest to rid myself of this unbearable dread.

True, Christianity tells us that if we repent for our sins God will not send us to hell; but this never felt quite right to me because no matter how hard I repented I still felt a deep sense of guilt that I could not get rid of. And I just could not live with that guilt.

Guilt never left me, Kathleen. No matter what I did I always felt guilty. It was a part of me just like my shadow was a part of me. But the strangest thing about my deep and irrepressible feelings of guilt was that I didn't feel I was responsible for all the guilt that I suffered from. That was my dilemma, then. I felt guilty for more than I felt I should be guilty for; and it was this paradoxical state of consciousness that forced me to leave my family, my friends, and my country to search for the Way.

Well, Kathleen; to make a long story short I found the Way; and because I live the Way today I no longer suffer from this paradoxical state of consciousness that you are suffering from today. But I will do everything in my power to rid you of this false sense of fear that is keeping you from living a full and happy life...

You love your mother, Kathleen; I know this. But you know that Grace Kendal is not your biological mother. Knowing this, I understand that you had a compelling need to find out who your birth mother was; so you sought her out.

And you did find your birth mother and got to know her and were disappointed because she was an alcoholic, as was your brother; but at least you got that compelling need to know out of your system and you were free to get on with your life.

Obviously, you were a young lady in a very unique situation in life. You were brought up by a mother who was a nun for twenty years and a father who was a monk for an equal number of years, so Christianity had to be to you what water is to fish; but somewhere along the way you stepped outside the Christian paradigm that you were brought up in or you would not have said what you did about Jesus Christ.

I don't know the details, but I can empathize with you because I too was forced to question the divinity of Jesus Christ; I too was forced to step outside the Christian paradigm to find my true self. Not that one can't find their true self within the Christian paradigm; but it makes it awfully hard for one to do so.

And Christianity does not sanction people who leave its fold to look elsewhere for answers to the most important question that one can ask in life—*who am I?* To be quite honest with you Kathleen, I don't know how anyone can be a Christian today given how far the spiritual consciousness of society has evolved. But be that as it may, the point is this: why does Christianity continue to be so obstinate in its demands upon Christians?

The answer is simple: **Christianity preaches Love but rules by Power**. And what is the fundamental source of Christianity's power? Two words: spiritual ignorance.

As long as Christianity can keep Christians in the dark about soul's true situation in life it will have power over them; so any move towards enlightenment threatens the power base of Christianity. And when this happens Christianity musters its forces and rallies against the "evil-doers."

Kathleen, I have been called a "devil-worshipper" by some of the good Christians of St. Jude because I dared to take a different spiritual path to God from the path that Jesus brought to the world; and all because I threatened their Christian faith.

It took Christianity three hundred and fifty years to admit that it was wrong about Galileo, so it does not have a very good history of humility; how long then is it going to take Christianity to admit that Jesus Christ is not the only way home to God?

I doubt it ever will, because the exclusivity of Jesus being the savior of the world is Christianity's chief source of power and control over people, and I do not believe it will ever relinquish this misconception.

If this is the chief source of Christianity's power then we should look into it a little more; so if you will indulge me, let me point out to you how this one misconception has spawned other lies that are responsible for the false consciousness that keeps souls trapped in a state of perpetual spiritual ignorance.

To make the claim that Jesus is the savior of the world Christianity has to posit that souls are damned and have to be saved; and what does Christianity do to make this claim? Quite simply, it makes the claim that souls are born in a state of original sin. This original sin is man's first sin, committed by Adam and Eve, man's first parents, when they ate the forbidden fruit from the tree of knowledge in the Garden of Eden.

Man's original sin is passed on genetically by the act of procreation; so every person born in the world is tainted with man's first sin. And the only way to cleanse oneself of this stain is to become a baptized Christian. And how does baptism do this?

Here's what Christianity says about baptism. God sent his only Begotten Son Jesus into the world to die for the sins of the world; and it is the death of Jesus upon the cross that washes away the stain of original sin. And only by accepting Jesus Christ can a damned soul be saved. That's the awesome power of Christian baptism.

And that is the source of Christianity's power base—the idea that souls are born damned because they are stained with man's first sin; and only through Jesus Christ can we be saved, because God sacrificed Jesus on the cross for the salvation of the world.

So Christianity's first lie that Jesus Christ is the savior of the world cannot be sustained without **the second lie that man is born in a state of original sin.**

In other words, Christianity precludes all other spiritual paths to salvation as long as we continue to believe that we are born in a state of original sin which only Jesus Christ can wash away for us through baptism; and that is why Christianity has always opposed other religions—because it wants to be the sole savior of the world.

But this wasn't enough to keep souls fettered to spiritual ignorance. Christianity had to go one step further. The idea that the human body was only the vehicle for a pre-existent soul so threatened Christianity's power base that it denied soul's pre-existence by claiming that soul is created at the moment of human conception.

By claiming that soul is created at the moment of human conception Christianity could now say that we only live one life that is damned from birth by original sin until we accept Jesus as our savior and are baptized into Christianity.

And that is the third lie that Christianity has created to hold onto its power base—the inconceivable concept that man's immortal soul is created at the moment of mortal human conception—**the lie that we only live one life.**

Now, it's only fair Kathleen that you ask me how I can be absolutely certain that Christianity is lying about man's spiritual situation; and my answer is this: only by stepping completely outside the Christian paradigm can we see the lies that Christianity holds onto to sustain its power base.

Like you, I stepped outside the Christian paradigm; and as you are suffering now for daring to go against the mighty lies of Christianity, so too did I suffer. But I persisted, Kathleen. I dared to step all the way out and I explored many spiritual paths in search of an answer to the question that haunted me—*who am I?*

You see Kathleen, soul, our true self, has a need that is far more compelling to find God than you had to find your biological parents; and when this need to find our divine Creator possesses us nothing in the world can stop us. This is why you feel as strongly as you do about abortion. But just in case you don't get my point, let me explain.

Christianity says that abortion is wrong. It says that it is an act of murder (*thou shalt not kill*). But if I may, let me ask you this: how can one murder an immortal soul? In itself, this is illogical. Nonetheless, we cannot sanction murder simply because soul is immortal; that would be insane. So why does Christianity condemn abortion, then?

The answer is simple. Christianity maintains that a fetus is a person because soul is created at the moment of human conception; and by having an abortion one kills a person and denies salvation to the unborn child. Ergo, it is murder and a sin against God. So the fundamental question of the abortion issue is this: is a fetus a person?

Christianity says yes because it holds the belief that soul, our immortal spiritual and true self is created at the moment of human conception; but what if soul, the individuating consciousness of our true self, pre-exists the human body? What if soul, the inner self that is who we really are, is not created at the moment of human conception; does abortion then become an act of murder?

In other words Kathleen, if soul pre-exists the human body (which I know it does), then terminating a pregnancy by an act of abortion does not deny that soul life. It does not deny that soul a chance to be saved, as Christianity would have us believe. Why? Because that soul can simply choose another body to be born into; that's why.

This whole line of reasoning sounds absurd to Christianity because it is so obtuse about the true spiritual nature of man that it cannot see past its own power-based interests; and it will not even entertain such a notion because it would completely undermine the lie that we only live one life which Jesus died upon the cross to save. So, Kathleen; the three fundamental lies of Christianity are: 1. **that Jesus is the sole savior of the world**; 2. **that man is born in a state of original sin**; and 3. **that we only live one life**.

Once you grasp this simple fact that Christianity is founded upon a structure of carefully crafted lies you will begin to make sense of the hold that Christianity has upon your psyche and why it is so difficult to break free; but I will help you because I've been there, and it pains me to see other people suffer this kind of unbearable anguish.

241

Kathleen, I know that you are still a young lady and much of what I have said may take time to sink in; but all I am attempting to do here is this: to offer you an alternative to what you have been brought up to believe. You have made a great start by breaking free of the lie that Jesus is God; but that is not enough to free yourself of your fear of going to hell. So I have to get rid of your anguish by explaining to you exactly what it was that Jesus came into the world to do; so bear with me, please…

To understand Christ's mission on earth one has to understand soul's true situation in life. Contrary to what Christianity teaches, we do not have a soul; rather, Soul is who we are. Soul is one. Soul comes from God and returns to God by way of the life process. Life, then, is the vehicle that God uses to expand its consciousness; and Soul (God's consciousness) grows through life experiences. This is why life is so precious.

Deep down inside we all know that we are on a mission from God, but our human consciousness clouds our spiritual awareness, and God-conscious men like Jesus come into the world to wake us up to our inherent divine purpose.

That is what makes Jesus so special. His mission in life was to awaken man to his divine purpose, which is to expand the consciousness of God; and the only way we can do this is to become aware of our spiritual nature. Christ's teaching therefore provides a means for us to awaken to our spiritual nature; but it is not an easy teaching to live.

The essence of Christ's teaching lies in his words *"For whosoever will save his life shall lose it; and whosoever will lose his life for my sake shall find it"* (Math. 16: 25).These are puzzling words, as are Christ's words that we cannot enter heaven unless we first become as little children: *"Except ye be converted, and become as little children, ye shalt not enter into the kingdom of heaven"* (Math. 18: 3). But how can we both die and become as little children? It is impossible to do, is it not?

Obviously Christ's teaching is an elaborate metaphor for self-transformation; and the only way to understand Christ's teaching is to live his sayings, which are the means by which we transform our human consciousness and become aware of our spiritual nature, for

242

"whosever heareth these sayings of mine, and doeth them, I will liken unto a wise man which buildeth his house upon a rock" (Math. 7: 24).

Kathleen, as much as I would like to I cannot go into the detail I would like to here, because it would take too long to explain each and every saying of Jesus; suffice to say that the whole of Christ's teaching is a cryptic code that has to be broken to be understood. Once the code has been broken all the sayings fall into place and reveal the spiritual genius of the remarkable man called Jesus Christ.

Here, then, is the key that will decode the sayings of Jesus: we have two selves; one human, and one spiritual. Soul, our spiritual self, takes on a human body. It is not created at the moment of human conception, as Christianity would have us believe; but it lies dormant in us until life experiences awaken it. It follows that the more life we live, the better the chances of waking up spiritually. But even a full life is not enough to wake soul up.

This is why souls reincarnate. We are born back into life over and over again until we wake up to our spiritual nature; and only then can we move on to a higher plane of consciousness, or what Jesus called the kingdom of heaven.

Christ's teaching therefore is nothing more than a means to speed up the process of waking us up to our divine nature; and as mind-boggling as his sayings may be, they are all part of the spiritual technique that can be summed up in one word: **self-sacrifice.**

We have to sacrifice (transform) our human self-consciousness to wake up spiritually. This is why the death of Jesus upon the cross becomes such an important symbol for Christianity. It is unfortunate that his death has been taken so literally, because it distorts his message of self-transformation; but be that as it may, the point is that by living Christ's sayings we sacrifice our human self (ego) and wake up our dormant spiritual self.

But who wants to sacrifice their ego? How many people do you know besides your mother that have voluntarily lived the way of the cross? Not many, right? This is why I have the respect that I do for your mother, Kathleen. She is a special lady who exemplifies what it means to be a good Christian.

However, as much as I admire your mother for her commitment to Jesus Christ I have to tell you that we part company when it comes to her Christian faith. It is one thing to believe in Jesus, but quite another to believe in the Church born of his life and teaching because Christianity is diametrically opposed to Jesus Christ's teaching.

This is the most profound irony that I have ever experienced, Kathleen; but when I finally woke up spiritually the whole puzzle of Christianity fell into place for me. And here is what the puzzle revealed: **Christ's sayings are a teaching of spiritual liberation while Christianity is a religion of spiritual enslavement.**

The irony lies in the fact that one can liberate oneself spiritually by living Christ's way of the cross, but if one lives the way of the cross within the paradigm of Christianity one constrains their spiritual freedom; and this can be the cause of so much anguish that it can drive one to extremes, as it did you for example.

Why did you abort your unborn child, Kathleen? Why did you go to that extreme? Did you want to make a statement, as you young people are fond of saying today? Did you want to say to your mother, *"I believe that a woman's rights over her own body are more important than the rights of her unborn child?"* You could have had your child and given it up for adoption as your birth mother did, but you chose instead to defy Christianity by having an abortion; why the extreme, Kathleen?

You defied Christianity because that was the only way you could break free of its hold upon you. But after you had your abortion you began to feel guilty; and now you're afraid of going to hell because you cannot honestly repent for what you did and you think God cannot forgive you. You are living proof of what Christianity can do to a person—torture them to the bitter end. This is why Christianity is not a religion of love and spiritual liberation; it is a religion of power and control. And it controls people with guilt and fear; guilt for sinning, and fear of going to hell.

Kathleen, have you asked yourself why in your heart you cannot repent for your sin of abortion? Why you cannot make a perfect act of contrition? Is it not because somewhere deep within you know that you had to do what you did to preserve your spiritual integrity? You knew intuitively that you had to defy the false god of Christianity that had all that power over you? Is that not why you had your abortion?

Had you had your abortion and not told anyone it would have been a different story entirely; but because you felt compelled to tell your parents, especially your mother, you were crying out for understanding. *"Please, mom,"* you pleaded, *"try to understand why I have to do it. I know it's going to break your heart, but I have to do it. I have to!"*

You didn't understand why you had to do it, but deep within you knew that this was the only way you could make the final break from the hold that Christianity had upon you; but you underestimated the Church's power over you; that's why you're afraid now of going to hell. Right or wrong?

Now, Kathleen; the only way we can rid you of your fear of going to hell is to shed some light on this whole subject of eternal damnation…

Does hell exist? That's the question we have to ask first. And if it does exist, why does it exist? Does it exist to punish souls that have transgressed against God? Would God send a soul to hell for eternity because it went against God? Is God that cruel?

The most absurd thing about trying to make sense of this idea of hell is that it presupposes that we know what God would do, which no one can know; so we can rule out why God would send a soul to hell, then. That is, if hell exists at all.

Let's suppose that hell does exist though. And let's further suppose that God does not send a soul to hell for eternity. Why then would hell exist?

"And if thy right hand offend thee, cut it off, and cast it from thee; for it is profitable for thee that one of thy members should perish, and not that thy whole body should be cast into hell," said Jesus (Math. 51: 30).

Knowing that Jesus Christ's teaching was an elaborate metaphor to teach us how to live the spiritual life, what did he mean by saying that the whole body would be cast into hell if one did not cut off the offending hand?

If Jesus did not mean for one to cut off his offending hand literally (which many Christian fanatics over the years have done), then it follows that the body that he refers to going to hell would not be the literal body; it would have to be the same metaphorical body that he refers to above in his saying. And what body would that be?

By "offending hand" Jesus meant a mental attitude, or habit. For example, I heard of a man who lived alone in the bush who read the Bible daily and who literally cut off his right hand because he could not stop masturbating. He believed that masturbation was a sin, and he could not stop sinning; so he cut off the offending hand that sinned.

Now, Kathleen; wouldn't it be ironic if he couldn't help himself and began masturbating with his other hand? What would he do then? Would he not go on suffering the insufferable anguish of being a sinner?

Do you see what I'm trying to say? This man's anguish would be no different than the anguish that you are going through now. You believe that you have sinned by having your abortion, and you are suffering the grief of spiritual anguish.

But if Jesus did not mean for one to literally cut off his offending hand then he had to be referring to his mental hand; or, if you will, the thought that creates the habit that creates the state of consciousness that keeps one from waking up spiritually.

In other words, Jesus was saying that we have to sacrifice that part of our self-consciousness that keeps us spiritually asleep; the part of our self-consciousness that is not pure enough for us to realize our spiritual self.

All of Christ's teaching has to do with sacrificing that part of our self-consciousness that keeps us in a state of spiritual sleep; this is why his teaching is so difficult. It demands constant self-sacrifice; but it is not easy to "die daily," as St. Paul expressed it.

The point I want to make is this: if Jesus was referring to one's mental body, then by implication he told us that sin is a state of mind—which is exactly why Shakespeare would say, "There is nothing either good or bad but thinking makes it so."

So, Kathleen: in itself sin does not exist. Sin is a state of mind. This is why John Milton said in his epic poem *Paradise Lost*, "The mind is its own place, and in itself can make a heaven of hell, a hell of heaven."

All Jesus was doing then was telling us how to purify the consciousness of our mind, because the more pure our mind is the more we become aware of our spiritual self, and when he said that we have to die to our life to save our life he meant that we have to die to that part of our self-consciousness that is not pure enough for our spiritual self to become aware of itself. This is why he said that we have to become as little children, because the mind of a child has not been tainted by life yet.

The self that Jesus meant for us to sacrifice is that part of our mental self that keeps us from realizing our spiritual nature, what St. Paul referred to as "selfsame thing" because it is impossible to tell which self is which.

So we can be certain that the mental self is real; and when Jesus said that it was better to cut off an offending part than for the whole body to be cast into hell he implied that the mental body will continue to exist in hell after one dies.

Now follow the logic if you will, Kathleen. If Jesus was referring to the mental body in his metaphor, and if the mental body is the vehicle for soul as Jesus implies, then it follows that soul will remain trapped in the mental body after death.

This is what Jesus meant by hell. And this is why his spiritual liberation teaching takes on such an incredible sense of urgency— because life is short, and we can die any minute and damn ourselves to hell.

Of course, one will ask the question: does the mental body exist after death? Or, to express it differently, does our human consciousness exist after death?

We believe that soul exists after death, but if we are to make any sense of Christ's teaching we have to posit that our mental self exists also. In other words, our spiritual self (soul) takes with it the consciousness of our mental self (ego) to the other side when our physical body dies; and if our mental self is not pure enough for our soul to become aware of itself, then it will remain trapped in our mental self forever—that is, if one believes that we only live one life.

247

Christianity wants us to believe that we only live one life. That way it can have all the power it needs to keep one a prisoner to Christ's spiritual liberation teaching; but if we live more than one life then it means that soul will have another chance to liberate itself, and another chance, and another chance until it finally gets it right.

So yes, Kathleen; hell does exist. But it is only eternal within the Christian paradigm that we only live one lifetime. I don't believe that we only live one lifetime. In fact, I know that we live more than one lifetime (I have memories of some of my past lives); so what I'm telling you is drawn from my own understanding of what hell is and isn't.

Of course you can believe me or not, that is entirely up to you; but remember this Kathleen: our beliefs are handed down to us, as your Christian beliefs were; but the more life we experience the more conscious we become, and the more conscious we become the more we see through the lies that keep us fettered to spiritual ignorance.

But having made the choice to break away from your Christian beliefs by daring to go against them with your abortion you are free now to choose another paradigm to live by, a non-Christian paradigm if you will, that will allow you more freedom to become the person you were meant to be. In other words, Kathleen; you don't have to suffer the anguish of going to hell. You suffer because Christianity still has a hold upon you. But I have offered you another paradigm to live by, and if you choose to do so your heartache will go away all by itself. *I promise you that it will.*

Don't misunderstand me, though. I'm not suggesting that you throw the baby out with the bathwater if you do decide to shift your center of gravity all the way out of the Christian paradigm; all I'm saying is this: there is a great divide that exists between Jesus Christ's teaching and Christian dogma; and to dismiss Jesus Christ along with Christianity would not be very wise. In other words, learn from Jesus but don't take Christianity too seriously. Jesus was a great teacher of the Way who sacrificed his life to bring his teaching to the world; but he was not what Christianity has made him out to be.

The Jesus Christ of Christianity is a mythological God-man, and he only exists because people do not want to know the real truth about his teaching; but you do, and it is your choice now to live in fear of hell or not live in fear of hell. Is that clear?

Kathleen, this would be a good place to end my letter; but I have a few more points I would like to make because the context has been established to give them the best possible expression, so please bear with me a while longer.

If sin is a state of mind, which I believe it to be, that creates the impure state of consciousness that keeps soul asleep, the question we have to ask ourselves is this: can this state of sin-consciousness be eliminated by confessing one's sins to a priest? Can an act of perfect contrition purify one's sin-consciousness?

I think not. But proving this is impossible, because the idea of confession is so deeply rooted in Judea-Christian culture that it would take the second coming of Jesus Christ to displace this mind-set with the truth of the Spiritual Law of Accountability, otherwise known throughout the ages as the reconciling Law of Karma.

Forgiveness of sin through Holy Confession is another lie. In short, **forgiveness of sin is the fourth and most insidious lie of Christianity.** By convincing people that priests have the power to forgive sins Christianity holds all the cards.

Kathleen, man is basically lazy. It is a known fact of life that man will take the path of least resistance; so if he is offered an easy way to salvation he will take it. And what could be easier than to kneel down at the eleventh hour after a life of lying, cheating, and stealing and whisper into a priest's ear, "Father forgive me, for I have sinned"?

If you could only see how absurd this proposition is you wouldn't stop laughing for a whole month; but because this Christian mind-set is such a part of your life you cannot possibly see the humor. *But believe me, it is humorous!*

Sin consciousness is impure consciousness, and sins are karmic transgressions. What I mean by this is that anything that we do that violates the Spiritual Law of Karma is a sin, or what Christianity calls a transgression against God.

Christ's teaching infers karma with the reference to reaping what we sow; and today this spiritual insight has been rendered into the cliché "what goes around comes around." Specifically this means that we will get back the kind of energy that we send out into the world. In other words Kathleen, if we put out negative energy we will get back negative energy; and if we put out positive energy we will get back positive energy.

So it follows logically that the whole mystery of spiritual liberation (salvation) lies in one's ability to live a karmically responsible life; and by this I mean that we have to be conscious of how karma works. And if I may Kathleen, let me spare you years of anguish and explain to you exactly how the Law of Spiritual Accountability works.

The key word is freedom. Freedom is what we are after in life. "There is a doctrine uttered in secret," says Socrates in Plato's *Phaedo,* "that man is a prisoner who has no right to open the door of his prison and run away."

This prison, Socrates goes on to explain, is the kingdom of man's senses; his sense of smell, taste, touch, sight, and hearing. Man lives within the realm of his five senses; but the self-consciousness created by living a life of the senses is not pure enough to wake soul up from the sleep of life. So, says the great philosopher, the only way to open the door of our prison and escape is to purify our self-consciousness; and we can do this by separating the soul from the body by "the habit of soul gathering and collecting herself into herself."

The essence of Plato's philosophy has to do with living the kind of life that will liberate soul from the prison of the senses, which in essence is a life of virtue. As we strive to live the virtuous life of goodness, kindness, compassion, forgiveness and so on we separate the soul from the body and liberate ourselves from the prison of spiritual sleep.

Christ's teaching offers us a key to spiritual liberation by way of his sayings. As we live his sayings we separate soul from the body and wake up spiritually. And the path of Buddhism also offers us a key to liberation by way of "compassion" and "detachment." We learn to detach ourselves from a life of the senses. That's how we can break the eternal cycle of life and death and open the door to nirvana (heaven) in Buddhism.

Christianity however says that we can whisper our sins into a priest's ear, and by the power vested in him by the Holy Church of Jesus Christ he can forgive our sins and open the door to our prison of spiritual sleep; but if I may be so bold Kathleen, did you ever feel spiritually enlightened and free after you came back from Saturday night's confession?

I never did. And I doubt that any other Christian did because sin-karma (the impure consciousness of our spiritual indiscretions) cannot be instantly removed by confession; it has to be transformed by an act of doing. This is why Jesus stressed that his sayings had to be *lived*, because in the act of *living* them one purifies his sin-consciousness.

But wouldn't it make a lot more sense to know what creates sin-consciousness in the first place? Wouldn't it be wiser to just live a karmically responsible life so one does not have to go through the anguishing process of self-transformation?

Believe me Kathleen, I came to this conclusion only after I realized that I was the author of my own misfortunes; only after I realized that the kind of energy that I put out into the world would eventually come back to me. It took years to become conscious of the spiritually reconciling Law of Karma, and the conclusion that I came to was that the fundamental currency of this Spiritual Law of Karma is spiritual freedom.

Do you remember Christ's parable of the talents? The gist of this parable was about the investment of our energies. If we invest our energies wisely they will work for us and multiply; but if we invest our energies unwisely they will stay the same and not work for us. And Jesus went on to teach us how to invest our energies wisely: *"Lay not up for yourselves treasures upon earth, where moth and rust doth corrupt, and where thieves break through and steal. But lay up for yourselves treasures in heaven, where neither moth nor rust doth corrupt, and where thieves do not break through nor steal. For where your treasure is will your heart be also"* (Math. 6: 19-20).

It would take a whole book to decode Christ's teaching, Kathleen (which I hope to write one day); but I will break it down for you into its simplest terms now so you can have a working formula to consciously live by as you make your way through life.

251

As I said, the basic currency of karma is spiritual freedom. So the freedom that we give to life is returned to us in direct proportion; meaning, the more freedom we give to life, the more freedom life gives to us. And conversely, the less freedom we give to life, the less freedom life gives to us. This is what Jesus meant when he said, *"For unto every one that hath shall be given, and he shall have abundance; but from him that hath not shall be taken away even that which he hath"* (Math. 25: 29).

In other words, much gathers more and less gathers less; and Karma is the Spiritual Law that governs the ways of man. So we cannot get away with anything we do in life because Big Brother Karma has his eye on us every second of the day, and it would be foolish to live an irresponsibly karmic life because our own karma would only come back to bite us in the backside. Knowing this we would not be able to shout as Gloucester in *King Lear*, "As flies to wanton boys are we to the gods. They kill us for their sport."

Freedom implies karmic responsibility, Kathleen; so the working formula for spiritual liberation (happiness, peace of mind, and wholeness of self) is to respect the sanctity of individual freedom. **We get what we give, and learning how to give people their freedom is what the enlightened spiritual life is all about**. And the more skilled you become in doing this, the more freedom you will have; for such is the Spiritual Law of Karma.

Kathleen, having been brought up in a Roman Catholic home where one's mother is an ex nun and one's father an ex monk I would think you had little exposure to other spiritual paths, so it would be safe to assume that the concept of karma is somewhat alien to you; but only now has this dawned upon me, and I apologize for diving in so deeply. So if you can bear with me a while longer, I will take you up for air.

In the simplest terms possible, karma is our relationship with life. Let me give you an analogy to help explain what our karmic relationship with life is.

Life is like a Central Bank. Our soul has an account with this Central Bank. This account is our relationship with life. In other words, we all have an account with the Central Bank of life, and our account can have a credit or a debit. If we have a credit, then Life owes us and has to pay us back; but if we have a debit we have to pay life back.

Karma, then, is all about what we owe life and what life owes us; and we credit or debit our account according to how we live our life. For example, if we live our life by giving out negative energy— such as lying, cheating, and stealing—we debit our account and life will demand payment (usually by way of personal tragedy, because suffering burns off karma); but being blind to how karma works we cry foul and shout, "As flies to wanton boys are we to the gods. They kill us for their sport!"

But the simple truth is that the fault does not lie in the stars; it lies in us. This is what I mean by spiritual ignorance. If we do not know about the Law of Karma we blame God or the Devil for the ills that befall us; but neither God nor the Devil have anything to do with the choices we make in life. We are responsible for the karma that we create; and if we create good karma life has to reward us with good fortune, for such is the divine law of life. For example; if we want to have love in our life we have to give love to life. Life has to return the love we have given, because life is governed by the Spiritual Law of Karma.

Kathleen, this means that life basically is not unfair. Life has to maintain balance in the world because the divine law demands it. But we cannot see this because we are blind to how the spiritually reconciling law of life works.

However, the more spiritually discerning we are in the choices we make, the more conscious we will be of karma; and when we finally understand how karma works in our daily life we will come to the same realization that all wise men have come to—that the best way to live life is to simply be a good person, because being a good person creates good karma, and good karma keeps us balanced and makes life a joy to live.

If I may now, let me quote one of my favorite passages from the Bible to bring my point home about karma. The Preacher in *Ecclesiastes* begins by asking what I consider to be the most profound existential question that we can ask in life: *"What profit hath a man of all his labor which he taketh under the sun?"* In modern language this can be translated into the simple question, **"What is the purpose of our life?"**

The Preacher tells us that all life is vain and meaningless; but he does finally see through the emptiness of life and sums up his life-wisdom thusly: *"...of making many books there is no end; and much study is a weariness of the flesh. Let us hear the conclusion of the whole matter: Fear God, and keep his commandments; for this is the whole duty of man. For God shall bring every work into judgment, with every secret thing, whether it be good or whether it be evil"* *(Ecclesiastes* 12: 12-14).

The Preacher is talking about karma bringing every work, good or evil, into judgment; for Karma is the Law of God that governs life.

And this, my dear Kathleen, brings my long (and I hope not too boring) letter to fitting closure. I could not have expressed the sum of my own life-wisdom better than the Preacher has in *Ecclesiastes*, for I too have concluded that ultimately the purpose of life is to simply live it with karmic responsibility.

I spent years trying to find an answer to the Preacher's question, and I did work it out eventually; and I have passed my answer on to you now because you have reached out and asked for my help. I know my letter will take a long time to digest, if you choose to think about it at all that is; but just in case you don't want to go through the whole letter over and over again, let me stress the most important point: **there is no eternal damnation in hell; that is a lie created by Christianity to have total control over you**.

Hell does exist, but not as Christianity believes. It is a temporary place of karmic purification. But we need not get into that here. Suffice for you to know that your fear of hell is ill-founded, and foolish; so please drop your fear of hell because it will only make you miserable, and you are much too young to be miserable.

Secondly, sins cannot be forgiven because they are a karmic debt with the Central Bank of life; and the only way a karmic debt can be paid back is by resolving it through good karma. Kathleen, you can drop this notion that sins can be forgiven simply by going to confession and repenting for your sins, because that will never happen. And please don't worry yourself sick about your abortion. It was not a sin.

Your abortion was an act of personal courage, that's all. It is only a sin because Christianity says it is a sin, not because abortion violates the Law of Karma. No karma has been incurred with the unborn child because the soul has not yet entered the fetus. It enters the fetus when the child is born and takes its first breath of life.

Christianity says that soul is created at the moment of human conception, thereby making the fetus a person; but in *Genesis* it is written, *"And the Lord God formed man of the dust of the ground, and breathed into his nostrils the breath of life; and man became a living soul"* (Genesis 2: 7). So, Kathleen; fear not about having murdered your unborn child. It was not a person yet until the breath of life (meaning soul) was breathed into it.

Of course, this point of view will be contested and dismissed by Christianity; but what else is new? If something doesn't fit into the Christian paradigm, it is dismissed; so don't worry about it. If there is one thing that I have learned about Christianity, it is that you can never win. You are always at its mercy. So why waste your energy?

Live your life, Kathleen. Live it, as Nietzsche would say, as though the day were now. Take your courses, do your social work, find yourself a nice man, and make a good, honest, and decent life for yourself. *Go out there and follow your bliss!*

Sincerely,
Oriano

P.S. Please let me know if your heartache goes away.

11. THE BLACK HEART OF THE ONION

Cathy told me over lunch. One of the office staff at the hospital told her over coffee in the cafeteria. Michael, Grace Kendal's son, had a terrible skiing accident. "I heard he's paralyzed from the neck down," Cathy said.

I never know what to say whenever I hear news like that, so I just let it sink in. Cathy stared at me, waiting patiently for my response. I had started my novel and Grace was on my mind, and the news that her athletic son had suddenly become a quadriplegic affected me in a way that I could not explain. I grimaced. "Paralyzed from the neck down?"

"That's what I heard," she said.

"How reliable is that?" I asked, hoping it wasn't true.

"Oriano, rumors like that around the hospital aren't rumors; they're fact."

"Good God—"

"Sad, isn't it?"

"Where is he now?"

"In the city, I imagine."

"Can you find out which hospital for me?"

"They may have shipped him off to Toronto. I'll see what I can find out."

"Please," I said, and got up from the table. I had lost my appetite. Cathy had her coffee and went back to work at the hospital.

I had planned to proof my morning's writing and go cross country skiing, but I couldn't work on my novel; so I changed clothes and went skiing instead. I left Cathy a note and drove out to our trail; but instead of taking the same trail I decided to branch off and break a new trail. I needed the workout to process Michael's accident. But as fatiguing as breaking a new trail was, my emotions finally erupted: *"That poor kid! My God—"*

I continued trudging through the snow trying to imagine what his life would be like now. Christopher Reeve came to mind. He fell off his horse and severed his spinal cord and was paralyzed from the neck down also. I remembered reading that he required a breathing device and had to be fed and bathed, a totally dependent life; but Christopher Reeve, who ironically played Superman in the movies, had courageously adjusted to his new life and made the most of it, using his celebrity name to start a foundation for research on paralysis and spinal cord injuries; what would Michael do?

"And what am I going to do?" I asked myself, stopping to reflect.

I had modeled my story on the Kendals, but without Michael; and now Michael's accident was going to radically change their lives and the chemistry of my novel. *"What the hell do I do now?"* I cried out, in a moment of creative panic.

It was as though all of Michael's fear had become mine, and I had to let it out; but my voice startled some birds and they took flight. This brought me back to my task of breaking trail. But that didn't last long. I continued to plod my way through the snow thinking about what I should do. "I can't really do anything until I find out for certain," I thought; but it didn't take long to learn of Michael's situation.

When I got home Cathy, who had dinner almost ready, told me that Michael was definitely paralyzed from the neck down and that his parents were sending him to Toronto for a complete assessment; they wanted the most professional diagnosis available.

"So it's true, then?" I said, all hope now gone.

"I'm afraid so," she said, trying not to show her emotions.

I said nothing. We ate dinner in silence. Cathy cleaned up the kitchen and called Martha, an elderly friend whose husband had recently passed. It was Monday, and their regular coffee night; so Cathy left to pick her up. I watched TV.

"So, what the hell does this mean?" I asked myself, as I flicked channels.

I didn't want to think about it, but the symbolic implications forced themselves upon me: *"Two kids, both adopted. One has an abortion to defy her faith, and the other goes to confession and takes communion every Sunday and then has a skiing accident that paralyzes him from the neck down; what the hell does that mean?"*

I stopped working on my novel for several days, going skiing every day after making lunch for Cathy who preferred eating at home

257

over hospital cafeteria food; and for two or three hours on the trail I thought about the turn that my novel had to take.

I hadn't planned to include Michael. I had outlined it to be a mother-daughter story. I had been looking for years to find a real-life model for my abortion story idea, and then Grace and her daughter came into my life and I couldn't have asked for better material to model my abortion story on because I could now give it real-life gravitas.

I had already drafted a story to try out the conflict that the multiple life perspective on abortion would have when put up against Christianity's belief that we only live one life, but I couldn't make my story real enough; so I put it aside and forgot about it.

But when Kathleen told me about her abortion I took it out to see if I could rework my idea with her and her mother as my real-life models; that's why Michael's accident threw me. I didn't know how exactly, but I knew that his tragic accident had just changed the chemistry of my novel.

I couldn't deny the feeling that Michael belonged in my story as much as Kathleen, but how? I knew that my novel was going to go beyond the scope of abortion because of my Platonic relationship with Grace; but I had very little to do with Michael. He was just there, flitting in and out of the house with no presence to speak of. But now he loomed so large in my mind that I could not stop thinking about how to work him into my story.

Kathleen's abortion had taken my story out of the realm of ethereal archetypes and made it so visceral that it intimidated the hell out of me; but I just could not see where Michael would fit into it. But I had to fit him in. He belonged there.

I knew there were symbolic implications, because when Grace tripped and broke the head off Michael's statue an ominous chill ran up my spine; but I didn't want to include Michael in my story because I didn't want my novel to be a fictional parallel of Grace and her family. That would have been too obvious, and probably libelous; and then it hit me—*the image of Grace pushing the wheelchair!*

I was working my way back from a long workout on my new trail, cold and wet from sweating in freezing temperature, when the sudden flight of a dead-still partridge directly in front of me made such a noisy flutter that it startled me.

I stopped and watched the partridge bee-line it to a spruce tree; then I smiled, and out of the blue the image of Grace Kendal pushing a wheelchair flashed across my mind, as though it had been startled free by the flight of the partridge. *"It was Michael!"* I shouted; suddenly realizing who was in the wheelchair.

I couldn't believe it. I had seen Michael's accident before it happened. I had to continue skiing. I was too excited. Winded, I slowed my pace to an easy glide; my mind still working frantically to make sense of it all.

"I saw it," I muttered to myself, still in shock at foreseeing Michael's paralysis. "It has to go into my story," I said, doing my best to recall my vision of Grace. "It has to mean something that I'm not seeing; it has to—"

At home, after dinner, I said to Cathy, "Here, I'd like you to read this."

"What?" she asked.

"Just read this page," I said, handing her my notebook.

Cathy did, and then looked up at me. "Is that Grace's son in the wheelchair?"

"Yes. Now look at the date at the top of the page."

Cathy looked and her eyes popped. "How did you know?"

"I didn't. It just came to me today while skiing that it was Michael I saw in the wheelchair. I wrote that image down because I knew it might be relevant to my novel, but I had no idea that it would be this important."

"How important?" Cathy asked.

"The symbolic implications are staggering," I replied.

"What do you mean?" she asked.

"Grace's son is an innocent. Michael's a good Roman Catholic boy. Decent, well-mannered, and dutiful to his parents and the Church. Grace wanted him to go to university, but Michael wasn't university material; so he took some college courses to get himself into the police academy, and he did get accepted by the OPP. Brandon told me a couple of weeks ago at the post office. He would've made a good cop, Cathy."

"Sad, isn't it," Cathy sighed.

I grimaced at the thought of that young man spending the rest of his life in bed and a wheelchair cared for his every need. "My God, what will that do to him?"

It was too much for me to imagine, and for days I could not write. I did not have any work to go to because it was traditionally my slow time of the year, so I just read and went cross country skiing to let my creative unconscious work out the story for me—another technique that I had also picked up from my mentor Hemingway.

On my fourth day I came home from skiing early and took out my notebook and read through all my talks with Grace, and all the thoughts and ideas and insights that I had recorded in the heat of the moment, and I could not help conclude that my novel was destined to be written; but it was too much. It overwhelmed me symbolically.

I thought I had worked it out in my story outline with Grace being the good Roman Catholic mother whose daughter's abortion forced her to rethink her faith, but with Michael's accident I knew that my story had to go where it was called to go; but I couldn't handle that, and I was terrified. *"I know, I know; if not me, who?"* I cried out in the still bush air the next day as I worked my new trail. *"But why me?"* I screamed.

I was born a Roman Catholic who could not live within the confines of my faith, and I suffered unbearable anguish. And then it happened. The shocking experience that compelled me to begin my quest out of the cave of spiritual ignorance, and the pain and suffering that it cost to free myself of the hold that the Archetypal Shadow Christ had upon me awakened me to the Way and set me apart from society forever; that was why me. I had no choice. It was divinely ordained. That's why Grace and I met...

Grace Kendal was a Bride of Jesus Christ for twenty years before she left her Order and married a servant of Jesus Christ, who like herself had outgrown the confines of his ascetic monastic Order, and they adopted two children and brought them up within their expanded ex-monastic but nonetheless constraining faith; but then life happened and changed the dynamics of their family unit.

Kathleen stopped believing in the divinity of Jesus Christ and had an abortion to defy the moral authority of the Church. Her conviction that a woman should have the right to control her own body compelled her to have an abortion and shout to the world that she was free to do with her body as she deemed. Deep in her soul she was aware of the sanctity of the spiritual freedom that governs soul's destiny in life, and with her decision to have an abortion she began her own quest out of the cave of spiritual ignorance; but little did she know what price she would have to pay for her spiritual freedom.

But I knew. That's why I answered her letter. I was one of the lucky ones that had escaped from the stifling darkness of Christian ignorance, and I had no choice but to help her because it was the unwritten law of the Way; but to bridge the great divide that separated the original message that Jesus gave to the world and Christianity—that scared the hell out of me, because who knew what forces I would unleash?

All the conversations with God in the world and quests for Shambhala and endless repasts on chicken soup for the soul would not do the seeker one iota of good until he was willing to pay the price for spiritual freedom, but few people were willing to do that; so I knew how protective people could be when their faith was threatened. That's why I was terrified of writing the novel that was expected of me.

Christians are not kind when it comes to defending their faith. They can be as cruel as cruel can be, and what would I be doing but threatening their faith with my spiritual perspective that embraced all paths back home to God?

But what choice did I have? My whole life was one long and lonely indefatigable quest for authenticity; and I had to be me. I had to write my novel to bridge the great divide that existed in Christianity; but I did not have to be stupid about it, did I?

The only way to write my novel was to tell both sides of the story and let the reader draw his own conclusions; and I had to write Michael into my story, because unlike his spirited sister who defied her family faith Michael symbolized the spiritual paralysis that the great divide of Christianity was responsible for.

And so I went back to work. Every morning I got up at four, took a deep breath for courage, and invoked my Muse. *"Thy will, not mine,"* I implored, abandoning to my creative unconscious; and I dove into my story with all the fear and excitement that accompanies free-falling into the unmanifest world of a new novel...

For five weeks I worked on my first draft when I met Grace Kendal by chance one Saturday morning in the grocery store in St. Jude. Cathy was making blueberry cheesecake and needed another package of Philadelphia Cream Cheese, so I put down my manuscript and drove to the store to purchase the cheese for one of my favorite desserts.

Being unfamiliar with the newly renovated store because Cathy and I did our grocery shopping in the Superstore in the city, I was hunting down the cheese counter when I bumped into Grace; and my heart skipped a beat. I hadn't seen her since I had painted her house and walked out without saying goodbye.

"Oriano?" she said, surprised. Her smile was warm and inviting. *"How nice to see you? How are you? How are you?"* she asked, putting her hand on my shoulder.

I looked into her eyes and smiled. "I'm fine, Grace. But more important, how are you doing? I heard of Michael's accident. I'm so sorry, Grace; so sorry—"

"It's God's will, Oriano. God's will," she said, her voice breaking and tears quickly coming to her beautiful but now very sad eyes.

"I heard nothing can be done. Is that true, Grace?" I asked.

"Yes. We had him assessed in Toronto, but there's nothing more they can do. Maybe someday they will find a cure for paralysis. He's going to be confined to a wheelchair just like the movie actor Christopher Reeve. My little superman—"

Grace broke into full-fledged sobbing. I didn't know what to do. But just as suddenly as she started she stopped and took out her handkerchief. "It's God's will, and we have to make the best of it. What else can we do?"

I never felt so awkward in my life, and I didn't know what to say; but I knew that the divine law of synchronicity had brought us together again for a reason, so I abandoned my fear and dove right in just as I had done every morning with my novel—

"Grace," I said, feeling the archetypal energies of our unique relationship rising to blend with the raw existential energies of the moment, "I don't know how to comfort you in your situation, because it's beyond me; but I feel for you. I honestly do—"

"I know you do, Oriano; I know you do. So, how have you been? I haven't seen you for quite some time. I never did get to invite you and Cathy for dinner, did I?"

"Grace; your plate is full. Will you ever have an empty plate? It's so full now—"

She smiled, but her heart was not in her smile. Tears came to her eyes. Just then, as merciful coincidence would have it, a young contractor friend walked down the aisle with a cell phone to his ear. As he approached I heard him say, "I'll catch you later," and he folded his cell phone and was about to put it away. "Gerry," I said; "can I use your phone for a second? I have to call Cathy."

"Sure," he said, and handed it to me.

"Excuse me a minute, Grace," I said, and called Cathy and told her that I was talking with Grace Kendal and would be late. "Take your time," she said.

I handed Gerry the phone back and thanked him and turned to Grace and said, "Will Michael be coming home soon?"

"We're going to bring him home in the spring. He's in rehabilitation now. He has to get accustomed to his breathing apparatus and wheelchair. That's going to take a lot of patience and counseling. He's so depressed he can't stop crying. I pray to St. Jude every day, Oriano. I was going to go up with Brandon today, but he wouldn't let me. He said I needed a break. There's so much to do before he comes home. We're going to need assistive devices for lifting him in and out of the tub and getting him in and out of bed; and we were going to build a new deck anyway, but now we have to build a ramp for his wheelchair. He's going to be in a wheelchair for the rest of his life, and he's so depressed he wants to die. He refuses to see anyone. But he can adjust. I know he can. Christopher Reeve adjusted. He's making the most of his life. I'm looking into his foundation. I think it will do Michael the world of good if he got involved in Christopher Reeve's charity work. But we have to get him settled in first. He's going to need a lot of counseling and all the love we can give him. O my precious Jesus; why did I insist that we move here? Why, Oriano? Why? I'm never going to forgive myself. Never—"

"I don't know what to say, Grace," I said, my voice choking. "I guess in the end it all comes down to God's will; and we have no choice but to trust God."

"O, my precious Lord," Grace uttered, putting her hand to her heart. "I'm in your hands once more, dear Jesus. Please give me strength—"

I waited a moment or two, and then said, "Grace, will you call me when you get Michael settled in? I'd like to come up and visit him."

Yes, or course. We'd love to have you. Brandon and I hold you in the highest regard. Yes, of course I will. But I am keeping you, aren't I?"

"Not at all. Am I keeping you, Grace?"

"No. Brandon's in the city for a district school board meeting and then he's going to visit Michael. I'm just doing some shopping to get out of the house."

"You're free, then?"

"Yes."

"Then what do you say we walk over to the café for a cup of tea?"

"Oh, yes; that would be nice. But what about Cathy? Isn't she's expecting you?"

"This is more important," I said, with a warm smile.

Grace smiled back, and we checked out our few items and walked over to the St. Jude Café and found a private corner in the quiet dining room. The waitress took our order and I looked at Grace and said, "How are you coping, Grace?"

She looked into my eyes, and for the longest time just stared at me. The silence was pressing, and it started to make me uneasy. Then in a calm, measured voice, she said, "I have always been a martyr for my faith, Oriano. Why should I feel any different now?"

I didn't know what to say. Grace sounded distant, almost cold; as though she had already resigned herself to a fate of endless martyrdom. "I would imagine your faith is what's going to see you through this, Grace," I heard myself saying.

"Yes; where would we be without our faith, Oriano?" she said, and smiled; but her smile unsettled me. It was forced, defensive; and I braced myself for what I feared.

264

She continued to stare at me, still smiling. I thought it was my imagination at first, but her smile began to turn into a subtle, familiar grin.

"I think I shared this with you already, Grace," I said, deliberately to thwart the shadow side of her personality that I sensed had surfaced; "but I was led to believe by a very abrasive and short-tempered ophthalmologist in the city that I was going to go blind. My eyes were my life, Grace; and from the moment I walked out of his office until I got a second opinion from another ophthalmologist in the eye clinic in Waterloo I had trouble holding it all together. Fortunately the solar burns in my eyes were stationary and not degenerative, so I wasn't going to go blind; but in those two weeks I suffered more anguish than I did in my entire life. We all suffer in our own way, Grace. My suffering was foolishly self-inflicted, so I had no one to blame but myself; but I learned to live with it. Your pain and suffering is not self-inflicted. Michael's accident was his fate; or God's will, as you say. But you are his mother, and his pain and suffering is your pain and suffering; so Grace, thank God you have your faith to keep you strong—"

"Where is your faith, Oriano? What do you believe in?" she asked, in a flat, metallic voice that confirmed my suspicion; and a cold chill ran up my spine.

Her question threw me. I expected her to question me on my blindness scare, but she didn't. She went straight to the point, as though this was her final chance to resolve the issue of our spiritual dissonance and win me over. She continued to stare at me.

"Faith," I replied, with a nervous smile, "was my downfall. It's ironic, but it was because I believed too much that I almost ruined my eyesight. I impaired my eyes, Grace; but I thank God that I'm not blind today. I have three solar burns in my eyes, but I can see better today than when I had twenty-twenty vision. You want to know what I believe in, Grace; and I'll tell you. I believe in man's desire to know more than he is capable of understanding; I believe in man's quest for truth, and God, and love—"

"*I believe in Jesus Christ, Oriano,*" she abruptly cut in. "Jesus said, '*I am the way, the truth, and life; and no one comes to the Father but through me.*' That's what I believe in; and I am a martyr for my Lord Jesus. I have to sacrifice my life for my savior. What are you a martyr for, Oriano? Your writing?"

Her tone was menacing, confrontational. "Not at all," I replied.

"What, then?" she came back at me, oblivious to everything but her desire to get out of me what she could not in all the time that I had worked at her house.

"I've already been bought with a price, Grace," I responded. I realized that I could not thwart her shadow personality, so I had to deal with it head on or suffer the indignity of her unresolved Christian self. "I have no need to martyr my life anymore. I died to my life to find my life, and I just live now. I am, Grace; and life is merely something that I do. That's the end of all spiritual paths. But can I say the same for you?"

She did not reply. She just stared at me, her blue and brown eyes boring into my impenetrable soul. I had challenged her inauthentic self just as it had challenged me, and her steely cold eyes behind her sad beautiful eyes told me that she knew that I knew; but true to its nature, the archetypal shadow self cannot reveal itself—

"I live too, Oriano," she was forced by the sheer gravitas of my personality to confess. "I may not live the life that I want to live, but I live too—"

Suddenly she broke down. Tears began streaming down her cheeks; but she made no effort to wipe them, and I made no effort to console her.

A minute or so later she stopped, wiped her face with the table napkin, and said, "What did you tell Kathleen, Oriano? She's stopped going to confession because she doesn't believe in sin any more. What did you tell her?"

"So that's it. That's why she's behaving so strangely," I said to myself, and sat back in my chair to catch my breath. I thought carefully before replying, and then I looked Grace in the eye and very calmly said, "I told her to live her own life. I told her not to be afraid of going to hell, because that myth does not fit into the evolving spiritual consciousness of the new millennium—"

"You told her too much. My daughter has lost her faith, and I don't know if you're responsible for that or not; but I fear for her soul—"

Grace stopped, once again suspended in no man's land; but I didn't know what to say, so I just waited. Finally, feeling obligated to respond, I said, "Fear drove Kathleen to reach out to me, Grace; her fear of going to hell. Can't you see how much psychic damage this nonsense of eternal damnation can do to an innocent soul like your daughter? Kathleen asked for my help, and I couldn't turn her down—"

"But did you have to destroy her faith? She refuses to repent for her sin of—"

Grace caught herself and stopped short of saying the word. I snickered; I couldn't help myself. "She told me, Grace."

"Then you know?" she said, affecting ignorance.

"Yes, of course. That's why I replied to her letter asking for my help."

"But what did you say to her? She adamantly refuses to repent for her sin—"

"Abortion, Grace," I cut in. "Not sin; abortion. Kathleen made a statement to the world with her abortion, and I for one am proud of her. And so should you be."

"Of taking the life of her unborn child? You want me to be proud of my daughter for that? *Oh my precious Jesus—*"

"Grace, Grace; must you be so righteous? You Christians don't have a monopoly on morality, you know. That's why I burnt three holes in my eyes, because of blind faith. Ironic, isn't it? I just about went blind because I believed blindly. What makes you so sure that abortion is a sin? Because the Church says so? There are more things between heaven and earth than can possibly be dreamt up by your faith, Grace; and spiritual freedom is one of them. Kathleen was hurting, and she asked me to take her heartache away like I took her headache away; and I did my best to help her—"

"But at what cost, Oriano? The price of her faith? What does she have to live for now, I ask you? What? *Oh my precious Jesus. I lost one child, and now Michael—*"

Grace broke down again. She put her hands to her face and cried inconsolably. Just then the waitress came over to see if we wanted more hot water for our tea and I put my forefinger to my lips and she walked away quietly.

When Grace finally uncovered her face she wiped her eyes and looked at me and in a very calm, soft voice said, "Oriano, you're not a bad man. I know that you are not. I have looked into your heart, and it is good; but I cannot understand why you would believe what you do. I simply cannot understand you, Oriano—"

"You may not understand me, Grace; but I understand your quandary. I puzzle you because I'm a good person but not a Christian. But has it ever occurred to you that your faith may be wrong? Tell me, Grace; do you believe in your heart of hearts that there is such a thing as eternal damnation? Do you honestly believe that God would condemn a soul to hell for eternity? Do you honestly and truthfully believe that?"

"I don't want to, but it is my faith. I took a vow of obedience to accept the Word of God as it is revealed through our Holy Mother Church, and I cannot doubt my faith; I cannot. It's who I am. You don't have any faith, Oriano; and I feel sorry for you—"

"Please, don't waste your pity on me. I'm sorry if what I wrote Kathleen has upset you; but I didn't expect her to reveal my letter to you—"

"But she's my daughter. We share everything—"

"Then why can't you share her joy? Why can't you share her need to find her own path in life? Why do you have to impose your faith upon her?"

"Because I fear for her soul, that's why. I am her mother, after all—"

"And does that entitle you to determine her destiny? Is she not entitled to her own life, Grace? Didn't Kathleen say that she's a free spirit?"

"My daughter is free to live the life she chooses. I only want her to live it in Jesus Christ. Is that asking too much of my daughter?"

"Yes, it is Grace. Kathleen doesn't believe in the divinity of Jesus. She believes that Jesus was a man. A remarkable man, but a man nonetheless. She doesn't believe that he's the Son of God and savior of the world. Why can't you let her have her own beliefs? If there is such a thing as sin, Grace; it has to be interfering in another person's karma—"

"That's the word she used," Grace interrupted. "She went on and on about this karma thing and I didn't know what she was talking about. Did she get that from you too?"

"Yes," I said, with a rueful smile. I didn't want to go there, but I had to bring some clarity to her quandary. "Jesus makes reference to karma, Grace. Karma isn't some kind of strange virus from another planet that's going to infest the soul of humanity. On the contrary; karma is the slow burning love of God. Karma is the healing balm that restores balance to the world. Karma is the law of spiritual accountability that brings soul back home to God. It's not something to be afraid of, Grace—"

"I shouldn't be talking to you," she said, suddenly realizing that she was in mortal danger of being infected by the simple truth of the Way. "Why I let myself come here, I don't know; but I have to be going," she said, and stood up.

"Before you leave, let me say just one thing more; if I may?"

"What?" she asked, with fright in her eyes.

"I know how difficult it must be for you, Grace; but I know that when a person's beliefs are threatened they cling to them more tightly than ever, so I do know where you're coming from. But please, if you believe in the power of love, let your daughter find her own way in life—"

"I pray for my daughter every day, Oriano. I pray for her just as I pray for you."

"For me?" I said, feigning shock.

"Yes. I pray that one day you will come back to Jesus."

I wanted to laugh, but decency forbade me; so I said, "I never walked away from Jesus, Grace. I walked away from Christianity. And I think we should just leave it at that."

I stood up also and we walked to the cash register and I gave our waitress a ten dollar bill and told her to keep the change. Grace wanted to pay for her tea, but I refused. As we walked back to the store where I had parked my car, I broke the painful silence—

"Grace, is it so difficult to love your daughter unconditionally?"

Grace turned to me, and with a glazed look in her eyes, replied, "Jesus loves you, Oriano. One day you will realize that and come back to him. I will pray for your soul."

"Thank you, but that's not necessary. I do hope that you and Kathleen can work it out. And I am so sorry for Michael, Grace; so sorry—"

She smiled, and in her deepest martyr's voice said, "Who are we to question the will of God? Goodbye, Oriano," she added, giving me her hand to shake.

There was something so final in Grace's voice that my heart sank to my feet, because I knew that this was where my novel parted company with reality; and I could not believe what I had just experienced. I shook her hand, knowing that barring the natural coincidences of everyday life this was the last time I would ever be talking with Grace Kendal.

"Perhaps in your next life, Grace," I whispered softly, with an ironic smile; and I turned and walked to my car. Grace kept on walking home, up the long steep hill to her new home that overlooked the town of St. Jude that had called her to her destiny...

It would have been so easy to write my novel as I had experienced it, but I didn't want to just write about life as it was; I wanted to write about life as it could be. I had learned from Hemingway. He tried to write the straight autobiographical novel and *Green Hills of Africa* got panned by the critics, proving to himself that without the alchemy of imagination he could not transform the raw stuff of life into literary gold, which he did in the two fictional stories that were inspired by the same safari, "The Short Happy Life of Francis Macomber" and "The Snows of Kilimanjaro," and the gold that I was after was the spiritual growth of my fictional Grace because I had come to believe that art was the miracle of the possible; and for three days I puzzled over my conversation with Grace in the restaurant, which I recorded in my notebook the moment I got home.

It was painfully obvious that she clung to her faith more tightly now than she had ever done in her life, but in my novel I wanted her to take her daughter's abortion as a God-given opportunity to expand her faith, because her love for her daughter transcended her faith; and I wanted to have it liberate her from the choke-hold of Christianity. So my conversation with Grace in the St. Jude Café shocked me back into reality, because the real flesh and blood prototype resisted the creative pull of my archetypal ideal.

TEA WITH GRACE

Grace Kendal was a real person with one brown eye and one blue eye. She was a married ex nun whose whole life was her Roman Catholic faith, and my fictional Grace was a married ex nun whose daughter's abortion provided the catalyst that she needed to liberate herself from her suffocating faith; but I had no intention of having my Grace walk away from her Church as I brought her to the painful realization that Jesus was not the only savior of the world. Jesus was the way, the truth, and the life; but he wasn't the only way into the kingdom of heaven, and my goal was to transform my Grace from a faithful Roman Catholic ex nun into a thoughtful, spiritually enlightened new millennium Christian.

That was the only way I could fulfill the symbolic implications of our Platonic relationship. In real life it was not going to go there, because Grace had used up all of her courage for God; but in my imagination I could take her there, and I was going to make every effort possible to do so because all the symbols pointed in that direction.

In my mind's eye I saw Grace pushing a wheelchair across a bridge, but I knew that would never happen now. I didn't understand what the omniscient guiding force of life was trying to tell me with the image of Grace pushing her son in the wheelchair across the bridge, but after my conversation with Grace in the St. Jude Café it came to me.

Grace was Michael's mother. Symbolically, she represented the Holy Mother Church; and Michael, her adopted son, represented the innocent Christian. Grace loved her adopted son as the Holy Mother Church loved her adopted children, and she had to take care of her son because Michael was a quadriplegic now just as Christianity took care of its spiritually paralyzed children. I realized now that Michael's paralysis symbolized the spiritually paralyzing faith of Christianity, and Grace pushing her son across the bridge in the wheelchair symbolized Christianity's efforts to take her spiritually crippled children to the other side of the great divide; but I knew that was never going to happen, because heaven does not accept spiritual cripples.

Life had made Michael a physical cripple just as Christianity makes spiritual cripples of its children; but to make my story work I had to have Michael walk again, and there was only one way that I could ever hope of doing that...

Karma is a personal responsibility, and everyone has to earn their own way into the kingdom of heaven; so I had to expand my Grace character's faith to provide the spiritual environment that would then translate into a miraculous cure for her son's paralysis. *"As above, so below"* was the working premise of my story.

I had to make it happen in the spiritual realm before it could happen in the physical realm; and the only way I could do that was to cure Grace of her spiritual paralysis first by expanding her faith, and this would create the spiritual conditions for the patron saint of hopeless causes to cure her son of his paralysis. *That was the challenge of my novel!*

So after I came to terms with my conversation with Grace in the St. Jude Café I went back to my notes and found all the signs that pointed to bridging the great divide that Grace was called by her destiny to do, and three signs shouted symbolic fulfillment.

The signs were the three burnt bulbs that I had changed for Grace at her home, which represented the three levels of human consciousness: 1, waking everyday consciousness; 2, the unconscious; and 3, higher, or spiritual consciousness.

The first burnt bulb that I changed was in the entranceway closet on the main floor (waking, everyday consciousness); the second bulb was at the bottom of the basement stairs (the unconscious); and the third was at the top of the stairs to the upper level of the house (higher, or spiritual consciousness).

When I read my notes on the three bulbs that I had changed I shook my head in disbelief. *"I couldn't have made this up if I tried!"* I exclaimed to myself.

Every time I changed a burnt bulb our conversation had to do with shedding the Light of the Way into that part of Grace's life that inhibited her from expanding her faith. I could not believe it: three burnt bulbs changed, and three conversations shedding the Holy Light of the Way into the respective level of Grace's personal consciousness.

That was real. Divinely choreographed or not, it actually happened; so why was Grace so recalcitrant then? Why did she cling to her faith more tightly now when all the signs pointed for her to free herself from its choke-hold?

It puzzled me. It was on the strength of these three signs that I wanted to continue our Platonic relationship; but that didn't happen, and I could not figure out why. Cathy came into the picture and despite herself saved the day for me; but it still puzzled me why Grace failed to see the signs that pointed to her liberation.

It had to be her Roman Catholic faith. It blinded her to all the signs that the divine law of synchronicity had provided for her; but I had to change that in my novel. I had to implore my imagination to awaken Grace to the guiding Light of the Way.

I had all the signs to work with, and in my novel I had to wake Grace up a little at a time with each sign that synchronicity had provided for us; and by the time her daughter had her abortion she would have enough courage to free herself from her faith and provide the spiritual conditions that would answer her prayers to St. Jude to cure her crippled son. Grace would get her miracle, but only if she cured herself first.

That was my story on one level; but there was another level as well, and to tell that part of my story I had to rely upon another symbol that was provided for me by the mercifully law of synchronicity, the symbol of the black heart of the onion…

It amused me, all the signs and symbols that came to me from the moment I began working on Grace's house; but the symbol that amused me the most was the onion heart. It was the most astonishing synchronicity that I had ever experienced while working on a new novel, and I had experienced many synchronicities when writing.

This one was so poignant that it felt like God was laughing with me in its revelation of what I had to do with my story, but I knew that it would only make sense in the context of the Platonic ideal of my story; and I implored my Muse for all the inspiration that I would need to transform the reality of my story into a literary work of art.

I was facing an enormous task, which I didn't want to do in the first place. I knew that I had a story in Grace Kendal from the moment we met, but I had no idea that it would take on the importance it did; and it overwhelmed me. That's why I asked God to

273

give me a sign to convince me that I was going in the right direction with my story.

I wanted to know if I was right in my efforts to peel away the four lies of Christianity one by one until I got to the heart of the religion that I knew had been transformed into the opposite of what Jesus had intended with his teaching; and once again the merciful divine law of synchronicity gave me a sign that struck me dumb.

Because Cathy wanted to get as much cross country skiing in as she could before the season ended I waited for her to get off work so we could go together and to make life a little easier for her I put dinner on in the slow cooker in the morning; that way when we came home from skiing dinner would be ready.

On the day that I asked God for a sign to confirm that I was on the right track of peeling away the four lies of Christianity so I could bridge the great divide that existed between the religion that grew out of Christ's life and teaching and the true meaning of his teaching of spiritual liberation, I decided to put a pot roast in the slow cooker.

I peeled the potatoes and carrots and added them to the roast, four or five cloves of garlic, a couple of stalks of celery cut into diagonal pieces like my carrots, and then I cut my first onion on the end to peel it; but I noticed that it was black in the center.

I sliced the outer layers of the skin and peeled them off and then stood the onion on one end and cut it through the center. "That's odd," I said to myself. I hadn't seen a black onion center before. I looked at both sides of the onion, and each center looked like half of an elongated black heart. And then for some reason I was strongly nudged to count the layers of the black heart. I pried them apart gently and counted four, and it didn't take more than a split second to make the connection and I burst out— *"Incredible! I asked for a sign, and here it is: the four lies of Christianity!"*

It was too much. I had to stand back. I looked at the onion to make sure I wasn't dreaming. I picked up the two halves and stared at them. They were real. I studied them, and they were white right through to the center whose four innermost layers made up the tightly encased black heart of the onion just as the four lies of Christianity made up the tightly woven black heart of the religion that Grace clung to with all her heart, and I knew beyond a shadow of a doubt that I was on the right track with my novel.

I knew that Christ's teaching of spiritual liberation worked. I had taken the sayings of Jesus into the marketplace and lived them with pathological commitment, and I died daily; and with each death that I died I stored my treasures in heaven where the thieves and rust and moths could not steal and corrupt them; and the more treasures I stored, the more spiritually conscious I became until one day I reached critical mass and my little self could no longer contain all the spiritual consciousness that I had realized with Christ's sayings and I burst out of the womb of my little self and gave birth to my spiritual self in my mother's kitchen one day while she was kneading bread dough on the kitchen table.

But that didn't happen in a miraculous burst of glorious light as one might imagine; my spiritual birth stole upon me like a thief in the night, quietly and with no fanfare. I was standing in the doorway of the kitchen talking with my mother when suddenly, for no apparent reason, I was imbued with the feeling that I was immortal. I *knew* with all my heart and soul that I was immortal. I simply *knew* that I would never again doubt the immortality of my own existence, because I could never die. *I knew this!*

This feeling of immortality was so complete that it imbued every fiber of my being, so I knew that Christ's teaching worked if one had the courage to live it; but I also knew that the four lies of Christianity that I had written about to Kathleen did just the opposite of Christ's teaching, which was to keep soul asleep to its divine nature.

I took the black halves of the onion heart and threw them into the garbage pail under the sink, and the good part of the onion I added to my roast; and then I peeled three more onions, which were all good, and added them also; and when we came home from skiing Cathy made a garden salad, I poured the wine, and we sat down to a lovely dinner.

"Cheers, darling," I said, holding up my glass.

"Cheers, sweetheart," she said, and we touched glasses.

I took a sip, and then said, "I've decided not to take any more jobs until spring. I want to work on my new novel. You won't mind, will you?"

"No. Why should I? You had a pretty good year last year, so you can take time off to write your novel. How is it coming?"

I wanted to share the symbol of the black heart of the onion, but I had also learned from Hemingway that to talk about a story before writing it would rob it of its magic; so I just said, "I know where I'm going with my story now, but as much as I'm going to love working on it this one's going to be really tough."

"Why?" she asked.

"I'm taking on Christianity," I replied.

"What's so different now? You've always taken on Christianity. I can't see why this story should be any tougher."

"Not this time, Cathy. I'm going to the very heart of the issue. This one's about a woman who has awakened to her true self through her love for Jesus but who has stopped growing spiritually because her faith won't let her; but I have to get her to expand her faith to make my story work, and I don't know if I can do that. It's a paradoxical conundrum that no one's ever been able to resolve, and I have to be very creative to make it work."

"This is about Grace Kendal, isn't it?"

"Yes."

"Are you sorry you didn't continue your relationship with her?"

"No. I know now it wouldn't have worked."

"Why not?" Cathy asked, with a glimmer of triumph in her eyes.

"Because Grace is too ensconced in her faith," I replied.

"Ensconced?" she queried.

"Grace is too fixed in her faith. She can't dislodge herself."

"Maybe she doesn't want to," Cathy said.

"Oh, she wants to. She's desperate, Cathy; but she can't. She has too much invested in her faith to dislodge herself from herself. She's outgrown her Christian life, and you know very well what happens when we've outgrown our life—"

"We suffer. I know that. Do you think that's why her son had his skiing accident?" Cathy asked, with uncanny insight.

"Karma doesn't work in a vacuum," I answered, with a wry smile. "We're all in this together, Cathy; and if we can't break out of our spiritual impasses on our own, then life is forced to break us out with pain and suffering. It could be breast cancer, an automobile accident, losing a job, the sudden death of a child, or whatever; that's

276

just the way life works. Nobody understands it, but suffering *really* is good for the soul. Suffering is how the merciful law of karma reconciles soul with God and gets our life back on track. Grace had no idea why she was called to St. Jude, but she was tested and found wanting; and now she's suffering. I really do feel sorry for her. She's trapped between a rock and a hard place, and I can feel her pain. And that's the challenge of my novel. I have to get her to transcend her life. I have to free her from herself; but will she let me?"

"I'm glad I'm not a Christian," Cathy said, and took a sip of wine.

"Me too. Well, here's to my new novel," I said, holding up my glass again.

Cathy clicked my glass, and then said, "Do you have a title yet?"

"I'm thinking of calling it whatever name I give to my Grace character."

"Why not just call it Grace? You can change her last name. She's going to know it's about her anyway, so why pretend to hide it?"

I laughed. "Here's to Grace, then!"

"To Grace," Cathy said, to my delight; and bright and early the next day I officially titled my new novel *Tea with Grace, A Story of Synchronicity and Platonic Love.*

OTHER BOOKS BY OREST STOCCO

Letters to Padre Pio

Jesus Wears Dockers,
The Gospel Conspiracy Story

Old Whore Life
Exploring the Shadow Side of Karma

Healing with Padre Pio

Why Bother?
The Riddle of the Good Samaritan

Just Going With the Flow
And Other Spiritual Musings

Keeper of the Flame

My Unborn Child

What Would I Say Today If I Were to Die Tomorrow?
Reflections on the Life of a Seeker

On the Wings of Habitat
A Volunteer's Story

ABOUT THE AUTHOR

Orest Stocco was born in Panettieri, Calabria, Italy. He immigrated to Canada and studied philosophy at university. A student of Gurdjieff's teaching for many years which opened him up to the Way, his passion for writing inspired such works as *Keeper of the Flame* and *Healing with Padre Pio.* He lives in Georgian Bay, Ontario with his life mate Penny Lynn Cates. His personal dictum is: *life is an individual journey.*
Visit him at: http://www.oreststocco.com
Spiritual Musings Blog:
http://www.spiritualmusingsbyoreststocco.blogspot.com

ME AND MY SISPHYEAN ROCK

www.ingramcontent.com/pod-product-compliance
Lightning Source LLC
Chambersburg PA
CBHW031103260626
47172CB00001B/193